... her stories.

...eing a nurse and
...e romance novels I've
...a young teen.

...started writing at a very young age and loved to read, devouring everything in sight. As a teenager, she volunteered as a Candy Striper at a nursing home and fell in love with nursing. She worked several part-time jobs to put herself through nursing school, and one managing job and two degrees later, she found she could embark on an old dream: writing. Now Laura is thrilled to combine her favourite careers into one – writing medical romances for Mills & Boon.

The Single Dads

COLLECTION

July 2019
**Captivated by the
Single Dad**

October 2019
**Falling for the
Single Dad**

August 2019
**Surrender to the
Single Dad**

November 2019
**Spellbound by the
Single Dad**

September 2019
**Seduced by the
Single Dad**

December 2019
**Fairytale with the
Single Dad**

October 2019
(Christmas Special Edition)
**Christmas with the
Single Dad**

November 2019
(Christmas Special Edition)
**Snowbound with the
Single Dad**

Snowbound with the Single Dad

SCARLET WILSON

DIANNE DRAKE

LAURA IDING

MIX
Paper from
responsible sources
FSC
FSC C007454

This book is produced from independently certified FSC™ paper
to ensure responsible forest management.

For more information visit: www.harpercollins.co.uk/green

Printed and bound in Spain
by CPI, Barcelona

MILLS & BOON

First Published in Great Britain 2019
By Mills & Boon, an imprint of HarperCollins*Publishers*
1 London Bridge Street, London, SE1 9GF

SNOWBOUND WITH THE SINGLE DAD © 2019 Harlequin Books S.A.

Her Firefighter Under the Mistletoe © 2013 Scarlet Wilson
Christmas Miracle: A Family © 2010 Dianne Despain
Emergency: Single Dad, Mother Needed © 2009 by Laura Iding

ISBN: 978-0-263-27947-4

HER FIREFIGHTER UNDER THE MISTLETOE

SCARLET WILSON

This book is dedicated to my good friends
Jane Bell, Kirsten Gallacher and Lorna McCririe,
who all enjoy getting into the spirit of Christmas!

CHAPTER ONE

Bzzz… bzzz…

The noise jerked Jess out of the delicious tranquil state that had been enveloping her.

Her eyes blinked at the bright light outside, the fuzziness of her brain trying to adjust and make sense of it all.

Her pager usually woke her in the dark of the night—just like it had three times last night. Having it wake her in the middle of the day was an entirely new experience.

A baby with RSV had kept her awake most of the night in Paediatric ITU, and when the ward had finally quietened down around an hour ago, she'd brought her coffee in here to do some paperwork.

Fat chance. She touched the coffee cup on her desk. Stone cold. Had she even managed a sip before she'd wiped out?

How long had she been asleep? She wriggled in her chair, rolling her shoulders back and trying to ease the knots out of her back.

Bzzz… Bzzz…

She glanced at the number. A and E. Another admission. Probably another respiratory problem.

It was Glasgow, at the start of November, but it felt like the middle of winter. The temperature had dropped dramatically in the last few days and paediatric emergency admissions had soared. Trips and falls on the slippery pavements had resulted in a whole host of strains, fractures and head injuries. Asthma and respiratory complaints were through the roof. Infections and nondescript viruses were causing mayhem with new babies and toddlers.

Just as well she didn't have anyone to go home to. She hadn't seen the inside of her house for days.

She picked up the phone and dialled A and E. 'It's Dr Rae. You were paging me.'

The voice was brusque, skipping over any pleasantries and getting straight to business. 'Assemble a flying squad. Nursery minibus in the Clyde on the city outskirts. Unknown number of casualties. We're waiting for more information from emergency services. You need to be ready to leave in five minutes.'

She was on her feet in seconds and throwing open the door, her tiredness, sore muscles and fatigue instantly forgotten. 'I need a flying squad,' she yelled, glancing down the corridor as the sister of the ward hurried towards her, 'Where's Jackie? I want her with me.'

Jackie appeared at her side in an instant. 'What is it?'

'Nursery minibus in the Clyde.'

The experienced nurse's face paled. 'In this weather? In these temperatures?'

'Go!' The ward sister waved her hand at them. 'Leave everything else to me.'

Jess started jogging down the corridor, heading for the stairs. It took less than a minute to reach A and E and one of the staff thrust a green suit into her hands. She climbed into it immediately, noting the fluorescent 'Doctor' sign on the back. It was essential that all staff could be picked out easily in an emergency. One of the paramedics thrust a pair of gloves towards her. 'Take these, you'll need them out there.'

She glanced at her watch. It was only two-thirty in the afternoon. At least a few hours of daylight left. She prayed they wouldn't need more than that.

'Let's go!'

The shout came from the front doors. Jackie appeared at her side again, similarly clad in a green jumpsuit with 'Nurse' emblazoned across the back. They picked up the pre-packed paediatric emergency kits and headed outside.

Jess climbed into one of the emergency vehicles and fastened her seat belt as the sirens sounded and they headed out onto the motorway. She turned to the man sitting next to her, 'I'm Jess, paediatric consultant. Have you heard any more?'

He nodded. 'Stan, emergency service co-ordinator. Lots of problems. Someone sideswiped the minibus and sent it down a thirty-foot slippery bank and straight into the Clyde.'

Jess tried to stop the sharp intake of breath. Her brain was into immediate overtime, imagining the types of injuries the children could have sustained.

'How many?'

He shook his head. 'Still waiting for confirmation. Three adults, at least ten kids.'

'Age range?'

'From two to five. We're getting more information all the time. The other nursery minibus missed everything. They didn't even know there had been an accident. The police are there now, collecting details of all the kids.'

Jess swallowed, trying to ignore the huge lump in her throat. The flying squad wasn't called out too often. She was the consultant on call—it was her job to be here. But that didn't mean her stomach wasn't churning at the thought of the scene she was about to face.

Yes, she could appear calm. Yes, she could use her skills

and clinical expertise. Yes, she would do everything that was expected of her and beyond.

But would she sleep tonight?

Probably not.

There was a crackle of the radio and some voices she couldn't distinguish. The driver turned his head. 'Five minutes. They've called out the rapid response and specialist rope rescue team. They should arrive just before us. Let's hope Callum got out of bed on the right side today.'

'Who is Callum?'

The words were out of her mouth automatically, before she even had a chance to think. 'And what's the specialist rope rescue team?'

None of this sounded good. All she could think about was the children involved in the crash. What did this mean for them?

Stan's face was pale. 'It means that the banking is too dangerous for our crews to work on, that, plus the added complication of being in water means we need the specialist crew.'

'Will it delay me getting to the children?'

Stan averted his eyes, obviously not wanting to give her the answer. He hadn't answered the other part of her question. He hadn't mentioned Callum. And the driver's comment had made her ears prick up. *Let's hope he got out of bed on the right side.*

The last thing she needed right now was a prima donna firefighter getting in her way when she had kids to attend to. 'Is Callum a bit on the crabbit side, then?' she asked as they pulled over to the side of the road. A bad-tempered man she could deal with. As long as he didn't interfere with her job.

'Only on a good day,' muttered Stan as he jumped from the rescue vehicle.

Jessica opened the door carefully, to avoid the passing traffic on the busy road. The police had cordoned part of it off as best they could. But the constant flow of traffic was unnerving.

The cold air hit her straight away. Biting cold, sneaking under the folds of her jumpsuit, made her wish she was wearing a hat, scarf and fleece and not just the thin gloves she'd been handed.

She flinched at the sight of the crash barrier, twisted beyond all recognition and lying like a useless piece of junk at the side of the road.

There were raised voices to her left. She turned just in time to see a broad-shouldered man snap on his harness and disappear down the side of the banking, with the vain words 'Risk assessment' being shouted after him by his colleagues.

A sense of unease came over her body. A vague awareness trickling through her. Callum—that's what they'd said. It couldn't possibly be Callum Kennedy, could it? She hadn't seen him since school and had no idea where he'd ended up. But there was something vaguely familiar about the body that had just disappeared over the edge.

Her footsteps shortened as she reached the edge of the steep bank. Someone touched her shoulder, looking at the sign on her back. 'Oh, good, the doctor. Let's get you harnessed up.'

She lifted her legs as she was clipped and harnessed and talked through the motions of the descent. Her bag was sent down ahead. A burly firefighter appeared next to her. 'You'll go down with me. Have you done this before?'

She peered over the edge again. Thirty feet of steep descent. How many times had the minibus rolled on the way down?

She could see it now, lying on its side in the Clyde,

the icy cold water surrounding it. There was a flurry of firefighters around it. Some on top, trying to get through the windows, some on the banking, surrounded by other pieces of equipment.

'Get me down there.' Her eyes met the firefighter's and the whispered words grew more determined. 'Get me down to those children.'

He nodded and spoke into the radio clipped to his shoulder. 'The doc and I are on our way.'

She took a deep breath and turned with her back towards the water, edging down the side of the bank in time with the firefighter. It was slippery work. A thin layer of frost had formed over the mud at the side of the bank, her simple shoes giving her literally no grip. The firefighter's firm hand in the small of her back kept her from slipping completely. Even through her gloves the biting cold was already making her fingers numb.

She looked over her shoulder. 'How much further?'

'Keep your eyes straight ahead, please.'

Her anxiety was building. She wanted to get down. She wanted to help those kids. But she needed to get down there in one piece.

'Who is Callum? Is it Callum Kennedy?'

The firefighter's eyes gave a spark of amusement. 'Know him, do you?'

She wrinkled her nose. 'I'm not entirely sure. I think so. I went to school with a Callum Kennedy, but I didn't get a good look at him before he went over the edge.' She shrugged her shoulders, 'I'm not even sure he would recognise me now.'

The firefighter gave her a little smile, 'Oh, I'm sure he would.'

'What does he do exactly?'

'He's the head of the rope rescue unit. He'll be in charge

down here.' They were inching closer and closer to the bottom.

'And is he any good?' She bit her lip. It might seem a little cheeky, but Stan had already mentioned he could be crabbit. She needed to know that he wouldn't get in her way. That he wouldn't stop her doing her job with these kids.

'Put it this way—if me or my kids were stuck anywhere that a rope rescue was needed?' He lifted his eyes skyward. 'I would be praying to the man upstairs that Callum would be on duty that night. He's the safest pair of hands we've got—particularly near kids.' He caught her around the waist. 'That's us. Let me just unhook you from this line—but we'll leave your harness on. You'll need it to get back up and they'll hook you up to another one if you're near the water.'

'Where's the doc?' came the shout.

Jess swivelled around, looking for her bag. 'I'm here. I'm coming.'

Several of the firefighters were forming a line, passing two little kids along to the edge of the bank. Jackie appeared at her side. 'Let's go.'

They reached the kids just as they were placed on warm blankets on the ground. Jess worked quickly, gently feeling over their little bodies for signs of injuries as she spoke to them in a quiet voice.

'Need some help?'

She nodded at the firefighter next to her. 'Heat them up. There are no obvious injuries. But they're in shock.' She turned back to the minibus. Now she was closer she could see every dent, every bash, every hole in the metalwork.

It made the chill seem even worse. 'Are these the first two?'

The man next to her nodded. 'Do we have a number yet? How many kids are injured?'

'Twelve. That's the figure we have for the moment. Just awaiting confirmation.'

She moved over to the side of the slippery river's edge as an adult was passed along and dealt with by the paramedics. She could see the hive of activity going on within the bus, hear the whimpering cries of the children.

'Can I get over there? Do you need me to get into the bus?' Her anxiety was building. She couldn't stand here and do nothing. It just wasn't in her nature. She needed to be at the heart of the action. It was her job to prioritise, triage and treat the sickest kids. She needed to be next to those children.

Her voice must have carried in the cold air, because a head whipped up from the bus. The man was lying across the windows, reaching down to grasp a squirming child, and his eyes connected with hers.

'Stay *exactly* where you are.'

Callum. Callum Kennedy. Absolutely no mistake.

She saw him flinch visibly as his brain made the connection of who was standing on the riverbank.

He'd recognised her? After all these years?

The cold hard air hit her lungs. She must have sucked in a bigger breath than normal. Her skin prickled.

How did she feel about seeing Callum Kennedy thirteen years on?

Unprepared.

Like a seventeen-year-old again, standing in a dark nightclub and willing herself not to cry as they broke up. It had been the right decision. The sensible decision. They had both been going to university, she in Glasgow and he—after a wait of a few years—in Aberdeen. Their relationship would never have worked out. It had been best for them both.

It just hadn't felt that way.

She pushed her feet more firmly into the ground, trying to focus her attention. Callum's gaze hadn't moved. It was still fixed on her face.

She could feel the colour start to rise in her cheeks. It was unnerving. But why the flinch? Was she really such an unwelcome sight after all this time?

Or maybe she was imagining this—maybe he'd no idea who she was at all.

Callum couldn't believe it. He was holding a child firmly by the waist, while a colleague released him from his seat belt.

But Callum's eyes were fixed on the flyaway caramel-coloured hair on the riverbank. Running up and down the thin frame that was in no way hidden by the bright green jumpsuit.

A sight he hadn't seen in thirteen years.

A lifetime ago.

His childhood sweetheart, here on the banks of the Clyde, at the scene of an accident.

He'd always wondered if he'd come across her sometime, some place.

As a firefighter he'd been in and out of most of the A and E departments in the city. But in all these years he'd never glimpsed her, never seen her name on any board.

He knew that Jessica had gone to university to do her medical training, but had no idea where she'd ended up, or which field she'd specialised in.

And now he knew. She was somewhere here in Glasgow, specialising in paediatrics. Why else would she be here?

Would she even remember him? It looked as though she had—even though he'd filled out considerably since the last time they'd met. She, on the other hand, looked as if she'd faded away to a wisp.

Although he could see her slight frame, the most visible changes were around her facial features and structure. And it wouldn't have mattered how many clothes she was bundled up in, he would have noticed at twenty paces.

It struck him as strange. The young Jessica he remembered had had an attention-grabbing figure and a personality to match. Every memory he had of her was a happy one. And for a second he felt as if they could all come flooding back.

There was a tug at his arms, followed by a sensation of relief and a lightening of the weight in his arms. He pulled upwards automatically. The little guy's seat belt had been released.

He pulled him up and held him to his chest, capturing the little body with his own, holding him close to let a little heat envelop the shivering form. The little boy wasn't even crying any more. He was just too cold.

He held the boy for a few seconds longer. He looked around four, just a year younger than his own son Drew. He couldn't help the automatic paternal shiver that stole down his spine at the thought of something like this happening to his son. It didn't even bear thinking about.

His only relief right now was that he hadn't signed a consent form for the school to go on any trips this week, meaning that his little Drew was safely tucked up inside the primary school building.

The temperature in the minibus was freezing, with water halfway up its side-on frame. They were going to have to move quicker to get these kids out in time.

'Callum! Callum! Pass him over, please.'

Oh, she'd recognised him all right. The authoritative tone made no mistake about that.

'Okay, little guy, we're going to get you heated up now.' He ruffled the little boy's hair before he passed him over to the arms stretched out towards him. He didn't have time to think about Jessica Rae now. Too much was at stake.

He thrust his head back inside the minibus. 'How are we doing?'

John, one of his co-workers, lifted his head. 'I'll have two more for you in a second. But I need some more light in here.'

Another voice shouted from the darkness, 'I think I've got one with a broken leg and another unconscious. Can we get a paramedic or a doctor in here?'

Callum lifted his head back up. The light was fading quickly, even though it was only afternoon. Winter nights closed in quickly—by four p.m. it would be pitch black. He didn't think twice. 'I need a paramedic or a doctor over here, please.'

He could see the quick confab at the side of the river. Jess was issuing instructions to the nurse with her and the paramedics and ambulance technicians at her side. Things were going smoothly out there. Two of the children and one of the adults had already been transported back up the slippery bank. The latest little guy was still being assessed.

Jess moved to the side of the bank. He could see the impatience on her face as she waited for her safety harness to be clipped to the harness point on the shore. She shook her head at the waders she was offered, grabbed at a hand that was offered and started to climb towards the minibus.

It was precarious. The Clyde was not a quiet-flowing river. It was fast and churning, the icy-cold water lapping furiously at the side of the minibus as it penetrated the interior.

The minibus was moving with the momentum of the river and Jess slipped as she climbed over the wing of the minibus, the weight from her pack making her unstable. She was just within Callum's reach and he stretched out and grabbed the tips of her fingers with a fierce, claw-like grip.

'Yeowww!' Her other hand flailed upwards then closed over his, and he steadied her swaying body as she thudded down next to him.

The red colour in her cheeks was gone, replaced with the whiteness of cold. 'Thanks,' she breathed, the warm air forming a little steamy cloud next to them.

'Fancy seeing you here,' he murmured, giving her a little smile. It had been impossible to spot from the riverbank, but here, up close, he had a prime-time view of the thing he'd always loved most about Jess—her deep brown eyes.

The smile was returned. That little acknowledgement. That in another time, another place...

The memories were starting to invade his senses. Jessica in his arms throwing back her head and laughing, exposing the pale skin of her neck—skin that he wanted to touch with his lips.

His brain kicked back into gear. This was work. And he never got distracted at work.

'Have you done anything like this before?'

She pulled back a little. It was the tiniest movement, a flinch almost, as if she was taken aback by his change of tone.

She shook her head and her eyebrows rose. 'An overturned minibus in a fast-flowing river with lots of paediatric casualties?'

The irony wasn't lost on him. He might do this sort of thing day in, day out, but Jess was usually in the confines of a safe, warm, comfortable hospital.

She hunched up onto her knees and pointed at the harness. 'I've never even had one of these on before, let alone abseiled down a hillside.' She wiggled her hips and tried to move her tether. 'These things aren't too comfortable, are they?'

It struck him—almost blindsided him—how brave she was being. The Jessica Rae he'd known at school hadn't even liked contact sports. He closed his eyes as an unguarded memory of other activities of a physical nature swam into his mind.

Focus. Focus now.

He knelt upwards and grabbed her around her waist, trying not to think about how it felt to be touching Jessica Rae again after all these years. Trying not to remember how her firm flesh used to feel beneath his fingers. What had happened?

'I'm going to lower you down, Jess.' He peered through the side window next to them, which had been removed. 'Your feet will get a bit wet because there's some water on the floor. Are you okay with that?'

She nodded. She didn't look scared. She didn't look panicked. But there was a tiny little flicker of something behind her eyes. She looked in control.

He shouted down into the minibus. 'John, I'm going to lower the doc down. Can you take care of her?'

She started. 'Take care of me?' It was almost as if he'd just insulted her. 'Don't you mean take care of the kids?'

But Callum wasn't paying attention. He was back in rescue mode. 'There are two kids in the back who need your attention. One unconscious, the other with a broken leg. It's too cramped in there to take your bag down. Shout up and tell me what you need.'

Their eyes met again as she shrugged off her pack. 'Ready?' She nodded and he lowered her down slowly into the waiting arms of the firefighter below, praying that things would go to plan.

* * *

'Sheesh!' Her feet hit the icy cold water and it sent the surge of cold right up through her body. No one could stand in this for long.

It took her eyes a few seconds to adjust to the gloom inside the minibus. The mottled daylight was still sending shadows through one side of the bus, but Callum's body and those of the other firefighters lying across the windows was blocking out the little light that was left.

A flashlight was thrust into her hands. 'Here you go, Doc.' She turned it on immediately. The first sight was the way the water was lapping quickly around them. She felt the vaguest wave of panic. 'Is the river rising?'

John nodded. 'Not quickly enough for us to worry about.' His eyes didn't quite meet hers.

Work quickly.

She noticed his black trousers ballooning around his ankles and gave him a little nod. 'Did you say no to the waders too?'

He smiled. 'No room for waders in here, Doc. Space is limited.'

She nodded and she shuffled around him towards the kids. 'Are any of the kids in water?' Her feet were already numb. There was a real danger of hypothermia setting in for any kid exposed to these temperatures.

'Four.'

'Four?' She could feel a flare of panic. She was one person. How could she attend to four kids?

Callum stuck his head in the gap. 'Start with the two at the back, Jess. As soon as you've stabilised them and they're safe to move, my men will get them out. The other two don't appear injured.' He pointed to the front of the bus. 'My men are getting them out as quickly as possible.'

He looked towards the back of the bus. 'The little girl is called Rosie.'

His voice was calm, authoritative. The kind of guy in an emergency who told you things would be okay and you believed him—just because of the way he said it.

She pushed her way back to a little girl with masses of curly hair, still strapped into her seat. Her leg was at a peculiar angle, and it hadn't taken a doctor to make an accurate diagnosis of a fracture. The little boy behind her, strapped into the window seat, was unconscious, but she couldn't possibly get to him until she'd moved this little girl. She took off her gloves and put her hand round the girl, feeling for a pulse at his neck and checking to see he was still breathing. Yes, his pulse was slowing and his chest was rising and falling. But in these cold temperatures hypothermia was a real risk. She had to work as quickly as possible.

The water was lapping around their little legs and would be dropping their temperatures dramatically.

She shouted up to Callum, 'I need you to pass me down the kit with analgesia—I need to give Rosie some morphine. It's in a red box, in the front pouch of the bag.' She waited a few seconds until the box appeared then shouted again, 'And an inflatable splint.'

She spoke gently to Rosie, stroking her hair and distracting her, calculating the dosage in her head. It was too difficult to untangle the little girl from her clothes and find an available patch of skin. The last thing she needed to do was cause this little girl more pain. She took a deep breath and injected it through the thick tights on her leg, waiting a few minutes for it to take effect. 'Pass me the splint,' she whispered to John.

The positioning on the bus was difficult. 'I'm sorry, honey,' she whispered, as the little girl gave a little yelp as she straightened her leg and inflated the splint around about it to hold it in place.

'Is she ready to be moved?'

'Not quite. Can you get a collar? In fact, get me two. Once I've got that on her, you can move her.'

It was only a precaution. The little girl didn't appear to have any other injuries apart from her leg. She seemed to be moving her other limbs without any problems, but Jess didn't want to take a risk.

It only took a few seconds to manoeuvre the collar into place and fasten it securely. The cold water was moving quickly. It had only been around the children's legs when she'd entered the vehicle—now it was reaching their waists. Time was absolutely of the essence here.

She was freezing. How on earth would these children be feeling? Kids were so much more susceptible to hypothermia because they lost heat more quickly than adults.

Another firefighter had appeared next to John, and they held a type of stretcher between them. Space was at a premium so Jess pushed herself back into the corner of the bus to allow them to load the little girl and pass her up through the window to Callum.

Time was ticking on. The sky was darkening and the level of the freezing water rising. She squeezed her way into the seat vacated by the little girl and started to do a proper assessment on the little unconscious boy, who was held in place by his seat belt.

'Anyone know his name?' she shouted to the crew.

'It's Marcus.' The deep voice in her ear made her jump.

'Where did you come from? I thought you were on the roof?'

'The water's too cold to have anyone in it for long. I told John to go ashore and dry off.'

'Tell me about it. Try being a kid.'

There was an easy familiarity in having Callum at her side. It didn't matter that she hadn't seen him for years, it almost felt as if it had been yesterday.

Callum had changed, and so had she. The skinny youth had filled out in all the right places. His broad shoulders and muscled chest were visible through his kit. The shorter hairstyle suited him—even though it revealed the odd grey hair. They were only visible this close up.

'What do you need?'

He was watching as she checked Marcus's pulse, took his temperature, looked him over for any other injuries and shone a torch in his eyes to check his pupil reactions.

She shook her head. 'This is going to have to be a scoop and run. He's showing severe signs of hypothermia. His pulse is low and I can't even get a reading with this thing.' She shook the tympanic thermometer in the air. 'So much for accurate readings.'

She placed the collar around his neck. 'I don't want to waste any time. I can't find an obvious reason for him being unconscious. His clothes are soaking—right up to his chest. We can't waste another second. Can you get me some kind of stretcher so we can get him out of here?'

Callum nodded. 'Get me a basket stretcher,' he shouted to one of his colleagues. He gestured his head to the side as the stretcher was passed down. She stared at the orange two-piece contraption, watching while he took a few seconds to slot the pins into place and assemble it. It had curved sides, handholds, adjustable patient restraints and a lifting bridle.

'This is the only way we'll get the casualties back up the steep embankment. Jump back up, Jess, we need as much room as we can to manipulate this into place.' A pair of strong arms reached down through the window to-wards her and she grabbed them willingly. It pained her to leave the little boy's side, but there wasn't time for egos or arguments here.

The cold air hit her again as she came back out into the open. If she'd thought standing in the icy water had been bad, it was nothing compared to the wind-chill factor. Her teeth started chattering.

'How…many more patients?' she asked the firefighter next to her.

'We've extricated all the adults. There's another two kids stuck behind the front seat, but their injuries are minor and they're not in contact with the water. We'll get to them next.'

'Has someone looked them over?'

He nodded. 'Your nurse and one of the paramedics. They had another kid who was submerged. She'll be in the ambulance ahead of you. We've just radioed in.'

The minibus gave another little lurch as the currents buffeted it. 'This thing had better not roll,' came the mumble from next to her.

Jess wobbled, trying to gain her balance. She hadn't even considered the possibility of the bus rolling. That would be a nightmare. There was a tug around her waist, and she looked to the side of the riverbank where one of the rope crew was taking up some of the slack in her line. The stretcher started to emerge through the window. At last. Maybe she'd get a better look at Marcus out here.

Callum's shoulders appeared. He was easing the stretcher up gently, guiding it into the arms of his colleagues.

The minibus lurched again. Callum disappeared back down into the depths of the minibus with a thud and a matching expletive. The firefighter next to her struggled to steady the weight in his arms, the stretcher twisting and its edge catching her side-on.

She teetered at the edge of the bus, losing her footing on the slippery side.

It seemed to happen in slow motion. She felt herself fall backwards, her arms reaching out in front of her. The firefighter who'd knocked her with the stretcher had panic written all over his face. There was a fleeting second as he struggled to decide whether to decide to grab her or maintain his hold on the stretcher.

What was it that knocked the air from her lungs? The impact of hitting the water? Or the icy water instantly closing over her head? Her reaction was instantaneous, sucking inwards in panic, instead of holding her breath.

The layers of clothes were weighing her down, as were her shoes. She tried to reach for the surface. The water hadn't been that deep, had it? She was choking. Trying to suck in air that wasn't there—only murky water. Then the overwhelming feeling of panic started to take over.

CHAPTER TWO

CALLUM HIT THE bottom of the river-filled minibus with a thud, the icy water doing nothing to slow the impact. What little part of him had remained dry was now soaked to the skin.

There was a splash outside, followed by some panicked shouts. Callum was instantly swept with a feeling of dread. The jolt had been a big one. *Please, don't let them have dropped the stretcher.*

He was on his feet in seconds, his arms grabbing at the window edge above him and pulling himself up onto the side of the bus.

The stretcher was steady, the child safe and being passed along the line. The crew around him, however, was panicking.

'Where's her line? Wasn't she wearing a line?'

Oh, no. His head flicked from side to side, searching frantically for any sign of Jess. She was the only female river-side. Everyone else was safely ashore. They could only be talking about her.

'Can you see her? Can anyone see her?'

Callum didn't hesitate. Not for a second. He saw where the outstretched fingers were pointing and jumped straight into the Clyde.

The water closed around his chest, leaving him up to his

neck with barely a toehold on the river's bed. Even after the water in the minibus, being fully submerged in the fast-flowing Clyde was a shock to the system. Every part of his body seemed to react at once. Everything went on full alert, hairs on end, trying to pull heat back into his centre.

He looked around him, shouting at the guys still on top of the bus. 'Where? Here?' He pointed to the riverbank. 'Tell them to pull in her line!'

The Clyde was murky and grey and several pieces of ice, broken from the river's edge, floated past.

He swept his arms around under the water. He couldn't see a thing. Not even a flash of the bright green jumpsuit she'd been wearing. The water wasn't too deep as he was on tiptoe. But he was a good foot taller than Jess, with a lot more bulk and muscle. Even he could feel the hidden currents pulling at his weight.

Every man working on the minibus had been wearing a line—except him. He took a few seconds to follow the lines from the riverbank to the bus, until he located the one that led directly into the river.

The firefighters on the bank were having the same problem. It took a few moments of frantic scrambling to ascertain which line belonged to Jess. They started to reel it in and Callum waded through the water towards it.

There! A flash of green as she was tugged nearer the surface.

He grabbed, lifting her whole body with one arm, raising her head and chest above the water's surface.

For the briefest second there was nothing, just the paler-than-pale face.

Then she coughed and spluttered, and was promptly sick into the river. He fastened one arm around her chest, pulling her back towards him, supporting her weight and lifting his other arm to signal to the crew to stop pulling in her line.

'I've got you, Jess. It's okay.' He whispered the words calmly in her ear. The cold wasn't bothering him now. There was no heat coming from her body, but he could feel the rise and fall of her chest under his hands. He could feel her breathe.

Relief. That was the sensation sweeping through him. Pure and utter relief.

He always felt like this after a rescue. It was as if the anxiety and stomach-clenching that had been an essential part of his momentum and drive to keep going just left him all at once. More often than that, after a rescue he would go home and sleep soundly for ten hours, all his energy expended. Building reserves for the next day so he could do it all again.

Even Drew understood. And on those nights his little body would climb into bed next to his father and cuddle in, his little back tucked against Callum's chest—just the way Jess's was now.

She coughed and spluttered again. He could hear her teeth chattering. She still hadn't spoken. Was she in shock?

There would be an investigation later. An investigation into why the paediatric consultant helping them had ended up in the middle of a fast-flowing icy river.

But right now he wanted to make sure Jess was okay. He started wading towards the riverbank, keeping Jess close to his chest. Several of his colleagues waded in towards him, sweeping Jess out of his arms and wrapping them both in blankets.

One of the paramedics started pulling out equipment to check her over. Callum pulled his jacket and shirt over his head. The cold air meant nothing to him right now—

he couldn't be any colder anyway. He gratefully accepted a red fleece thrust at him by one of his colleagues.

He pulled it over his head. There was instant heat as soft fleece came into contact with his icy skin. Bliss.

Two basket stretchers with a firefighter on either side were currently being guided up the steep, treacherous slope. The two kids with hypothermia. He could see the ambulance technicians waiting at the top of the bank, ready to load them into the waiting ambulances.

'Stop it!'

He turned, just in time to see Jess push herself to her feet and take a few wobbly steps.

'I'm fine. Now, leave me alone.' She pulled the blankets closer around her, obviously trying to keep the cold out.

He turned to one of his colleagues. 'See if someone will volunteer some dry clothing for our lady doc.'

Jess stalked towards him. Her face was still deathly pale, but her involuntary shivering seemed to have stopped. She pointed to the stretchers. 'I need to get to the kids. I need to get them to hospital.'

Callum shook his head. 'Jess, you've just been submerged in freezing water. You need to get checked over yourself. The kids will go straight to Parkhill. One of your colleagues will be able to take care of them.'

She shook her head fiercely. '*I* will take care of them. I'm the consultant on call. Neither of my junior colleagues has enough experience to deal with this. Two kids with hypothermia? It's hardly an everyday occurrence. Those kids need me right now.'

One of the firefighters appeared at his side with a T-shirt and another jacket. Callum rolled his eyes. 'You've still got a stubborn streak a mile wide, haven't you?'

He handed the clothes over to her. 'Get changed and I'll get you back topside.' She shrugged off her jumpsuit, tying the wet top half around her middle, hesitating only for a second before she pulled her thin cotton top off underneath.

In just a few seconds he saw her pale skin and the outline of her small breasts against her damp white bra. It was almost translucent. She pulled the other T-shirt over her head in a flash. But not before he'd managed to note just how thin she was.

Jess had always been slim. But slim with curves. What had happened to her?

She zipped the jacket up to her neck. Meeting his eyes with a steely glare. Daring him to mention the fact she'd just stripped at a riverside, or to mention her obviously underweight figure.

Callum knew better.

He'd learned over the last few years to pick his battles carefully.

Now wasn't the time.

He signalled and a couple of lines appeared down the side of the steep incline. He leaned over and clipped her harness. Her whole bottom half was still wet—as was his. Spare T-shirts and jackets could be found, but spare shoes and trousers? Not a chance.

'You do realise we go back up the way we came down?'

She sighed, but he couldn't help but notice the faint tremble in her hands. An after-effect of the cold water? Or something else?

He stepped behind her and interlocked their harnesses. 'The quickest way to get you back up is to let me help you.'

He could see her brain searching for a reason to disagree.

'You want to get back up to those kids?'

She nodded. Whatever her reservations, she'd pushed them aside.

'Then let me help you. It's like abseiling in reverse. Lean back against me.'

She was hesitating, still keeping all the weight on her legs, so he pulled her backwards towards him. He felt a little shock to feel her body next to his.

It had felt different in the water, more buoyant, the water between them cushioning the sensation. But now it was just clothes. Wet clothes, which clung to every curve of their bodies.

Her body was tense, stiff, and it took a few seconds for her to relax. He wrapped his arms around her, holding onto the lines in front of them, and gave them a little tug. His lips accidentally brushed against her ear as he spoke to her. 'We let the lines take our weight. If you just lean back into me, I'll walk up back up the incline. Just try and keep your legs in pace with mine. It feels a little weird, but it'll only take a few minutes.'

He let her listen, digest his words. He could feel her breathing sync with his, the rise and fall of their chests becoming simultaneous. She put her hands forward, holding onto the same line as he was, reaching for a little security in the strange situation.

He wrapped his hands around hers. His thick gloves were in place, to take the taut strain of the line.

He felt the tug of the line and started to walk his legs up the slope, taking her weight on his body. He looked skyward. Praying for divine intervention to stop any reactions taking place.

It was the weirdest sensation. The last time their bodies had been locked together she'd been seventeen and he'd been twenty-one. A whole lifetime had passed since then.

A marriage, a divorce, a fierce custody battle—and that was just him. What had happened to her?

His eyes went automatically to her hand. He'd always

imagined a girl like Jess would be happily married with a couple of kids by this age. But even through her wet gloves he could see there was no outline of a wedding band. Not even an engagement ring.

Something clenched at him. Was it curiosity? Or was it some strange thrill that Jess might be unattached?

His head was buzzing. He couldn't even make sense of his thoughts. He hadn't seen this woman in years. He hadn't even *heard* about her in years. He had no idea what life had flung at Jessica Rae. And she had no idea what life had thrown at him.

Drew. The most important person in his world.

A world he kept tightly wrapped and carefully preserved.

Drew's mother, Kirsten, had left after the divorce and costly custody battle. She was in New York—married to her first love, who she'd claimed she should never have left in the first place, as he was twice the man that Callum was. Callum had been a 'poor substitute'. Words that still stung to this day.

By that point, Callum couldn't have cared less about her frequent temper tantrums and outbursts. He had only cared about how they impacted on Drew.

Drew was the best and only good thing to have come out of that marriage.

He didn't intend to make the same mistake twice.

He'd never introduced any woman to Drew in the three years following his divorce. No matter how many hints they'd dropped.

But his immediate and natural curiosity was taking over. He didn't have a single bad memory about Jessica Rae. Even their break-up had been civilised.

Seeing her today had been a great shock, but her warm brown eyes and loose curls took him straight back thirteen years and he couldn't resist the temptation to find out a little more when it was just the two of them. They were around halfway up now. 'So, how have you been, Jessica? It's been a long time since we were in a position like this.'

He was only half-joking. Trying to take some of the strain out of her muscles, which had tensed more and more as they'd ascended the slope. Was Jessica scared of heights?

Her voice was quiet—a little thoughtful even. 'Yes. It has been, hasn't it?' She turned her head a little so he could see the side of her face. 'I'd no idea you were a firefighter. Didn't you do engineering at uni?'

She'd remembered. Why did that seem important to him?

'Yes, three years at Aberdeen Uni.' He gave a fake shudder. 'These would be normal temperatures for up there.'

'So, how did you end up being a firefighter?'

Was she just being polite? Or was she genuinely curious? He'd probably never know.

'There was a fire in the student accommodation where I stayed. We were on the tenth floor.' He tried to block out the pictures in his mind. 'It gave me a whole new perspective on the fire service. They needed to call out a specialist team and specialist equipment to reach us.' He didn't normally share this information with people. But Jess was different. Jess knew him in ways that most other people didn't.

'That must have been scary.'

Not even close. There was so much he was leaving unsaid.

The terrifying prospect of being marooned on a roof with the floors beneath you alight.

The palpable terror of the students around you.

The look on the faces of the fire crew when they realised you were out of reach and they had to stand by and wait, helpless, until other crew and equipment arrived.

'Callum?'

'What? Oh, yes, sorry. Let's just say it made me appreciate the engineering work involved in the fire service's equipment. I joined when I finished university. It didn't take me long to find my calling at the rope rescue unit. I still do some other regular firefighting duties, but most of the time I'm with the rescue unit.' He wanted to change the subject. He didn't want her to ask any questions about the fire. 'What about you? Are you married with four kids by now?'

It was meant to be simple. A distraction technique. A simple change of subject, taking the emphasis off him and putting it back on to her.

But as soon as the words left his mouth he knew he'd said the wrong thing. The stiffness and tension in her muscles was automatic.

They were nearing the edge of the incline and he could see movement above them. The flurry of activity as the stretchers were pulled over the edge and the paramedics and technicians started dealing with the children.

'Things just didn't work out for me.'

Quiet words, almost whispered.

He was stunned into silence.

There was obviously much more to it than that but now was hardly the time or the place.

And who was he to be asking?

He hadn't seen Jessica in thirteen years. Was it any of his business what had happened to her?

The radio on his shoulder crackled into life. 'We've got the last two kids. Minor injuries—nothing significant. There's an ambulance on standby that will take them to be checked over.'

'Are all the ambulances heading to Parkhill?' She sounded anxious.

He lifted the radio to his mouth. 'Wait and I'll check. Control—are all paediatric patients being taken to Parkhill?'

There was a buzz, some further crackles, then a disjointed voice. 'Four classified as majors, eight as minors. Two majors and six minors already en route. The adults have gone to Glasgow Cross.'

'Give me your hand!' A large arm reached over the edge and grabbed Jessica's wrist, pulling them topside. Someone unclipped their harnesses and tethers, leaving them free of each other.

'Doc, you're requested in one of the ambulances.'

Jess never even turned back, just started running towards the nearest ambulance, where one of the hypothermic kids was being loaded.

Callum watched her immediately fall back into professional mode.

'Scoop and run,' she shouted. 'Get that other ambulance on the move and someone get me a line to Parkhill. I want them to be set up for our arrival.'

Callum looked around him. The major incident report was going to be a nightmare. It would probably take up the next week of his life.

He grabbed hold of the guy next to him. 'Any other problems?'

The guy shook his head. 'Just waiting to lock and load the last two kids. The clean-up here will take hours.'

Callum nodded. 'In that case, I'm going to Parkhill with the ambulances. I want to find out how all these kids do. I'll be back in a few hours.'

He jumped into the back of one of the other ambulances, where the paramedic and nurse were treating the other hypothermic kid. 'Can I hitch a ride?' He glanced at the nurse, who was balanced on one leg. 'Did you hurt yourself?'

The paramedic nodded.

'Ride up front with the technician. We're going to be busy back here.'

The nurse grimaced, looking down at her leg. 'I'm sure it's nothing. Let's just get these kids back to Parkhill.'

Callum jumped back down and closed the doors, sliding into the passenger seat at the front. Within seconds the ambulance had taken off, sirens blaring. Great, the paediatrician had ended up in the Clyde and the nurse had injured her ankle. The major incident report was getting longer by the second.

It wouldn't take long to get through the city traffic at this time. He pulled his notebook from his top pocket. It was sodden. Useless, soaked when the minibus had tipped and he'd landed in the water.

'Got anything I can write on?'

The technician nodded, his eyes never leaving the road, and gestured his head towards the glove box, where Callum found a variety of notebooks and pens.

'Perfect. Thanks.' He started scribbling furiously. It was essential he put down as much as could for the incident report, before it became muddled in his brain.

The number of staff in attendance. The number of victims. The decision to call out the medical crew. Jessica. The descent down the incline. The temperature and depth of the water. Jessica being called onto the minibus. His first impression of the casualties. The way the casualties had been prioritised. The fact that Jessica had landed in the water.

The feeling in his chest when she'd disappeared under the water.

He laid the notebook and pen down in his lap.

This was no use.

He wasn't thinking the way he usually did. Calmly. Methodically.

He just couldn't get her out of his head.

It seemed that after thirteen years of immunity Jessica had reclaimed her place—straight back under his skin.

CHAPTER THREE

THE AMBULANCE DOORS were flung open and Jess heaved a sigh of relief. Her team was ready and waiting.

The A and E department would be swamped. There were twelve kids with a variety of injuries to look after, as well as all the normal walking wounded patients and GP emergency admissions that would have turned up today.

Everyone would be on edge. The place would be going like a fair.

Her team sprang into action immediately as she jumped down from the ambulance.

'Is the resus room set up for these two kids?'

'All prepared, Dr Rae. Fluids heating as we speak. Harry Shaw, the anaesthetist, and Blake Connor, the registrar, will help you run these kids simultaneously. You're drookit, Jess. Wanna get changed?'

A set of scrub trousers were thrust into her hands and she gave a little smile. Her team had thought of everything.

Harry appeared at her side. 'I take it it was freezing out there?'

'Baltic.' The one-word answer told him everything he needed to know.

The second ambulance arrived and both kids were wheeled into the resus room and transferred to the trolleys. Jess ducked behind a curtain and shucked off her soggy jumpsuit, replacing it the with the dry scrub trousers. If only her underwear wasn't still sodden.

Her team was on autopilot, stripping the freezing-wet clothing from both kids and bundling them up in warming blankets.

She walked out from behind the curtains. Harry Shaw was standing at the head of one of the trolleys, doing his initial assessment. 'What can you tell me?'

She looked up as Callum appeared at the doorway and handed her a sheet of paper. 'Thought this might be useful,' he said as he walked away.

She stared at what he'd scribbled for her. *Temperature of the Clyde is currently minus five degrees centigrade. Moving water takes longer to freeze.*

It was just what she needed. The temperature to which these kids had been exposed was very important.

She walked over to Harry. 'This is Marcus, he's four. He was unconscious at the scene but I can't find any obvious sign of injury. Showing severe signs of hypothermia. As far as I know, his head was always above the water, but we couldn't get the tympanic thermometer to register on-site.'

Harry nodded. 'I need baseline temps on both these kids. Has to be a core temperature, so oesophageal temperatures would be best.'

More paperwork appeared in her hand from the receptionist. 'Nursery just called with some more details.'

Her eyes scanned the page and she let out a little sigh. 'This is Lily. She's four too. She was submerged at the scene—but no one can be sure how long.'

Harry was one of the most experienced paediatric anaesthetists that she knew. He'd already realised that Lily was the priority and left Connor to take over with Marcus. He was already sliding an ET tube into place for Lily. He took a few seconds to check her temperature. Both cardiac monitors were switched on and the team stood silently to watch them flicker to life.

Jessica's heart thumped in her chest. What happened in the next few minutes would determine whether these kids made it or not.

'Marcus's temp is thirty degrees. Moderate hypothermia,' shouted Connor.

She watched the monitor for a few more seconds. 'He's bradycardic but his cardiac rhythm appears stable. Any problems with his breathing?'

Connor shook his head. 'He's maintaining his airway. His breathing's just slowed along with his heart rate.'

Jessica's brain was racing. She was the paediatric consultant. This was her lead. But Harry was an extremely experienced anaesthetist. She wanted to be sure they were on the same page.

She turned to him. 'Warmed, humidified oxygen, contact rewarming with a warming unit, rewarmed IV fluids and temperature monitoring. Do you agree?'

He gave her a little smile over the top of his glasses. 'Sounds like a plan. I've paged one of my other anaesthetists to come down.' The nursing staff started to flurry around them, carrying out the instructions. Jessica felt nervous.

Hypothermia was more common in elderly patients than in children. Every year they had a few cases come through the doors of A and E, but she wasn't always on duty. And most of those kids were near-drownings—kids who'd been playing on frozen rivers or lakes and had slipped under the water.

Blake Connor, her registrar, looked up from Marcus's arm. 'I've got the bloods.' He rattled off a whole host of tests he planned to run. 'Anything else?'

She shook her head. 'Right now, we're working on the

assumption that he's unconscious due to his hypothermia. There's no sign of any head injury or further trauma. Keep a careful eye on him. I want to know as soon he regains consciousness. He'll probably be disorientated and confused. Most adults with a temperature at this stage start undressing. We might need to sedate him if he becomes agitated.' She scribbled in the notes then spoke to the nursing staff.

'We're aiming for a temperature gain of around one degree every fifteen minutes. Keep an eye on his blood pressure and watch for any atrial fibrillation. Is that clear?'

The nursing staff nodded and she looked around. 'Anyone seen Jackie? She was the one who brought Lily in. I need some more information.'

One of the paramedics touched her arm. 'She fell, coming back up the slope. We think she might have fractured her ankle. Once we'd dropped Lily here my technician took her along to Glasgow Cross.'

Jess felt a twinge of guilt. It was her fault Jackie had been on the scene. She'd wanted the expertise of the experienced nurse at the site. Now, because of her, Jackie was injured. It didn't seem fair.

'Lily's temperature is lower than Marcus's. It's twenty-eight degrees.' Harry had just finished sliding the oesophageal temperature monitor into place. He glanced at the monitor. 'She's borderline, Jess. What do you want to do?'

Jess pulled back the warming blankets to get a better look at her small body. Lily was right on the edge, hovering between severe and moderate hypothermia. It was a wonder she hadn't gone into cardiac arrest.

'How's her respiratory effort?'

Harry was sounding her chest. 'For a child who was submerged I'm not hearing any fluid in her lungs. Just a few crackles. She is breathing, but not enough to keep me happy.'

'Wait a minute, folks.' Jess held her hand up as the monitor flickered, going from a stable but slow heart rate to a run of ectopic beats. She shook her head.

Time was of the essence here. She needed to make a decision.

Lily was deathly pale. All her surface blood vessels had contracted as her little body was focusing its resources on keeping her vital organs warm.

Her lips and ears were tinged with blue, showing lack of oxygen perfusing through her body.

Her eyes fell on Lily's fingers and toes. Their colour was poor.

No. Their colour was worse than poor.

The blueness was worse.

The tinkle of the monitor indicated Lily had gone into cardiac arrest. Jessica leaned across the bed and automatically started cardiac massage with the heel of one hand.

It clarified things and made the decision easier.

'Harry, we're not going to wait. Call the team. Let's get her to Theatre and begin extracorporeal rewarming. Can you phone ahead? Let them know we are resuscitating.'

One of the nurses nodded and picked up the phone in the resus room. 'Paediatric ECMO in Theatre ASAP. Yes, it's one of the minibus victims. Four-year-old female, submerged, with a core temperature of twenty-eight degrees. She's arrested and currently being resuscitated. Dr Shaw has her intubated and they'll be bringing her along now.' She replaced the receiver. 'Theatre one will be waiting for you.'

A wave of relief washed over Jessica. There was no drama. No struggling to find theatre time. It sounded as though the theatre staff was already prepared for the possibility of one of the hypothermic kids needing ECMO.

Extracorporeal membrane oxygenation worked with cardiopulmonary bypass to take over the function of the heart and provide extracorporeal circulation of the blood where it could be rewarmed and oxygenated. It had only been used in a few cases of hypothermia with cardiac arrest in the last few years, but had had extremely positive results with good outcomes for patients.

Lily was going to be one of those patients.

Jessica was absolutely determined.

Two porters appeared at either side of the trolley, ready for the move.

As they swept down the corridor towards the lifts she caught sight of Callum again, taking notes and talking to one of the nurses. He was still here?

She hadn't had a chance to think about him. She had been too busy concentrating her energies on keeping this little girl alive. She could feel the cold flesh under her hand as she pumped methodically, trying to push blood around Lily's body. Trying to get some oxygen circulating to her body and brain.

This was somebody's child. Somebody's pride and joy.

Their reason to get up in the morning and their reason to go home at night.

Any minute now some poor, frantic man and woman would turn up in A and E anxious to get news of their daughter.

Praying and pleading to hear the best possible news. Trying not to think about the pictures their brains had been conjuring up ever since they'd heard about the minibus crash. Struggling to remember to breathe as they made the journey to the hospital.

A journey that probably seemed to take twice as long as it normally did.

Their 'normal' day had changed beyond all recognition. Had they kissed their daughter goodbye that morning before they'd dropped her at nursery? At the place they'd assumed she would be safe?

Had they spent a few brief seconds taking her in their arms and feeling the warmth and joy of cuddling a child before they'd left her that morning? Or had they given her the briefest kiss on the top of her head because they had been in a rush to get to work? Because they hadn't realised it could be the last time they kissed their child.

Would they spend the rest of their lives regretting signing a consent form to say their daughter could go on the nursery trip? The one that could have cost her life?

All these thoughts were crowding her brain. Any time she had to resuscitate a child she was invaded with *what-ifs*?

But the *what-ifs* were about her own life. She'd spent the last three years thinking about the *what-ifs*.

What if she'd been driving the car that night?

What if she hadn't been on call?

What if her husband hadn't stopped to buy her favourite chocolate on the way home?

The lift doors pinged and they swept the trolley out. She lifted her head. The theatre doors were open and waiting for them.

One of the perfusionists was standing by, already scrubbing at the sinks, preparing to insert the catheter lines that could save Lily's life.

This was why she did this job.

This was why after a year of darkness she hadn't walked away. She might not have been able to save her own child but she would do her damnedest to save *this* one.

* * *

Callum stared at his watch. It had been six hours since he'd last seen Jessica sweeping down the corridor, her thin scrub trousers clinging to her wet backside, her hand pumping the little girl's chest.

He'd felt physically sick at that sight.

Not because he wasn't used to dealing with casualties. Casualties of all ages and all descriptions were part and parcel of the job.

But seeing the expression on Jessica's face wasn't.

Everything about this situation was having the strangest effect on him. The sight of Jessica hadn't just been unexpected—it had been like a bolt out of the blue.

They'd been childhood sweethearts who'd broken up when life had moved on and they'd never moved in the same circles again. He hadn't even heard anything about Jessica over the last few years.

Her words on the steep embankment had intrigued him. *Things just didn't work out for me.*

It made his brain buzz. There was a whole world of possibilities in those words. But he didn't feel as if he could come right out and ask.

Particularly when the sick kids were the priority.

And his lasting memories right now were the way her body had felt next to his. The way they'd seemed to fit together so well again—just like they always had.

It was the first time in a long time that he'd felt a connection to a woman.

The first time in a long time he'd ever *wanted* to feel a connection to a woman.

Sure, he'd dated on a few rare occasions, but nothing had been serious. He'd never introduced anyone to Drew. It was almost as if he didn't want to let anyone into that part of his life.

Would he ever feel ready to change that?

The doors opened at the end of the corridor and Jessica walked through. She looked absolutely exhausted. There were black circles under her eyes and her skin was even paler than it had been earlier.

He was on his feet in an instant. 'Jess? How did it go?'

She reached out to touch his arm, her brown eyes fixed on his. 'The next few hours will be crucial. We've done everything we can. Lily's temperature is coming up gradually. Now it's just wait and see. I've just spoken to her parents.' Was that a tear in Jess's eye?

It was there—written all across her face—how much those words pained her. How much she hated it that things were out of her control. The only thing left to do was wait.

She flicked her head from side to side. 'I need to get a report on all of the other kids. I need to find out how they are all doing.'

'No.' He rested his hand on her shoulder. 'You need to take a break. Come and sit down. Have a coffee, have something to eat. You must be running on empty, you know that can't be good for you.'

He could see the struggle in her eyes. 'I just can't, Callum. There were twelve kids in that accident. I'm the consultant on call. They're my responsibility.'

Callum glanced at the notes in his hand. 'Four have already been discharged. Another four have been admitted to the paediatric unit with mild hypothermia, a head injury, and some bumps and scrapes.'

Her eyes widened. 'How do you know all that?'

He gave her a little smile. 'It's part of the investigation after any major incident for the rope rescue crew. I always need to find out the outcomes for the victims. We need to look over everything that we did to make sure there were no mistakes.'

'And were there?'

He frowned. 'Apart from our doctor ending up in the Clyde? And your nurse fracturing her ankle?'

A little smile danced across her weary face. 'I don't think you have much control over tides and currents—no matter how much you want to. And Jackie? That's my responsibility. It was me who asked her to come on the rescue.'

He shook his head. He hadn't been able to shake the picture from his mind of Jessica falling into the icy river. It had made him feel sick to his stomach and would have to form part of his investigation.

'It's my job to make sure everyone is safe at the rescue site. It's my responsibility, not yours.'

Her shoulders relaxed a little. This was probably the first normal conversation she'd had all day. 'Do you want to fight me for it?'

'Will I win?' he quipped.

'Did you ever win?' she quipped back equally quickly.

He smiled. This was the Jess he'd once known.

He glanced at his notes. 'What about the other kids? I know about Marcus and Lily, but that still leaves another two.'

'One was Rosie, she was on the bus next to Marcus. The other is a little girl called Kelly. Both have broken limbs and were taken to surgery by the orthopaedic surgeon.'

'I'll need to follow them up for the report.'

She paused for a second, as if trying to find words. 'It was nice to see you today, Callum, even though it wasn't the best of circumstances. I'm glad you're doing well.'

Something sparked in his brain. She was just about to say goodbye. And he didn't want her to. He didn't want this to be the last time he saw Jessica Rae for another thirteen years.

'But how are you doing, Jess?' The words were out before he had a chance to censor them. Should he really be asking her something like that?

Her eyes lowered, breaking contact with his. Had he offended her? He could see her taking a deep breath.

'If you need any assistance with the investigation, feel free to come back and talk to me.' It was a deliberate sidestep. A deliberate attempt to move the conversation back to something more professional.

'I'll need a statement from you about the events.' He would. It wasn't a lie. Any event like this always needed information from all the professionals involved. Not least the one who had landed in the middle of the Clyde.

'That's fine, but can we do it some other time? I really want to check on the kids.'

What she needed to do was to rest. She looked as though a long night's sleep would do her the world of good. But he already knew that wasn't going to happen.

'Of course we can do it some other time. I need to follow up the adults at Glasgow Cross—I'll do that tomorrow. Then I'll come back here to see how the kids are doing.' He hesitated, just for a second. 'Will you be available at any point tomorrow?'

He was hopeful. He was more than hopeful. This might be work, but more than anything right now he'd like to see Jessica again. Any way he could.

She nodded. 'Leave it until later in the day. I'll be busy first thing in the morning with ward rounds and reviews.'

He gave her a little smile and he couldn't help the words that came out of his mouth. 'I'll see you then.'

There was a moment of hesitation, a flicker of something going through her eyes, and it struck straight at his heart. Was it panic? Was it fear?

Her shoulders had pulled back a little, moving away

from him, and the urge to reach out and pull her back towards him raced through his mind.

Why would the simplest of words cause this reaction? Jessica had always been a fun-loving, gregarious young woman. And even though he hadn't seen her in thirteen years this seemed wrong to him. Out of character.

But did he even know Jess's character any more?

It took a few seconds, but Jess seemed to gather herself and gave him the slightest flash of her brown eyes. 'Tomorrow's fine, Callum. I'll see you then.'

She turned and walked down the corridor. He couldn't tear his eyes away from her.

Now, when she was wearing only thin green theatre scrubs, he could see that her weight loss was dramatic. He flinched, remembering having seen the outline of her ribs on the riverbank. Now he could see her legs and hips. Hips that had been pressing up against his earlier.

He'd reached the bottom of the corridor, near the nurses' station in A and E. He recognised one of the sisters— they'd gone to a few study days on some aspects of community safety.

He walked over to her. 'Hi, Miriam, how's things?'

The older woman looked up and shot him a friendly smile. 'Hi, Callum. I take it you were dealing with the kids in the minibus?'

He nodded. 'Not the best day of my life. One of your doctors was out helping us—Jessica Rae?'

Miriam looked confused for a second then waved her hand. 'Oh, you mean Jessica Faraday. I know she's reverted back to her maiden name but I can't get used to it. She's fabulous. One of the best consultants we've got. The kids were certainly in safe hands with her.'

Callum could feel himself furrowing his brow. 'Jessica Faraday? She was married?'

Miriam finished typing something on the computer. 'Yeah.' She was distracted, concentrating on the words in front of her.

'But she's not now?' Callum couldn't help but probe. Curiosity was killing him.

Miriam met his eyes. 'Sadly not.'

Things just didn't work out for me.

Jessica's words echoed in his brain. He still didn't know what they meant, and it just didn't seem right to be asking someone else. It didn't matter that Miriam was a colleague—one he'd spoken to on many occasions—he just didn't feel he could ask anything personal about Jess.

It was an invasion of her privacy. He had no right to ask anything about her. It didn't matter that his curiosity was currently burning so fiercely in his stomach it would probably cause an ulcer.

Suddenly he was conscious of what he'd just done. He'd been around hospitals long enough to know that even the simplest and vaguest questions could be entirely misinterpreted.

Miriam had gone back to her paperwork—not in the least interested in why Callum was asking questions about Jessica. Thankfully, she had a hundred other things to worry about. The last thing he needed was rumours starting to spread in a hospital. He didn't want anyone to get the wrong impression.

What was the wrong impression?

He had no idea what he thought about all this.

All he knew for sure was that the haunted look in Jessica's eyes was going to stick in his brain for the rest of the day. And probably most of the night.

This was wrong. He shouldn't be thinking about her at all.

He had Drew to worry about. His little boy was his

entire life and he didn't want anything to get in the way of that. He *wouldn't* let anything get in the way of that.

The custody battle had been fiercely fought, sapping all his energy and strength. And whilst he'd been on dates in the last year or so, no woman had really attracted his attention. No woman had ever been introduced to his son.

And that was way he intended to continue.

He should walk away.

He should run.

But somehow he knew that come tomorrow afternoon he would be right here.

Right here, waiting for Jessica.

CHAPTER FOUR

CALLUM STARED AT the clock and pulled out his cellphone again. *How is Drew?* he typed.

Drew had been clingy last night. Definitely not normal for him. He hadn't wanted to go to bed and had just said he didn't feel good.

After a day stuck in the freezing-cold Clyde, all Callum had wanted to do was hold him close. So he'd broken all his own rules and let Drew come into bed beside him.

There hadn't seemed to be anything obvious wrong with Drew. His temperature hadn't been raised. He hadn't had a rash. But he'd had a restless night and when he'd stirred his porridge around his plate that morning Callum had looked at the pale little face and had known he couldn't send him to school today.

Thank goodness for good friends. Julie and Blair were always willing to help out any way they could.

His phone buzzed.

Not eating and a little tired. But managing to watch the TV. Don't worry. Julie.

Don't worry. Fat chance.

The door next to him opened. Jess. He stood up straight away and walked over to her. 'How are you? Are you okay?' She looked a little better today. There was some colour in her cheeks, her caramel-coloured hair hung in waves around her shoulders and her pink woollen jumper gave the illusion of some curves.

There it was again. The little surge he'd felt yesterday when he'd seen her. That buzz of attraction. He hadn't imagined it. He hadn't imagined it at all.

She gestured down the corridor. 'I'm fine. Honestly. No ill effects.' She gave him a little smile. She was definitely a little more relaxed today but, then, Parkhill was her comfort zone.

'How are the kids?'

Her expression was still serious. 'We've still got two in ITU, both serious but stable. Four were allowed home yesterday, another four were kept for observation overnight but are being discharged today. The last two will be in for a few days, both have different kinds of fractures.'

He gave her a knowing smile. 'Busy day, then?'

She let out a little laugh. 'What? No way. We've only had another thirty admissions on top of the accident yesterday. It's practically been a walk in the park.'

'Thirty? Is there some kind of outbreak?'

She nodded. 'Yip.' She handed over a set of case notes to the secretary next to them. She folded her arms across her chest. 'It's called a Scottish winter.'

'What do you mean?'

She gave a little shrug. 'It's like this every year. Asthma and chest infections flare up and there's always an outbreak of norovirus somewhere. Public health had to recommend closing two nurseries yesterday.' She waved her hand. 'We've got a baby with chickenpox in ITU. Oh, and the usual slips, trips and falls. We're thinking of putting a sign on the door of ward 1C saying *Only people in fibreglass may pass these doors.*'

He couldn't help the smile dancing across his face. 'It's that bad?'

She gave a little sigh. 'It's just how things are. That, and all the parents that come to the desk and give it laldy.'

He smiled. 'Now, there's a word I haven't heard in a while.'

She rolled her eyes. 'It's the most accurate description. I said it the other day to one of the Spanish registrars and he was totally lost. Thing is, it's never the parents with the sickest kids who cause a scene, it's the ones who probably shouldn't even be in an A and E department and don't think they should be waiting.'

'We get our fair share in the fire service too. Last month it was a guy who called 999 every time his house fire alarm went off.'

'Did he have a fire?'

Callum shook his head. 'Nope. He just kept burning his toast and thought we should come out.'

'Thank goodness. I thought it was just us that got the crazies.'

He looked over at her. Although her outward appearance had improved since yesterday, he could still sense the tiredness in her body.

'Are you sure you want to do this today? We can do it some other time if it doesn't suit you.'

She shook her head. 'You're going to need the statement at some point and it's probably best I do it while it's all still fresh in my mind.'

'Have you got time for a coffee?'

She glanced at her watch. 'Actually, I've got a couple of hours.' She looked around her. 'Can we get out of here for a little while? I need to cover for someone tonight so I'll be here until tomorrow.'

He bit his tongue. From the look of her she'd already covered last night too. Did she really need to do it again? The thought of getting her out of this place was very appealing. Maybe some fresh air and a change of scene would lessen the tiredness in her eyes. There was no way he'd say no to her.

'Sure. As long as you don't mind travelling in a fire and rescue vehicle.'

Her eyes widened. 'You've got a fire engine sitting outside?' He could hear the edge of excitement in her voice. It was almost everyone's childhood dream to ride in a fire engine.

He laughed. 'No, I've got the four-by-four. But I'm on call and can be paged at any time, so I need to be ready to go.'

'Oh.' She looked a little disappointed. 'Does that mean you can't go anywhere?'

He shook his head, his heart clenching a little as he realised she'd looked a little sad at the prospect. 'Of course I can. But let's not go too far. That way, if I get paged I can drop you back here quickly. Is there somewhere local you'd prefer?'

She nodded. 'There's an Italian coffee shop that does great food and some killer carrot cake about five minutes' drive from here. Just let me grab my bag and coat.'

He stood for a few seconds until she reappeared at his side, wearing a thick purple wool coat and pink scarf. He smiled. 'I take it you came prepared today.'

'After yesterday? I've honestly never been so cold. The first thing I did last night was put on the fire, find the biggest, snuggliest pair of pyjamas I could and pull my duvet in front of the fire.'

The picture was conjured up in his head instantly. Snuggly pyjamas might not be the sexiest nightwear he would normally think of for a woman, but it still brought a smile to his face.

They walked outside into the cold air and she automatically moved a little closer to him, letting his body shield her from the biting wind. It was all he could do to stop his arm reaching out to wrap around her waist.

He felt on edge. He hadn't seen her in years. She had a whole other life he knew nothing about. Little things started to edge into the corners of his mind. Who did Jessica have to snuggle up to after a stressful day at work? Had she spent the night alone in front of the fire?

Curiosity was killing him. Particularly after the comment Miriam had made the previous day about Jessica reverting to her maiden name.

He had a burning sensation to find out why. It suddenly seemed really important—even though it shouldn't. Did Jessica feel the nervous edge that he did?

But Jess seemed relaxed around him. She shot him another smile as she climbed into the car. 'You would have been horrified. I even resorted to bedsocks last night!'

'Were they pink?' He started the car and pulled out of the car park.

'How did you guess?'

'Because some things don't change.' Pink had always been her favourite colour. The words had come out before he'd had time to think about them. Because nothing could be further from the truth. Things had changed, for both of them—probably more than they could ever have imagined.

Thirteen years was a long time.

There was silence for a few seconds, as if she was thinking the same kind of thoughts that he was.

She gestured to the side. 'This way.' She waited until he changed lanes. 'I guess I always did like pink,' she said quietly. She touched the collar of her coat. 'I've even got a pink coat, I just didn't wear it today.'

Another little memory sparked into his brain. Jessica's wardrobe. She'd had the biggest array of clothes he'd ever seen. He shot her a smile. 'Knowing you, you've probably got a coat for every colour of the rainbow.'

She tilted her head to the side as if she was racking her brain. 'Emerald green.'

He raised his eyebrows.

'That's the colour I'm missing. I need to get an emerald-green raincoat and the rainbow will be complete.' She pointed in front of them. 'It's just over here. Pull in to the left.'

He halted just in front of the Italian-style coffee shop, walking around and opening the door for her.

The heat hit them as soon as they walked inside, along with a whole host of mouth-watering smells.

He pulled out a chair and helped her off with her coat, before sitting across from her and bringing out his array of paperwork. But his brain wasn't focusing on the paperwork.

Taking Jessica out of her own environment felt a little odd. It felt personal but this was business. A professional meeting. Nothing more, nothing less. No matter how casual it seemed.

No matter how *easy* it seemed.

Why did he have to keep reminding himself about that?

He pointed to the menu. 'What do you recommend?'

'Anything and everything. There won't be a single thing in here that you don't like.'

The waitress appeared at their side.

'Just a latte for me, please.'

'No.'

He couldn't help it. Her thin frame was too much for him. He was resisting the temptation to just order her some mushrooms, a portion of lasagne and some garlic bread. Things they used to eat together a long time ago and he knew that she liked.

He couldn't help but wonder who was looking out for Jess right now. Surely her friends had spoken to her quietly and told her she'd lost too much weight? It didn't matter that he hadn't seen her in years, he couldn't stand by and say nothing.

The waitress looked a little taken aback. Callum's eyes ran down the menu. 'You need more than just coffee. Order something else.'

He could see her take a deep breath, getting ready to argue with him. But he shook his head, the smallest of movements, then reached over and touched her hand. 'Don't.'

He kept his gaze steady. They'd been friends for such a long time. It didn't matter that he hadn't seen her in years. It didn't matter that fate had thrown them together. He had no idea what had happened in the last few years for Jess—and she might never tell him. But he could focus on what was in front of him.

The one thing he could do something about.

And she knew him. She knew him well.

She would know that he would never cause a scene, but she would also know that when he was determined, there was no way around him.

Her brown eyes were fixed on where his hand was touching hers. Was she annoyed? Did she think it inappropriate? Because he'd only done what had felt natural—and it didn't feel inappropriate to him.

He could see the long exhalation of breath, the relaxing of her shoulders, then she lifted her long dark eyelashes to meet his gaze.

The long dark eyelashes that used to tickle his cheeks.

The thought came out of nowhere, triggering a whole host of memories in his brain. Now, *they* could be inappropriate.

Jess's fingers moved under his. She looked at the wait-ress. 'What's the soup?'

'Minestrone or tomato and herb, both served with crusty bread.'

Jess pressed her lips together. 'I'll have the minestrone. Please.' She handed the menu over.

'I'll have the same—the soup and a latte.' Something fired in his brain and he remembered what she'd said in the car. 'And carrot cake—for both of us, please.' It wasn't what he would normally eat at this time. The paperwork was still in front of him. But right now it was the least of his concerns.

Would she tell him what had happened to her in the last few years? And, in return, would he be able to tell her about Drew?

He took the bull by the horns. 'You're thin, Jess. A lot thinner than you used to be. I'd rather have bought you a three-course meal than a plate of soup.'

'Who said I was letting you buy it?'

He smiled. There it was. The spark that had seemed missing at times. The spark that took him back thirteen years.

Every now and then it flared, reappearing out of no-where. Then the thin veil would come back down and the Jessica that he had once known would disappear.

He leaned back in the chair. Sparring with Jess now felt as natural as it had years ago. 'Oh, you're letting me. I can assure you of that.'

'Still a stubborn bossy boots, then, Callum?'

'I had a very good teacher,' was his automatic response. But it only took a second to know what he really should do. He stretched across the table and took both her hands in his. 'Actually, I'm still a concerned friend.'

He could sense her pull back a little. See her wariness at his actions.

'We haven't seen each other in years, Callum. We lost touch. You've no idea what's happened in my life and I've no idea what's happened in yours. If that accident hadn't happened yesterday, our paths might never have crossed again.'

'And that would have been a real shame.' He shook his head. 'I'm not glad the accident happened. I'm not glad those kids were injured. But I am glad our paths have crossed again. It's nice to see you.' His voice was low and the words said quietly. He hoped she could see the sincerity in his eyes.

She paused for a moment then said, 'It's nice to see you again too.' She gave him a little smile. 'You always were a pest when it came to food.' She had a glint in her eye, and he could see her visibly relaxing, sinking a little further into her chair and leaning her elbows on the desk so they were closer.

His reaction was entirely natural—he leaned forward too. 'Jessica Rae, I've no idea what you're talking about.'

She raised her eyebrows, her smile spreading across her face. She placed her head on her hands. 'What about the cookie incident, then?'

He stifled a laugh.

The memories came flooding back. A visit to the cinema with Jess asking him to hold her coffee and cookie that he'd bought her while she went and washed her hands. They'd been running late and the film had already started by the time they'd fumbled to their seats. It had taken Jess a few minutes to lift the napkin from her purchase and the scream she'd let out had caused the whole cinema to jump in shock.

'It was only a tiny nibble.' He shrugged his shoulders.

'It was a giant-size bite! And then you let me think that it was the boy behind the counter—you were going to let me go and complain.'

He couldn't stop laughing now, with the still indignant look on her face thirteen years later. 'Just as well the crumbs gave me away, then.'

Jess started to laugh too. Her shoulders shook as she bent forward and then threw her head back. Jess didn't have a delicate, polite laugh. It was loud and wholehearted, as if it came all the way from her toes.

There was something so nice about this. The way her skin glowed and her eyes sparkled when she laughed like that. The ease and familiarity of being with someone you felt comfortable around. Someone you shared a history with. Someone who made you feel as if you could look into their eyes and trust what they said.

Someone who wouldn't run out on you and your child.

Where had that thought come from?

The door to the café opened and a woman and her child bundled in out of the cold. The little boy's nose was glowing red underneath his woolly hat. He looked around the same age as Drew.

Callum pushed all thoughts of Drew's mother out of his head and leaned forward to pass a comment to Jess. But the expression on her face stopped him dead.

She'd gone from hearty laughter to deathly pale—almost as if she'd been caught unawares. He bit his tongue, stopping himself from asking what was wrong.

He had to give her time. He had to give her space. If Jess wanted to tell him something she would.

There was silence for a few seconds as he could see her gathering herself.

She nodded at his paperwork. 'This could take some time. Shouldn't we get started?'

The barriers were going up again. She was closing herself off from him. Going back to business as usual. 'What do you need from me?'

The waitress appeared and put down two bowls of steaming-hot minestrone and a basket of crusty bread. 'I need you to relax for a bit. I want to see you eat. Once you've finished we'll do my paperwork. I need a detailed statement from you.'

He didn't want the veil to come down. Because when it did Jess had the strangest look in her eyes, almost vacant, as if she was removing herself from the situation. It was obvious that she wasn't feeling any of the same strange sensations that he was. His brain was currently mush.

Being around Jess was flaring up too many memories in his mind. Sharing memories with Jess was both warming and setting off alarm bells in his head. He'd been awake most of the night, thinking about all the good times that they'd had together.

He hadn't even told her about Drew yet. And did he want to? He had no idea what he wanted to do about any of this. Could he be friends with Jessica or was it just a recipe for disaster? He'd just have to wait and see.

CHAPTER FIVE

IT WAS THE middle of the night. The snow had given way to sleet and was currently battering the windows in the old Glasgow hospital.

Whilst the ward was dark, most of the windows were adorned with festive lights. A Santa, a snowman and a reindeer stood out twinkling against the black night sky outside. A tree with multicoloured lights flickered at the end of the ward, and strings of icicles were hanging from most of the windows outside the ward bays.

A few little bodies shifted under the starched white hospital sheets and coloured blankets. Almost everyone was sleeping—unusual for a children's ward—with only a few little murmurs here and there. Alongside most of the beds were chairs and stools with an array of uncomfortable parents trying to catch a few hours' sleep as they watched over their children.

Jessica padded along the ward in her soft-soled shoes. She loved Christmas in the children's ward. Although most people in her circumstances would want to avoid this place, it was actually the one place at this time of year that gave her a little solace.

There were always people worse off than you.

Actually, no there weren't. No parent should outlive their child.

Here, in the ward, she felt safe. Everyone knew what had happened. No one asked awkward questions. If she needed a few moments on her own, she got them.

If she needed to be amongst people and in company, it was here.

If she needed to feel of value, there was no doubt she was needed here. There was always a little one to cuddle. There was always a parent to talk to in the quiet hours of night—to give some kind of explanation, to give some kind of comfort.

Mostly, she just liked to watch the kids sleeping.

There was nothing more comforting than watching a child sleep.

Tonight she was watching Grace Flynn, a seven-year-old with a rare form of aggressive bowel cancer. She'd had her tumours operated on twice.

Grace was a beautiful child. She wanted to be a ballerina, or an air hostess, or a teacher. She changed her mind every day. But she was becoming frailer and frailer with every visit. The chemotherapy and radiotherapy were having ravaging effects on her body. The surgeries were taking their toll. The battle was becoming harder and harder.

So tonight she was taking a little pleasure in watching Grace sleep. Watching the rise and fall of her little chest.

Moments like this always pained her. What was worse? Your child dying suddenly, with no chance to say goodbye, or dying slowly, painfully right before your eyes?

Her brain couldn't even begin to compare those issues. All she knew was that she would do everything in her power to help Grace and her parents.

Hopefully Grace would be able to be discharged home with her family tomorrow and get to spend Christmas at home.

She would love that. She might be the model patient

but she always had a smile on her face when she was discharged home.

Jessica walked down the corridor, watching the twinkling lights on the windows and appreciating the stillness of the ward.

It wasn't always quiet in here. Some nights it went like a fair. Some nights she didn't even see the inside of her on-call room. Then there were other nights like tonight.

She sat down at the nurses' station and tapped a few keys on the computer, bringing up the file of one of the kids admitted earlier. She would never have been able to sleep anyway.

Images of Callum were currently swimming around in her brain.

It was the oddest of feelings.

Because she didn't know how she felt.

For the last few years she'd been sad. She'd worked hard to put one foot in front of the other and try and come out the other side. And now she finally felt as if she'd reached a plateau.

She didn't cry non-stop any more. She didn't spend every day wishing she didn't need to get out of bed. She wasn't insanely jealous of every woman pushing a stroller in the street.

Oh, she still had moments when things crept up on her and caught her unawares. When she needed a few minutes to gather herself or to wipe the stray tear that appeared on her face.

But things had eased. It was still the first thing she thought about every morning and the last thing she thought about at night. But it didn't fill her every waking moment of the day any more. She'd allowed herself to think about other things. To care a little about other things.

And work was her biggest comfort. It helped her tick

along. It gave her a sense of purpose. A little confidence that she did have a life worth living.

Then something like this happened.

A blast from the past, totally unexpected. Totally unprepared for.

Callum was evoking a whole host of memories. Most of which were good. Some of which were distinctly edged with tinges of pink—the way all teenage first-love memories were.

It was a little unsettling. Not just seeing Callum but the whole host of *what-ifs* that had her flooded her mind afterwards—some of which had permeated her dreams.

What if she'd married Callum? What would her life have been like? Would they still have been together after all this time?

She tried to push the thoughts away. It felt disloyal. Disloyal to the memory of her husband, Daniel, and her little boy, Lewis.

Daniel had been the love of her life. She'd been blissfully happy. She'd thought they'd grow old together. She'd *expected* them to grow old together.

But as much as she'd loved Daniel, the loss of Lewis was even worse. As if someone had ripped her heart right out of her chest and squeezed it until every last drop of blood was gone.

The pain had almost killed her.

Maybe that was why her brain was drifting into unchartered territories. If she'd stayed with Callum, Daniel and Lewis would never have featured in her life.

She would never have suffered such torment and hurt at their loss. She wouldn't have found herself wondering if she wanted to go on. To live a life without them.

Maybe Callum was a safe memory.

She opened her eyes, looking around to see if anyone

had noticed her hunched over the keyboard. Two of the nurses were standing at the door of one of the rooms but they hadn't noticed a thing.

Her pager sounded and she was on her feet instantly. ITU. She had three kids in there right now. The baby with chickenpox and Marcus and Lily from the accident. She started saying silent prayers in her head as she walked swiftly down the corridor. She looked around. It was the dead of night and there was no one else about so she took off. Her soft running footsteps echoed up and down the passages of the long building until she reached the doors and squirted her hands with gel before entering.

The doors swung open. The steady whoosh-whoosh of the ventilators was the first thing that she heard whenever she stepped inside. In most instances it was a soothing sound, often not reflecting the serious condition of the patients inside. She took a quick look around the unit. It was brighter than the rest of the hospital, even though some of lights were dimmed.

She recognised a figure next to Lily's bed and walked over quickly. Pauline, the sister in ITU, was great. She'd been there for ten years, had a whole wealth of experience and, more importantly, good instincts. Jessica trusted her judgement, and she also valued her friendship. She'd been a pillar of strength for Jess in the last few years.

'What's up, Pauline?'

Pauline shook her head. 'She's gone from bradycardic and hypothermic to the opposite. Tachycardic and high temp. Isn't it amazing how kids go from one extreme to the other?'

Jessica cast her eyes over the monitor. Thirty-six hours ago Lily had had a heart rate of fifty and now it was one hundred and sixty. 'Darn it. The ECMO should be keeping her heart rate and temperature steady. She must have an infection somewhere. How's her suctioning been?'

Pauline's lips pressed together. She hated it as much as Jess did when kids got sicker. 'She's been suctioned every four hours and there's been no increase in her secretions.'

Jessica rolled her shoulders back, trying to relieve the tension in her neck and shoulders. Everyone knew that ECMO could have complications—bleeding, infections, neurological damage and kidney damage.

Jessica unwound the pink stethoscope from her neck. 'I'll have a little listen to her chest. It was clear earlier and her chest X-ray was fine, but you know how things can change.'

She placed her stethoscope on Lily's little chest and listened for a few seconds then frowned. 'I can hear crackles in her lungs. Can I have her chart? I'll get her started on IV antibiotics right away.' She scribbled on the chart handed to her. 'Are you okay to make these up or do you want me to do it?'

Most of the nurses in ITU had extended roles. The IV antibiotics could be sent up from the hospital pharmacy but that would take time. Time that Lily essentially didn't have. Pauline nodded her head. 'It's fine. I'll do it. It will only take a few minutes.'

Jessica continued to make a few notes. 'I'm asking for another chest X-ray. I want to see if there's any change from this morning. And I'll be about for the next few hours. Let me know if you have any concerns.'

'Not planning on having any sleep tonight, Jess? You know that's not good for you.' There was concern in Pauline's voice. And it was sincere—she always tried to look out for Jess.

Jess just gave her a little smile and kept writing. Sometimes she just liked to keep her head down.

'I meant to ask you, how do you know Callum?'

The question took her by surprise. She felt on guard, even with a woman she'd always trusted. But Pauline's face was open and friendly. 'Callum Kennedy?' she asked.

'Yeah, the fireman—the rope rescue guy. He was on the phone earlier, enquiring after the kids. He knows we can't give him any specific details. He just wanted to check everything was okay. Apparently he was in yesterday too. The staff say he's gorgeous.'

Callum was in here yesterday? Why hadn't she known that? 'What did he say?'

Pauline's eyebrows rose. 'He said you went way back— that you were old friends.'

She was obviously piquing Pauline's interest, and it made her wish she hadn't asked. Jessica felt the colour flare into her cheeks. What on earth was wrong with her? Callum was a good-looking guy and in a gossip hive like a hospital it was obvious people would comment.

Pauline was still talking as she adjusted the controls on Lily's monitors. 'Even David knows him. Says he's played five-a-side football against him. Apparently he's single.' She gave a little laugh. 'He also says the firefighter football team are a bunch of break-your-leg animals. He says he always volunteers to be goalie when they play against them.'

David. The solitary male staff nurse in ITU who was usually the butt of everyone's jokes. Just as well he was fit for it. He always gave as good as he got. And it was good to have a male in a predominantly female environment. Some babies responded better to a male voice—even seemed to be soothed by it.

And he always told any little boy who woke up scared and ventilated in ITU that the same thing had happened to him as a kid.

Some people were just destined to work with children.

Then again, David had just given her a vital piece of information. Callum was single. It seemed ridiculous. He was a gorgeous man, with a good job, and was fun to be around. Women would be beating a path to his door. Why on earth was he single? And, more importantly, why would she care?

'Jess? What's wrong?'

'Nothing. Nothing's wrong.' She could hardly look Pauline in the eye. Pauline was too perceptive by half. Her cheeks were practically bursting. She felt like some crazy teenager again.

'Jess, honey, no one would ever dare say these words to you. But I will because I care about you. Things are looking easier for you, Jess. Your mood has lifted, you don't have quite as many dark circles under your eyes. And once you start eating again...'

'What do you mean, Pauline?'

Pauline bit her lip. 'I mean that if you and Callum have history, *good history*, that might be a good thing.' She hesitated then continued, 'It might be something to embrace instead of run away from.'

'You think I run away from things?'

Pauline reached over and touched her arm. 'I think that you're ready. I think it might be time to start living your life again. I think it might be time to lift your head above the parapet and see what's out there. Whether that's Callum or someone else.' She gave Jess's arm a little squeeze. 'The next step will be hard, Jess. It might be easier if you took it with someone you used to know.'

She looked at Pauline's hand on her arm. The same place that Callum had touched her. The touch that had made every tiny hair on her arm stand on end and little unfamiliar sparks shoot up her arm. It had felt odd.

She wasn't sure how she felt about any of this. She'd spent

a long time with one man and the thought of another—
even one who was familiar—was alien to her. There was
still that burning edge of disloyalty. Right now she couldn't
even consider that Callum could be anything but a friend.
No matter how her body reacted to him. It didn't help that
her confidence was at an all-time low.

She caught a glimpse of her reflection in one of the
windows in ITU. She hardly recognised herself these
days. Even she was aware of how thin she was.

She'd once been proud of her figure. She'd liked the
glow about her skin. But all that had been lost in the last
three years. She barely even looked in a mirror any more.
She got her hair cut when it took too long to dry in the
mornings. She only put make-up on to stop people com-
menting on how pale she looked. What man could ever
find her attractive now?

'It's only work, Pauline, nothing else.' The sadness in
her voice surprised even her. Why were thoughts like this
even entering her mind?

'But maybe it could be something else?' Pauline had
raised her eyebrows and there was a hopeful tone in her
voice.

Everything about this made her uncomfortable.

'If it hadn't been for the accident, our paths would never
have crossed again. It's just some crazy coincidence. Callum isn't interested in me.'

'Isn't he? Well, he apparently asked after you while he
was in.'

'He did?' She hated the way her heart had given a little
jolt at those words.

Pauline finished checking the controls on the ECMO
machine and recorded them in the log. 'Yes. He did.' She
stared at Jess. 'All I'm saying is there's a world of possibilities out there. Just leave yourself open to a few.' She

hung the chart at the end of the bed and moved across to the next patient.

Jessica gazed at her reflection in the glass. A world of possibilities.

How on earth would she cope with those?

CHAPTER SIX

CALLUM WAS BORED. Bored rigid.

He usually liked coming to study days. There was always something new to learn in his job and some networking to be done. But this guy had been droning on for what seemed like hours. It felt like he was saying the same sentence over and over again. It didn't matter that the clock had only moved on ninety minutes, it felt like groundhog day.

The door at the back of the auditorium opened and he heard a little murmur around him, accompanied by the sound of over a hundred firefighters straightening up all at once. He turned sideways, trying to see what had caused that effect. Had the chief officer just come into the room?

No. It wasn't the chief officer. It was a woman with caramel-coloured hair and a sway to her step. His mouth fell open. Jess?

All of a sudden he was paying attention to what the man at the front of the room was saying. 'Ladies and gentlemen, I'd like you to welcome Dr Jessica Rae. She's a paediatrician at Parkhill, the children's hospital in Glasgow.'

Callum tore his eyes away from Jessica for a moment—something none of the other men in the room were doing—to look at his programme. It had someone else's name on it for the next lecture.

'Dr Rae is filling in for Dr Shepherd, who had an unexpected family emergency today. We're very grateful that she could find the time to step in for us. Dr Rae will be talking to us about paediatric smoke inhalation and immediate treatment.'

Callum watched as Jessica walked to the front of the room. Her hair was shining and resting in curls on her shoulders. And she was dressed cleverly in layers to hide how thin she was, and in bright colours to complement her skin tone.

'Hey, Callum, isn't that the lady doc from the minibus accident?' the firefighter sitting next to him whispered.

'Yes, it is.' He still hadn't taken his eyes from her. She was wearing a bright blue dress that was draped and gathered at the front. She looked good. She had more colour about her face today and was wearing bright lipstick.

'Wow. She looks gorgeous.' He turned and squinted at Callum, in the way only a friend could. 'Didn't you say you knew her from years gone by?'

Callum shifted uncomfortably in his seat. He knew exactly what was going on in Frank's head. 'Yeah. She's an old friend.'

Frank let out the lowest of whistles. 'Wish my old friends looked like that.'

The hackles at the back of Callum's neck immediately rose. Frank was only voicing what every appreciative man in the room was thinking. But that didn't mean that he liked it. He wanted to put a cocoon around Jess and protect her. Hide her away from the leering glances.

He hadn't seen her in more than a week and, boy, was she a sight for sore eyes. The fact that thought had sprung into his mind alarmed him. Why, all of a sudden, was he annoyed by the fact that other men found her attractive? What right did he have to feel like that?

More than once this week his hand had hovered over the phone, thinking of a reason to phone Jess again. Looking for any excuse just to speak to her.

But then his rational side had kicked in and brought him back into reality.

Too bad reality was looking kind of blurry right now.

Jess stood up at the podium and looked around the room. When her eyes rested on Callum he saw her give a little start, before she gave him a nervous smile.

'Hi, folks. I recognise some of the faces in here today because unfortunately, in our lines of business, our paths frequently cross.' She pressed a button and the presentation appeared on the wall behind her. 'I'm going to give you some up-to-date information on the best things you can do for a child with smoke inhalation.' She lifted her hand and gestured around the auditorium. 'I'm sure it's something you've all had to deal with.'

Jessica was confident at work. She was in control. That much was clearly evident. She could probably have done this presentation with her eyes shut. And it was nice to see her that way.

Her voice was steady and clear. 'We don't expect any of you to do anything more than the most basic first aid. I'm sure you're all aware that the paramedics and ambulances aren't always on scene immediately, so my job today is to give you enough information to feel confident in your first responses.'

She lifted her hand, pressed a button on the remote and the screen behind her changed. Then she turned back and gave the room a dazzling smile. 'Now, let's begin.'

It was officially the quickest thirty minutes of her life. She hadn't hesitated that morning when a colleague had asked her to cover for him. As a paediatric consultant at a teaching hospital she was often asked to give lectures to medical students and people in other disciplines. This was a walk in the park for her.

If only there wasn't a great big distraction right in the middle of the room.

Callum was definitely the proverbial elephant in the room today.

She spent the whole thirty minutes trying to avoid looking at him. She was sure that if she caught a glimpse of his green eyes she wouldn't be able to concentrate at all.

It was strange. She should have felt happy that there was a friend in the room, but instead she felt almost like a student undergoing an examination. It was just as well the firefighters went easy on her and there were only a few questions at the end. That was the beauty of talking just before the coffee break—no one wanted to hang around for long.

As soon as she'd finished the room emptied quickly. Her heart started to thud. Would Callum leave without speaking to her? Maybe he had to network with some of his colleagues and wouldn't have time.

'Hey, Jess. That was a nice surprise.' She started at his voice and turned around quickly as someone jostled him from behind and pushed them even closer together. It looked as if it was a stampede towards the strong smell of coffee.

Her hand went up automatically and rested on his chest. She could feel the heat of his body through his thin black shirt. 'Hey, you too. I didn't expect to be here. Just filling in for a friend.'

'What happened?'

'Mark Shepherd's wife has cancer. She had a bad reaction to her chemo, so he wanted to stay home with her.'

'I'm sorry to hear that. How are the kids from the accident doing?'

She raised her eyebrows. 'You mean you haven't already phoned today?'

He squirmed. 'Okay, I admit it. I'm a bit of a stalker.'

She laid her hand on his arm. 'But only in a good way. We've got four still in, but they're all improving. With kids we just take things one day at a time.'

Callum nodded slowly. He held his elbow out towards her. 'Have you time for some refreshments before you leave?'

'Hmm, firefighter coffee. Is it as bad as I think it will be?'

'Scandalous! We're very serious about our coffee, and we're even more serious about our cakes. I can guarantee you a fruit scone.'

'Something does smell pretty good around here.' She put her hand through his crooked elbow. 'Why do I get the impression that you're trying to fatten me up, Callum?'

He rolled his eyes and pressed his other hand to his chest. 'Tragedy, you've caught me out.' His face broke into a wide grin. 'Let's call it *looking out for a friend*.'

Her heart gave a little flutter. 'Friends? Is that what we are again, Callum?'

'I certainly hope so.' There was something so nice about the way he'd said those words. Not a moment's hesitation. He didn't even need to think about it for a second.

Friends. She liked that word. It felt safe.

They walked across the corridor to the coffee room. The queue had died down a little and she had a little time to peruse the cakes in the glass cabinet. The firefighters certainly did take their coffee seriously. This was an outlet of a popular coffee house, with all their famous tempting products on display.

He placed his arm on the counter and slid a tray in front of her. 'What can I tempt you with?'

Now, there was a question.

The thoughts that flooded her mind almost made her blush.

'I'll have a light caramel latte with two shots and a piece of the banana and nut loaf, please.' The words were automatic. She was used to ordering in one of these coffee shops—she didn't need to think twice.

He seemed pleased. Pleased that she didn't spend forever fretting over what to eat and drink. Patience had never been Callum's strong point.

They waited a few minutes while the barista made their coffee. 'How did you manage to wangle a franchise in here?' she said. 'I didn't think it would be allowed.'

He pointed to a sign near the door. 'Neither did we, but the coffee was getting worse and worse and tempers were fraying. They asked what we wanted and we told them. The profits from this franchise don't go back into the overall company. We have a ballot every year to decide which charity to support.'

He gave a little shrug. 'It works in our favour and in theirs. We get to support the charity of our choice, and they get to put us on their website talking about their contributions to charity. It's good publicity for them.' She smiled at the poster supporting research into Alzheimer's disease. 'Why did you pick that one?'

He picked up the tray and carried it over to a vacant table. 'We get lots of accidental house fires started by older people with memory problems—putting things in the oven or on the hob and forgetting about them. Some have early signs of Alzheimer's. We often go out and do community safety visits and fit fire alarms for anyone referred to us. It seemed a natural pick.' His voice lowered and she could sense the sadness in it. 'It caused us three fatalities last year.'

They sat down and Jess sipped her coffee. It was just as good as it was in every shop in the country. 'I think it's a great idea. I wonder if the hospital would consider it? The hospital kitchens are great, but the staff canteen is run by an outside firm. It's nowhere near as good as this.'

'I can give you some details if you want.'

'That would be perfect.' She leaned back in her chair. 'You could quickly make me the most popular woman in the hospital.'

'I'm sure you're that already.' His voice was low and he was looking up at her from over the top of his steaming cup of coffee.

She couldn't help the little upturn at the corners of her lips. When had the last time been that she'd had a man flatter her? It had been so long ago she couldn't remember.

Sure, there had been the odd unwanted leering comment, the kind that made your stomach turn—and not in a good way.

But this was different. It hadn't been invited. Or expected.

It was just—well, a nice comment. The kind that sent a little rosy glow all through you. Something she hadn't felt in a very long time.

It was kind of weird how she felt about all this. That first glimpse of Callum on the riverbank had been a total shock. And the way her body had reacted—her *natural* instinct—had been even more of a shock.

Because her natural instinctive response to Callum had been very physical. It hadn't helped that they'd been thrust together—in more ways than one—and parts of her body that had seemed dead had suddenly sparked into life.

It was taking time to get her head around all this.

And, to be frank, she was struggling.

In a way she wished she could be that naïve seventeen-year-old again, thinking that her heart was breaking as she left her first love behind.

If only she'd known then what she knew now.

That wasn't the thing that broke your heart. Not even close.

But all her memories of Callum were good. They were safe. Even if they came with a heavy dose of passion and teenage angst.

She didn't feel afraid around Callum. And she liked the way he was looking at her. It made her feel as if she was finally worth looking at again.

Pauline's words echoed around her head. *A world of possibilities.*

'Callum, I need to speak to you about something.'

The words jerked Jess out of her daydream. A well-stacked blonde was directly in her line of vision, her boobs inches from Callum's nose. Were those real?

'We need to talk about the meeting tomorrow at city headquarters. I need to give you a report to review before you go.'

Strange things were happening to Jess. The hackles had just gone up at the back of her neck and she felt an intense dislike for this extremely pretty and apparently efficient blonde. What on earth was wrong with her? She was never like this.

'Hi, Lynn. I'm actually in the middle of something right now.'

'What?' She glanced over at Jessica—whom she'd completely ignored—with renewed interest. 'Well, I'll let you finish up. But I'll need to see you in five.'

She turned to sweep away. Jess felt a smile sneak across

her face as she realised Callum hadn't stared once at the boobs on display.

'Actually, I'll be a bit longer than that.' He gave a wave of his hand. 'I'll come and find you later.'

Lynn shot him a look of surprise, but Callum wasn't even looking at her any more. His attention was completely on Jessica.

Jess's heart gave a little flutter. She'd just recognised the sensation she'd felt a few seconds ago on Lynn's approach. Jealousy.

It was almost as if she'd landed in the middle of the icy-cold Clyde again, with the freezing water sweeping over her skin.

There was something very strange about all this. Being around Callum was making her feel again, something she thought would never happen. She'd been switched off for so long that she wasn't recognising everything straight away.

This was dangerous territory. She would have to take baby steps.

But all of a sudden it didn't seem quite so scary.

She gave Callum a little smile. 'So, tell me more about uni.'

She had to start somewhere and it was as good a place as any.

'Daddy, I don't feel good.'

Callum was sleeping but the little voice jerked him straight out of the weird dream that was circulating around his brain. Jessica dressed in a clown suit. Where did these things come from?

Yesterday had been fun. They'd spent most of the time together reminiscing. Talking about their past seemed to relax Jess. And he liked her like that.

He also liked the fact he was spending time with someone he trusted. Someone he didn't need to feel wary around. Somebody who wouldn't let him down.

But right now his paternal radar was instantly on alert. Drew was standing in the doorway, his eyes heavy with sleep and his hand rubbing his stomach. This was the second day he hadn't felt great. The second night Callum had put his dinner untouched into the bin.

Over the last two weeks Drew's symptoms seemed to flare up and then die down again.

He lifted up the corner of his duvet. 'Come over here so I can see you.'

Drew scuttled across the room and straight under the cover next to his dad. Callum pressed his hand to his head. He didn't feel warm—no obvious temperature. 'What's wrong, big guy? Do you feel sick?'

According to Drew's primary teacher half the class were off with a sickness bug. Maybe some of them had even ended up in Jessica's hospital. Rumours were circulating that it was norovirus.

Just what he needed. He still had the accident report to complete and there had been another incident at work today that would need to be followed up.

'Not sick, Daddy. Just a rumbly tummy.'

'Are you hungry? Is your tummy rumbling because you didn't eat any dinner?' He glanced at the clock. Two a.m. 'Do you want Dad to make you some toast?' It wasn't an ideal situation but if it settled Drew and got him back to sleep quickly, he could live with it.

Drew lay back against the pillows. 'No. Not hungry.' He moved a little closer. 'Just rub my tummy, Daddy, that will make it better.'

'You're sure? Do want a little drink of water?'

Drew shook his head and closed his heavy eyes.

Callum's hand automatically moved into position, very gently rubbing Drew's tummy in little circles. What could be wrong?

He hated to overreact. He hated to be an over-anxious father. But the truth was he had very few people he could bounce things like this off.

His friends Julie and Blair were the obvious choice but he wasn't going to call them at this time of night.

He glanced at the clock again. Maybe he would take Drew back to the GP in the morning. The trouble was, he hated going to the GP with a list of vague symptoms. A list of *not much but maybe it could be.*

It made him feel paranoid. It made him feel as if he wasn't coping. And that was the last thing he wanted anyone to think.

Did single mothers feel like this too?

Drew was the most precious thing in the world to him. He couldn't live with himself if he brushed something off and it turned out to be serious.

Maybe he should have asked Jessica yesterday. She was a paediatrician, she knew everything there was to know about kids.

But he hadn't thought about it and that made him feel a little guilty. He hadn't even told her about Drew yet. Should he have? Theirs was a professional relationship. Nothing more, nothing less. But a tiny little part of his brain was nagging away at him, thinking that maybe it could be something else.

He still hadn't got to the bottom of her words. *Things just didn't work out for me.*

She'd been really careful today to keep steering the conversation back to him—or work, whenever he'd asked anything vaguely personal. She'd mentioned her mum and dad, a few old friends they'd known years ago. But nothing about herself.

Maybe he should wait until he found out what that meant before he gave it another thought.

He cuddled up with his little boy. Drew was his top priority right now.

The first person he looked at in the morning and the last person he looked at at night.

And that's the way it would stay.

CHAPTER SEVEN

THE WARD WAS quiet and he'd no idea where Jessica was. The nurse had just pointed down in this general direction.

He walked past a few windows, seeing children lying in beds with anxious parents next to them.

His heart clenched slightly. He would hate to be in that position. Thank goodness Drew usually kept in good health. He still hadn't got to the bottom of that stomach ache. The GP had basically fobbed him off and Callum didn't blame him because when they'd finally got an appointment, Drew had been full of beans and jumping around the place.

It was always the same with kids.

The ward sister he'd met a few times was standing next to one of the doors. 'Hi, Pauline.'

She gave him a knowing smile. 'Hi, there, Callum. And who might you be looking for?'

He sighed. He'd known from the first time he'd met her that Pauline could read everyone instantly. Why even pretend it was anything else? He still hadn't seen Jess, so this might work in his favour.

He leaned against the doorjamb and folded his arms. 'Let's just say I'm looking for our favourite doc.' He lifted his eyebrows. 'All work-related, of course.'

Pauline nodded. 'Of course.' But the smile was spreading further across her face. She lowered her voice. 'I think our mutual friend will be very pleased to see you.'

He felt something flare inside him. That acknowledgement—no matter how brief—reassured him. Pauline and Jess were good friends. If Jess was talking to anyone it would be Pauline. It gave him a little hope. It also gave him the courage to ask the question that had been gnawing away at him.

He hesitated for a second. 'Pauline—about Jess.'

She raised her eyebrows, as if he was about to say something she didn't want to hear. She was protective of Jess and that was nice.

'Jess told me that things didn't work out for her. And I know she's reverted to her maiden name.' He unfolded his arms and held out his hand towards her. 'I wonder if you could tell me what happened. I get the feeling I'm treading on difficult ground.'

Pauline bit her lip and glanced over her shoulder. Her eyes met his. 'You're right, Callum, it is difficult ground but I think that it's something Jess really needs to tell you herself.' Her eyes looked down, as if she was hesitant to say any more. 'Life hasn't turned out the way she expected. Jess should be married with a family to love and I'm hoping that's what she'll get. Just give her a little time.'

She pointed to the next set of doors. 'She's down there. Go and say hello.'

Was this better or worse?

His curiosity had just scaled up about ten notches.

He wanted to give Jess time to tell him—he really did. There was just that little edge of wariness. That lingering feeling left by a previous experience.

Jess was nothing like Kirsten, Drew's mother. They weren't even in the same ballpark. But it didn't stop his slightest sense of unease as he walked down the corridor.

He pushed the feelings to one side. He'd already made up his mind about what he wanted to do next. He wanted to see how Jess would react. And he wouldn't know unless he tried.

Finally he caught sight of Jess's caramel-coloured hair. She was sitting talking to a little girl with curly hair with her leg in a bright pink fibreglass cast. It was Rosie, from the minibus accident.

He stuck his head around the door. 'Knock, knock.'

Jess looked surprised to see him. 'Callum, what are you doing here?'

'I phoned and left you a message. Didn't you get it?'

She shook her head then turned to the woman sitting next to her. 'Carol, this is Callum Ferguson. He's one of the fire rescue crew who were at the accident. He helped get Rosie out of the bus.'

'It's him, Mummy! It's him!' Having a cast on hadn't seemed to limit Rosie's movements. She wiggled over to the edge of the bed. 'The one I told you about.'

Rosie's mum stood up and held out her hand. 'Callum, my daughter has been talking about you non-stop. She seems to think you're a superhero. She saw you abseil down the side of the riverbank.'

Callum felt a little rush of blood to his cheeks. This was the last thing he had been expecting. He shook his head and knelt down beside the bed. 'You're much braver than me, Rosie. You tumbled down the bank in the minibus. That must have been really scary. The way I got down wasn't scary at all.'

Rosie held out her hands and reached round Callum's neck, giving him a big hug.

Jessica was watching. Watching—and trying to keep the smile from her face at his appearance. Callum seemed totally at ease, not in the least fazed by the little girl's action. Thank goodness. She had him on some sort of pedestal.

But it was kind of nice. Almost as if he was used to being in contact with kids.

Callum leaned back and tapped the pink cast. 'How is your leg? I love the colour of your cast.'

Rosie smiled. 'Thank you. Dr Rae and I have the same favourite colour. That's why I picked pink.'

'Well, I think it looks great. Your leg will be all better soon.'

Jess stood up and gave Carol and Rosie a smile. 'I'll leave you two. You can give me a call if you need me.' She nodded her head towards the door. 'Callum?'

She could smell his aftershave. It wasn't familiar. It was different from the one he'd used the day they'd abseiled back up the slope. It was more spicy, with richer tones. She liked it.

They walked along the corridor. Callum waved his hand, in which he had a big brown envelope. 'I've typed up the statement from the other day. I need you to read over it and sign it.'

She felt a flutter of disappointment. Business. Purely business. That's why Callum was here. Not for any other reason. A strange lump was forming in her throat. Once she'd signed the statement she would have no reason to ever see Callum again.

Her heart had leapt when he'd appeared. She hated it when it did that. She kept telling herself over and over again that this was nothing. This meant nothing. Just some wild, crazy coincidence that their paths had crossed again. This was work-related.

He turned to face her and she tried hard not to stare at his chest, which was instantly in her view.

She raised her eyes to meet his bright green ones. It was

one of the first things she'd ever noticed about Callum, his startling green eyes.

'I can read the statement now, it will only take a couple of minutes.' There was no point turning this into something it wasn't. She saw him glancing at his watch, it was nearly six o'clock in the evening. He would be finished for the day—just the way she should be. Was he worried about being late? Did he have a date? Maybe that blonde from the fire station?

She hated the way that thought made her stomach curl.

'Have you finished for the day?'

'What?'

He'd moved a little closer and was towering over her, an impatient edge to his voice.

'I mean have you finished? You can't be on call again. I want you to come somewhere with me.'

She pulled back a little. There was something a little weird about him. Was he nervous?

She looked around her. The ward had quietened down. All patients had been seen, all prescriptions and instructions written. 'Yes, yes, I'm finished.' She was feeling a bit bewildered. A few seconds ago she had been sure everything was business as usual. He needed a signature to get the job finished so he could be on his way. And that had made her sad.

Now what?

A smile broke across Callum's face. 'Then get your coat.' She was turning towards her office when she heard him mutter something under his breath. 'You've pulled.'

She let out a burst of laughter and spun back around. 'Did you just say what I think you did?'

It had been a joke between them. A daft teenage saying that both had used years before. But it came totally out of the blue and instantly took her back thirteen years.

Callum's shoulders were shaking. 'Sorry, I couldn't resist it.'

Jessica stuck her hand around the office door and pulled out her woollen coat. There was a flash of bright pink. 'Think you can cope?' she asked as she wound her purple scarf around her neck and fastened the buttons on the bright coat.

He just nodded. 'You did warn me about the bright pink coat, and knowing you I wouldn't have expected anything less. Do you have gloves?'

She stuck her hands in the coat pocket and pulled out a pair of purple leather gloves. 'Sure. Why?'

'It's a nice night out there. Just a little dusting of snow. I'd like to walk instead of drive. Are you okay with that?'

She pulled out a woolly hat and stuck it on her head. 'I'm game if you are. But you've got me curious now. Where are we going?'

He gestured towards the door. 'Let's find out.'

They walked quickly through the lightly falling snow. It was pitch dark already—darkness fell quickly in winter in Scotland. The streetlights cast a bright orange glow across the wet pavements.

'So where are you taking me?'

Callum drew in a breath. He was still getting over the fact he'd asked her. It had been totally instinctive. He'd only made the decision once he'd set foot on the ward—particularly after what Pauline had said to him. The words had come out before he'd even had a chance to think about them. A signature would have meant he'd have no excuse to see Jesssica again. And he wasn't quite ready for that.

Drew was at mini-kicker football tonight. He went every week with Julie and Blair's son. One week Callum gave them dinner and took them, the next week Julie and Blair took them. Drew wouldn't be home until after eight o'clock.

'That would be a surprise.'

'Hmm…a surprise. How do you know I still like surprises?'

He gave her a little smile. 'It's an educated guess. Some things are just part of us—like our DNA. I'm working on the premise that the fundamentals haven't changed.'

They turned a corner and started walking along one of the main roads. It was busier now, the crowds jostling along all seeming to be headed in one direction.

The strains of Christmas music could be heard above the buzz of the crowds around them. Jess stopped a few times to look at the Christmas displays in some of the shop windows. Finally, he placed his hand in the small of her back as he guided her around the corner and into George Square.

'Oh.' He heard the little bit of shock in her voice as the recognition of where they were sank in. The square was bustling, packed with people here to see the annual switching on of the Christmas lights. A huge tree stood in the middle of the square, already decorated and just waiting for the lights to be lit. The Lord Provost already stood on the stage, talking into a microphone and trying to entertain the crowds.

'You brought me here? I can't believe you remembered.' Her voice had gone quiet, almost whispered.

This had been one of their first dates, coming to see the annual switching on of the Christmas lights in George Square. He hadn't planned this. He hadn't even thought about it. But as he'd driven to the hospital tonight he'd heard the announcement on the radio about the switch-on. It had almost seemed like a sign—a message. He'd had to

ask her to come along. If only to try and take a little of the
sadness out of her eyes.

'There's so many families,' she said as she looked
around, dodging out of the way of a little girl with long
blonde hair running straight for them.

'Yeah, there always are.' Lots of people brought their
families to the turning on of the lights. It was entirely normal. But he couldn't help catch the little edge of something
else in her voice.

'Over here.' Callum put his hand on her back again
and guided her over to one of the street-vendor stalls. The
smells of cloves, mulled wine and roasted chestnuts were
all around them. Callum bought two cups and handed one
over to her.

'Want to take a guess at what colour the tree lights will
be this year?'

Jessica leaned against one of the barriers, sipping her
mulled wine and watching the people around them. It was
obvious that her brain was trying to take in their surroundings. 'They were purple the first year that we came here.'

'And they were silver the year after.' He kept his voice
steady.

'And red the year after that.'

It was clear that they both remembered and for some
reason it was really important to him that it was imprinted
on Jess's brain just as much as it was on his. Half of him
had been sure she would know why he'd brought her here,
while the other half had been in a mad panic in case she'd
turned around with a blank expression on her face.

'They were blue last year,' he murmured, not really
thinking.

Jess spun round, the mulled wine sloshing wildly in her
cup. 'You were here last year?'

Yes. He'd been here with Drew. But it had turned out

Drew didn't really like the turning on of the lights. It was almost as if there was a little flare of panic in Jess's eyes. Did she think he'd been here with another woman?

Maybe this was it. Maybe this was time to tell her about Drew. It seemed natural. It was a reasonable explanation for what he'd just said. But the look in her eyes, that and the wistful tone in her voice when she'd remarked on the families, made him think twice.

'I was here with some friends.'

'Oh.' She seemed satisfied with that answer and rested her forearms back on the barrier.

The crowd thickened around them, pushing them a little closer together as people jostled to get a better place at the barrier. Callum wound his arm around her waist, holding her firmly against him, to stop anyone coming between them. The countdown around them started. Ten, nine…

It was the smallest of movements. Jess rested her head on his shoulder then a few seconds later he felt her relax a little more and felt some of the weight of her body lean against him.

A grin spread across his face. It wasn't like anyone could see it but it had been automatic and was plastered there for the world to see. Three, two, one.

'Woah!' The noise went around the crowd as the lights flickered on the tree, lighting up the square in a deluge of pink and silver.

'Pink! It's pink!' Jess yelped, as the wine sloshed out of the cup and she turned to face him. Her eyes were sparkling, her excitement evident. It was the first time since he'd seen her again that she looked totally carefree. Totally back to normal.

Her face was right in front of his, her brown eyes darker than ever before and their noses almost touching. He could see the steam from her breath in the cold night air. He placed his cup on the barrier and brought his hand to her hip, matching the hold of his other hand, and pulled her a little closer. He gave her a smile.

'My plan worked. I told them that pink was your favourite colour and that you'd be here.'

She let out a laugh and placed her hands on his shoulders. She didn't seem annoyed by him holding her. She didn't seem annoyed at all. In fact, if he wasn't mistaken, she was edging even closer.

Her dark eyes were still sparkling, reflecting the twinkling lights around them, 'Oh, you did, did you? I bet that took a bit of planning, especially as you didn't even know if I'd agree to come on a walk with you.'

He pulled her even closer. 'Oh, I knew. I was absolutely sure you'd come with me.'

He could turn back the clock. He could flick a little switch right now and this could be thirteen years ago. Standing almost in this exact spot.

She tilted her head to the side. 'Well, that was a bit presumptuous, wasn't it?'

He shook his head. 'I don't think so. But this might be.'

He bent forward. People around them were still cheering about the Christmas lights, breaking into song as the music got louder in the amplifiers next to them.

But Callum wasn't noticing any of that. The only thing he was focused on was Jess's lips.

And everything was just like he remembered. Almost as perfect.

The last time round Jess had tasted of strawberry lip gloss, and this time she tasted of mulled wine. He could sense the tiniest bit of hesitation as he kissed her, so he took it slowly, gently kissing her lips, teasing at the edges until she moved her hands from his shoulders and wrapped them around his neck, kissing him right back.

And then everything *was* perfect.

CHAPTER EIGHT

CALLUM LISTENED TO the NHS helpline music with growing impatience. It was funny how all rational thought flew out of the window when your child was in pain.

Drew was clutching his stomach again. He was pale and feverish, and he couldn't even tolerate fluids. But the pain was making him gasp and sob and Callum was feeling utterly helpless.

He glanced at his watch. It would be nearly midnight by the time the NHS helpline put him through to one of the nurses—and he told Drew's story *again*—then they would have to drive out to one of the GP centres. Who knew when his son would get some pain relief?

No. He couldn't wait that long.

As a member of one of the emergency services, he hated it when people used the services irresponsibly. But this didn't feel irresponsible. This did feel like an emergency. And he could explain later why he hadn't been prepared to wait for the helpline.

Jessica was on call tonight. Should he take Drew to Parkhill?

He hadn't even told her about Drew yet, and this would be a baptism of fire. But as Drew's father he couldn't think of anyone he would trust more with his son. He'd seen Jessica at work. He'd heard her colleagues talk about her.

She was undoubtedly a great doctor, who cared about her patients.

He was supposed to be taking Jessica out for dinner in a few nights' time. He'd been hoping to tell her about Drew then, and also to explain why evening dates could prove to be difficult. After a day of work he really didn't like to ask someone to babysit his son. He wanted to spend time with him. And he was hopeful that Jess would understand that. But now that would all have to wait.

Within minutes he had Drew bundled up into his booster seat, still in his pyjamas and wrapped in a fleecy blanket.

The roads were coated with snow and deadly quiet. Anyone with a half a brain was tucked up in bed. The only other traffic on the roads at this time of night was the gritters. He made it to the hospital in record time, parked in one of the emergency bays and carried Drew inside in his arms.

'I need to see Jessica Rae right away.'

The receptionist looked up, her face unfamiliar. 'Can you give me your details, please, sir?'

'Jessica Rae—I know she's on duty tonight. I want her to check over my son.'

The receptionist plastered a weary smile on her face. 'Give me your son's details. I'll get one of the doctors to see him.'

Callum felt his patience at an all-time low. 'Page Jessica Rae for me—*now*!'

One of the triage nurses appeared at his side and gave a knowing smile to the receptionist. They were probably used to frantic parents, but it didn't excuse his behaviour. 'Come with me, sir, and I'll start the assessment procedure for your son.' She reached over and brushed Drew's fringe out of his eyes, taking in his pale colour and the sheen on his skin. 'Let's get some obs.'

Callum felt himself take some deep breaths as he followed the nurse down the corridor. She was ruthlessly efficient, taking Drew's temperature, heart rate and blood pressure, then putting some cream on the inside of one elbow to numb the area and prepare it for a blood sample to be taken. As she scribbled down Drew's history, then held a sick bowl to let him retch into it, she gave Callum a tight smile.

'I know you asked for Dr Rae, but she's in surgery right now. She will see your son, but he needs some other tests done and some blood taken in the meantime. I'm going to ask one of the other doctors on duty to see Drew right now.'

There was something in the way she said the words. The quiet urgency in them. As if she suspected something but wasn't prepared to say it out loud. She had that look about her—the nurse who'd seen everything a dozen times and could probably out-diagnose most of the junior doctors.

'What do you think's wrong?'

She gave the slightest shake of her head. 'Let's leave that to the doctors, shall we?'

He tried his best not to erupt. To tell her that he didn't want his son to wait a second longer.

She glanced at him as she headed to the curtains. 'I'll get the other doctor now. The sooner Drew is seen, the better. Then we can get him some pain relief.'

He nodded automatically. Pain relief for his son. That's what he wanted more than anything. Anything to take the pain away from Drew.

'Dr Rae, there's a kid with an acute abdomen in A and E. Father is insisting you see him.'

Jessica pulled off her gown and gloves and dumped them in the disposal unit. 'Really? What's the name?'

'Kennedy. Drew Kennedy.'

She shrugged. She was the consultant on call. She'd see any kid with an acute abdomen anyway. 'I don't recognise the name, but tell them I'll be right there.'

She gave her hands a quick wash, trying to place the name. None of her friends had a son called Drew. And the surname? Well, there was only one Kennedy that she knew.

Her stomach gave a little sinking feeling as she rounded the corner into A and E. It couldn't be, could it?

No. Not a chance.

It couldn't be a nephew as Callum didn't have any brothers or sisters.

And Callum would have mentioned something as important as having a son. Wouldn't he?

But as she walked over to the curtains she recognised the frame hunched over the little figure straight away.

She froze.

She wanted to turn on her heel and run away. She wanted to disappear out of the hospital and take a minute to catch her breath. To try and get her head around the thousand thoughts currently spinning around in her brain.

But that was the second that Callum looked up. And his relief at seeing her was plastered all over his face.

She'd seen that look a hundred times. The parent worried out of their mind about their child. Hoping against hope that their worst fears weren't about to be realised.

Professional mode. No matter how she felt, or what her questions were, she had to move into professional mode right now. There was a sick little boy to be dealt with.

She kept her voice steady and calm. 'Callum? I didn't expect to see you.' She picked up the chart, her eyes skimming over the notes and observations. 'Is this your son?'

Calm. Rational. That's how she was hoping she sounded.

Callum had the good grace to look embarrassed. 'Yes. This is Drew.' There was a shake to his voice. He really was scared for his son—he must be. He'd deliberately brought him here and asked for her, even though he'd known she would have questions. 'He's five and he's had a sore stomach on and off for the last two weeks. We've been back and forth to the GP with no diagnosis. But tonight he's much worse.' He lowered his voice. 'Sorry. I was going to tell you about Drew at dinner on Saturday.'

Her brain was still stuck on the 'five' part. She tried not to wince as she glanced at the date of birth. Drew was almost the same age as her son Lewis would have been.

She tried not to let the tight squeeze around her heart affect her. Everything was so unfair. Callum had the little boy she should still have. A little boy he hadn't even mentioned.

She took a deep breath and looked over at the little boy on the bed. The junior doctor had done everything he should, but he hadn't made any provisional diagnosis. Which meant he was stumped.

'Hi, there, Drew. I'm Dr Jessica. Do you mind if I have a look at your tummy?'

'No. Daddy, don't let them touch my tummy again.' She could hear the distress in the little boy's voice. The fear of someone touching a part of him that was already very painful.

She looked at the chart, making sure he'd been given some analgesia. 'Hasn't the medicine helped your sore tummy? It should have made it feel a little better.'

The little boy shook his head. 'It's still sore.'

'Can you tell me where it hurts if I promise not to touch?'

He nodded. His face was pale. 'It started in the middle but now it's over here.' He pointed to his left side.

She pointed to the IV in his arm. 'I'm going to put a little more medicine in here. It will work really quickly and help your tummy.' She nodded towards the nurse. 'Can I have point two milligrams of morphine, please?'

She waited a few minutes until the nurse returned with the syringe and ampule for her to check before administration. She prescribed the dose and signed the ledger before giving Drew the analgesic. She placed her hand on his forehead and bent down to whisper in his ear, 'It will start to work really quickly, I promise.'

Some doctors didn't agree with giving analgesia to paediatric patients before a diagnosis was made. They thought it could mask abdominal symptoms and delay a diagnosis. But Jessica had read a whole host of studies with evidence that analgesics reduced pain without interfering with diagnostic accuracy. Besides, Jessica could never leave a child in pain.

Right now, Drew was showing most of the signs and symptoms of appendicitis, but the pain for appendicitis was associated with radiating to the right, not the left.

She bent down and whispered in Drew's ear. 'Okay, I know I'm a lady doctor but I need to have a little check of your testicles. Do you know what they are?'

He shook his head.

She lifted her eyebrows. 'Your balls.'

He gave a little giggle.

She nodded. 'All I'm going to do is have a little feel to make sure they are where they're supposed to be. It will only take a few seconds, and it won't hurt, okay?'

He nodded and she checked quickly. It was important with boys to rule out a twisting of the testes, but everything seemed fine.

She did another few tests, one—the McBurney's—the classic indicator of appendicitis. But nothing was conclusive.

Drew's guarding was evident. Something was definitely going on.

The nurse appeared at her side. 'Drew's blood tests are back. They're on the system.'

Jessica gave a nod. No wonder the junior doctor had been puzzled. *She* was puzzled. 'Let's get an IV up on Drew and I'm going to order an abdominal ultrasound to see if we can get a better idea of what's going on.'

She walked over to the nearest computer and pulled up Drew's blood results. His white-cell count was up, just as expected in appendicitis. She gave a little nod of approval as she saw the junior doctor had grouped and cross-matched his blood too, in case surgery was needed at a later time.

She looked over at Drew again. He was curled up in a ball, guarding his stomach like a little old man. And the strangest feeling came over her.

She unhooked her pink stethoscope from her neck. 'Drew, I'm just going to have a listen to your chest. It will only take a few seconds.'

She placed her stethoscope on his chest, waited a few seconds then took a deep breath and repositioned it.

She looked sideways at Callum. 'Has Drew ever had a chest X-ray?'

He shook his head. 'I don't think so. He's never had any problems with his chest. Why? What's wrong?'

Jess signalled to the A and E nurse. 'Can you arrange a portable chest film for me—right away?'

The nurse nodded and disappeared for a few minutes. There was always a portable X-ray machine in the emergency department.

Callum walked over to her. 'What is it?'

She placed her hand on his chest. 'Give me a minute. I

need to check something.' She wrinkled her nose. 'Have you ever had a chest X-ray?'

He rolled his eyes. 'Jess, I'm a fireman. I spent years working with a regular fire crew. Every time I came out of a burning building I had a chest X-ray.'

She nodded, it made sense, 'Right. So you did. And no one ever mentioned anything?'

He shook his head. 'Are you going to tell me what's going on? I'm going crazy here.'

She reached over and touched his hand. It didn't matter how upset she was right now. She'd even pushed aside the conversation she wanted to have with him right now. 'Callum, do you trust me?' Drew was the only thing that currently mattered.

His eyes flitted from side to side. Panic. Total panic. He ran his hand through his hair. 'Yes, of course I do, Jess. Why do you think I brought Drew here and asked to see you? There's nobody I trust more.'

The horrible reality right now was that she understood. She understood that horrible feeling of parental panic. That *out-of-control* sensation. She did. More than he would ever know.

She wrapped her other hand over his. 'Then just give me five minutes. Let me have a look at a chest X-ray for Drew. I promise, I'll explain everything.'

She saw his shoulders sag a little, saw the worried trust in his eyes.

She was telling herself that she would do this for any parent. That she *had* done this for any parent. But her conflicting emotions were telling her something else entirely.

The X-ray only took a few minutes and she pushed the film up onto the light box. It took her less than five seconds to confirm her diagnosis.

'Can you stay with Drew?' she asked the nurse.

'What is it?' The stricken look had reappeared in Callum's eyes, but she shook her head, pulled the chest X-ray down from the box and gestured with her head for him to follow her.

She opened the door to a nearby office and pushed the film back up on the light box inside. She flicked the switch and turned to face Callum.

'Drew has a condition called situs inversus.'

'What? What is that?'

She took a deep breath. 'It literally means that all his organs are reversed, or mirrored from their normal positions. Everything about Drew's symptoms today screamed appendicitis. Except for the positioning of the pain. Most people have their appendix on the right side. One of the true indicators of appendicitis is pain in the right iliac fossa.' She pointed to the position on her own abdomen to show him what she meant. 'But Drew's pain is on the other side—because his appendix is on the other side.'

'What does this mean? Is it dangerous? And how can you tell from a chest X-ray?'

She placed her hand on his shoulder. 'Slow down, Callum. One thing at a time.'

She pointed to the chest X-ray. 'Drew's heart is on the right side of his chest instead of the left. I can see that clearly in the chest X-ray.' She pointed at the lungs. 'I can also see that his left lung is tri-lobed and his right lung bi-lobed. That's the reverse of most people. This all gets a little complicated. It means that Drew's condition is known as situs inversus with dextrocardia, or situs inversus totalis.'

She tried to explain things as simply as she could. 'This is a congenital condition, Callum, it's just never been picked up. It could be that either you or his mother has this condition. It seems less likely for you as it would have been picked up in a routine chest X-ray.' She gave her head a little shake. 'It could be that neither of you has it. It's a recessive gene and you could both be carriers. Around one in ten thousand people have this condition.'

'Is it dangerous?'

She bit her bottom lip. 'It can be. Particularly in cases like this, when things can be misdiagnosed. But Drew's been lucky. Some people with this condition have congenital heart defects, but as Drew's been relatively unaffected that seems unlikely. It's likely if he had a congenital heart defect he would have had other symptoms that meant the condition would have been picked up much sooner. We'll do some further tests on him later. Right now we need to take him for surgery. His appendix needs to come out. How about we take care of that now, and discuss the rest of this later?'

He was watching her with his deep green eyes. She could see that he'd been holding his breath the whole time she'd been talking. He let it out in a little hiss. 'Will you do the surgery?'

The ethics of this question were already running through her mind. She had treated the children of friends on a number of occasions. It wasn't something she particularly liked to do—but in an emergency situation like this, the child's health came first.

'I'm the physician on call tonight. So it's up to me to perform the surgery. Would you like to find someone else to do it? That's always an option if you feel uncomfortable.'

He was on his feet instantly. 'No. Absolutely not. I want you to do it. I trust you to do it.' He looked her straight in the eye. 'There's no one else I would trust more.'

Things were still bubbling away inside her. It wasn't the time or the place, but she still had to say something.

'This isn't exactly ideal, Callum. And I'm not entirely comfortable about it. The surgery isn't a problem. There will be a registrar and an anaesthetist in Theatre with me. I'll need to go over the risks with you and get you to sign a consent form.'

She hesitated and let out a sigh. 'I kissed you a few days ago, Callum, so that complicates things for me. Obviously I didn't know about Drew...' she held up her hand as he tried to interrupt '...because you chose not to tell me. So, because I haven't met your son before, and don't have a relationship with him, that makes things a little easier.'

Her hands went to her hair and she automatically started twisting it in her hands, getting ready to clip it up for Theatre. She kept her voice steady. 'I'll perform your son's surgery and look after him for the next few days. I'll take the time to explain his condition and give you all the information that you need. After that? I have no idea.'

'Jess, please just let me explain.'

'No, Callum. Don't. Don't make this any more complicated than it already is. I've got more than enough to deal with right now.' She pointed back through the open door towards the curtains, where Drew was still lying on the trolley with a nurse monitoring him. 'Make yourself useful, go and sit with your son.' She walked out of the room, muttering under her breath, 'You don't know how lucky you are.'

Callum watched her retreating back and took her advice.

The nurse gave him a smile as he appeared back at Drew's side. 'You were lucky,' she said. 'Our Dr Rae is a fabulous paediatrician. Not everyone would have picked up that diagnosis.'

He gave a little nod. That didn't even bear thinking about. If he'd taken Drew elsewhere and some other physician had missed this...

It made him feel physically sick to his stomach.

He stroked his hand across Drew's forehead. His son

was a little more settled, the morphine obviously helping to a certain extent. Drew was the most precious thing in the world to him. He couldn't stand it if something happened to his son.

It was obvious he'd hurt Jessica's feelings by not telling her about Drew. And he wished he could take that back.

But it was too late now.

He'd explain to her later—once this was all over. He really didn't tell women about Drew. Drew was precious. He was a part of his life he kept protected, tucked away. And he had intended to tell Jessica about him. He'd just wanted to wait a little longer until he was sure they might have some kind of a chance at a relationship.

A relationship? Where had that come from?

He hadn't had a real 'relationship' since he'd broken up with Drew's mother. But Jessica was different. She was Jessica. His Jess. Someone he'd known a lifetime ago. And someone he hoped he could trust around his son.

Someone he could introduce to his son without wondering about other motives. Whether they might only really be interested in him, and not his son. Whether they might only be interested in dating a firefighter. Or some other crazy reason.

There wouldn't be any of that with Jess.

Jessica was a paediatrician. She must love kids. Why else do this job?

And she'd been interested in him when he'd been a pre-university student with no idea about his potential career prospects. So he didn't need to worry about that.

Drew opened his eyes and stared at him. 'Where did the nice lady go?' he murmured.

'She'll be back soon. She's going to make your tummy better.'

'Is she? Oh, good.' His eyelids flickered shut again.

He'd make it up to Jess.

He would. And he'd try to get to the bottom of the haunted look in her eyes.

He just had to get his son through this first.

Jess pressed her head against the cool white tiles in the theatre changing room. It was no use. She couldn't take the burning sensation out of her skin.

Thank goodness this place was empty. As soon as she'd slammed the door behind her the tears had started to fall.

It was so unfair. Callum had a son the same age as Lewis. Or the age Lewis would have been if he'd survived. A little boy he got to cuddle every day. To read stories to.

What kind of conversations did a five-year-old have with their parent when they were lying in bed at night, talking about their day?

A little boy he'd got to dress in his school uniform and photograph on his first day of school.

All the memories that Jess wished she had.

All the memories she'd been cheated out of.

Just when she'd thought she was getting better.

Just when she'd thought she could finally take a few steps forward.

Of course she had friends who had children the same age as Lewis would have been. She hadn't cut them out of her life. She couldn't do that.

She was a paediatrician, for goodness' sake. She couldn't spend her life avoiding children of a certain age. That would be ridiculous.

But sometimes it was difficult. And they were good enough friends to sense that. To know when to hold her close. To know when to give her a little space. It was a difficult path, a careful balance.

But this was different.

This was Callum.

An old friend, who was evoking a whole host of memories.

First Callum had appeared in her life. Then he had kissed her.

He'd raised her hopes, given her a glimmer of expectation that there might be something else out there.

And now this.

She was hurt. She was upset.

Upset that Callum hadn't told her about his son.

But the horrible coiling feeling in her stomach was something else.

She was jealous.

Jealous that Callum had a son and she didn't.

It was horrible realisation.

She'd seen the interaction between them. The stress in Callum's face when he was worried sick about his son. The slight tremor in his hand after she'd explained the surgery and the possible complications and he'd signed the consent form. The trust in his little boy's eyes, for him, and, more worryingly, for her.

She gave herself a shake. Children looked at her like that all the time.

The doctor who could make them better. The doctor who could take their pain away.

So why was it different that this was Callum's son?

An appendectomy was routine to her. Even though Drew's appendix was on the opposite side of his body. It shouldn't complicate the procedure for her. It was just a little unusual.

Maybe it was something else?

Callum was trusting her. Trusting her with his son.

And although she was worthy of that trust, it terrified her.

Because she knew what it was like to lose a child.

Other people in this world had lost a child. Other parents in this hospital had lost—or would lose—a child. She'd had the horrible job of losing paediatric patients and dealing with the bereaved parents herself.

But this felt very different.

No one in her circle of friends had lost a child.

She wouldn't wish that on anyone. Ever.

No parent should outlive their child.

No parent should spend the rest of their life looking at the calendar and marking off all the milestones that their child had missed.

She started to open packs and change, putting on a fresh set of theatre scrubs and tucking her hair up into the pink theatre cap. She had to get her head away from those thoughts. She had to get her head back into surgeon mode.

She walked through to Theatre and nodded to the anaesthetist, who was poised ready to start scrubbing at the sink.

Her registrar appeared at her side. 'I was just looking at the chest X-ray of the little boy for the appendectomy. Fascinating, I've never seen a case of situs inversus before—have you?'

She shook her head. 'No, I haven't.'

Alex started scrubbing next to her.

He was staring ahead at the blank wall as he started automatically scrubbing his hands, nails and wrists. 'I'll probably never see one again in my career. This might be interesting to write up.' He turned sideways, 'Can't there be complications in these kids? Heart defects and other problems? Some kind of syndrome?'

He was starting to annoy her now. He was clinically excellent, but a little too removed from his patients for Jessica's liking. In her book caring was an essential component of being a paediatrician.

'Yes, there can be a syndrome—Kartagener syndrome. People with situs inversus may have an underlying condition called primary ciliary dyskinesia. If they have both they are said to have Kartagener syndrome.' She started scrubbing her nails with a little more ferocity. Just what she needed—a registrar who permanently thought the glass was half-empty.

She preferred the other approach—the glass half-full approach. Especially when it came to children.

'You know, Alex, I've got a really sick little boy out there. His dad only brought him to our A and E department because he's a friend of mine, and the GP has been fobbing off his son's symptoms for days.' She shook her hands to get rid of some of the water then started to dry them on a sterile towel.

'I'd like you to think about that before we start. I'd like you to stop thinking about this little boy as a case for a medical journal. Think about him as a little boy who loves playing football, watching cartoons and eating chocolate cereal for breakfast. Think about him as the light of someone's life. Because the patient comes before the disease in every set of circumstances.'

She pointed to the door.

'Out there we have a father who is worried sick about his little boy. And even though I've been clear with him and given him the rundown of the surgery and the complications, he's sitting out there right now, wondering if his little kid will have peritonitis, develop septicaemia or be the one in a million who will have a reaction to anaesthetic.'

The theatre nurse came over and held out her gown for her. She thrust her arms into the sleeves and snapped her gloves in place. 'So let's make sure that I don't have to go out there and give him any bad news.'

She glared at him and stalked over to the theatre table. You could have heard a pin drop.

She knew she'd been harsh.

She never acted like that at work.

And the staff in here all knew her personal set of circumstances. They understood exactly where she was coming from.

Harry Shaw, the elderly anaesthetist—who stood in as Father Christmas every year with his grey hair and beard—gave her a smile.

His voice was low. 'You can do this, Jess.' He gave a little nod of his head. 'It'll be a walk in the park.'

She watched as the trolley was wheeled in. She could only pray it would be.

CHAPTER NINE

'Wow—just wow.'

'What are you talking about, Pauline?'

The sister from ITU gave her a smile and pointed behind her at the delivery guy, who could barely be seen beneath the beautiful spray of pink, purple and orange gerberas. Jess was on her feet in an instant, reaching up and touching one of the petals. 'Aren't they gorgeous?'

Pauline was quicker, pulling the card from the top of the bouquet. She spun it around. 'Hmm… "For Dr Jessica Rae."' She held the card next to her chest as Jess reached over to snatch it. 'I wonder who these could be from?' She took a few steps away. 'I'm guessing Mr Tall, Dark and Very, Very Handsome. Otherwise known as Callum Kennedy.'

Jess felt her cheeks flush. 'Stop it!' She grabbed the card, putting it into her pocket without reading it.

Pauline tutted. 'I'm disappointed. He's a member of the emergency services, he should know better.'

'Know better about what?'

Pauline waved her hand. 'That we don't allow flowers in ITU.'

Jessica accepted the huge bunch of flowers and gave Pauline a smile. 'But these flowers aren't for ITU, these flowers are for me.' She pushed open the door to her office and placed them on her desk. 'Wow. Where on earth did he get these at this time of year?'

Pauline stood in the doorway and folded her arms over her chest. 'Must have paid a pretty penny for them.' She turned on her heel and walked away. 'It must be love.'

Jessica's stomach plunged. 'No, Pauline.' She pointed at the flowers. 'These are just a thank-you for looking after Drew.'

'Honey, a thank-you is a bunch of flowers from a supermarket. An enormous bouquet, delivered by a courier, that's a whole lot more.'

Jess sank down into the nearest chair. 'Oh.'

'Oh? That's all you can say? Just "Oh"?' She sat next to Jess.

'What did the card say?'

Jess bit her lip. Did she really want to get into this conversation? She dug into her pocket again and pulled the card out. Pauline was right, this wasn't just a thank-you. And she had a sneaking suspicion what it might be.

She read the message.

This was gigantic apology *and* a thank-you.

'What is it?' Pauline leaned forward and touched her hand.

'It's an apology.'

'An apology? What's Callum got to apologise for?' Her eyes narrowed, she was automatically moving into protective mode.

'It's…it's awkward.'

'What's awkward about it?'

Jess let out a sigh. 'He didn't tell me about Drew. The first time I found out was when he brought him in with appendicitis.'

Pauline's mouth fell open. 'How long have you known this guy?'

'Since I was a teenager. But I hadn't seen him in thirteen years. And I hadn't kept up with what was going on
in his life.' Her voice dropped. 'Just like he hasn't kept up
with what's happened in mine.'

'You haven't told him?' Pauline's voice was incredulous.

'It hasn't come up.'

'Just like his son didn't come up?'

Jess put her head in her hands and leaned on the desk.
'This is a mess.'

'Yes. It is.' Pauline never pulled her punches. It was one
of the things that Jessica liked best about her.

She placed her hand at the side of her face. 'So, this
guy—who you used to know thirteen years ago—and you
only met again a few days ago, and brought his son to A
and E, even though he hadn't told you about him?'

Jessica nodded.

'He brought his sick son to see *you*.' She emphasised
the word strongly. 'Even though he knew that might make
you mad. Even though he knew you might have a thousand
questions. It was more important that he thought about
the health of his child and—after seeing you in action—
brought him to see a doctor he trusted with the health of
his son. Doesn't that tell you what you need to know?'

Jessica flopped her head back into her hands. Someone
else saying the words out loud made it all seem so much
more straightforward. So much simpler.

She felt Pauline's hand on her back. 'Jess, what is it
that you want?'

'What do you mean?'

'I mean, what are you ready for? I thought it was time
for you—time to take some steps and move on. Callum
seemed like a good idea. But maybe he's got as much bag-
gage as you do.'

'And if he does?'

Pauline rolled her eyes. 'You need to think about this, Jessica. What do you want?' She pointed to the flowers. 'Are you ready to accept Callum's apology and whatever else that might mean?'

'I don't know. I mean I'm not sure. I was hurt that he didn't tell me about his son.'

'And what about Drew?'

'What do you mean?'

Pauline moved her hand to her shoulder. 'Look at me, Jess. I'm going to ask a hard question. How do you feel about having a relationship with someone who has a son?'

Jess's head landed back on the desk. 'I don't know. I mean, I *really* don't know. Drew's lovely. He's a great little boy. I've spent a little time with him on the surgical ward. He's made a good recovery and he's ready for discharge.'

'Is he ready for you?'

'What do you mean?'

'Do you and Callum actually talk to each other? Where's Drew's mother? She hasn't been to visit. She isn't named on the consent form.' Pauline dropped her voice and said almost hesitantly, 'Is she dead?'

'No. I don't think so. When I asked Callum to sign the consent he said something about Drew's mother being in America and him having full custody. I'm not really sure what happened there. I know she's been on the phone to the ward staff a few times every day.'

'Ah, so there's no other woman to get in the way?'

'Pauline!'

She smiled at Jessica. 'So what? I'm being a little mercenary. I have a friend to think about.'

Jessica's eyes drifted over to the flowers. They were beautiful and the irony of the blooms wasn't lost on her. Gerberas were her favourite flowers—had been for years.

She was surprised that Callum had even remembered that, but there was something nice about the fact that he had.

She stood up quickly. 'I need to go for a few minutes.' She looked about the unit. 'Is everything okay in here? Do you need me to see anyone before I go?'

Pauline shook her head. 'Everything's fine and, don't worry, I'll look after your flowers for you.'

Jessica rolled her eyes and hurried down the corridor. She glanced at her watch. Although the hospital allowed parents to stay with their children at all times, most parents went away for an hour or so each day to freshen up and change their clothes.

The surgical ward had been a no-go area for the last few days. Callum was there constantly with his son. Just as she would have expected.

She'd had to review Drew a few times every day. His recovery was going well and it was likely she would discharge him today.

But every time she'd been anywhere in the vicinity Callum had tried to speak to her. She'd fobbed him off as best she could. The flowers were the biggest message yet that he was determined to apologise and pursue this.

She just wasn't sure how she felt.

Her stomach churned as she walked down the ward. It was ridiculous. She spent all day, every day in the presence of kids. Why on earth would this little boy be any different?

Because he was Callum's.

Because this could be something entirely different.

If only she could be ready for it.

Drew had a little DVD player on his lap and was watching the latest Disney movie. Although he had his clothes on, the curtains were pulled around his bed and lights in the room dimmed. Most children who'd undergone an anaesthetic took a few days to recover fully. A nap time in the afternoon was common—and when most of the parents took their chance to go home, shower and change.

'Hi, Drew.' Jessica took the opportunity to sit down next to his bed. 'What are you watching?'

He turned the screen around to show her. She nodded in approval.

'So, how are you feeling?'

'I'm good. When can I go back to mini-kickers?'

She wrinkled her nose. 'Is that some kind of football?'

He nodded. 'I go every week with my friend Joe. I love mini-kickers. It's my favourite.'

'Well, we can't have you missing your favourite for long. Lie back and let me have a little look at your tummy.'

His wound was healing well. The edges were sealed and there was no sign of infection.

'This is looking great, Drew. The stitches that I used will disappear on their own. But you also have some stitches inside your tummy and if you do too much, too quickly, then it can hurt.'

'Tomorrow?' He was serious. His little face was watching her closely.

So this was how a five-year-old boy thought. Couldn't see past the football. There was something so endearing about that.

She laughed. 'No. Not tomorrow. Maybe two weeks—if you're feeling okay. Do you like school? Because if you do, it will be all right to go back to school next week.'

He wrinkled his nose. 'School's okay. I like school dinner. Mrs Brown makes the best custard.' He leant forward and whispered in her ear. 'The custard here isn't nearly as good.'

'Really? I always thought the custard here was quite good.'

He shook his head and gave her a look of disgust. 'Oh, no. Mrs Brown's custard is *much* better.'

He was a lovely little boy, with Callum's searing green eyes and a real determined edge about him. They were so alike she could have picked him out from a room filled with a hundred kids.

'What's your favourite subject at school?'

It was something that preyed on her mind from time to time. She'd often wondered what her own son would have enjoyed most at school.

'Dinosaurs or volcanoes.' Drew was absolutely definite about what he liked. He tilted his head to one side. 'And I quite like the sticky tray.'

'The sticky tray? What's that?'

'For making things. I was making a Christmas card for my dad a few days ago at school. I've picked blue card and I was sticking a snowman on the front.'

'Ah.' Jess gave a smile. 'What were you using for the snowman? Was it some cotton wool—like the kind we have in here?'

'Yes. It got kind of messy. The glue stuck to my hands and then the cotton wool got all puffy.' His face was all screwed up, as if he was remembering the mess he'd made.

Jessica leaned across the bed. 'It doesn't matter if you made a mess. I'm sure your dad will love it.'

'But I'm not finished yet. I still need to put some glitter on. I want to put some stars in the sky.'

'And that will be gorgeous, Drew. Then it's my job to get you back to school so you can finish it.'

Drew shook his head. 'That one got a bit messy. Can't you help me make another one?'

Jess hesitated. Everything in her head was screaming no.

She was a hospital consultant. She had a hundred other things to be doing right now.

But for the strangest reason none of them seemed particularly important. Here was an opportunity to do something nice. To do the first real Christmassy thing she'd done in...goodness knew how long.

She hadn't even put her Christmas decorations up for the last three years. It had hardly seemed worthwhile when she wasn't really in the mood. They were lying stuffed in a box in her loft somewhere. Maybe she should think about pulling them out.

She smiled at Drew. Yes, she could go and ask one of the play advisors to come and help Drew make a card.

But he had a really hopeful look in those green eyes.

How could she possibly say no?

She walked over to one of the play cabinets and pulled out a drawer. The hospital's own kind of sticky tray. She lifted up the vast array of coloured card and fanned it out like a rainbow in her hand. 'What colour card would you like?'

Callum strode down the corridor. He hadn't meant to be so long. But three nights of sleeping in a hospital chair did strange things to your body.

He'd stepped out of the shower and had only meant to sit down for a few seconds at home. The next thing he knew he had a crick in his neck and was hopping about the place, trying to get dressed in the space of five seconds.

If he was lucky, today would be the day he got to take his son home. And as much as he liked going to the hospital and getting to see Jessica every day, he'd much rather have his son safe at home.

He'd promised Drew's mother that they could Skype tonight. She usually did it every week with Drew and had been annoyed that she hadn't been able to see him while he'd been unwell.

It was just as well children were so resilient. Drew had seemed to get over his mother's abandonment within a matter of weeks. Probably because he'd been surrounded by people who loved him. But Callum could never forget the impact it had had on his son. What kind of a woman did that?

He turned the corner, ready to head into Drew's room, and stopped dead.

It was a sight he'd never expected to see.

Drew looked nothing like the child he'd been a few days ago, pale-faced and in pain. Today he had colour in his cheeks and sparkle in his eyes.

Drew and Jessica. Paint was everywhere. Cotton wool was everywhere. Glitter was everywhere, including smudged all along Jessica's cheekbones. But most importantly Drew was smiling, Drew was laughing. His attention was totally focused on Jessica. And the way he was looking at her...

It tugged right at Callum's heartstrings. Kirsten, his ex-wife, had never been the most maternal woman in the world. And since she'd left Drew had never really had a female presence in his life, that female contact. Sure, there were his friends Julie and Blair, and Julie was fabulous with Drew. But he didn't see her every day—didn't have that kind of relationship with her.

This was the first time he'd realised what his son had been missing out on.

He felt a sharp pain in his stomach. He'd always felt as if introducing Drew to any of his girlfriends would have been confusing for a little boy. Taking things a step too far. He wanted to protect Drew from all of that. And to be truthful he'd never been that serious about any of them. He couldn't stand the thought of different women yo-yoing in and out of his son's life.

Then there was that lingering dread of introducing Drew to another woman, only for her to change her mind and speed off into the sunset, leaving him to pick up the pieces.

But maybe he had been wrong? Maybe he'd been cheating his son out of so much more.

Jess seemed so at ease with his son. But, then, she should, she was a paediatrician, she loved kids. It was the field she'd chosen to work in.

It made him even more curious. Why didn't Jess have kids of her own? It was obvious she would be a natural.

It almost seemed a shame to interrupt this happy scene, but he had to. He wanted to know if he could take his son home. He cleared his throat loudly. 'What's going on in here?'

Drew's eyes widened in shock. 'Hide them, Dr Rae! Hide them!' He cupped his hands over whatever it was he'd been making.

Jess jumped to her feet and stood in front of the table they were sitting at, opening up her coat to block his view. She gave Callum a wink then turned her head over her shoulder towards Drew. 'It's okay. He can't see a thing. Put them in the envelopes now.'

There was the loud sound of shuffling behind Jessica's back, along with little-boy squeals of excitement.

But Callum was kind of stuck in the view right in front of his eyes. Jess was wearing a red woollen dress, which clung to her every curve, leaving nothing to his imagination. He was kind of glad that her white coat normally covered this view. He didn't want everyone else seeing what he could.

Jess sparkled. Literally. Blue and silver glitter along her cheekbones.

He lifted his thumb up and touched her cheek. 'You got a little something on here.' He brushed along her cheekbone then his fingers rested under her chin. He half expected her to flinch and move away, but she didn't. She stood still, fixing him with her deep brown eyes.

A man could get lost in eyes like that.

If he wanted to.

He stared down at his thumb. 'Is this a bit of a give-away?'

She shook her head and glanced over her shoulder again. 'How are you doing, Drew? Nearly done?'

Drew held up two giant white envelopes, looking ever so pleased with himself. 'Done!'

He stood up, but stayed behind Jessica, putting his hands on her hips and sticking his head around. 'Wait till you see what I've made you, Daddy.'

Callum knelt down. 'I can't wait. I'm hoping we can go home some time today. What do you think, Dr Rae?'

Jess brushed her hair back from her face, leaving traces of glitter everywhere, including shimmering in the air between them. 'Oh, wow! I guess we went all out with the glitter, then.'

'I guess you did.' She was still smiling at him. Not avoiding him. And not avoiding Drew. Did this mean she'd finally forgiven him? She might give them a chance at... something?

'What do you think, Doc? Is Drew ready for discharge?'

He could almost see the silent switch—the move back into doctor mode. 'Yes, I think he is. His wound is healing well. We've done a few other tests—an ECG and an ultrasound of his heart. There's been no sign of any problems.' Her face became serious and the smile disappeared for a few seconds.

'Right now I'm assuming that Drew's situs inversus in straightforward. But I understand you might want to talk to someone about it. So, even though I don't think Drew will need any kind of follow-up, I've asked for one of the other consultants who specialises in genetic conditions to give you an appointment so you can discuss any concerns that you have.'

Callum pulled back a little. 'But why? Can't I just talk to you?' The words she was saying made sense, but that didn't mean that he liked them.

She shook her head. 'I don't think that's a good idea. I performed Drew's emergency surgery, but I probably have a conflict of interest here.'

He raised his eyebrows. 'A conflict of interest, what does that mean?'

'You know what that means, Callum.'

'But you must have treated a friend's kid before?'

She nodded slowly and stepped a little closer, lowering her voice and glancing in the direction of Drew. He'd become bored by their chatting and was now doing a jigsaw at one of the nearby tables.

'Yes, I have treated children of friends before—but usually only in an emergency. I wouldn't willingly be the paediatrician for any of my friends' kids. It crosses too many boundaries—complicates things and leads to confusion all round.' She tilted her head to the side and gave him a little smile. 'I'm sure you understand.'

'Actually, I don't.' He folded his arms across his chest. 'What do you mean?'

'Friends. Is that what we are?'

'Of course.'

He didn't like it. He didn't like it at all. It didn't matter

that the concept of only being friends with Jess had cir-
culated in his mind for days.

In the cold hard light of day he didn't like that.

He wanted more.

He wanted to be more than friends.

The kiss had started something.

No. That was rubbish. Something had started more than
thirteen years ago.

There was unfinished business between them.

'What if I don't want us to be friends?'

Her head shot up. 'What?' There was that fleeting look
across her face again. She was hurt. But she wasn't getting his implication. She was thinking he didn't *even* want
to be friends. Not that he wanted something more. It was
time to put that right.

He stepped closer and placed his hand on her hip. 'What
if I wanted us to be more than that?'

Her pupils widened and her tongue shot out and licked
her lips. Her eyes darted to the side, obviously to see if
anyone was watching. He pressed his fingers a little more
firmly into her hip, pulling her closer to him.

Drew hadn't even noticed what they were doing, he was
still engrossed in his jigsaw.

'I'm not entirely sure what you mean,' she murmured.

'Truth be told—neither am I.'

His other hand settled on her other hip, feeling the wool
under his fingertips, along with the outline of her hip. He
still had to find out what was going on with Jessica. He
was no closer to that than he'd been a few weeks ago. She
played her cards close to her chest.

But Drew was happy. He'd warmed easily to Jessica.
He liked her. She made him smile. And after what he'd
witnessed today he was willing to take some baby steps.

'But let's find out.'

She lifted her hand and touched the side of his face, her hand trembling. She bit her lip. 'What if I'm not sure?'

'Then we take it slowly. We find out together. Are you willing to try that?'

His heart was thumping against his chest wall. An answer had never seemed so important. He wasn't even entirely sure what he was asking. This was all new territory for him. New territory for them both.

He glanced over at Drew. 'How about a date? A family date?' He'd never done that before. It wasn't just a step for him—it was a leap. But maybe now was the time to find out.

He could see something fleeting pass through her eyes. A moment's hesitation. Did she want to say no? Did she want to walk away?

There it was again. Her tongue licking her dry lips. What kind of effect was he having on her?

'Let's embrace the time of year. I promised Drew I would take him to see Santa at Cullen's Garden Centre in Largs on Saturday. They usually have a huge play park and real live reindeer for the kids to see. Do you want to come along?'

A nervous smile came across her face. 'A play park? Is that really a good idea after an appendectomy?'

He pulled her body next to his and gave a sexy smile. 'Oh, I think we'll be fine,' he whispered in her ear. 'We'll have medical supervision.'

The smile on her face seemed genuine now. 'I guess you will.'

CHAPTER TEN

HER BEDROOM WAS a mess.

No, her bedroom looked as if a tornado had swept through it.

Every jumper and pair of jeans she possessed was scattered across her bed. Along with every raincoat, woollen coat, hat, glove and scarf. It was a beautiful eruption of colour, but Jess was still standing in her bra and pants. No further forward than she'd been an hour ago.

She picked up the phone next to her bed and pressed the automatic dial. 'Pauline? Help.'

Her friend sounded as if she'd just woken up. 'What is it, Jess?' she groaned.

'What do I wear?'

'Tell me you're joking.'

'No. Why?'

'You phoned me at this time in the morning to ask me what to wear to meet Santa?'

Pauline already knew about the date. She just didn't appreciate the agonising Jessica was doing over her wardrobe.

Jess sagged down onto the bed. 'Please, Pauline. Tell me what to wear.' She sounded pathetic and she knew it. This was the behaviour of a teenage girl, not a grown woman with a responsible job.

But Pauline's voice came through loud and clear. 'I would have thought that would be obvious, Jess. You're going to meet Santa—you wear red. Wear your Christmas jumper—the one you wore on the ward last year. Drew will love it. And your skinny jeans and your big red boots. There. That's you sorted. Anything else, or can a girl get back to sleep?'

The picture was forming in Jessica's mind. She hadn't even considered her novelty knitted jumper with the great big Christmas pudding on it. It would be perfect. She stood on tiptoe and yanked it out of the back corner of her cupboard. 'Thanks, Pauline. I'll see you tomorrow.' She hung up the phone and held the jumper in front of her for a second before quickly pulling it over her head. Pauline obviously had better vision than she did. The jumper, along with her skinny jeans and red chunky boots, was perfect. She even had a red coat she could wear too.

She glanced at the clock again. She couldn't believe she was this nervous. It seemed ridiculous. This was a simple trip—a chance to get out of Glasgow and have a nice drive along the Ayrshire coast until they reached the garden centre outside Largs.

She should be calm about this. She should be relaxed. She fastened her red coat and wrapped her scarf around her neck. The forecast today said it would be cold—really cold—so she wanted to wrap up warmly.

Her make-up was already on. Even though she hadn't managed to choose her wardrobe, when she did wear make-up it was always the same—some light foundation, some mascara and a little bit of red lipstick. It seemed to give her the little bit of colour she always lacked.

There was a toot outside and her heart leapt into her mouth. Oh, no. They were here.

Why had she agreed to this?

What if Drew decided that he hated her?

What if she just found this all too hard?

She walked down the stairs and sat on the bottom step for a few seconds, taking a few deep breaths. She could do this. She had *chosen* to do this. And she had to remember that.

No one was forcing this on her—no one.

Callum had lit up something inside her that had been dead for a long time.

And no matter how much she tried to deny it, it had felt good.

Then there was Drew. He was a gorgeous little boy. Being in his company was easy. With his big green eyes and determined manner it was easy to like him.

The fears she'd had about constantly comparing him to Lewis weren't there. Lewis was a totally different little boy.

She took a sharp breath. That thought.

She did that frequently. Still thought about Lewis in the present tense—as if he was still there. Did all mothers do that? Did all parents who had lost a child still think of their child in the present tense?

Was that good or bad? She wasn't sure.

Things were changing. She was changing. Yesterday she'd even pulled the box out of the loft with her Christmas decorations and tree. It had been hard to look at them again, the pink and purple globes brought back so many memories of previous happy Christmases in this house. So last night when she'd been shopping in the supermarket she'd bought a whole host of new decorations—silver ones. It felt different. It felt right.

The pink and purple ones held too many memories. The silver ones were new. With space available for memories of their own.

The car tooted again and she stood up, trying to ignore

the fact her legs were shaking. She stared at herself in the mirror in the hall, taking in the look of absolute fear on her face.

She picked up the fake-fur-trimmed hat on the table in the hall and stuck it on her head. 'You can do this,' she told her reflection. She closed her eyes for a second.

Harry Shaw's face drifted into her mind. The expression on his face that day in Theatre when she'd just been about to operate on Drew. *You can do this, Jess. It'll be a walk in the park.* And he'd believed it. She had been able to tell by the expression on his face.

She opened her eyes and stared at her reflection again, adjusting her hat in the mirror. She looked herself in the eye and repeated the mantra, 'You can do this, Jess. It will be a walk in the park.'

She gave herself a little smile then headed out to the car, pulling the door closed behind her.

Now, if only she believed that.

Callum's fingers were drumming nervously on the steering wheel. Drew was happy. He was watching his favourite DVD in the back seat of the car, oblivious to his father's tension.

Callum squinted at the address again. This was definitely the right number. And he was definitely in the right street. He peered at the front door again. It was lovely, white with a stained-glass panel. He was sure he could see movement behind it. What was taking Jess so long?

He looked up and down the street. This was definitely one of the nicest areas of Glasgow. The street was filled with well-kept town houses with private drives and neat gardens. Wouldn't a town house be a little big for a single woman?

He shook that thought out of his head as the door opened

and Jess came out. She was dressed in red today with a dark hat pulled over her ears.

There it was again. Even though he kept trying to ignore it. He was sure if they had him on one of those twenty-four-hour cardiac monitors his heart rate would shoot up every time he saw her. Jess was definitely wreaking havoc and adding to his chances of heart disease.

She gave him a little wave as she pulled the door closed behind her and started down the steps. Instead of walking around to the passenger side, she stopped and pulled open the rear door. 'Hi, Drew, how are you doing?'

Drew looked up from his DVD. 'Hi, Dr Jess. I'm good. Can I go to mini-kickers this week instead of next?'

She laughed. 'I can see five-year-old boys obviously have a one-track mind. I tell you what—let me think about it. Let's see how you do with Santa today.'

'Okay.' He pointed to the TV in the rear of the driver's seat. 'Do you wanna watch the dinosaurs too?'

She gave a little smile as she glanced at Callum. 'No, thanks. I'd better sit up front with your dad in case he gets lonely.'

'Aw, okay, then.' His eyes fixed on the screen again as she closed the door and walked around to the passenger side.

She slid in and started to unfasten the buttons on her coat. 'I was so worried about how cold it was going to be I totally forgot about the fact we'd be in the car for an hour.' She pulled her hat off her head, leaving her curls sticking up in all directions.

She seemed happy. She seemed relaxed and Callum felt himself heave a sigh of relief. He'd been so worried about this.

Worried that she'd change her mind.

Worried that she'd phone him and back out.

And although her face seemed relaxed, he'd noticed the way her hand was gripping her bag. Take things slowly. That's what they'd agreed.

He started the engine again and they pulled out onto the motorway, heading down towards Ayrshire. It was a bright day, with just a little nip in the air. Not quite cold enough to freeze yet and little chance of ice.

The road to Largs was always busy. It wound through various towns all haunted by a million sets of traffic lights, but the scenery made up for the slow-moving traffic.

'I didn't expect it to be so busy.' Jessica had leaned back in her seat and was changing radio stations for most of the journey. 'I thought people only went to Largs in the summer for the ice cream.'

He smiled. 'When was the last time you were in Largs?'

She frowned. 'I think I was a child. We were going to Millport for the weekend and had to get the ferry from Largs.'

'Did you get your picture taken on Crocodile Rock?'

She gave a little gasp. 'Hasn't every Scottish child got their picture taken on Crocodile Rock?'

He laughed. 'I've not taken Drew there yet. Maybe that's a trip for the summer.'

'What's Crocodile Rock?' came the little voice from the back of the car.

Jessica twisted round in her seat to talk to him. 'It's a rock that looks like a crocodile. Some people painted it red, white and black years ago and when I was a young girl everyone went to Millport in the summer and got their photo taken standing on Crocodile Rock.'

'But crocodiles are green!'

Callum tried not to laugh. Only a child's logic could say something like that. 'I'll show you some pictures of it later, Drew. I've got a photo taken standing on the rock. If you like it I'll take you over in the summer to see it.'

'Does it bite?'

'No, silly, it's a rock.'

Drew settled back into his chair. 'How far until we see Santa?'

Callum glanced at the road signs. 'About another ten minutes. We'll be there soon.'

'I'm hungry.'

'So am I,' Jess piped up. 'We'll get something to eat when we stop, okay?'

It was almost a relief to hear her say that. Even better was the sound of her stomach rumbling. It was like music to his ears.

She pressed her hand over it. 'Oops, sorry!'

It didn't take long to reach the garden-centre car park and Drew's DVD was instantly forgotten when he saw all the 'Santa's Grotto' signs. 'Look, Dad!' he shouted. 'They've got a sleigh and everything!'

He was out of the car like a shot and over at the painted barrier advertising Santa at the garden centre.

Jessica felt her stomach churn. He was so excited he was practically jumping up and down. It was so nice to see. So nice to experience. Lewis had been too little to really comprehend Christmas. Although he'd liked the presents, he'd still been a little scared of the man in the big red suit.

She felt Callum's arm around her waist. 'Everything okay?' Sometimes she felt as if he could almost read her mind. As if he knew when her thoughts were drifting off and taking her out of the present time and place.

She reached over and put her hand on his chest. 'I'm fine. I guess we'd better get in there before Drew bursts his stitches.'

They walked through the garden centre, past the blue-lit trees lining the driveway and fake snowmen and animals. Inside the garden centre they had a path to Santa's Grotto and another to meet the reindeer. Callum went to the nearby desk to buy tickets. It was already getting busy in the centre, with lots of families and children arriving all the time.

The entrance was gorgeous. It was filled with a huge variety of pre-lit trees, sparkling in a variety of different colours. There were shelves and shelves of lighted ornaments, coloured parcels, little nativity scenes, sequin-covered trees and models of little Christmas villages playing music. On the surrounding walls were thousands of tree decorations, all hanging in different colour schemes to make selections easier.

All around the place children were squealing with delight at seeing something new or squabbling over their favourite tree ornament.

Jessica felt a little hand slip into hers. She looked down and Drew was staring up at her with anxious eyes. She knelt down next to him. 'What's wrong? Don't you feel well?' She couldn't help it, she was immediately moving into doctor mode.

He shook his head. 'I couldn't see my daddy,' he whispered.

Jess smiled. From down here, in amongst the jostling throng of people, it was hard to make anyone out, particularly for a little boy who had been running to and fro between the attractions. But her bright red coat would be easily visible. When she stood up she could clearly see Callum's back at the ticket booth, but she wasn't a little boy.

She slipped her hand out of her red leather glove and grabbed Drew's hand again. The heat was rising in the garden centre so she unfastened the zip on his jacket. It was even nicer holding hands, skin to skin. Drew seemed relieved to have found her. His immediate trust in her was so apparent.

Callum appeared next to them and waved the tickets. 'All the visits are timed. We can't see Santa until eleven-thirty. Want to get something to eat and then we'll go and see the reindeer?'

They nodded and followed him into the busy café. 'Have a seat, you two, and I'll get us some food.'

Jessica and Drew sat down at one of the nearby wooden tables. The whole café was decorated for Christmas with tinsel, garlands and Christmas holly wreaths hanging all round the walls. There was a cup filled with crayons on every table along with ready-made Christmas colouring sheets. Drew wasted no time and started to colour in a picture of the North Pole. 'Have you given your daddy your card?'

He shook his head. 'We posted the other one to mum in America. Dad helped me write the envelope. But I hid his under his pillow this morning.' Drew giggled. 'He won't find it until we get home.'

Jess smiled, watching Callum's back as he pushed his tray along the rack, picking up food as he went. He hadn't even asked her what she wanted to eat. She had a sneaking suspicion he was trying to feed her up. And she didn't feel insulted or annoyed. It was kind of nice that someone wanted to look after her.

The tray landed on the table a few minutes later with a glass of milk and a bacon roll for Drew, some toast with scrambled egg for her, and a full breakfast for Callum. He lifted some other plates onto the table with some home-baked scones, along with a caramel latte for Jess.

He really did have the best memory in the world. All the things in the world she liked.

'Okay, everyone?' he sat down in the seat next to Drew

and admired his crayoning. 'Let's eat and then we'll have a walk around the garden centre while we wait for our turn.'

Jessica looked around the room. It was full of families, all here either to buy a Christmas tree or pay a visit to Santa's Grotto. It had been such a long time since she'd been to a place like this.

She used to love visiting garden centres—especially around Christmas. She could easily have spent all her time off visiting one after the other, buying something in every place that she visited.

Something on one of the walls caught her eye. Little silver and red hearts, bunched together with bells to be hung from a Christmas tree. They were beautiful and just the sort of thing she would have picked in years gone by.

Callum followed her line of vision. 'Do you like them?'

She nodded slowly. A lump had appeared in her throat and she was too nervous to talk. She tried to clear her throat. 'I…I've changed my colour scheme. They would be perfect.'

He reached across the table and touched her hand. It was as if he knew. As if he'd just looked inside her head and saw that for a second she was struggling. 'Then we'll stop and get them before we leave. They look beautiful.' He took a sip of his coffee. 'Will your tree be red and silver this year?'

She shrugged. 'I bought some new silver decorations yesterday. I hadn't got much further than that.'

'Didn't you see the sparkly red ribbon near the door? It was on one of the trees.' Drew gave a little sigh. 'It was lovely.' Then he said quickly, 'But it's for a girl. It would be nice on your tree.'

'What colour scheme do you guys have?'

Callum choked on his coffee. 'You're joking, right? There's no colour scheme in our house. It's like a hotch-potch with every colour of the rainbow.' He smiled at Drew. 'Our colour scheme is whatever Drew's made at nursery or school that year. Right, son?'

Drew nodded and laughed. 'I've made lots of decorations. Daddy puts them all up on the tree.' He leaned forward and whispered in Jessica's ear, 'He says it doesn't matter if they're wonky.'

She felt a little tug at her heartstrings. She could just imagine their jumbled tree with haphazard decorations all made by a little boy. She wished hers could look like that.

Her silver and red decorations would seem drab in comparison. Suddenly the step she'd decided to take didn't seem nearly far enough. Not by a long shot.

She picked up a crayon and started to help Drew with his drawing. Callum's eyes were on her. He must have questions. But when could she tell him?

When could she tell him that there was a reason she wanted to take things slowly? It seemed almost deceitful when he'd invited her on a trip with his son.

He was still watching and smiling cautiously as he split the scones and put butter and strawberry jam on them. It was official. He was trying to feed her up. And he was doing a good job—it was the most she'd eaten in months.

But she didn't have the normal feelings she had around food. Mostly she was uninterested or dissociated herself from it. These last few weeks she'd started to notice the beautiful aromas of food again—instead of just the smell of coffee. In the garden centre today food smells were abundant. From the freshly baked scones and other cakes to the smells of bubbling soup, bacon and toasted cheese. Today was probably the first time in a long time she'd felt truly hungry.

'Is it time to go and see Santa yet?' Drew could barely contain his excitement and it was so nice to see.

Jessica stood up and held out her hand towards him. 'Why don't we go and see the reindeer? Maybe your dad will be able to take a picture of them for you. How cool would it be to show your friends at school that you met one of Santa's reindeer?'

Drew jumped up like a shot. 'Oh, yes, Daddy! Could I take it in for show and tell?'

Callum was smiling again and stood up. He looked at his watch. 'We've still got half an hour to kill. I think we can take some pictures of the reindeer.'

Drew sped down the path ahead of them, giving Callum a few seconds to reach and grab Jessica's hand. It didn't feel strange. It didn't feel unnatural.

Just as holding Drew's hand earlier hadn't felt unnatural. In fact, it had felt entirely normal.

An older couple was walking down the path towards them and stood aside to let Drew barrel past them. The older man laughed. 'What a lovely family,' he remarked.

Jessica felt herself catch her breath. Her feet were still moving, still walking down the path, but she felt every muscle in her body stiffen.

That's what they must look like.

A family.

An ordinary family.

She felt Callum squeeze her hand. He could sense it. He could sense her unease again. It must be killing him that he didn't know what was going on.

She so wanted to tell him. She so wanted to tell him right now before she burst into tears in the middle of Santa's Grotto.

Guilt was crawling all over her skin. Was this a betrayal? A betrayal of the memory of Daniel and Lewis— the people she'd thought she would spend the rest of her life with?

She could feel that horrible tight feeling spreading across her chest. Her breath was catching in her lungs.

Callum's feet stopped moving and his hand slid out from hers, turning her round to face him and sliding his arms around her waist. She couldn't lift her head to look at him. It was too hard right now as she was struggling to breathe.

This was wrong. Wasn't this usually the stage that single men ran away? When they heard someone mention something about a family?

Instead, Callum was taking it all in his stride. He pulled her a little closer and whispered in her ear, 'Just breathe, Jess. I don't know what's wrong, but this is a good day.' His voice was steady and calm. 'Wherever you are, know that I'm right here. Breathe.'

His hand rubbed gently up and down her back. A few people wandered past. Drew had raced on ahead and was out of sight. To the rest of the world it must just look as if they were taking a few seconds for a sneaky cuddle. Only Jessica knew the demons she was currently fighting in her head.

Gradually, the feeling across her chest started to ease. Her muscles started to relax. Callum released his grasp and pulled back, stroking her hair from across her face. 'Okay?'

She nodded. She didn't know what to say right now. How on earth could she explain what had just happened? What had caused that reaction in her?

He took her hand again. 'Ready to see some reindeer?'

It was as if he knew better than to ask right now. But even though his gaze was kind she could see the questions in his eyes. There was no judgement, only wonder.

She squeezed his hand. 'I would love to see the reindeer.'

They walked down the path to the outside stall where

the reindeer were. Drew was already standing agog. Of course none had a red nose, but the names of Santa's reindeer had been stencilled across the top of the stalls.

It was a wide paddock, with two members of staff—albeit dressed in elf costumes—on duty at all times. Jessica didn't know what she'd been expecting, but the reindeer seemed happy. They walked to the fence, and under the guidance of the staff allowed the children to stroke their coats and touch their antlers. They seemed healthy and in good condition.

Jessica had heard horror stories in the past about animals kept in children's play parks but it certainly wasn't the case here. In fact, the staff seemed enthusiastic, answering all the children's questions about the reindeer upkeep, with a few North Pole stories flung in for good measure.

'Can I get my picture with Comet, Dad?'

Callum nodded and knelt down as Drew posed next to the reindeer. Jessica waited until he'd finished then gave him a nudge. 'Go and stand next to Drew so I can take a picture of the two of you.' He obeyed and she snapped away happily. These would be great photos for Drew's show and tell at school.

'I want a picture with Dr Jess too!' shouted Drew.

Jess flushed. 'It's just Jess, Drew. You don't need to call me Dr Jess any more.'

Callum raised his eyebrows at her, obviously wondering if she would object to having her picture taken, but she swapped places with him and put her arm around Drew, letting Comet take pride of place in the background of the picture.

It was so easy to be around them. Drew had so much energy. No one would guess how sick he'd been a week ago. And Callum was every bit the doting dad that she'd expected him to be. It was so nice to see. And so easy to be a part of.

'Is it time yet, Dad?' Drew was bouncing up and down on the spot.

Callum looked at his watch. 'It's nearly eleven-thirty. Want to go down to the grotto?'

'Yippee!'

It was only a few minutes' walk. The path was lined with frost-covered decorations and houses. Christmas trees with green lights and gold stars lined the path, with red berry lights around the door of the grotto. Drew couldn't resist peering through the windows.

The garden staff had certainly gone all out to create a kids' paradise. They had staff dressed as elves, working away in a pretend workshop, piled high with sacks of toys. A little train ran around the outside of the whole complex with another elf driving it and children and parents in the carriages. 'Do we get to go on that too, Dad?'

Callum shrugged, 'I expect so.'

Jessica stood on tiptoe and whispered in his ear, 'I think that's part of the way out. Probably to make sure you don't stay in here too long.'

The queue moved along quickly and Callum showed Drew's ticket. An elf hurried over. 'Drew Kennedy? Come over here until we check and see if your name's in the naughty or nice book.' She held out her hand towards Drew.

His eyes widened like saucers and he turned to Callum, who smiled. 'Go on,' he urged.

'They asked me his name when I bought the tickets,' he said. 'They also asked me to choose which one he'd like best from a list of toys.'

'Wow. They've really thought of everything here, haven't they?' She looked around. 'You know, I'd love to bring some of the kids from the hospital here. You know, the ones that spend half their life stuck in a ward? Things are so well organised here, it could be perfect.'

'Why don't you ask before we leave if there's any way you can arrange it?'

She gave a little nod then nudged Callum. 'Look!'

Drew gave a little gasp as the elf pretended to find his name on the Nice list. 'Fabulous!' she shouted. 'That means we can go in and see Santa.'

'Come on, Dad. Come on, Jess,' shouted Drew as he tugged at the elf's hand.

Santa's Grotto was beautiful, filled with lots of fake snow and an icy blast of cold air. Santa was bundled up in the most padded costume and thickest beard Jessica had ever seen. And he had the patience of a saint. He took each child in turn, never hurried, never concerned about what was going on around him, and sat him or her on his knee, asking lots of questions.

Drew was totally enthralled. 'Tell me everything you want for Christmas,' Santa said with a wink towards Callum and Jessica.

Drew immediately reeled off a list of typical things a five-year-old boy wanted—a dinosaur, a racing car, a dress-up soldier's outfit. Then he stopped and pulled Santa down towards him, glancing towards his dad and whispering in Santa's ear.

Jess had a brief feeling of panic. Drew's eyes were on her the whole time he spoke to Santa. What was he asking for?

Santa smiled over at them both then spoke so quietly to Drew that neither of them could hear what he was saying. A few seconds later he handed Drew his present.

'Can I open it now, Santa?' he asked.

Santa nodded towards them. 'You'll need to ask.'

Drew jumped down. 'Can I, Dad? Can I?'

Callum swung Drew up into his arms. 'Say thank you to Santa and we'll go on the train. If you're good, you can open your present when we get to the car.'

'Yippee!' He squirmed around in Callum's arms. 'Thank you, Santa!'

They headed over to the train and Jessica laughed as Callum tried to squeeze his large frame into the carriage beside them. 'Budge up,' he said. 'It's a tight squeeze in here. This train is obviously designed for elves.'

The train ride was perfect. It started inside in the snow-covered landscape with snowmen and trees and wound its way outside to the garden centre, which was covered in a dusting of real snow and glistening in places with ice. The garden-centre staff had decorated huts to make them look as if they were still part of Santa's village.

After a few minutes the train came to a halt outside one of the buildings at the edge of the garden centre. It was a decorated barn. Jess and Callum looked at each other. They could hear the joyful squeals of children from inside. 'What on earth is in there?'

They waited as everyone alighted from the train, the elf standing at the front.

'Is there something else in there?'

The elf puffed out his already red cheeks. 'It's the winter wonderland—a children's playground.' He nodded his head at Drew. 'Your day's not over yet, pal.'

They walked inside and were hit with the wave of heat as soon as they crossed the threshold. The noise level was incredible. Every child who had visited Santa that morning had obviously ended up in here.

Around the edges of the playground were a variety of bedraggled parents sitting at tables, trying to make themselves heard above the noise.

Drew edged a little closer to his father. Jess knelt down next to him. The noise must be intimidating to a small child.

'Is there anything you'd like to go on?' she asked. Her eyes swept around the room and she put her hands on his shoulders. 'It's probably not a good idea to go on the trampoline or bouncy castle yet when you've had stitches in your tummy. But you could go over to the craft tables or into the games room if you wanted.'

Drew's hand slid into hers. 'Come into the games room with me.'

She nodded and gave Callum a smile as they made their way to the other side of the barn. He leaned over. 'This isn't like him. Normally he'd have made a beeline straight for the bouncy castle and dived straight on.'

Jess looked down at the little figure next to her. 'He's still in recovery mode. Being in hospital is a big thing for a kid. And having an anaesthetic takes a lot more out of them than you'd expect.' She rolled her eyes. 'Anyway, a bouncy castle or trampoline is the last thing he needs to be on right now.'

Callum gritted his teeth. 'Yeah, about that...'

'What?'

'I sort of bought Drew a trampoline for Christmas. He asked for it months ago and I bought it just the week before he was ill. It's sitting in the garage, waiting to be assembled. Am I going to have to say that Santa lost it?'

'What? No.' She shook her head. 'It's another few weeks yet. By then Drew should be fine. His stitches will be healed and he should be back to normal. But please tell me you've bought one of those big safety nets.' She waggled her finger at him. 'If you dare bring him into Casualty with a head injury because he's bounced off...'

He held up his hands. 'Whoa! No chance. With you on

duty and knowing the abuse I would get, I can assure you the safety net is ready.' He slipped his arm back around her shoulders as they headed into the games room.

He bent his head lower. 'Anyway, I remember the days when you weren't quite so safety-conscious.'

'What do you mean?'

He started to laugh and pretended to fumble in his pocket. 'Wait until I get the list out. First, there was the day you decided we should all jump into the harbour. Then there was the time you thought it was good idea to try out that thirty-year-old sled…'

'That was a family heirloom!'

He raised his eyebrows. '*Was* being the operative word.'

She stifled a laugh. Callum brought back so many good memories. Things that she'd forgotten about for so long. Things that she'd locked away inside the part of her mind that had stopped her from feeling joy any more.

It was so good to finally set it free again. It was so good to have someone to share this stuff with.

It was a bit quieter in the games room, with tables set with board games and a few electronic game machines. Drew didn't hesitate. He dropped Jessica's hand and raced off to watch the football game being played at the end of the room. Then he hesitated, turned round, took off his coat and hat and dumped them in her lap.

Callum pointed to one of the benches at the side. 'What do you say to another coffee? We could be in here for a while.'

'Sure. Thanks.'

The heat was building already. Jessica unfastened her coat and pulled off her hat and gloves. Callum disappeared to the coffee stand for a few moments and she leaned back against the wall.

Wow. So this was the stage Lewis would have been at.

Her eyes drifted around the quieter games room and then to the noisy throng outside.

Which room would he have wanted to be in? Would he have been in the thick of things, wreaking havoc outside? Or would he have been in here, like Drew, plotting his fantasy football side?

She let out a little laugh. How on earth did five-year-old boys know how to do that?

It was so nice to sit in here and watch all the kids at their various ages and stages. And even though she was thinking about Lewis, she was thinking about Drew too.

She watched as there was a minor clash of heads outside on the bouncy castle, and for the first time she didn't go into doctor mode and run forward to intervene. It was minor—their parents could deal with it—and she didn't want to leave Drew unsupervised. Callum had trusted her to watch over his son, even if it was only for a few minutes, and strangely she was enjoying it.

She hadn't been asked to come with them as a doctor. She'd been asked as a…what? A friend? A girlfriend? A potential lover?

All the things she would have immediately shied away from a few months ago. But with Callum it all felt so easy. One look from those green eyes and she tingled right down to her toes. One brush of his hand and her whole body craved more.

It was taking her time to get used to these feelings again.

To *admit* to feeling them.

To let herself feel them without being overwhelmed by sensations of guilt and betrayal. Slowly but surely she was starting to let those feelings go.

She thought about the photo currently in her living room. A beautiful photo of Daniel and Lewis, caught wrestling on the floor together, laughing together with unbridled pleasure. It was the image that stayed in her head.

Right there, caught in that moment of happiness forever.

They would always be part of her life—a wonderful part of her life—but the shades of grey around that picture were moving.

She was starting to move.

Starting to see a life past that.

'Jessica.' Her head shot up. Drew was waving her over. 'Come and see my score. I'm the top striker!' He was jumping up and down on the spot, clearly delighted. She ran over and gave him a hug. 'Well done, Drew, that's fantastic!'

He hugged her back with the exuberance that only a five-year-old could show. It felt good. It felt natural. It felt right.

Baby steps, her brain whispered. Just keep taking baby steps.

Callum walked around the edge of the winter wonderland with the two coffees, trying not to let his 'health and safety at work' hat annoy him. The coffee area should be cordoned off to minimise the risk of scalds to all the hyperactive children who were racing around the place.

He froze at the edge of the games room. Jessica and Drew were hugging in front of the giant TV, Drew obviously excited about something.

But that wasn't what made him freeze.

It was the expressions on both their faces.

Drew's was one of pure innocence and pleasure. The joy of sharing his delight with a mother figure. The way he'd wrapped his hands around her neck and was talking nineteen to the dozen in her ear.

And the way Jessica was looking at Drew.

Like he was the best thing she'd ever seen.

It had the strangest effect on Callum. He should be happy. He should be glad that his little boy felt so comfortable around the woman he hoped would be his girlfriend.

He should be delighted that they obviously had a mutual admiration society going. So many of his other friends had told him tales of woe about new potential partners and children not getting on—this obviously wasn't the case here.

But there was the weirdest feeling in the pit of Callum's stomach.

He knew there was something else. He knew there were parts of herself that Jessica still had to reveal to him. And it didn't matter what his memories of Jessica were. It didn't matter what effects one look of those brown eyes had on his body. It didn't matter how much he kept trying to push any little nagging doubts aside.

The fact was he wanted more. More than she was currently giving.

He wanted everything. The whole package.

Whatever that might contain.

But until he knew exactly what that was, he had a little boy to put first. He couldn't risk Drew's feelings or emotions. He could see the trust in his son's eyes. He could see the way he was already forming pictures in his mind—pictures that included Jessica.

Those pictures were starting to form in Callum's mind too, but he had to be sure. He had to be certain about Jessica before things went any further. It didn't matter how much he wanted to kiss her. It didn't matter how much he wanted to hold her in his arms. After a few short weeks he knew exactly where he wanted this relationship to go.

Drew was reaching up, touching one of Jessica's curls and tucking it behind her ear as he talked to her. Jessica caught his hand in hers and planted a kiss on his palm.

That was what he wanted for his son. So much it made his stomach ache.

Jessica looked over and caught sight of him. She frowned, obviously seeing the expression on his face, and gave him a little wave. She ruffled Drew's hair and pointed back at the big screen before moving over towards Callum and taking the coffee from his hand. 'Thanks for that. What's up?'

'Nothing. Nothing's up.'

She tilted her head to one side. 'Are you sure? You looked unhappy.'

She was staring at him with those big brown eyes. *She was worrying about him.* The irony wasn't lost on him.

And she looked happier. She looked more relaxed than he'd seen her in a while. If he could forget the episode earlier, today would have been a perfect day.

There was a little sparkle about her, a little glow. Glimmers of the old Jess shining through.

She glanced over her shoulder to where Drew was engrossed again in his game. There was something different in her eyes, something playful.

She gave him a cheeky smile then grabbed his arm and pulled him round the corner, out of the line of sight of everyone. 'I wonder if I can make you feel better,' she whispered, then she leaned forward and wrapped her arms around his neck, rising up on tiptoe and kissing him gently on the mouth.

And at that precise moment all rational thought left the building.

CHAPTER ELEVEN

HER PAGER SOUNDED again. It was the fourth time in the last hour, but she'd been stuck in Theatre, performing surgery on a very sick baby with a necrotic bowel.

She pulled her theatre mask and cap off as the tiny baby was wheeled out of Theatre and off to ITU. She'd probably spend most of the night there, but she had to answer this page first.

She couldn't believe how tired she was. It was weird. For the last three years work had been her sanctuary. A place of focus. A place where she didn't have time to think about anything else.

And things here were good. Marcus and Lily, the two children with hypothermia, had both made a steady recovery and been allowed home. All the children from the accident had now been discharged and would be looking forward to Christmas with their families.

Christmas with a family. Something she hadn't even thought about for the last few years.

But the last few weeks had been different. Spending time with Callum and Drew had brought a whole new perspective to her life.

Life didn't just revolve around the hospital any more.

She didn't just wake up in the morning and stay there for as long as possible, only going home when the nurses eventually flung her out, then falling asleep straight away for the next day.

Work wasn't the first thing she thought about when she woke up in the morning. That was usually Callum and his green eyes—or Drew and whatever event he was looking forward to at school that day.

It was amazing how differently she felt about things.

In fact, tonight she'd been almost sorry that she was on call. She'd have preferred to spend more time with Callum and Drew.

For the first time in three years she was actually looking forward to Christmas. To spending it with people she loved. To have a Christmas when the focus wasn't just on being alone but sharing the time with others.

There was still the odd moment where she felt guilty. Usually in the depths of night when the feelings crept up on her unawares. When little voices in her head asked if she really deserved a second chance at happiness.

After all, she'd had her happy-ever-after. She'd been married to the love of her life and had had a beautiful son. Why should she get that chance again?

Was it fair?

Slowly but surely Callum and Drew were edging their way into her heart. Even just thinking about them brought a smile to her face.

It made her try to push the other voices away. Push them away into some dark place where she wouldn't hear them any more.

Her pager sounded again and she picked up the phone. The sister in A and E answered straight away.

'Bad news, Jessica. It's Grace Flynn. She's been admitted again. Her bloods have come back whilst we've been paging you—they're awful.'

Jessica's heart plummeted. Grace was a long-term patient. A seven-year-old with a rare form of invasive bowel tumours. She'd operated on another tumour only a few weeks ago and things hadn't looked good.

Children with cancer always had a wide team of staff looking after them at Parkhill. Grace had a paediatric consultant, a specialist oncologist, herself with her surgical skills and a whole host of specialist nurses. Even though doctors weren't supposed to have favourite patients, she'd been treating Grace for so long that she couldn't help but let the little girl have a special place in her heart.

'Have you sent her up to the ward or is she still in A and E?'

'The registrar's seen her and sent her up to the ward while we were waiting for her blood results and ultrasound. She knew her and thought she'd be more comfortable up there.'

Of course. Javier, the Spanish registrar, was familiar with the case. He'd dealt with Grace on a number of occasions over the last year. 'Ultrasound? Is there a chance her bowel is blocked again?'

She heard the sigh at the end of the phone. 'Put it this way, after a conversation with one of the other consultants he gave her a bolus of morphine and set up a continuous opioid infusion.'

Jessica sucked in her breath. News she didn't want to hear. Not for a child.

'I'll go straight up now,' she said. 'I can review the test results when I get there.'

Jessica replaced the phone and hurried up to the ward.

It didn't matter that she knew this was inevitable for Grace. It didn't matter that the doctors, family and nurses had already had discussions about future plans for Grace's care.

Her frail little body couldn't go through another round

of surgery—or chemotherapy or radiotherapy. Her body had already taken all it could.

The best they could do for now was to keep her comfortable.

She pulled up the test results and her heart plunged when she saw them. Nothing was good. The blood results and ultrasound could only mean one thing. She read the notes that her registrar had written, the record of pain relief and a few further comments by one of the other consultants involved in her care and called in tonight.

There was nothing to disagree with. She would have done exactly the same things that they had done.

Grace's mum, dad and brother were sitting at her bedside, along with one of the other paediatric consultants involved in her care.

Jessica stood in the doorway for a second, trying to collect herself. She was trying to keep her professional face in place and doing her best not to cry.

Grace's mum looked up and rushed over, enveloping her in a huge, crushing hug. 'Oh, thank you for coming up to see her. I knew you'd come.'

This was breaking Jessica's heart. She had still had a tiny little glimmer of hope in her eyes—as if at any moment one of the doctors would suggest something different—something completely out of the blue that no one had thought of. But it just wasn't possible.

If there was any surgery in the world Jess could do right now to save this little girl she wouldn't hesitate. But it just wasn't to be.

Her eyes met Grace's dad's. They were strong, resolute. Resigned to their fate but determined to give his little girl as much as dignity as possible. He gave her the tiniest nod, but didn't move from his place, holding his little girl's hand.

Jess moved into the room and sat down in a chair in the corner. The lights in the room were dimmed and Grace's little chest was barely moving up and down.

Her heart was breaking. She was finding it difficult to think straight. The tension in the room was palpable. They all knew what was about to happen.

Parkhill was a children's hospital and the sad fact of life was that children did die. But it wasn't a common occurrence. None of the staff here were used to it. None of them wanted to be.

Every child's death impacted on every member of staff that worked here.

She felt a hand on her shoulder. Pauline. 'Sorry, Jess, but I need you in ITU for the baby.'

She nodded and stood up. She still had a job to do, no matter how difficult things were right now.

She walked over to the bed and stroked Grace's hair. There was a horrible pressing feeling in her stomach. She honestly couldn't do anything more for Grace, and there was a baby in ITU who needed her now.

But she couldn't just walk out of here and say nothing. This might be the last time she saw this little girl alive.

Then it came to her, the poem that she and Grace had made up one day Grace had decided she wanted to be a horse rider. It had been a wonderful daydreaming session, when Grace had decided the name and colour of her horse, where it would be stabled and how famous it would become.

Jessica bent down and whispered in her ear, 'Riding across the fields, the wind is in your hair, holding onto Cupid's reins, as if you don't have a care. Racing through the grass, and tearing round the bend, all on a magical mission, to reach the rainbow's end.'

She felt tears forming in her eyes. In Grace's daydream

that day she'd reached the end of the rainbow and found the mythical pot of gold. If only something like that came true.

She took one final look. One glimpse of the family that was about to be changed forever.

The walls were closing in around her. Suffocating her. She gave the family one final smile and left, her feet carrying her swiftly down the corridor before she unravelled any further.

Her phone beeped. Again.

She pulled it out of her pocket. *Drew and I are picking you up at nine a.m. to make sure you actually leave.*

She smiled. She was exhausted, both physically and mentally. The baby she'd performed surgery on had needed constant review throughout the night. It had been touch and go for a while. But finally, around six a.m., the little mite had seemed to turn a corner.

She rubbed her eyes. What time was it now? She looked around for the nearest window. Was it even daylight yet? Dark winter mornings were notorious in these parts. It was frequently still dark in the morning when kids were walking to school.

There was a smudge in the background of the window. The first few edges of a rising sun. She dug in the pocket of her scrub trousers to find her watch. Just before eight a.m. A feeling of dread crept over her. She knew where she had to go next.

Almost as if someone was reading her mind, the phone next to her started to ring. One ring tone instead of two. An internal call.

Pauline picked up the phone swiftly. 'ITU Sister Jones. Yes, yes. I see. I'm really sorry.' Her eyes skittered towards Jessica, who felt her stomach tighten. 'I'll let her know. Have they? Okay, thanks for that.' She replaced the receiver and turned to face Jess, her face grave.

Jessica felt sobs rise up in her chest. Pauline's arm quickly came round her shoulders. 'Jess, it's been a big night. You were in surgery for hours, then with Grace's admission and the time you've had to spend in here...' Her voice tailed off.

'I should go back down. Back down and see the family.'

Pauline shook her head. 'They've gone home. Grace's brother was exhausted and Grace's parents decided they had to go home. They'll come back later today to make arrangements. John Carson, the other consultant, is meeting them then.'

It made sense. They would be exhausted. It would have been the worst night of their life. And John Carson had been sitting with them last night. He knew them inside out and had been involved in Grace's care from diagnosis.

Pauline placed both her hands on Jess's shoulder. 'Go home, Jess. That's what you need to do.' She glanced at the phone that was sitting on the desk. 'Go home with Drew and Callum. It's the best thing you could do right now. It's what you need right now.'

She nodded. She didn't even need to say the words.

This had probably been the second-hardest night of her life.

She'd felt herself unravel at some points. Felt as close to breaking point as she'd ever been. The only glimmer on the horizon had been the one in her heart.

Three years was a long time to nurse a broken heart. To go home to an empty house. To feel as if there wasn't much reason to get up in the morning. To wonder if anyone would miss you if you were gone.

Thank goodness she'd met Callum again. With his

come-to-bed eyes and his sexy smile. The one that could stay in her thoughts for hours.

That tiny little black cloud that had still been hanging over her head needed to be banished forever. It was time to stop avoiding the subject and let him know why she found some things so hard.

She knew in her heart that he would understand. That he would support her. And that was all she could ever want. Spending time with Callum and Drew had become the most precious thing in the world to her. Something she didn't want to live without.

She gave Pauline a hug. 'Tell John I'll be available if he needs me.' She walked down the corridor and into the changing rooms. She didn't want to wait a minute longer.

If there was one thing she'd learned it was that life was too short. Life was for living.

There were only two faces in the world she wanted to see right now. And they both had a place in her heart.

Callum glanced at the clock. Two minutes to nine. Just as well this wasn't a school day. His fingers were tapping nervously on the steering wheel.

He couldn't work out why he was on edge. He just knew he was.

It was time. It was make or break.

He wanted this relationship to work. He wanted it to move on. But for that to happen there needed to be honesty between them.

He needed to know.

He needed to know what had happened in Jessica's life.

Drew had spent most of the night talking about Jessica. The glow in his eyes had told Callum everything he needed to know. His little boy had fallen just as hard as he had.

He watched the door of the hospital, willing Jess to appear, and finally she did.

She looked shattered. She obviously hadn't slept a wink last night.

Her coat was barely pulled around her shoulders and he could see her eyes searching the car park.

He gave the horn a beep and waved to her. Her face lit up and she hurried over. He expected her to jump straight in but she didn't. Instead, she opened the rear door, gave Drew a quick hug and dropped a kiss on top of his head.

'We've been waiting for you,' Drew said solemnly.

'And you've no idea how happy I am to see you,' she answered. Callum turned, watching as she enveloped Drew in another quick hug. She looked truly happy to see him—to see them both. He didn't know whether to leap for joy or let that little cautionary voice in his mind rear its ugly head.

She closed the rear door and opened the front passenger door, climbing in and sinking into the seat next to him.

'Hard night?' He could see the furrows in her brow, etching deep lines into her normally smooth forehead.

She gave a little sigh and a shake of her head, glancing across her shoulder at Drew. 'More than you can ever know.'

The words hung in the air between them. He could tell there was so much she wanted to say—but couldn't because Drew was in the car.

His little hand stretched over and touched Jessica's shoulder. 'Jess, are we going home now? Are you going to watch my movie with me? I've got my duvet on the couch for us. We can snuggle up.'

A wide smile spread across her face. Relief. Relief at the thought of getting away from the struggles of the hospital and spending the day with them. Stress free.

He felt his stomach clench a little more. Was he wrong

to do this today? To ask her about her past and to put her on the spot about their future?

Part of him wanted to leave it, to stay in this happy limbo they were in. It felt like a safe place. But deep down he didn't want a safe place. He wanted much more. He wanted to be able to shout from the rooftops that he and Jessica were together. He wanted to make plans for a future for the three of them together, as a family.

He wanted to wake up every morning with Jessica by his side.

He wanted to be there to support her through whatever had happened.

He wanted to be a family.

And the only way to do that was to get rid of the elephant in the room.

He pulled out into the Glasgow traffic and started along the street. It was after nine so the morning rush was dying down. 'Want to go somewhere for breakfast before we get home?'

She shook her head. 'A duvet day with a film sounds perfect. I don't want to delay that for a second.' Her stomach gave a growl. 'But I'm starving. Do you have any bacon at home?'

'Daddy! Give her the chocolate we bought her!' Drew's voice echoed through the car. 'We bought you your favourite, Jess.'

Callum smiled and reached across her, opening the glove box and pulling out the orange-flavoured chocolate. It had been her favourite years ago, and he expected it still was. He put the chocolate in her lap. 'That will keep you going until we get home. We stopped to pick it up on the way here.'

Silence. Absolute silence in the car.

He knew instantly that something was wrong.

Thank goodness Jess was sitting down because the colour drained instantly from her face and she looked as if she might pass out.

She swayed—even though she was sitting in the seat.

They were heading through the busiest part of town. There was nowhere to pull over and the traffic was a little heavier here so he needed to keep his eyes on the road.

'Jess? Jess? What's wrong?'

Was she sick? Maybe it was nothing. Maybe she was feeling faint because she'd been on her feet all night and hadn't had anything to eat. That would be just like Jess. Too busy to sit down for a few minutes and think of herself.

But he had the strangest feeling he wasn't even close.

'Stop the car.' Her voice was quiet, almost a whisper.

'What?'

'Stop the car!' This time she was definite.

He could see the flare of panic in her eyes. She absolutely meant it.

His head flicked from side to side, trying to see if there was anywhere to stop in the midst of the queued traffic. 'I can't, Jess. There's nowhere to go. You'll need to wait. What's wrong? Do you feel sick?'

'I'll get out here.' She flung open the door and jumped out of the car. Her bag was still sitting in the footwell of the car.

Callum was stunned. What on earth had just happened?

'Daddy? Where's Jess gone?'

'I don't know, Drew.' He looked frantically up and down the street in the direction she was walking, trying to find somewhere to pull over.

What on earth had gone wrong?

This was supposed to be a good day. How on earth could a chocolate bar cause a reaction like that?

All the nudging doubts he'd had about putting Jess on

the spot vanished. Drew looked near to tears, sitting in the back of the car hugging his toy to his chest.

Something had upset Jess but she, in turn, had upset his son.

He couldn't have that. He couldn't have that at all.

This was crazy. And he couldn't let it go on a moment longer.

He'd been wrong. He'd been wrong not to sit her down and ask her right away what was going on in her life.

He'd been blindsided by her. She brought back a whole host of good memories and feelings. He loved being around her. She was beautiful—inside and out. He could see that. Even in the times she tried to hide it away.

He wanted things to work out between them.

His heart twisted as he watched the forlorn figure scurrying down the street and a whole new sensation swept over him.

He loved her. He loved Jess.

Just like he had years before.

Only this was different. This was a grown-up kind of love.

One that realised that nobody was perfect and everyone had history. And in his heart he knew she felt the same way—about him and about Drew.

So what on earth had gone wrong? He had no idea what had just happened.

But the one thing he knew for sure was that he needed to find out.

She was going to be sick. She was going to be sick everywhere.

She couldn't think or see straight.

Her hand reached out and grasped the wall, trying to steady herself.

A woman stared at her on the way past. She looked horrified. Did she think Jess was drunk at nine in the morning? Because that's the way she felt right now.

Her hand was gripping something tightly, her knuckles blanched white, her fingers growing numb.

Her hand was shaking. No, her whole body was shaking.

She leaned over and retched, trying to ignore the people walking past and looking at her in horror.

Unravelling.

She'd felt like that earlier on—in the middle of the night when she'd known Grace was about to die. She'd felt as if she hadn't had the strength to be there, hadn't had the strength to do the job she was supposed to be doing.

And now this.

Her whole world had just tilted on its axis.

In an instant. In a flash.

She stared at her hand, willing her fingers to open.

All this over a bar of orange-flavoured chocolate.

She heard the thud of feet running along the pavement. Felt a hand on her back. 'Jess. What is it? What's wrong?'

She could hear it all. The confusion in his voice. The concern.

She should have told him. She should have told him before.

Then he would have looked at her in pity and walked away. Then she wouldn't have dropped the walls around her heart and let him and his son in. Then she would have stayed safe. Locked in her own fortress where nothing could penetrate her heart and leave her exposed to hurt again.

She should have told him before.

But that would have made it all real.

Not the fact that it had happened. Not the fact that her

husband and son had died. But the fact that she was telling him—telling him, as she prepared to move on with her life.

Because up until this point she hadn't really told anyone—she hadn't needed to. All her work colleagues already knew and bad news travelled fast, following you like a billowing black cloud. She was used to people whispering behind her then averting their eyes when caught.

Maybe this was what she deserved. Why should she get a chance at a happy ever after with a new family? Maybe she didn't deserve it.

All the doubts and feelings of guilt were rearing their ugly heads. How could she forget about her husband and son? How dared she?

Callum looked utterly confused. He bent down and picked up the bar of chocolate. 'You're retching over this?'

The look on his face said it all. He was at breaking point. She'd known for the last few weeks that Callum was holding back—stopping himself from saying what he wanted to.

She looked at the bar of chocolate in his hand. It must seem so pathetic, but it didn't feel that way to her.

'You don't understand—'

'You're right. I don't.' His voice was soft and he stepped closer to her, touching the side of her cheek. 'So tell me, Jess.' He glanced over at his car parked at the side of the road, where he'd left Drew on his own.

She couldn't bear to look. Couldn't bear to look at the little boy who'd won a place in her heart. Not while she felt so guilty. Frustration was building in her chest. She wanted to say so much but just couldn't find the words. They all seemed to get jammed in her throat. 'I lost them. I lost them this way.' She pointed to the bar of chocolate in his hand.

'Lost who? What way?' He looked totally confused.

'Jess, I want to understand. Really, I do. But I can't until you tell me. It's time, Jess. It's time there were no secrets between us.'

Her legs wobbled underneath her. They couldn't take her weight any more and she felt herself crumple. 'My husband. My son.' Sobs racked her body. The words were out. They were finally out there. For everyone in the world to hear. For Callum to hear.

'What?'

She couldn't stop. Now the tears had started they wouldn't stop.

She felt his strong arms on her shoulders. 'What do you mean, you lost your husband and son?'

He was crouching now, on the ground beside her. She looked up into his green eyes. He was totally thrown by all this. Probably knocked sideways.

Her voice was trembling. 'My husband Daniel and son Lewis were killed in a road accident.'

His shock was palpable. 'What? When?'

'Three years ago.' Her shoulders were shaking now.

He shook his head, his disbelief apparent. 'Why didn't you tell me, Jess? Why didn't you tell me something like that?'

She was panicking now. People in the street were staring at them. 'I couldn't find the words. I didn't know how to tell you. I didn't know what to say.' Her breathing felt erratic, every breath a struggle. Her voice dropped, her eyes looking towards the horizon. 'It never felt the right time.'

Callum shook his head. 'How could you not tell me something as important as this?'

'How could you not tell me about your son?' The words shot out instantly. In blind panic.

He reeled back, looking as if he'd been stung.

She saw him take a deep breath and get to his feet,

reaching over, putting his hands under her arms and pulling her up with him. He looked about him. 'This isn't something to discuss in the street, Jessica.'

People were staring. People had stopped what they were doing.

She looked over at the car. Drew's little face was pressed up against the window. He looked frantic and her heart went out to him. He had no idea what was happening. Just that something was wrong.

If she felt upset and confused, how must he feel?

The chocolate bar was on the ground at her feet. Tears welled in her eyes instantly. 'I can't do this,' she whispered.

'Can't do what?'

She put her hands out. 'This. Us.' She looked over at the car. 'Drew.'

She could see sadness mounting in Callum's eyes. He didn't understand. He didn't understand this wasn't about him and Drew. This was all about her.

She shook her head. 'You don't get it. You don't understand. Daniel and Lewis—they stopped to buy me my favourite bar of chocolate the night they died. They stopped at a shop just round the corner from our house.'

Her voice was breaking, trembling as she remembered, the memories rushing up so clearly and strongly, as if it had just happened a few hours ago. 'He sent me a text.' She let out a huge gasp of air. 'Daniel sent me a text saying they'd be five minutes late because they'd stopped to buy me chocolate.' She shook her head.

'The next thing I knew the sister from A and E came to find me. I was standing outside the hospital, waiting for them, wondering what was taking so long. She'd been phoned by Ambulance Control—the crew had radioed in once they knew who they were dealing with.'

Callum hadn't moved. He was still standing over her,

his face unreadable. She must seem like a crazy woman, but everything seemed so clear in her head.

'What did she tell you?' His voice sounded a little wobbly too.

She looked up at him. She'd never seen his green eyes so full of conflict. She couldn't imagine how he must feel about all this. She'd never wanted to hurt him.

She'd never wanted to hurt Drew.

She took a deep breath, every part of the experience as painful now as it had been then. 'She told me Daniel had been taken to Glasgow Cross and Lewis was coming to Parkhill.' She looked off into the distance. It seemed easier to speak when she didn't have to look at him. 'That was normal after a RTA. The kids always came to us.'

'And then?'

He reached out and touched her hand, giving it a squeeze, willing her to have the strength to carry on. She could see tenderness written all over his face. She could almost reach out and touch the hurt he felt for her.

She'd been terrified to tell him. Terrified he would misunderstand.

She'd been right.

She looked at him. The tears were gone now. This was the worst part. This was the part that almost killed her.

'It was too late for them both. They were both dead on arrival. I never got to say goodbye, Callum. To my husband or my son.'

There was something so final about those words. So final, because she was saying them out loud. Her voice continued automatically—because she needed to get it all out. She'd held it in for so long. She'd wanted to tell him, but now it felt as if someone had released the dam and it had to all rush out.

'None of the staff knew what to do when Lewis arrived.

It's so different when it's one of your own. Somebody else's child is just as important but you have an emotional detachment that allows you to do the job, not to think about the hopes, dreams and fears of that little person in front of you. And to a certain extent you need that. But when it's one of your own…' She met his gaze. 'The child of a friend, colleague or loved one. It's like the world stops turning. You can't function any more, autopilot just doesn't work.'

She wanted him to understand.

She needed him to understand. Because it related to why she couldn't find the words to tell him.

And he must understand it a little. He'd been the parent with the sick child.

How could she have performed surgery on Drew if she'd known him like she did now? How could she have got through that op?

He was watching her steadily. She could see the rise and fall of his chest. His words were hoarse. It was almost as if he was seeing the whole picture in his head. Feeling her pain. 'They didn't resuscitate?'

She shook her head. 'There was no point.' She couldn't hide the forlorn tone in her voice. 'I think both of them probably died at the scene. It was strange—I always thought if something like that happened I wouldn't be able to do that. That I would resuscitate for hours and hours, no matter how hopeless. But it was totally different. I didn't want my son disturbed. I didn't want people to touch him when I already knew it was pointless. I just wanted to hold him.'

She wrapped her arms around herself at the memory of it. 'Someone phoned Pauline and she came down from ITU. I held Lewis for hours. And Pauline held me.'

There was silence between them. She didn't need him to say anything—she didn't want him to say anything.

She couldn't imagine how he must be feeling.

Well, she could, but only in part.

She remembered exactly how she'd felt when she'd first heard about Drew. It had been a total bolt out of the blue. And this was much worse than that.

Callum looked deep in thought—as if a hundred different things were spinning through his mind at once.

He couldn't stop looking at his car, where Drew was. She wished she could read his mind. Know what he was thinking. He dug his hands deep into his pockets. 'So, what's changed, Jessica? You may not have told me this before but it was still there. Still circling in your head every day.'

She felt a single tear slip down her cheek. It was so hard to put this into words. She looked at the little face staring out of the car window towards her and it made her heart ache. She so wanted to hold him. She so wanted to take him in her arms and give him comfort. Because she loved him. She loved that little boy—just as much as she loved his father.

Callum's face looked more than confused—he looked numb. As if he was trying to work out where his place in all this was. She'd done this to him. It had been her.

It was all her fault.

She was hurting people that she loved. Again.

'You don't get it.'

'No, Jess. I don't get it.' He reached over and pulled her towards him. For a second they stood in the street, their heads bowed, their foreheads touching.

If she could, she would stay this way forever. With Callum holding her as if he could take all her cares and worries away.

Because this was killing her. She hated herself right now. She hated hurting those that she loved.

'It was my fault, Callum. Don't you see? It was my fault that Daniel and Lewis died. If they hadn't gone to get me that chocolate, they wouldn't have been on the road at that time. They wouldn't have had that accident.' She reached over and grabbed his hand from his pocket. 'Just like you did today. You and Drew.' She shook her head as fiercely as she could. 'I can't have that. I can't have that on my conscience. Something happening to the people I love because of me.'

He lifted his head from hers and reached up and touched her cheek. His hand was freezing. They'd been standing out in the cold for far too long. Trying to dissect their lives in the middle of the street.

She knew this was ridiculous. Everything about it was so wrong.

She'd been hurt before. She was desperate.

How could this compare to losing her husband and son? It couldn't. And yet it was hurting every bit as much.

She'd started down that road. The one that was going to lead her to a new life. She'd started to feel again.

She'd started to trust.

She'd started to love.

And there would never be anyone as perfect for her as Callum and Drew. She could never feel as much as she did now.

And it was disintegrating all around her. Slipping through her fingers like grains of sand.

Callum shifted on his feet. He looked over towards the car again and something must have clicked in his head.

'What age was Lewis, Jessica?' His voice was sharp, abrupt.

'He was two. He was just two.' She was confused. It was a natural question. But it didn't seem quite right.

His eyes darted to the car. 'So he'd have been the same

age as Drew is now?' There was something in the way he said it. As if he was having a different conversation from her.

Her heart squeezed. The whole host of thoughts that she'd had at first about Drew came flooding into her mind. The comparisons with her own son, which had all faded as the weeks had progressed and she'd got to know this other little boy.

'Yes. Yes, he would.' Why was her voice shaking? Why did she feel as if she'd just sealed their fate?

'Oh, Jess.'

It was the little gasp in his voice. The way the words came out. As if his world had just crumbled in on itself.

He shook his head, very slowly. Were those tears in his eyes?

His voice was trembling. 'This was never about us, was it, Jess? This was never about me and Drew. This was about you—looking for a replacement family.'

'What? No.' She shook her head. 'Not at all.'

But Callum had switched off. It was almost as if he'd detached himself. 'You don't love me and Drew, Jess. You love the *idea* of us.' He was shaking his head again. 'I should have known.'

She couldn't believe this. She couldn't believe his brain was thinking this way. But she was so undone she couldn't think straight.

'I need you to love me, Jess. *Me*. And I need you to love Drew. For who *he* is. Not just the thought of a replacement for your own little boy. My little boy's already had a mother who walked away from him. I can't expose him to that again. I need you to love Drew with your whole heart. Love every inch of him—and every inch of me.' He was shaking his head again. 'You've broken my heart, Jess—truly you have.'

'But I do love you, Callum. I do. And I love Drew too.' Even as she said the words they sounded desperate. Like the last-ditch attempt to save something that was already slipping through her fingers.

This was over. This was finished.

It didn't matter that she'd been the one telling him she couldn't do this any more.

Part of her had still wanted him to tell her they could make it. That they could still have a chance of something.

But it wasn't to be. This was all too much for him. He hadn't signed up for this. That much was evident.

Her heart was breaking all over again.

She couldn't look at him. It was just too hard.

'We've both made a mistake here, Jess. I wanted you to be something that you just weren't ready to be. And you wanted us to replace something that you've lost.' He bit his lip. She'd never seen him look so shattered. So resigned to their fate. 'Neither of us can do that.'

His voice was tired. 'Get in the car and I'll drop you home. It seems we both have a lot to think about.' He took a deep breath and touched her cheek one more time. 'I'm sorry about your husband and son, Jess. I really am. I'm sorry that things just haven't worked out for us.' He pointed over his shoulder. 'But right now I have to put the needs of my son first.'

He shifted slightly, blocking her view of the car. 'I want you to say something—anything—to placate Drew until we drop you off. Can you do that for me and for Drew?'

'Of course,' she whispered. 'I would never do anything to hurt Drew.'

'Too late,' he whispered as he turned towards the car and walked away.

CHAPTER TWELVE

THE DOOR OPENED and Callum jumped about a foot in the air. Drew and his little friend walked through the door, football boots in hand.

'You're back already?' He rubbed his eyes. Hadn't he just sat down?

He couldn't believe it was that time already. Julie and Blair walked into the room behind the boys and Julie folded her arms across her chest.

'Boys, go up to Drew's room for ten minutes and play. I want to talk to Drew's dad.'

Blair gave a shake of his head as he crossed the room. 'Why don't I just start running the bath and put them both in it?' He glanced at Callum on his way past. 'You're in for it, mate.'

Callum straightened up instantly. Julie and Blair were two of his closest friends. He'd never had any problems with either of them. They'd been fabulous, helping him with Drew. But even though they had a good relationship, Callum knew that Julie wasn't a woman to be messed with.

He stood up and walked towards her. 'Is something wrong?'

She waited a second, tilting her head to listen for the sound of the boys' footsteps going up the stairs and out of earshot.

'You...' She pushed her sharp finger into the middle of his chest. 'You're what's wrong. Kitchen. Now.' She turned on her heel and walked through to his kitchen.

'Ouch.' Callum rubbed the middle of his chest and started to follow her. He had a sinking feeling Blair had known exactly what he was doing when he disappeared with the boys.

Julie knew her way around the house. The coffee machine—which was only used on special occasions—was sitting on the counter and filled with water. She switched it on and turned to face him, folding her arms across her chest again.

'Right. Spill.'

Callum sat down on one of the breakfast bar stools. 'Spill what?'

She threw her hands up. 'You're the one sitting in a dark living room, staring at Christmas-tree lights. Tell me, how long were you there for? One hour? Two?'

Yeah, the Christmas-tree lights. The hotch-potch of decorations, along with the new silver and red ones that Drew and Jessica had picked out at the garden centre. Another reminder of Jessica. Along with the picture of the three of them Drew had drawn at school that was currently stuck to the fridge. Or the photo Drew had put on his bedside cabinet of him sitting on Jessica's knee at the winter wonderland.

Or the fact she was haunting his dreams. Every. Single. Night.

Julie was waiting. Waiting with her steely glare for an answer.

'I've had a hard few days at work. It's been chaos.'

'Pull the other one, Callum, it's got bells on.' She hadn't moved. The coffee machine was starting to bubble next to her.

'I don't know what you mean.'

She shook her head and started clattering around, pulling cups from cupboards and thumping them down on his worktop. 'I'm the one who's been in the company of your little boy. Your little boy who's missing Jess. She's all he'll talk about, Callum—well, that and some promise Santa made him.'

'Drew said something?'

She nodded as she put the coffee in the machine. 'Oh, Drew said a whole lot. All about some fight and how he wanted to see Jess and you won't let him.'

Callum put his elbows on the worktop and his head in his hands. 'It's difficult, Julie. I found out something about Jessica—and it's made me rethink everything.' He shook his head. 'But Drew's hardly said a thing. He's asked a few times if she's coming round, but that's it.'

Julie pulled the chair out on the other side of the breakfast bar and sat down directly opposite him. She counted off on her fingers, 'Apparently on Monday he asked if she would be coming for dinner, on Tuesday he asked if she could go to the pictures with you both. On Wednesday he asked if she would be here after his Christmas party.' She let out a sigh. 'Whether you like it or not, Callum, this is affecting your little boy.' Her face was deadly serious. 'What did you find out?'

He hesitated. He hadn't spoken to anyone about this. It felt like a betrayal. His stomach was churning at the thought of Drew remembering every day that he'd asked after Jess. Protecting him seemed more important than ever. 'She wasn't truthful with me. She didn't tell me something really important.'

'Like you didn't tell her about Drew until you had to?'

He cringed. It felt like a low blow. And it was just what Jess had said. But from Julie's mouth it had been a lot more sarcastic. He nodded and held up his hands. 'I know, I know, but that was different.'

'Different how?'

Blair hadn't been kidding. He was in trouble.

He shook his head and waved his hands. 'Her husband and son died in a car crash three years ago. She didn't mention them at all. She just told me things hadn't worked out for her.'

Julie's hand had shot up to her mouth. He could see her take a deep breath. 'So, how did you find out if she didn't tell you?'

Trust Julie to cut straight to the chase. 'Well, she did tell me. But it was out of the blue. After she reacted badly to something and said she couldn't do this any more.'

Julie screwed up her face. 'Are you trying to talk in riddles?'

'I told you—it's complicated.'

There came the sound of shouts and splashes from upstairs. She shrugged. 'I've got time.'

Drew felt wary. The things that had been circulating through his brain for the last few days were all on the tip of his tongue. The things that had given him a pounding headache and kept him awake every night jumbled around in his head.

'It was all over a chocolate bar.'

'What?'

He couldn't keep his exasperation in check. He stood up, almost knocking his stool over, walking over to the counter and pushing some pods into the machine and propping the cups underneath.

Julie stayed silent. It must be killing her, not breaking the silence. But he knew exactly why she was doing it. She was forcing him to say all this out loud.

He placed the coffees on the breakfast bar and sat down

again. 'I bought Jessica her favourite chocolate bar and I gave her it when we picked her up. After a few minutes she freaked out and jumped out of the car before I even had a chance to pull over. She said she couldn't do it. She couldn't have a relationship with me and Drew.'

Julie raised her eyebrow. 'Over a chocolate bar?'

Total disbelief was in her voice. She was waiting for the rest.

Callum sucked in a deep breath. 'Apparently her husband and son had stopped to buy her chocolate the night they had the accident. If they hadn't...' His voice tailed off.

'If they hadn't—what?'

'If they hadn't stopped she thinks they wouldn't have been killed. They wouldn't have been on that part of the road at that time of night. She thinks the accident was her fault.'

Julie sat for a few moments, biting her lip. She looked up from the coffee cup she had continued to stir. 'No. She doesn't.'

'What?' It was not what he'd expected her to say.

Julie sighed. 'Oh, Callum. This is much bigger than I ever expected. Tell me what else she said.'

He racked his brain. Did he really want to share everything Jessica had said? He'd been mulling over this for days. Going over and over things in his head. Maybe it would be useful to get another perspective.

He looked at the picture pinned to the fridge. 'It's all about Drew, Julie. This all comes down to Drew.'

'Why do you think that?'

'Her little boy—her son was the same age as Drew. If he'd lived he would be five too.' This was the hardest part. The part he hated most. 'She's looking for a replacement, Julie. She's looking for a replacement for her son—and maybe her husband.'

Julie looked shocked. She stood up sharply. 'Tell me everything. Did she say anything else to you that day? Anything at all?'

He winced. 'She told me that she loved me. She loved me and Drew and she couldn't put us in the same position her family were in. She didn't want to hurt us.'

'She told you she loved you?' Julie's voice rose.

He nodded and stared down at his coffee. He couldn't even bear to take a sip.

'She told you she loved you?' This time she was practically shouting.

'Yes. But it doesn't make a difference. She didn't mean it. It's not us that she loves. It's just the idea of us.'

Julie walked straight over to him, barely inches from his face. She looked furious. 'And what did you do then, Callum? What did you do when she told you that she loved you both?'

A horrible, cold sensation swept over his skin. Every hair on his arms stood on end. His actions had seemed perfectly reasonable at the time. He'd been so upset for her. And so upset for them too. He didn't want to be replacement for what Jess had lost. He wanted Jess to love him and Drew the way that they loved her—with their whole hearts.

'I told her to get in the car and say something to placate Drew. I told her I'd drop her off.'

'Oh, Callum.' Julie turned away. She put her arms up to her face and stood still for a few moments.

'What? I have to protect my son, Julie. Drew's the most important thing in the world to me. I won't let anyone hurt him. Not even her.' The words came spilling out. Why did he feel as if he had to defend himself?

'Drew's been through all this before. He had a mother who treated him as if he wasn't good enough. Who walked away from him. How can I put my wee boy through something like that again?' He shook his head. 'I can't. I won't.'

Julie touched his arm. 'But Jessica isn't Kirsten, Callum. Not by a long shot. From all the stuff that you've told me about her, they couldn't compare. Surely you know that?' Her voice was wavering.

And his heart started to pound in his chest. He knew what she was saying was true. He had just needed someone else to say it out loud for him. Jess was nothing like Kirsten. He knew in his heart of hearts that Jessica would never have walked out on her son. A thought like that would never even have occurred to Jess. She was made in a totally different way.

Julie spun back round and there were tears in her eyes. She pointed to the stool. 'Sit down.'

It was *that* voice again. Do or die.

He sat down numbly. Julie should be on his side. So why did he feel as if she wasn't?

'Callum Kennedy, you've been my friend for four years. You know I love you. But sometimes you are a complete git.'

'What?'

'When you're wrong, Callum, you're *so* wrong it's scary.'

He was starting to feel sick now. Sick to his stomach. She had that horrible female intuition thing, didn't she?

'What do you mean?'

She started pacing around the kitchen, her arms flailing around her. 'This wasn't about a bar of chocolate, Callum. This was *never* about a bar of chocolate. This was about a woman learning to let go and love again. She's scared, Callum—she's terrified. And with your reaction— frankly—who can blame her?'

'What do you mean, she's scared?'

'You and Drew—you're not a replacement family for her.' Julie looked at him in disgust. 'You could *never* replace her family, Callum.' She pressed her hand to her chest. 'They will always be with her—in here—forever. This is something totally different. Don't you see?'

He was starting to feel panicked. The last sensation in the world he ever felt. Not even in the middle of a fraught rescue. But he was feeling it now. His mouth felt bone dry. The lump in his throat was as big as a tennis ball. He shook his head. 'No. I don't see. Tell me.'

Julie reached her hands across the breakfast bar and clasped his. She looked at the drawing on the fridge. 'Callum, we both know how your son feels about Jessica. It's written all over his face. But how do *you* feel about her?' She pointed her finger to his chest again, this time a lot more gently. 'How do you feel in here?'

The million-dollar question. The thing that kept his stomach constantly churning because no matter what he did the feeling wouldn't go away. The words he didn't want to say out loud. Because then he would have to admit to a whole host of things.

Her pointed finger felt like a laser burning a hole straight through to his heart.

He looked up. 'I love her.' He could feel his voice breaking. But he didn't want it to. He took a deep breath and tried again. 'I love her, Julie.' This time the words were stronger—more determined.

It felt like a weight had been lifted off his shoulders. The acknowledgement of saying the words out loud. Admitting to himself and his friend how he felt.

Julie sagged back down into the stool opposite him. She put her elbow on the breakfast bar and put her head on her hand. 'Then what you going to do about it, dummy?'

CHAPTER THIRTEEN

THE CANDLES FLICKERED around her.

They were beautiful, spilling yellow and orange tones along the pale cream walls in her house.

The Christmas decorations had been closing in around her. A permanent reminder of another Christmas alone. Sitting in the kitchen was different. The orange and pomegranate spice of the candles was soothing. She'd been trying some deep-breathing exercises. Anything to try and take her thoughts away from the constants on her mind.

Callum and Drew.

The door rattled then the doorbell started ringing and didn't stop.

'Jess? Jess, are you in?' The door rattled again.

Her heart started to race instantly. She recognised the voice. She'd recognise it anywhere. Something must be wrong. Drew. Something must be wrong with Drew.

She ran down the hall and yanked the door open. 'What is it? Is it Drew? Has something happened?'

Callum was stuck with his hand still in mid-air—frozen to the spot. It was almost as if he hadn't expected her to answer.

She looked down at the car parked at the side of the road. Drew wasn't in it. His car seat was empty.

Callum shook his head. 'No. No, it's not Drew. He's fine.' Then he paused. 'Well, actually, he's not fine.'

'What is it?' Her stomach was clenched. Was he in hospital? Had there been an accident?

Callum stepped forward, closing the gap between them. She could smell him. His distinctive aftershave was immediately invading her senses, bringing a whole host of memories. Bringing a whole heap of regrets.

He reached up and touched her cheek. 'He misses you. *We* miss you. That's what's wrong with Drew...' He paused. 'And with me.'

It was the last thing she'd expected to hear. She couldn't breathe. All her muscles contracted.

He put his hand on her shoulder. 'Jess, please. Can we talk?'

Her brain started to race. She was confused. She'd thought he hated her. The last time she'd seen him she hadn't been able to read the look on his face. Had it been confusion? Or resignation?

She felt overwhelming relief. Drew was fine. There hadn't been an accident. She couldn't help the way her brain worked. But, then, any parent would be the same—their first thought in a moment of panic would be for their child.

Parent. The word that had popped straight into her mind.

Her reactions to Drew were those of a parent. And her thoughts about Callum? She loved him so much it hurt to even be in the same space as him.

So, if this wasn't about Drew, why was Callum here?

She tried to focus. The messages between her brain and her mouth were getting muddled. There was so much jumbling around in there.

'Jess, can I come in?'

Her feet moved backwards automatically, creating space for him to come through.

He walked into the hall and glanced in the direction of the darkened living room. He took her hand and led her inside, bending down to switch on the lights of her Christmas tree.

Christmas lights. The ones she'd been trying to avoid. The new twinkling red berries and silver stars lit up the room. They had been her fresh start. But the chance to build new memories had been destroyed. All the tiny little hopes that had started to form. All the baby steps towards some new memories—like buying the new decorations with Drew—had been wiped out.

She was trying hard to focus. Trying to make sense of it all. Part of her was angry. This was the man she'd hoped for a future with. She might not have been truthful with him, but his reaction had still hurt.

'What are you doing here, Callum?' The tone of her words revealed the exhaustion she was feeling. Every bone in her body ached. She hadn't slept for days. She couldn't eat. The truth was she just couldn't go on like this.

His hands went to her waist and she gasped. His fingers were icy cold. It was only then she realised he wasn't wearing gloves or a jacket. Why on earth was he out on a freezing night like this with no jacket? Had he been in that much of a rush?

'I came here to apologise.' His voice was deep and husky. Was he being sincere? 'I came here to apologise for how I reacted the other day when you told me about your husband and son. I'm not proud of myself, Jess. I didn't understand.'

He was apologising. She felt shocked. Then she noticed the lines around his eyes and on his forehead. It was like a mirror image of her own face. Maybe Callum had had problems sleeping too. She shook her head. 'How could you understand? I would never wish something like that on you.'

'No. That's not what I meant.' He was babbling. 'Of course I don't know what it's like to lose a wife and child. But I didn't understand how you were feeling about us. Us—me and Drew. I got confused. I thought you were looking for a replacement. I thought you were using me and Drew as a replacement for your family.'

She pulled back. How could he think that? A million different things flew about her brain. 'But why? Why would you think that?'

Things started to drop into place. The questions. The expressions on his face. The age. This was all about Drew's age.

'Is this because Lewis and Drew would have been the same age?' For a second it felt as if someone had just dropped her back into the icy River Clyde. 'You think I would try and replace my little boy with another?'

No. It didn't even bear thinking about. How could any-one think that? She tried to keep calm. Sure, a few com-parisons had swept through her brain. She'd even been a tiny bit jealous of Callum when she'd first found out about Drew. But to think she would try and do something like that?

She ran her tongue across her dry lips.

Wow. Maybe it wasn't such a leap in the dark. If the shoe had been on the other foot, might that have occurred to her? If she was the one with a child and Callum had lost his wife and child, would she wonder if he was try-ing to replace them?

Maybe. Just maybe. Even if it was only for a few sec-onds.

He pulled her closer, his chest pressing against hers.

'Jess?' He could see she was lost in her thoughts. He stared at her with his dark green eyes and she could see the sincerity on his face. 'I don't think that. I don't think that now. I was shocked. I never expected something like that had happened to you. I couldn't make sense of it in my head.'

It was easy. It was easy to feel his arms around her. It felt so good to sense him touch her skin again. But there was so much more to say. She couldn't expose her heart to this kind of hurt again. She wouldn't survive.

'Is that what you came to say?' She was trying to distance herself from all this. She could accept his apology—if that's what he wanted to offer. She could accept it, and then walk away. No matter how good it felt to be in his arms.

'No. That's not what I came to say.' He reached up and brushed her curls behind her ear. 'I came to tell you that I'm sorry. I'm sorry and I love you. Drew and I love you. I know I made a mess of this, Jess, but please don't give up on us. We want you to be part of our lives.'

'But—'

'Shh.' He put his finger against her lips then traced it over her cheekbones and eyelids. The feel of his light touch on her skin was magical. She could forget about everything else that had happened and just let this touch lull her into a false sense of security that everything would be fine.

She opened her eyes and took a deep breath.

'Don't say no. Please, don't say no, Jess. I can't be apart from you. *We* can't be apart from you.'

'But why, Callum, why now?'

'Look at me, Jess. I haven't slept in days. Neither have you—I can tell. This...' he waved his arms in the air '...is driving me crazy. I didn't mean to walk away. I just wanted to protect Drew. I needed to know that you were there because you loved *us*, not just the idea of us.'

'But how could you ever doubt that?'

He tapped his finger on the side of his head. 'Because I wasn't thinking straight. When you told me about your husband and son, I went into defence mode—protecting my son, protecting my family.' His hand cupped the side of her face. 'But you're part of my family now, Jess. You, me and Drew. I love you. I don't want to do this without you.'

She felt herself start to shake. From one extreme to the other. Callum was looking into her eyes and telling her that he loved her. Telling her that he and Drew loved her, Jessica Rae.

She wanted to believe him. She really did.

But ten minutes ago she had been wondering just how to get through one night. And even that had seemed too much for her. Even that had been taking candles and deep breathing.

'I...I...I don't know, Callum.'

He pressed his hand to her chest. 'How do you feel? How do you feel when you see me and Drew?'

There was no doubt. No doubt for her at all. It was the one thing that was crystal clear. 'I love you. I love you both.' But even as she said the words she felt fear and she instinctively made to pull away.

Callum lowered his head so it was level with hers—so he could look straight into her eyes. 'I know you're scared. I get that now. I can deal with that. *We* can deal with that together—as a family.'

She lowered her gaze. 'But how, Callum? When I saw that bar of chocolate it brought so many memories back. What if something happened to you and Drew? I can't go through that again.'

He gave her a smile. 'I know you're scared. But it's a big old scary world out there, Jess. You and I work in it every day. And what makes it all right is the people around us.' He took her hand and placed it on his chest. She could feel his heart beating under her palm. Thump, thump. Thump, thump.

'I can't promise you that everything will be perfect. I can't promise you that nothing will ever happen to any of us. I can't promise you that I'll never stop to buy you a bar of chocolate again. There are some things in this life we have no control over.' His other hand wound through her hair. 'What I can promise you is that I'll love you faithfully for every second that I'm here. I'll do my best to keep you and Drew safe. And if you have fears, talk to me about them. I'm here for you, Jess. I've waited thirteen years to get the woman of my dreams. I'm not about to let you escape now.'

Thirteen years. It seemed like a whole lifetime.

It had been a whole lifetime—for both of them.

'Can you give me a chance, Jessica? Can you give us a chance?'

He knew. He knew she'd been scared. He knew it had all felt too much for her and she'd needed some space.

But the love that she'd felt for Callum and his son had never faltered—not even for a second. Instead, it was growing, every single day.

'I'd like that, Callum,' she breathed. 'I'd like that very much.'

She could see the sparkle appear in his eyes. 'Then wait here.'

He turned and vanished, leaving her standing in the living room with only the red and silver twinkling tree lights.

She heard her front door open and some muffled voices then a little giggle. A little boy's giggle.

Callum appeared at the doorway with Drew standing in front of him, clutching something in a Christmas box.

'Drew!' She couldn't help herself, she rushed over and

hugged him as tightly as she could. 'I've missed you. Have you been a good boy?'

Drew was bouncing on his toes. 'Watch out, Jess. You'll squash your present. I made it specially.'

She turned to Callum, shaking her head in wonder. 'But how? The car was empty. Where was he?'

It was then she noticed. Under his thick jacket and hat Drew was wearing his pyjamas and slippers. Callum wasn't the only one who'd left the house in a hurry.

Callum gave her a nod. 'I have some good friends—they helped me out, in more ways than one.'

His finger brushed her cheek again and he knelt down on one knee opposite in front of her. Drew sat on his knee and held out the box. 'This might not be the most traditional way of doing things, but it probably suits us best.' Callum smiled at his son. Drew had a huge smile plastered to his face. 'We want you to marry us, Jess, and stay with us forever. We promise to love you, for now and for always. Will you marry us, Jess?'

Drew's little hands were shaking with excitement. She reached out and took the little red box, pulling off the lid and looking inside. Her hands were trembling. A few hours ago she had been feeling helpless and miserable, expecting to spend another Christmas alone, just wishing for it all to be over.

This was the best present she could ever have hoped for.

Her eyes squeezed shut for a tiny second.

She opened them again. Yes, they were still there. She wasn't imagining this. It was really happening.

She looked inside the box. There was one of the tiny Christmas decorations that she and Drew had bought together. A tiny little red heart. Except this one had been twisted on to some tin foil to make a ring. There was a little piece of folded paper next to it.

'I made it. Jess. Do you like it?'

She looked into their smiling faces. This was hers. This was her family. For now and for always.

'I love it.' She lifted the makeshift ring out of the box and put it on her finger, watching as it gleamed in the twinkling tree lights. 'It's perfect.' She gave Drew a kiss.

He pressed the little bit of paper into her hand. 'This is the real one we've picked for you. Daddy says it's a pink diamond because pink's your favourite colour.' He looked a little sad. 'But we couldn't get it tonight.'

Jessica looked at the printout. It was beautiful. It was breathtaking. 'It's perfect.' She smiled and looked at the little red heart. 'But every Christmas I want to wear this ring, because you made it for me.'

She put her hands around Callum's neck to meet his mouth with a kiss. She couldn't have wished for anything more. A family, not just for Christmas but forever.

Drew was standing at the fireplace staring at the chimney. 'Can I write a thank-you letter for Santa?'

Callum frowned. 'But it's not Christmas yet. You've not had your presents yet.'

Drew gave him a little knowing smile. 'Oh, yes, I have. Santa and I made a deal. He's just delivered his present early.'

Jessica linked her arm around Callum's waist. 'It seems our son has been making deals without telling us. What else do you think he asked Santa for?'

She could see the gleam in his eye. 'Let's hope it's a little brother or sister,' he whispered as he bent to kiss her.

* * * * *

CHRISTMAS MIRACLE: A FAMILY

DIANNE DRAKE

CHAPTER ONE

FALLON O'GARA glanced at her watch, and the panic in her rose a little more than she'd expected. It was ten after one now, and she was late to meet her good friends and colleagues Gabby Ranard and Dinah Ramsey for lunch. Yet she couldn't bring herself to open the car door because she was about to take a big step, and it scared her. She'd fretted, paced, worried all night, and now it was time. Time to make a decision about Gabby's job offer, and finally think about returning to work for the first time since the plane crash. But she couldn't lay her hand on the doorhandle, let alone open the door and get out.

A loud tapping on the passenger's side window startled Fallon out of her dilemma. It was Gabby, standing there with Dinah. "I'm coming," Fallon called without opening her window, without making the slightest motion toward getting out.

"We've got the back table reserved," Gabby yelled. "And you know Catie. She can't wait to see you. She's standing at the front door right now, ready to cry." To prove her point, Gabby stepped back and pointed to the café owner standing with hankie in hand, on the verge of blubbering.

Fallon loved these people! They were the best. But being here at Catie's Overlook, her favorite restaurant in the world, was suddenly feeling like a mistake. She wanted to go in, wanted to accept that job offer Gabby had made to set up the practical details of White Elk's new women's hospital—buy the beds, hire the staff, hire the contractors to make the renovations. It was a kind, generous offer, since she'd told Gabby that she wasn't ready to go back to nursing at the main White Elk Hospital. But she was afraid to accept Gabby's offer. Afraid not to. Not sure what to do. Consequently, her hands were shaking, her breath was clutching in her lungs. But surviving an airplane crash… there were always the reminders, and for her one of them was the panic attacks.

Gabby took another step toward the front of the car, and simply smiled at Fallon. "Well, darn," Fallon muttered to herself. "Having lunch with my best friends should be an easy thing to do. I'll simply get out, go in, say…." Well, she wasn't sure what she'd say to Gabby, and Gabby did want an answer. "I'll eat, chat, go home." And forty-five minutes later, well into a heaped piece of chocolate cake, she still wasn't sure what she was going to say to Gabby.

"Well, should I order a celebratory flute of ginger ale?" Gabby finally asked. Gabby wasn't drinking alcohol as she had a baby on the way. "Assuming your answer to my offer is yes? And if it's not, could you explain that to little Mary here, because her mommy needs rest at this stage of the pregnancy and if you don't take this job, little Mary's mommy is going to be worn out by the time little Mary's born."

"Good guilt trip," Dinah commented, laughing.

Gabby patted her belly, smiling. "Just using what I have to, to get my way." She looked over at Fallon. "Seriously, I really do need you. Not because of my pregnancy but because of your skills. I trust you to do this job and do it well."

Fallon sighed. Her back was to the wall now; she had to be fair to Gabby. Yes, or no? She wanted a voice from the heavens to cry out the answer, but when none came, she braced herself, trying to force aside the awkward tension attempting to burrow its way out. It was a job made to order. One where she could build up some confidence, still be close to medicine, and work her life out from that point forward. Also, this was something she could do on her own terms. If ever there was an opportunity to step back into her life, the way it used to be, the way she wanted it to be again, this was it. And it was true what they said about the very first step being the hardest.

Looking into the faces of her friends, and over at Catie, the owner of the restaurant, she realized just how *not* alone she was in this. And it was time. She'd isolated herself for too long now. Months in rehab then hiding out in her cabin. She'd been through so much. But now was the right time to begin again. Suddenly, it all made sense. Surviving came in steps. It didn't happen the way most people believed, in one great event or whoosh. It trickled in, a little here, a little there. This was one of those trickles. Although a big one. But when she realized that it was what she had to do and, more than that, wanted to do, a sense of calm fell over Fallon, the first real calm she'd felt in months. So, she reached across the table and squeezed Gabby's hand. "Order the ginger ale. I'm ready to celebrate. And promise me you'll tell little Mary that I'll be making sure her mommy will get all the rest she needs for the rest of her pregnancy."

"Really? You're going to take the job?"

Fallon nodded, wondering if what she was feeling now was the calm before the storm. "I'll try, Gabby. That's the best I can give you right now. But I'm going to take it a day at a time, because that's about the only way I can handle my life. So, if that's agreeable to you and little Mary, I'll start work as soon as you want me to."

Gabby winked at Dinah. "Told you so."

"You were betting on me?" Fallon asked.

"Just the chocolate cake," Gabby said, "and it's Dinah's treat. She was pretty sure you'd eventually say yes, but she thought it would take more persuasion."

Fallon laughed. "In that case, I'm going to order another piece to take home with me."

It felt good being there with friends, being involved in something again. She glanced out the window to the Three Sisters. She'd avoided looking at them since she'd been home, didn't want to be reminded that her plane had crashed on the Middle Sister. Popular Indian lore said these three mountain peaks loomed over the valley, protecting everybody in their shadow. People here truly believed that. To be honest, she'd believed it too, until the accident. Now, to her, the Three Sisters were simply mountains. Yet in the brief glance she allowed herself she was surprised she wasn't panicking. So maybe going back to work *was* a good thing. Maybe the calm she was feeling was real. She wanted it to be.

"Bet or no bet, I'm glad you're doing this," Dinah said, putting her fork down halfway though her cake. "Eric and Neil are going to be thrilled." Eric Ramsey was Dinah's husband and Neil Ranard was married to Gabby; both men were doctors and co-owners of the White Elk Hospital.

The three friends chatted on, until suddenly they were interrupted.

"Fallon?" The familiar, deep voice cut through the talking at the table.

Fallon gasped. Felt her pulse double immediately. She hadn't seen or spoken to James in months, since just after her accident, when she'd made it clear that she couldn't be in a relationship with him any more. Because he'd just discovered he had a son, and she'd had plenty of her own issues to deal with, things she couldn't talk to James about. She'd done what she'd thought was best for both of them. But she was just taking her first steps back into normal life and she didn't feel like she could deal with James now.

"Fallon, how are you?"

Suddenly, her lungs felt so tight that she couldn't breathe and her hands were shaking so hard her muscles were practically seizing up. On top of it all, she was breaking out in a cold sweat. Head spinning. Chest aching. Nausea fast on the rise.

"Fallon?" Gabby whispered, leaning into her. "Are you OK?"

"Tell him to go away," she whispered. "Please, I don't want to see him."

Gabby looked back at Dr. James Galbraith, not sure what to make of this. "I don't know what to tell you, James. She doesn't want to see you."

"Please," Fallon begged, refusing to turn around and look at him. "Just go away, James."

"You didn't return my calls," he said, as if there were no other women sitting at the table. He stepped forward, stood directly behind Fallon and bent down. "We spoke soon after the accident, when I told you about my son. But then I called every day, for weeks, left messages on your voice mail until you canceled that number, and you never returned my calls. E-mails bounced back."

"I was a little busy," she said, turning her head away from him. "And I did leave you a message."

"*Once.* You said you were fine, that you were in a nice rehab facility, to please not bother you again. Then the next time I called I got the message that your cellphone number was no longer in use."

She scooted down in her chair, wanted to crawl under the table. "What are you doing in White Elk?" she asked.

"James is the new pediatrician at the hospital," Dinah commented. "He applied months ago, back when you were…" She stopped, glanced helplessly at Gabby.

"I'm so sorry, Fallon," Gabby said. "I wanted to tell you…but not yet. Neil and Eric hired James a while back, pending the completion of the new pediatrics wing. Now that it's completed, James is head of Pediatrics."

"And no one told me?"

"How could we?" Gabby said. "Fallon, you'd turned your back on everyone. Practically went into seclusion. And you made it clear to everyone that your relationship with James was over. But he was already hired before we knew that, and Neil and Eric weren't going to go back on their commitment to him. They wanted James from the moment they read his résumé. Knew he was perfect for the job. But with what you'd gone through…how *could* we tell you he'd moved here?"

Fallon looked up at James. "Why did you leave Salt Lake City? Why did you move here?" she asked.

"White Elk is where I wanted to be, Fallon. The way you talked about it when we were together, then what I found out about the hospital, how good it was, what a dynamic pediatric department they were setting up…"

"And me? Did I factor into that anywhere?"

Taking the cue, Gabby and Dinah slipped away from the table, not even seen by Fallon as they hurried out the door.

"Yes. At first, when I thought we were going to be together… Well, after we drifted apart, I still wanted to be here because the more I learned about White Elk, and the more I knew the reputation of the hospital, the more

I wanted to work here. You knew how bad my job was in Salt Lake…the hours, the demands. It was driving me crazy. I wasn't advancing, wasn't getting to practice the kind of medicine I wanted because I was always the back-up for my medical partners. And this…it was everything I've ever wanted in my medical practice and I couldn't walk away from it just because you'd walked away from me. But I didn't mean to upset you over it because, well…I thought we could still work things out between us."

"No, we can't." She started to twist, to look at him, but caught herself in time. Oh, how she wanted to look, though. To remember, to lose herself in him. Tall, with sandy blond hair and the most gorgeous blue eyes…eyes as clear as a mountain lake. But she couldn't. Wouldn't. She'd loved this man. Had wanted to spend a life with him. Then she'd let him down in ways he could never know about, ways that were so painful to her she didn't want to be reminded of what she'd done.

James straightened up, squared his shoulders, cleared his throat to break the tension of that awkward moment. "You wouldn't talk to me, Fallon. Wouldn't let me talk to you. I know you must have gone through hell after the accident, but you just withdrew from me. All that time we'd spent together in Salt Lake City…all the plans we were making. I thought we had something that would endure. Then after the plane crash…" He paused, swallowed hard. "I know I got busy with Tyler. And I know the timing was terrible, finding out I had a son just a week after the plane crash. One day I'm not a father and the next I've got a five-year-old son whose been literally dropped on my doorstep. I'll admit I was reeling from it, not handling it as well as I should. Is that why you stayed away from me, why you didn't even let me know where you were? Is it because I had to spend so much time with Tyler when you were facing so many problems? Did I hurt you, Fallon? Because I never meant to."

"You didn't hurt me," she said. "I told you at the time that I understood how much Tyler needed you, that I was fine by myself."

But there were also things that she hadn't told James… A few weeks before the plane crash she'd discovered she was pregnant. She'd been excited, because they'd even talked about having a family, even though they hadn't dated for long. And after they'd met when she'd been transferring a patient to the hospital in Salt Lake City where James worked, their relationship had developed quickly. But, still, the pregnancy had felt very soon. So Fallon had waited for the right moment to tell him the news. But the stress level of his job had been on the rise, and he had been working so many hours, had been tired, grumpy… So she'd kept it to herself, waiting for the right moment when things had calmed down for him.

Then the plane crash as she'd been returning home to White Elk, the surgeries, the anesthesia, the doctor's discouraging prognosis of her pregnancy, and…Tyler. To add to James's stress, he'd found out he was a father to a five-year-old he'd never known about. Everything had felt so confusing, and she had been in such bad shape. In his defense, James had been too. She had seen it. Felt how he'd been so torn between wanting to be with her and needing to be with his son, a child who desperately needed a good father. So she'd kept her secret, and never told James that she'd carried his son for six months and delivered him stillborn. And now it was too late.

Through those awful months, she'd kept telling herself she couldn't add to James's burden. Kept telling herself that she was doing the right thing by him and Tyler. Because if he'd known what she was going through, he wouldn't have left her side. But Tyler had needed him, too. *Needed him more.*

"No, you didn't hurt me, James. You'd never do that. But Tyler had to be your priority. If we'd stayed together, you'd have torn yourself up trying to divide your time between Tyler and me, and it had to be about Tyler. There wasn't any other choice you could make." That was something she had come to understand more than anything else about that time. James *had* to be a father first and if she'd stayed with him, that couldn't have happened. He'd have been too divided.

"But you couldn't have told me how you were feeling, how you were afraid I'd spend too much time with you and not enough with Tyler? We couldn't have talked about it?"

She shook her head, couldn't tell him that what she would have needed from him would have been too great. She'd survived the plane crash, but in so many little pieces. James would have wanted to be the one to put those pieces back together again, and the timing…it couldn't be helped. He'd just met Tyler. And only just learned how it truly felt to love a child so desperately.

And she'd lost hers…theirs. Lost her baby before James ever knew he existed. And not telling James, not letting him be part of those few months she carried their baby, was the unpardonable sin. Not letting him be there at the delivery of their son, and hold him the way she'd been allowed to for those brief moments… It was all too late now. What was done was done. She couldn't go back and change it, and she refused to go forward and hurt James. He didn't deserve that. And she…she didn't deserve a man as good as James. "I disappeared because I had issues to resolve, and physical problems to work out."

"Without me," he said. "Even after what we'd been to each other, you wanted to do it without me?"

"Our relationship was still new, James. A few weekends. Good weekends, and that unbelievable week together, lots of long phone calls in between. Plans, expectations and excitement. But it was so much, and so fast. After the crash I had time to think about it, to realize that..."

"That you didn't love me? Because you'd said you did."

"Maybe we were confusing our emotions." She hated this, hated saying something that wasn't true because she'd known quickly into their relationship that James was the one. But she'd gone so far beyond that now, and there was no way back. "Maybe what we thought we had wasn't real."

"I don't believe that, Fallon," he snapped. "Not a word of it. But if that's the way you want to do this between us..."

"Not *us*, James. Not any more. But since you're in White Elk now, we can still be friends..."

"And you think that's enough?"

"I think it's all there is." Not all she wanted, but all she could have.

"You're wrong, Fallon. I can see it in your eyes. Something you're not saying. Something you want to say to me, but won't."

She shut her eyes. Drew in a steadying breath, and pushed herself away from the table. "You're the one who's wrong. I've said everything I want to say. And now there's nothing else."

Drawing back from her, he studied her for a moment. "That first time I saw you in Salt Lake City, when you were transferring a patient to the hospital, I knew, Fallon. Knew that if I were the marrying kind, you'd be the kind

I'd want to marry. Then you turned me into the marrying kind. I didn't change my life and my entire outlook on a whim. I changed because I knew you, even in a short time I knew you, and knew you were the one worth making those changes for. You were so amazing and open and honest, and you went after life in such a big way. And I don't believe you've changed. Maybe you believe you have, but you're not the one standing here, looking at the same woman I saw back then. I am looking at her, though, and what I'm seeing more than anything else is…confusion. Pain."

The most open, honest woman…well, not any more. But to be honest would be to wound him in so many ways and, no matter what he said, she couldn't bring herself to do that. She just couldn't. So she stood and left the restaurant without another word. Without looking back. Without letting him see the tears.

CHAPTER TWO

"OK, HE lives here now," she reasoned as she stepped out of her front door for her morning walk. "A lot of people live here that I never see, and just because he's working here it doesn't mean that I'll have to run into him." In fact, knowing he was here was good because she could go out of her way to avoid him. Catie's Overlook was out now because, apparently, he lunched there. Of course, returning to White Elk Hospital wasn't going to happen now, no matter how much Eric and Neil wanted her back, as that's where James worked. But Gabby had offered her a permanent job at Three Sisters Women's Clinic and Hospital, and in time she might be able to face nursing duty there. Someday, when she wasn't so sensitive to mothers with new babies.

The good thing was, James should rarely have reason to be there. "It could work," she concluded. Then, in time, after she'd avoided him enough, the habit would sink in. Yes, that's the way it would be. Or else she couldn't stay in White Elk. And the thought of leaving was more than she could bear. But, realistically, it was a choice she might have to make.

It was a brisk morning. Just a few weeks away from Christmas, snow was beginning to pile up higher in the mountains, and it wouldn't be long before it found its way down to the lower elevations in more than just sprinkles and showers. She loved crisp mornings like this, when her breath was visible in white puffs, when the glistening of frost on the trees looked like diamonds. Heavy sweaters, snow boots, mittens and hot chocolate…her favorite things of the season, and she was glad she was well enough to be part of it. For a time she hadn't been sure that would happen, hadn't been sure she'd ever see anything outside the gray cement block walls of the rehab hospital. Those had been bleak days, days full of so much pain and so little hope. But finally coming home, especially at this time of year…

"How far do you go now on your morning walks?"

He startled her, and Fallon immediately retreated for her front door.

"You don't have to run from me," James said. He was standing at the edge of her cottage, his hand shielding his eyes, staring up at the Older Sister. "Wasn't it you who said, just yesterday, that we could still be friends?"

"What are you doing here?" she said abruptly.

"Taking a walk, *with a friend*. You got me into the walking habit, and it's something I look forward to in the mornings now. I thought maybe we could walk together, the way we used to. Just as friends, like I said."

"I walk alone," she snapped.

He turned to face her, the clean, sharp lines of face now coming into her full view. "But I thought you were open to having a friend? And the truth is, I really need a friend because I don't really know anybody here in White Elk, except you. So I thought it would be nice if the two of us could…"

"No, it wouldn't be nice," she said, trying to avert her eyes from him, trying not to let herself get caught up in what she knew would so easily catch her. "And I don't know why you're doing this to me, James. I made it clear that I can't get involved with you again."

"I'm sorry, Fallon. If I have to say that a million times before you believe me, that's what I'll do. I'm so sorry. We both went through a difficult time but I never meant to hurt you. And I know you say I didn't, but I must have in some profound way."

His voice was so kind, so sincere, so agonizingly patient it nearly melted her heart. "You didn't hurt me, James," she whispered, turning away. But he caught her by the arm and turned her back to him.

"Then what is it? For God's sake tell me, so I can make it right."

"There's nothing to make right. I…I've changed since the accident. And now all I'm trying to do is get on with my life. There's nothing more to say about it, James. There's nothing left of the *us* you want us to be. I can't be anything you want. I don't have anything left that we wanted together."

He sighed deeply. "So maybe all I want right now is a companion on a nice morning walk. Is that asking too much?"

She looked up at him again. "And Tyler?"

He shrugged. "I don't know. Haven't seen him for a couple of months. Don't even know where he is. His mother came and took him back for the second time, and I've been looking ever since."

Her heart broke for him, and she knew that being near him, trying to be his friend or even a casual acquaintance wouldn't work because she would be compelled to tell him the truth at some point. And break his heart even more. "I'm sorry it's not working out for you."

"So am I. He's my son. I have the right to be a part of his life. But Shelly keeps taking that away from me."

Dear God, it hurt him, hurt her. And she didn't want to keep doing this, over and over. But their circumstances were what they were. She'd made a bad choice and nothing about it could be changed. "We can't do this, James."

"I'm not doing anything, Fallon, but asking to take a walk with you. That's all. Just a walk. This morning. No expectations attached to it. I mean, aren't you the one who told me it was so much nicer having someone to walk with? Remember that?"

She had said that, during the most wonderful time of her life, hadn't she? Back before having James so close to her was a painful reminder of so many losses. "Walking, no talking. Those are my terms. And so you'll know, I walk two miles out then two miles back. The first part is uphill, at a brisk pace. I won't slow down for you. If you can keep up with me, fine. If not, the trail is clearly marked and you won't have any difficulty finding your way back."

Rather than be dissuaded, as she'd hoped he would be, he simply chuckled.

"What's so funny?" she asked.

"You. You haven't changed a bit. That's exactly the same thing you told me the first time we walked together—except the part about walking and not talking. But if you recall, I kept up pretty well for someone who wasn't used to executing a vigorous morning constitutional the way you were."

"I slowed down for you that time," she said, spinning around and heading off down the path at the side of her cottage. Heading quite vigorously, as James would call it. "This time I won't."

"And this time you don't have to." He caught up to her in several easy strides, matching her pace perfectly. "I'm in better shape, thanks to a very good teacher who convinced me about the merits of regular exercise."

She didn't answer him.

He chuckled. "You're not going to be easy, are you? Of course, I didn't expect that you would be. But I want to make this work between us, Fallon. Want to try it again. Start slow and steady and see what happens from there."

"You can do whatever you want, James. I can't stop you. But just be clear, you'll be doing it by yourself because I'm done with us."

"Because you've met someone else? Is that it?"

She was still at the point in this break-up, so raw from it, that she believed there could never be anybody else. She'd believed that the first time he'd kissed her, the first time he'd held her hand, the first time they'd made love. And while she didn't want to, she still did believe that. Especially now that he was here, now that the memories were so vivid. "There's no one else," she told him. "Just me, and I've changed." In deep, profound ways.

That's all she said, and they spent the next four miles in total silence. Fallon didn't speak, neither did James. For which she was grateful. It was nice having him tagging along, though. Felt normal. As normal as she'd felt in all these months. Then the walk ended and he made no pretense of wanting anything more. She expected he'd ask to come inside her cottage for some reason…a glass of water, or a cup of hot tea. She even thought he might allude to seeing her same time, same place tomorrow. But he didn't. When they reached her house he gave her a very casual "Thanks for letting me walk along" then trotted away.

OK, so maybe she was a little disappointed. Largely, though, she was relieved. It's what she wanted, what she demanded now. The only way she could deal with Dr. James Galbraith, and survive.

"And then I want to go on the Christmas train. They have hot chocolate, and we can feed the reindeer. And see the dinosaurs. They have lights on them."

"The dinosaurs have lights?" James teased, popping the stethoscope from his ears.

"All colors. But we can't get close 'cause they might be real."

"What might be real? The lights, or the dinosaurs?"

The freckle-faced six-year-old giggled. "The dinosaurs, silly."

"So the lights might not be real?"

Matthew Brower, or Matty as he insisted on being called, scrunched up his nose, trying to figure out the answer to James's question. "I think they're real, too," he finally said as James helped him down off the exam table. "That's why they light up...I think."

James tousled Matty's curly white-blond hair. "Sounds like the Christmas train is going to be fun. Do they allow adults to ride on it?"

Matty shrugged. "Just moms and dads, I think. Maybe grandpas and grandmas, too."

Well, for this month, and who knew for how long, that didn't include *him*. Didn't matter. Without Tyler, and worried about Fallon the way he was, James wasn't in a very festive mood for the holidays, anyway. "You have fun, Matty," he said, "and watch out for those dinosaurs. Especially the ones with the red lights. They're the tricky ones."

Matty rolled his eyes at James, like that was a fact every sensible person on the planet already knew, then he skipped out of the exam room while James gave final instructions to Mrs. Brower. Limited activity for another few days, plenty of rest, continue taking his antibiotics, and by the beginning of the week Matty's bronchitis would be completely gone. "Call me if you have any questions," he told her on the way out the door, "and if you don't mind, I'd like you to bring him in one more time so I can listen to his chest again. As a precaution. Just stop by when it's convenient, no need to make an appointment."

No appointment. He liked that. Wasn't used to the laid-back way medicine was practiced here, but he did like it. Looked forward to a long association. Though that was still pretty much up in the air, because if he truly made Fallon's life miserable by being here, he would rethink his decision.

"I think Matty's on the mend," Dinah Ramsey commented, as she passed James in the hall.

"On the mend and excited by something called the Christmas train...it has dinosaurs."

Dinah chuckled. "That's all my daughters have been talking about for weeks. Apparently, it's a big tradition here in the valley. For two weeks, it's a Christmas train for the children then for the next few months it's an old-fashioned steam locomotive taking skiers from slope to slope."

"Quaint," James said.

"Do you ski?"

"Sometimes. When I have someone to ski with."

"Fallon might be up to it, at least on the gentle slopes. I know she spent all her time on skis before..." Dinah stopped herself. "I guess that's not the best suggestion to make, is it?"

"It's awkward. But I'll have to get used to it."

"We all understand, James. It's been tough on everybody. Fallon's like an institution in White Elk. Everybody depended on her so much I think she was probably taken for granted in the past. Getting along without her is a tough adjustment on everybody at the hospital, and it's hard to know what to do around her sometimes. You know, like treading on eggshells. And your situation with her…"

"I think she's made it perfectly clear there is no situation."

Dinah gave his arm a sympathetic squeeze. "I'm sorry. For both of you. I hope it gets easier for you in time."

Time…something he had plenty of. He was a doctor and he was…nothing else. That's all there was. Six months ago he'd pictured himself as a man who'd be married by Christmas. And now… "I hope so, too," he told Dinah before Emoline Putters, the irascible ward clerk, shooed him off to his next appointment.

"Mrs. Shelly Geary, and her son Tyler," Emoline announced, shoving the chart into his hands. "She claims the boy has a cough, but I haven't heard him."

A surge of excitement shot through James, followed by a surge of anger and the dread he'd come to know so well. So it was starting over. Except this time he wasn't giving up. He was ready to fight for Tyler. Ready for a different ending to this chapter in his life. Maybe he couldn't win Fallon back, but he sure as hell was going to win custody of his son.

"How are you doing, Tyler?" James said, putting on a happy face when he walked into the exam room. He wanted the boy to smile, to be happy to see him again. Wanted to hug the boy. But that wouldn't be the case today. Both times before, when Shelly had dropped him off, Tyler had been sullen. Nothing had changed. Still, James's heart swelled the instant he saw his son because the last time Shelly had taken him away, he wasn't sure he'd ever see Tyler again.

"James," Shelly said, without the least bit of concern in her voice.

"In the hall!" he demanded, then exited the room.

She followed. "It's not like you think—" she started.

But James interrupted her. "What's different this time? Does Donnie want to keep him and *you're* the one who doesn't want him?" Donnie, the husband who didn't want to raise a son that wasn't his. That was the reason she'd brought Tyler to him the first two times and he had no reason to believe that wasn't the reason this time.

"You've got it all wrong. Donnie tries really hard, but Tyler gets on his nerves. And Donnie's got this new job now…"

"Save it, Shelly. I don't care about your excuses, and I sure as hell don't care about your husband." Two nurses in the hall raised eyebrows, and then James led Shelly into the empty exam room across the hall and slammed the door shut. "The only one who's important here is Tyler, and I'll swear if you've…"

"Tyler doesn't even try, James. He breaks things, and throws tantrums. Donnie works hard, and when he comes home at night he wants peace and quiet. Doesn't he have a right to have peace and quiet in his own home?"

A million things crossed James's mind, things he wanted to say, things he wanted to scream. But he wouldn't because none of it mattered. At the end of the day, all he cared about was Tyler and, God willing, he was going to get permanent custody of him this time. "Look, just get out of here. I don't give a damn why you're dropping him off, don't give a damn what Tyler's doing to make your husband angry."

"It won't be long, James. Just through the holidays, maybe, then things will settle down."

Things would never settle down for Shelly and, no

matter what else happened, Tyler wasn't going back into that situation. Not after the holidays, not ever, if he had his way. "Get out, Shelly. Get out of White Elk." With that, he brushed around her and went straight back to the exam room where Tyler was sitting. And shut the door. Shelly wouldn't come back, wouldn't say goodbye to her son. He knew that from history.

So did Tyler.

"I'm sorry, Dr. Galbraith, but I just can't do it. He wore me out chasing after him, and it's only been half a day. He's too...destructive, and I simply can't have him in my house." As proof, Mrs. Prestwick held up the headless porcelain figurine Tyler had broken. That, and the lamp for which James had already compensated her. "I hate to give you such sort notice, but you can't bring Tyler back here." Emphatic words. The same words he'd heard from Mrs. Powers and Grandma Addy...the three most highly recommended care-givers in White Elk. Three days, three bridges burned, and James was at his wit's end now. He had to work, had to take care of Tyler and, at this moment those two parts of his life were clashing in a big way. "I don't suppose you could recommend anyone else, could you?" he asked the gray-haired septuagenarian.

She shook her head, backing away from her front door as hastily as she could, practically shutting the door in James's face. He looked down at Tyler, who seemed preoccupied by the snowflakes falling on the evergreen bushes. "I thought you were going to behave," he said, trying to be patient. "We talked about it the last time you stayed with me and we talked about it just this morning. Remember? Remember how you promised me that you would be good?" For Mrs. Powers it had been about a dozen raw eggs and a pound of ground coffee, all stirred into a nice little cake in the middle of her kitchen floor…a floor that had enough slope that it had facilitated the slithering of that mess to a spot underneath the refrigerator, which had required James to move the fridge and do the cleaning. For Grandma Addy it had involved the hiding of her hearing aid in the trash can just before the trash had been tossed out. Luckily, Grandma Addy had a spare, but James was going to have to take time off work to take her to Salt Lake City and get fitted for another.

"Tell me, Tyler, why did you break Mrs. Prestwick's things?" He wanted to understand him. Wanted to get to know him and find out why he did what he did, but so far Tyler had resisted pretty much every effort James had made, just like the two previous times when James had taken care of him.

Tyler shrugged, still more interested in the snowflakes.

James huffed out the impatient sigh he'd tried holding in. Three days, and he was all out of ideas. Yet he couldn't get angry with Tyler. In spite of everything, he loved his son and didn't blame him for the bad behavior. It was a reaction to his life, to the way he'd been tossed around. Sadly, as hard as James tried to be responsive to Tyler, the boy always pulled away from him. First time, second time and this time. Nothing about that had changed. Nothing about the fact that he'd missed the first years of Tyler's life would change and he wondered if he'd known about Tyler all that time, if he'd had a hand in raising him, in being his dad, whether Tyler would be so destructive now. Things to wonder about, but things he'd never know since Shelly hadn't told him about Tyler until her husband had forced her into it. "Well, for now you're going to have to come back to work with me." And do what? James didn't have a clue. Not a single, solitary clue. "Look, Tyler, I don't know what it is you've got against these women, but we need to make arrangements for you while I'm at work." He held out his hand to Tyler, but Tyler reflexively shoved his hands into his coat pockets.

James could have pushed the issue, insisted Tyler take his hand, physically demanded it, but what good would that do? Upsetting a five-year-old that way didn't prove a thing and somehow James had the idea that the things Tyler needed proved to him were profound and deep. "What I need from you is some co-operation. I know you don't like being here, that none of this was your idea, but right now we've got to make the best of it. Figure out what's going to make you happy..." He glanced out to the road in time to see Fallon drive by. She was headed in the direction of home, and as he watched her car wind its way down the road, the longing hit hard.

He wondered again whether he could have handled things differently after her accident. She'd needed him and he'd clearly been divided. Her needs, Tyler's needs, adjusting to fatherhood...yet he'd always thought that he could get through it and give everybody what they required. Clearly, he'd been wrong and even now, while he didn't know what it was, he was convinced Fallon had needed something he hadn't been able to give her. The hell of it was, he hadn't even realized it at the time. It was all afterthought, and filled with so many unanswered questions. But he'd been desperate back then, doing his best. Yet Fallon had insisted she understood his absences, his distractions, his moods—in short, that she was OK without him. He'd believed her, too. Trusted her. After all, Fallon was a strong woman, even with her injuries. She was a fighter, and that was something else he trusted.

But maybe he'd taken that strength too for granted, the way people in White Elk had taken her competence for granted. Maybe the brave face she'd always put on for him hadn't been so brave. And he'd never realized it. Never once questioned it.

Then the morning Shelly had taken Tyler away from him, he'd gone to Fallon's hospital room to apologize for not being there for her as much as he'd wanted. But the room had been empty, the bed stripped of its linens. There had been nothing to suggest she'd ever been there. The nurses had told him she'd gone to a rehabilitation hospital, without telling anyone which one. Or, if they knew, their loyalty to Fallon had kept them from revealing it.

Could he have done things differently? Probably. Would it have made a difference to his relationship with Fallon? That, he didn't know.

"There's someone I want you to meet," he said, glancing down at Tyler then back at Fallon's car, which was turning onto a side street. He loved Fallon, and he loved Tyler. It was time to set at least one of his mistakes right. "Look, Tyler, we're going to make a quick stop before we go to the hospital, and I need you to be on your very best behavior. Do you think you can do that for me?"

Naturally, Tyler didn't respond. All he did was follow James to the car, and crawl into the back seat after James opened the door for him. Dutifully, the little boy fastened his seat belt then he sat there like a perfect little gentleman, hands folded in his lap, staring out the window.

For a moment James studied Tyler in the rear-view mirror once he'd settled himself into the driver's seat, wondering what went on in the child's mind. Wondering what he could do to find out.

Wondering what he could do to make Tyler accept him as his father.

CHAPTER THREE

"I WANTED to see how you're doing," James said, brushing the snowflakes from his hair.

She hadn't even had time to take off her scarf. "I'm keeping busy," Fallon said, being careful to keep her back to him lest any expression of excitement or expectation accidentally crossed her face. After all, he hadn't come back to walk with her after that first time, although she'd half expected him to. Maybe even subconsciously wanted him to. He hadn't called either, and she'd half expected that. But it was probably for the best. She was working now. Not so many hours, but the progress was steady and Fallon was pleased that they were moving in the right direction to get the Three Sisters Women's Clinic and Hospital set up and staffed. It felt good to be busy again, she had to admit.

"The hospital is coming along nicely. I'm in the process of ordering room equipment right now…beds, tables, those sorts of things. And I'm beginning to go through job applications, trying to figure out what kind of staffing we'll need."

"I'd intended on stopping by sooner, maybe taking another morning walk with you. But things have gotten pretty hectic, and—"

"And that's fine. I prefer my walks in solitude." Once

though, she hadn't. "It keeps life less complicated that way."

"Maybe it does," he said, almost under his breath. "Anyway, I saw you drive by, and as I was in the area I thought I'd stop by for a minute to see how you're doing."

Finally, she turned to face him. Not that she wanted to, but she had the feeling that if she didn't, he might linger there in the doorway indefinitely...standing there, waiting for something, anything, from her. This was so awkward. She'd made love to this man. Spent nights in his arms, laughing, talking, pouring out hopes and dreams, being happier than she'd ever been in her life. *Had had his baby.* And now the only thing between them was cold, white awkwardness. It hurt, and she couldn't be anything but unapproachable. Because being anything more only encouraged him, and he deserved better than make-believe encouragement. "Look, I appreciate you coming by," she said, fixing her stare on the floor for she knew what fixing her stare on his beautiful eyes would do. "But I've got catalogs to go through, and some phone calls to—"

"Bathroom. Now!"

The tiny voice came from behind James, and Fallon immediately stepped sideways to take a look. Gasped when she saw the child. Felt her heart start to race when she noticed his startling resemblance to James.

"Now!" the little boy said. His face was deadly serious. Full of anger. An expression much too old for someone so young.

"Down the hall," she said, pointing to it. "First door."

Without a word, the child scampered out from behind James and ran down the hall, leaving a trail of slushy water and dirty snow in his wake.

"Sorry about that," James said. "I told him to stay in the car."

"When nature calls…" Fallon said, her voice not quite steady. This little boy was so much like the one she'd dreamt her own little boy would be that all the emotion she'd been fighting to hold back for so long was now fighting against her. This moment of realization unnerved her so badly that she had to back up to the wall to steady herself. This wasn't her son, she knew that. But she felt the instant connection as this was her son's brother. "I assume…assume that's Tyler?"

"Shelly dropped him off again a few days ago."

She swallowed back her emotion. She had to. There was no other way to do this with James. "A-and are you happy?" She knew he was. Happy, worried. Relieved.

"More than you can imagine. Although being his dad scares me because it's a lot of responsibility I never expected to have…at least, not right away. Not without you."

"Give it time," she said, ignoring his last comment. "The adjustment for Tyler is just as big as yours. But you'll both do fine once you're used to each other." Thinking about James and Tyler getting to know each other, working out their lives together, caused a lump to form in her throat when she thought about their child, their little boy…how they'd never have the chance to work out their lives with him. But seeing Tyler made the loss so acute again, like those first days after she'd lost her own baby. Suddenly she had to spin away from James lest he see the tears welling in her eyes. "He's cute, James," she said, walking away from the door. "I'm guessing he's, what? Five or six? You may have told me, but I don't remember."

"Five."

"And still so active?" That was a polite way of describing what James had told her early on about Tyler's behavior.

In answer to her question, a loud crash coming from the bathroom sent them both running down the hall to the open door where Tyler was standing, totally unaffected by the mess he'd made pulling a shelf of lotions and cosmetics right off the wall. And it had taken some doing, as it was hung a good three feet higher than Tyler was tall.

"He must have climbed up on the sink," Fallon said, bending to pick up a bottle of lotion. Only the bottom of the bottle had broken and when she lifted the bottle from the floor, its bottom, along with its contents, remained there, leaving Fallon holding a bottomless, empty bottle.

"Tyler," James said, his voice so quiet and controlled it was brittle.

"I'm sure it was an accident," she said, not sure what else to say, or do.

"I'm sure it was *not*," James responded.

"Maybe we should ask Tyler," Fallon said, quite surprised that he seemed totally unaffected by the whole matter. Most children his age would be scared, on the verge of tears. But Tyler had his shoulders squared, his jaw set, his arms folded belligerently across his chest. Getting ready to do battle was what Fallon immediately thought of. This child was getting ready to square off with someone. "Was it an accident, Tyler?" she asked, suddenly feeling protective of the boy.

He didn't answer. Instead, he stared straight ahead at the hall, barely blinking.

"Tyler?" she asked again.

Again, no response. She glanced up at James, who seemed in agony. Then she glanced back at Tyler, and saw just a flash of that same agony, and the need to come to his defense in some way, to make the situation a little better for him, overtook her. "Look, Tyler, I'm not going to punish you for breaking my shelf. But here's what we're going to do. I'm going to go find some rags so you can clean up the lotions and everything else that spilled on the floor. And while I'm doing that, stand back so we can get the glass picked up. We don't want you cutting yourself while you're cleaning."

"We've been having a rough time," James admitted, not so much in defense of what Tyler had done as in explanation.

"I guess you have. And it looks to me like Tyler…" Before she could finish, James's cellphone rang, and he seemed almost grateful for the interruption. Too grateful, she decided as James walked away, leaving her there to make sure Tyler didn't do something to hurt himself. Half a minute later, James returned, red-faced.

"Look, I know I don't have a right to ask this, but…I have an emergency up on Pine Ridge, a child with a broken leg, and I really can't take Tyler with me. He's…" He glanced down at the boy. "He's having a rough time right now, as you've already seen, and I don't have anyplace else for him to stay yet. He's been through three babysitters in as many days, and I haven't had time to find someone else to look after him while I'm at work. I wouldn't normally impose on you, but it may be a compound fracture, and I need to get the child stabilized before transport…"

"Just go," she said, not sure why. "Take care of your patient, and I'll look after Tyler." She glanced down at Tyler, who was eyeing another hanging shelf and trying to inch his way in its direction without being noticed. "But only for a little while."

"You don't know how much I appreciate that," James said, the expression on his face turning into genuine relief.

"We'll talk when I get back, OK? I have so much I need to tell you."

Fallon reached out and took hold of Tyler's arm to keep him from moving any closer to his next target. "When you know how long this is going to take, call me, will you?"

Instinctively, James bent to kiss Fallon's cheek, but she jerked away from him. So he simply nodded then bent to Tyler who jerked away, too. "You be good, and don't break anything else, you hear me?"

Tyler stared him in the eye, not defiantly, though. And didn't answer. After several seconds James straightened up. "Like I said, we'll talk," he said, then turned and left, leaving Fallon alone with what she knew was going to turn the rest of her day into a royal disaster.

"So, Tyler," she said, pulling him out into the hall, "tell me why you broke my shelf, and why, right this very minute, you're thinking about breaking my other shelf."

The boy's eyes opened a bit wider, as if surprised that she could anticipate what he was thinking.

Fallon laughed. "You do want to pull down the other shelf, don't you? Are you surprised that I know what you want to do?"

Naturally, he didn't respond. But that didn't surprise her. The answer was in his eyes. Big, beautiful eyes, like his father's. So beautiful she ached with longing for what she'd lost. "So I don't suppose I can trust you to stand here and not go back into the bathroom while I go find a broom to clean up the broken glass, can I?" Silly asking the question when she already knew the answer. "Which means you get to go with me." She pointed in the direction of the utility room, but Tyler kept his eyes glued to the wall across from him. What kind of trauma had done that to him? What kind of upset had caused such a young child to be so removed? James hadn't told her much. Mostly, she'd heard just the anger from him over being left out of Tyler's life, over the things he missed. Anger that sank to the heart of what she'd done to him herself, how she'd left him out, too.

And seeing Tyler, even with his problems, reminded her of how selfish she'd been. She'd made a choice that couldn't be undone. Fought hard then lost. And never included James. It was the hardest thing she'd ever done because she'd loved that baby, wanted that baby. Should have been strong enough to carry that baby to term. But she hadn't been, and the day her doctor had come to her and told her it was over…

Now she ached that their baby wasn't in her arms. "Well, Tyler," she said, trying to shake off the glum mood settling over her, "I don't know if you're hungry, but I am. And I think ice cream is a good afternoon snack. Care to have some with me?" she asked.

Naturally, Tyler didn't answer. So Fallon decided to ignore him and hope that once she got the ice cream out of the freezer, he'd come to the kitchen. Bad reasoning, though. She'd been in the kitchen less than a minute when she heard a crash. A loud crash coming from the bathroom, followed by another… "Oh, my God!" she gasped, recognizing the sound of breaking glass.

Dropping the carton of ice cream on the floor, she ran to the bathroom to find that Tyler had pulled the second cosmetic shelf down. Along with it had come a large framed picture from the wall…its glass broken into hundreds of pieces and Tyler standing in the middle of the mess, his arms and hands bleeding.

Without a thought that she, herself, could get cut, Fallon ran straight to the boy, picked him up and got him out of the bathroom. But halfway down the hall he started fighting her, kicking and screaming.

"Leave me alone!" he wailed, balling his bloody little fists and thrashing out at her. "Put me down."

"Hold still." she said, trying to have a look at the gashes on his arms without letting go of him. Which was an impossible task because Tyler was in a fit of rage, fighting her with everything he had in him. "Hold still, Tyler. I need to see how badly you're cut."

"Don't you dare!" he screamed, still fighting against her. "Just put me down or I'll…"

He didn't finish his threat but he didn't have to. Fallon knew exactly what he wanted to do, and would do the instant she let him go. So she held on even tighter, grabbed her keys from the table next to the front door, and ran as hard and as fast as she could to her car, with Tyler still pounding and kicking. Once there, she managed to get the back door open and literally had to toss him inside and get the door shut in the same swift movement. Then she locked the car with the remote control, ran to the driver's side, and simply watched Tyler for a moment. He was crying, and kicking the back of the seat. But the rage was gone, and replacing it was fear and sadness. He was now just a sad, scared little boy. Problem was, when she got in, that could change.

And it did. The instant she was behind the wheel Tyler started his tirade again, kicking the back of the seat, screaming, crying. "Tyler," she said, keeping her voice perfectly calm, "you're going to be fine. I'm a nurse, and I'm going to take you to the hospital to have your cuts taken care of." She knew that the better way would have been to stop the bleeding, remove glass fragments, bandage the wounds before moving him, but that was impossible, and her biggest fear was that in his tantrum he might injure himself further, maybe drive a glass fragment in deeper, or open a wound even more. The hospital was her only hope.

"As soon as I call your dad!"

"I don't have a dad," Tyler yelled. "Donnie didn't want me any more, and I don't want any more dads! I hate James! And I hate you!"

"He sustained some pretty good cuts." Dr. Eric Ramsey motioned Fallon into the hall. "And he was so agitated I was afraid he'd harm himself, so I had to sedate him. Just lightly. I want to keep him in for a day or so to make sure he doesn't rip out his stitches. He's…um… He's feisty. And very angry right now. I hope James will agree to let him stay for observation."

"He was so upset, Eric. I couldn't get him calmed down, and the only thing I could think of was to get him into the car and get him to the hospital. And you're right. He's a very angry little boy. But I think it's more than that. Not sure what, though."

"So you don't know anything about him?"

"James just dropped him off and, to be honest, that was the first time I'd met Tyler. I know he's been a struggle when James has had him before. But I had no idea how much."

"Well, James is en route to Salt Lake City now with his patient. It's going to be a fast turn-around, so I suppose we'll hold off making any further decisions concerning Tyler for a while." Eric was a pediatrician, and head of trauma services for the White Elk Hospital. "I've left a message to have him call here as soon as he can. So, in the meantime, we'll wait and hope Tyler calms down."

And here she was, involved. "Then I guess I'll go and

sit in Tyler's room. He'll need a familiar face there when he wakes up."

"He's going to be asleep for quite a while. How about I prescribe a cup of coffee or something to eat? And I'll get it for you myself. You're looking pretty strung out, Fallon. I don't want you letting this get to you."

"I'm feeling pretty strung out, as a matter of fact. But coffee and food aren't going to fix that." Going home and getting away from anything involving James was the prescription she needed. Only right now that prescription wasn't going to be filled because Tyler was the priority, and she felt obligated to be with him as James wasn't. More than that, she wanted to sit with him.

"Want to work?" he asked, half teasing, half serious. "I'm down a nurse today. Dinah's home with the girls. It's their regular monthly girls' day out, and she won't miss it for the world. So…"

"You know Gabby would have your head if you lured me away from her."

"And I'm still protesting that she got you and we didn't." He faked a frown. "Neil wants you back so badly that he weeps openly when your name is mentioned. You know he's at odds with his wife for stealing you away from him."

Fallon laughed, and swatted Eric's arm playfully. "I love you both, but what I'm doing right now is good. I didn't realize how much I missed being useful and for now I like the job." Not the way she liked real nursing. But for a while, until she figured out what she really wanted to do with her life, it would do.

"Well, I'm glad you're back, even if it's with Gabby," he admitted, laughing.

Fallon looked down the hall of the trauma area and sighed. Yes, Gabby did have her. And she was grateful for that. Which meant White Elk Hospital was officially the past now. If only she could return to the past and stay there for ever.

"How is he?" James gasped, running through the door. "I just got the message. I was on my way back when I remembered to check my voicemail."

"Resting," Fallon said. She'd been sitting at Tyler's bedside well over an hour, simply watching the boy. He was even troubled in his sleep. She could see that in the way he tossed and turned and twisted in his covers. "Eric gave him a light sedative and I didn't want to leave him so I've been sitting here for a while, and he's doing well." Physically well, anyway. She wasn't sure about anything else.

"The cuts are all superficial," Eric said, stepping into the room. "He has a few stitches, and he's good to go as far as his injuries are concerned. But I'd like to keep him under observation for a while because he was so…I suppose the word to describe it is enraged. He was having a major temper tantrum when Fallon brought him in, fighting her as hard as he could, and I was afraid he'd hurt himself so I gave him something to take the edge off a little, and now I'd like to watch him for a day or so to see if there's anything else wrong with him other than his cuts."

James agreed quickly. "I wish I knew his history…if he's always like this or if this is new behavior. Because it's extreme. Children have their temper tantrums and that's part of learning how to cope with disappointment, but when I see a child like Tyler, who acts it out so violently, I'm inclined to look for something other than the momentary trigger of those emotions. I've had him three days this time and he's getting worse, so I think observing him for a day or two, running some tests to make sure he doesn't have some underlying medical problem, is a good idea. I appreciate the offer, and I'd appreciate it if you'd oversee his care, Eric."

"Look," Eric said, "I've got to get back to work. But, yes, James, I'll take over his medical treatment, observe him, run some preliminary tests. You know, blood tests, a general physical, maybe some X-rays, that sort of thing. So, until we know more, if you have any questions, call me. And feel free to sit with Tyler for as long as you like. I'm sure he'll be happy to have you with him when he wakes up."

"I'm not so sure of that," James muttered, slumping to the wall as Eric took his leave. "I'm really sorry about all this, Fallon. I didn't mean to drag you into it. This whole thing with Tyler has been…difficult."

"Have you talked to his mother about how he's acting? Maybe she knows what triggers the temper tantrums."

"Do you think she'd actually tell me anything? I mean, she didn't even tell me I had a son until her husband didn't want him any more. If Tyler had been a well-behaved child, I'm pretty sure she would have never revealed her little *secret* about his existence. So I have no reason to believe that she'll tell me anything about his behavior. The hell of it is, Fallon, that when she drops him off and leaves, I don't even know where she goes. Don't know where Tyler lives when he's not with me. They have a son of their own now, and Donnie, the husband, doesn't want Tyler around. I'd wanted to ask her some questions, so a couple of months ago, after she disappeared with Tyler for the second time, I hired an investigator to find them. But apparently she and Donnie move around a lot, and every time my investigator catches up to her, she moves again. So we start over." He sucked in a sharp, angry breath.

"Secrets. Her stupid damn secrets are killing me, and I can't do a thing about it."

Secrets… Reality sprouted in the form of a dull ache in her chest. "But you're going after custody?"

He nodded. "My first round didn't turn out so well. I didn't have the results of the DNA test back, although our blood types matched. And the judge wouldn't hear the case. To make matters worse, Shelly came back in the middle of that mess and wanted Tyler back, and the judge said I had no legal recourse at that point, that I had to let Tyler go. So I did, then I couldn't find him again."

"It must be awful for both of you, never knowing what she's going to do."

"This time it may not be up to Shelly to decide."

It was unthinkable, what Tyler's mother was doing to him. What she was doing to James. Poor child. Poor James. "And nothing's getting better yet, is it?"

He shook his head. "Tyler's so angry, and he's frightened, and I can't blame him. When I grew up I had great parents who took care of me, protected me. At his age, I probably had no concept that one, or both, of my parents could simply get rid of me the way Shelly did Tyler. I can't even imagine…"

"Well, however it works out in the long run, you have Tyler right now and I know you'll do whatever's best for him. And if there's anything I can do in the meantime to help him…"

"Actually, if you ever run onto a place where Tyler and I can live…"

"Where are you now?"

"We're staying in a hotel room. One room, with a microwave and a mini-fridge. Two beds, a television and a lamp. For me, it was fine. I wasn't in a hurry to find a house or a condo because this is the tourist season and

I know nothing's available. But the thing is, I won't get custody of Tyler if I don't have a stable home for him. And that little room isn't enough for him. He's bouncing off the walls, it's driving him crazy. So if you know of a place I can rent, or even buy… Oh, and a care-giver, too. As of this morning Tyler has exhausted the list of available care-givers in the area…at least, the ones with a recommendation from the hospital pediatric department. I'm pretty sure his reputation precedes him now, which will make the possibility of finding someone else to care for him while I'm working slim to none. So if you know someone who's up to a challenge…"

"Let me think about it. Make some calls, see if I can figure something out for you…for Tyler."

"It's not your problem, but I'd appreciate it." Stepping away from the wall, James bent and gave Fallon a quick kiss on the cheek, one from which she didn't flinch this time. "I'm sorry for so many things, Fallon. But I haven't had a lot of options lately."

"I know," she whispered, trying to push back the emotions straining to spring up in her. It was hard thinking of James and Tyler struggling so much. "And you did the right thing then. Still are. So, let me know how he gets along," she said. "Because I do care." He was her son's brother, how could she not care? "And in the meantime, if I can find you and Tyler a place to live…" Spinning away, too full of emotion and her own regrets to be near James any longer, Fallon had every intention of dashing for the exit, which was exactly what she did. But something tugged at her halfway there. It was an image of James and Tyler living in a small hotel room, an image of the judge taking Tyler away from James because James couldn't provide a proper home. It wasn't fair! But, then, life wasn't fair, was it? If it were, she and James and Tyler would be living together now, with the baby. The four of them as a family. Yet James and Tyler were stuck in a cramped hotel room and there was no way a judge would grant James the sole custody he wanted. And Tyler…he really did need a home, needed to be with James as much as James needed to be with his son. *The way she so longed to be with her own son.*

She understood that need in such deep, agonizing ways now, and it was causing the sprout of a plan to grow. One that sprouted then grew so rapidly it surprised her.

But could she do it? Could she take James and Tyler into her home temporarily? Give them the stability they needed, the stability the judge would demand? Could she do that and keep herself separated from them?

She shut her eyes, trying to fight off the plan. It was ridiculous, and James was right. It wasn't her problem. Yet behind her shut eyes she saw Tyler, looking so alone and frightened. Tyler without a home. Saw the judge pulling Tyler away from James. Saw the judge sending her son's brother back to a terrible home. That was the vision that turned her around and sent her right back to James.

"James," she said quietly, on entering the hospital room where Tyler was still sleeping peacefully. "I've been think-ing. It's not good to keep Tyler in a hotel room. He needs a home, someplace where he's going to feel safe. Someplace where he can live a normal life, where the judge can see stability. Since you can't find that right now, I think you two should come and stay at my cabin. It's not large, but I have a spare bedroom, plenty of space for a little boy. *For a little while.* There's a nice hill out back where he can sled and play in the snow.

"I mean, I realize it's not going to solve all his problems, or yours, but maybe it will help make things a little better in the meantime. And we can work out our schedules to watch him so he'll have some kind of consistency in his life, and you won't have to worry about finding someone else to look after him. I'm at home most of the time with my new job…at least, for now. And you can work your shifts around what I need to do. Eric and Neil are all into family these days, and I'm pretty sure that's what they'd want you to do."

"Why would you do that, Fallon?" James whispered, stepping quietly away from the bed, trying not to disturb the boy. "Considering the way we are now, why would you take us in?"

Because Tyler was lost, and she knew how that felt. Because James was at a confusing, frustrating place in his life and she knew how *that* felt. Because Tyler was so connected to her son. "Don't ask me personal questions," she said. "I'm not getting involved with you again. This is only a temporary solution to a bigger problem, *your problem*, and I don't want you getting any other ideas about anything. *Especially about us.* That's the only condition. Tyler gets the spare bedroom, you get the couch, and you both respect my privacy."

James looked down at Tyler then turned back to Fallon. "Do you really think he looks like me? People tell me he does."

Too much so, she thought. Because she was well on her way to losing her heart to the son, like she'd already done to the father. This wasn't good. Not good at all. But it wasn't about her, wasn't even about James. It was about Tyler. And as long as she kept that in mind, she'd be fine. "He does look like you." The way she thought their son would have.

CHAPTER FOUR

"WHAT was I thinking?" Fallon was exhausted from sheer worry by the time the end of the day rolled around. Intermittently, she was positive she'd done the right thing, allowing James and his son to move in temporarily with her. Then she was positive it was the worst thing she could have done. Back and forth, all day long. That, mixed with cold chills, shaking hands and throbbing head. For heaven's sake! After so many months fighting to be alone, she'd just gone and done the very last thing she'd wanted to do. "How could I have invited them?" she moaned on a weary sigh. Yet how could she have not done that? The bigger question, though, was how could she live with them and still remain disengaged from their lives?

She was already becoming engaged, especially with Tyler, and that was the problem. A huge problem because he wasn't her son. Wasn't a replacement for her son. Yet she had these motherly feelings toward him, feelings she couldn't have because she and James had no future together.

"It's a good deed, the right thing to do," she said, hoping that saying it aloud would convince her. "The thing any normal, decent person would do." No personal involvement permitted. "Good deed, good deed..." Besides, they wouldn't be staying long. "Good deed, Fallon. That's all it is."

The personal pep talk kept up as she prepared the bedroom for Tyler and the couch for James. No physical contact with James. No hugs, no kisses, no nothing. That, more than anything, was going to be the tough part, because there was no denying that she still craved his touch, his kiss. Craved every inch of him in a way she'd never known one person could crave another. "It's *just* a good deed…"

She *had* to keep her head about this. Because, maybe, just maybe, helping him through this rough patch would assuage some of her guilt. Or make it ever stronger.

Nevertheless, she was petrified that one little look from James could undo everything—her resolve, her resistance, both of them flying right out the window. Fighting against everything she'd hoped for in a life with James was the hardest thing she'd ever done. So she had to brace herself for that fight. Had to convince herself she was going to win it. Had to remind herself that she was doing this for James.

"Good deed," she said, heading to the kitchen to fix herself a cup of hot tea. "If I don't let my emotions get the better of me." Because she'd never stopped loving James, and she truly did care what happened to Tyler. Because she wasn't strong enough to completely divorce herself from the things she'd thought, for a time, she'd have in her life—the things she'd always wanted. Husband, children… "Because I'm crazy," she was repeating as someone rang the doorbell. At the same time her cellphone also jingled its Beethoven sonata. "Hello," she said, on her way to the front door.

"It's me. I didn't want to alarm you so after I knocked I called to tell you that I'm here with my things."

He was moving in tonight? Suddenly the thing she wanted, and dreaded, was happening, and she was a nervous wreck.

"Why now?" she said in wobbly greeting when she pulled open the door.

"Why not now?"

"Because I thought you'd move in once Tyler was released from the hospital."

"But I'm not working now, not on call, so I thought this was as good a time as any. Unless you don't want me yet, then I can…"

"What? Sleep in your car outside my house?"

Grinning, he looked almost as innocent as a young schoolboy. "Or bunk at the hospital in one of the on-call rooms until you're ready for us."

Why was it that just one smile was all it took and she was done for? "You don't have to spend your night in an on-call room."

"Then I can move in here, or is it back to the car?"

Now he was teasing her. She could see it in his eyes, in the way he couldn't keep a straight face even though he tried. Her old feelings were pummeling her now, and she had to duck her head to hide her feelings from James. Because what she could read in his eyes, he could read in hers. That's what had connected them initially. One look, she saw his soul. And he saw hers. "In here. I probably should send you back to the car, though," she said, trying to sound grumpy.

"Then I'll be right back." After dropping a duffle bag on the entry hall floor, he headed back out to his car then returned almost immediately with a couple of suitcases. "This is all I've got. Didn't bring any of the things with me from my apartment when I came here. Just a few clothes and some medical journals."

"What about Tyler's things?"

James shook his head. "Shelly didn't leave anything for him. I bought him a few clothes to wear, but I haven't had time to do much shopping for him yet. And he wasn't exactly easy to take to the department store the one time I did try. Let's just say that he was too exuberant with his opinion and we were kicked out within twenty minutes."

"Maybe I'll take him shopping when he's up to it. If that's OK with you."

"Oh, it's OK. I'd be grateful."

So there it was. One minute into the arrangement, resolve already flying away. She was getting involved. But it was with Tyler. Not James. That's what she had to tell herself. *It was for Tyler.*

Fallon stepped back as James walked fully into her house then she shut the door behind him. "You can have the spare room until Tyler moves in. It's down the hall, near the back. Bathroom is...well, you know where that is. And when Tyler's here you can have the couch in the living room, or there's one in the den. It's not as large, but you can shut the door and have your privacy. Take your pick. I'm upstairs, by the way, and there's no reason for you to come up there. My office is behind the stairs on this floor, so while you're here, it's your responsibility to see that Tyler stays out." She sounded like a cranky landlady all of a sudden, and it was all she could to do bite back a smile. Truth was, she'd rehearsed those words a few times. Out loud. Trying to sound churlish when she said them. She'd succeeded and she was a little proud of herself for it...proud that a little of that resolve was flying back through the window.

"Shall I have security bars installed at the bottom of the stairway?" James teased. "And another on your bedroom door?"

OK, so maybe she hadn't sounded as churlish as she'd wanted to. Resolve flying back out again. Then, to make matters worse, he didn't even try biting back his smile. It was broad, and so infectious Fallon glanced away so he wouldn't see the corners of her lips turning up. He always did that, always cured her disagreeable moods with a simple smile.

"Are you smiling, Fallon?" he asked.

"No," she lied.

"Can I see?"

"No."

"If I can't have a look, I have to presume that you're smiling."

"I don't smile."

"If you don't, it's a pity, because you have the most beautiful smile in the world."

She raised her head to look at him. "Flattery's not going to get you to the top of the stairs, James, if that's what you're trying to do here."

"I didn't think it would. And so you'll know, Fallon, I won't take one step up those stairs unless you want me to. The only thing that will get me to the top will be your invitation, and you have my word on that."

"Thank you," she whispered.

"It's not what I want, and you know that." Instinctively, he reached out, placed his fingers gently under her chin and raised her face to him even more. "I love you, and it's not going to be easy on me living here, knowing that you won't have me. But I'll respect your wishes. And your boundaries. Even if I don't agree with them."

"Thank you," she said again, fighting the urge to cry. He was so kind and good, and so…chivalrous. In time, after she'd pushed him away enough, he would realize he didn't want her any more. But for now he was being a perfect gentleman. Yet, God willing, if she could push hard enough, it would wear thin on him. Pray that day came quickly because, try as she may, she would slip. Sooner or later, she'd give in to that smile, to those twinkling eyes. Then she'd tell him her awful secret. And hurt him in ways she couldn't even imagine. "Look, I was about to fix myself a cup of tea. Would you care to join me?"

"Are you sure you want me here?" he asked, quite seriously. "I know you asked because that's just the thing you'd do. But do you really want me...*us*—here?"

"I wasn't sure about it when I asked you, and nothing's changed. But I'm not going back on my invitation. Tyler needs something other than a hotel room, and—"

"This arrangement is *only* about Tyler?" he asked, trying to sound neutral.

But Fallon heard no neutrality there...only hope, as she looked him square in the eye. "This is *only* about Tyler. I know what it's like to be...abandoned. That's what happened to me. My mother had me, didn't want me, passed me off to anybody who wanted to be charitable for a while and take me in. So I know why he needs stability, especially for Christmas."

"I'm so sorry, Fallon," he whispered, reaching out to stroke her cheek. "I didn't know that about you. You'd never told me, and you should have."

So many things she hadn't told him. She lurched back. "Don't do that, James. I just...I just can't deal with it." For a moment, she thought about taking his single room at the lodge. Shutting herself in with the microwave and mini-fridge. It wouldn't be so bad for a while, and she wouldn't have to deal with this. But James needed help with Tyler, and part of having them live there was that help. Truth was, she wanted to help. Tyler really did need that stability. "Look, I think I'm going to go upstairs for a while. Help yourself to anything you need, feel free to make yourself at home, kick around, open cupboards, get yourself familiar with what's here. Shout if you need something you can't find."

"I'm not sorry I touched you, Fallon. I'll respect the boundaries from now on, like I promised, but I'm not sorry."

"You're going to make this difficult for me, aren't you?"

"It's not my intention. But you know what? It's difficult on me, too. You know how I feel about you, but what you don't know is how I feel every time you push me away. It's killing me."

She thrust her hand to stop him. "Don't!" she said. "Don't tell me. Don't tell me…anything, because I don't want to know." Miserably, she already knew, but what James didn't fathom was how each time she pushed him away a tiny piece of her heart broke off. She was losing herself, one shred at a time, and the pain of it was unrelenting. It was a wound that would not heal. Not ever. And, she'd never show it to him. Because once he saw the weakness, he'd find his way in.

Stretching out on the couch in the den, James stared up at the ceiling, wondering if her bed was above him. He imagined that it was, and that she was sleeping there. He loved the way she slept…on her side, cuddled into a little ball. He remembered their first night together when he'd stayed awake hours, just watching her. He'd been tempted to disturb her, just to see if she would cuddle into him, but he hadn't. Second night, she'd cuddled into him, and he'd thought that was the way he wanted to spend every night for the rest of his life. "And we will, Fallon," he promised himself. "But I've got to find a way to convince you that you want it as much as I do."

Working on that solution was cut short by a phone call, though. It was Neil Ranard, informing him that every available medic in the White Elk Valley was being called out. The lodge on the Little Sister was on fire! Grease fire in the kitchen, spreading.

"Fallon!" James yelled, jumping up from the couch. "Medical emergency! Neil says he needs your help!"

She was down the stairs in a flash, blanket wrapped around her shoulders. "What?" she gasped.

"Fire. Lodge up on the Little Sister. He wants you in the ER, in charge of triage. Wants me in the ER, too."

Surprisingly, she didn't protest, didn't even think about it. Instead, she dropped the blanket to the floor and headed back to the stairs. "Give me three minutes to get ready," she called back over her shoulder on her way up. James could hear her footsteps pounding on the wooden floorboards upstairs. That was Fallon O'Gara preparing to do what she'd been put on this earth to do—be a nurse. It was a good sound to hear. Gave him hope for other things. Made him glad to know that Fallon wouldn't turn away when she was needed.

It was a good sign, seeing how the woman he'd come to love so quickly didn't turn away when she was needed. Except from him. Sadly, she'd found that easy to do.

Fifteen minutes after the initial callout, James and Fallon crashed through the emergency room doors together, shoulder to shoulder, and ran straight into a wall of volunteers and medical personnel alike. People Fallon knew, people who always responded when there was a need. People waiting for her instructions.

"How many doctors do we have?" she asked Emoline Putters, the night clerk in charge of the emergency desk.

"Two, so far. Dr. Galbraith and Dr. Ranard...Gabby.

She's on her way in as soon as Angela Blanchard gets there to look after Bryce. She'll be on light duty, considering her condition. Walt Graham may be heading into town, too. And Henry Gunther." A retired obstetrician and a semi-retired anesthesiologist.

"Dr. Eric Ramsey isn't here?"

Emoline, a tight-faced woman with gray- and brown-streaked hair pulled into a knot at the nape of her neck, shook her head. "He went out with Dr. Neil Ranard. First time back on the rescue for him. Dr. McGinnis went out with him, too. I've been trying to locate Dr. Stafford to come in, but so far he isn't answering his cellphone."

Fallon spun to face James. "How much experience do you have with treating burns?" she asked. It was a difficult specialty, took stamina. In her opinion, burns were the worst of the worst to tend, and she never assigned anyone to burns unless they had the experience. Some of the doctors who passed through here wouldn't treat burns unless absolutely forced to.

"I worked in the pediatric side of the burn unit back in Salt Lake City," he said. "I'm not a burn specialist by a long shot, but I can do the initial assessments and stabilize them. Get them ready to transport to a burn unit."

"Well, we're not set up with a specific burn room, but exam five is larger, probably the best one." She motioned for one of the volunteers to come over. Dave Ellis, the town dentist. "Dave, you go with Dr. Galbraith, and get the room ready. He'll tell you what he needs. You can hang the IVs and get the saline ready." She also signaled Catie, the owner of Catie's Overlook, to help. Catie would fetch, Dave would actually assume some of the medical duty.

"Who are these people?" James whispered to her.

"They're not trained to do the actual rescue out in the field, but I've trained them to help in the ER—they run errands, go after supplies, carry messages, do whatever they can to help the medical staff. In the case of Dave Ellis, he's got a fair amount of medical training as he's a dentist, and he can do pretty much anything we need him to."

"Amazing," he said, looking around at the expanding sea of these volunteers. At least fifteen of them had wandered in now.

"Yes, they are," she said, taking some pride in her little group.

"Not them. You. They're here because of you, aren't they?"

She looked up at him. Smiled. For a moment, an old longing filled her. She wanted to feel his arms around her, just a fleeting hug, but she stepped back before he saw the need reflected in her eyes. And he would. "They're here because this is where they want to be. It has nothing to do with me."

"I don't believe that," James argued. "Just look at the way they're watching you, waiting for instructions."

They were waiting for her and it was nice to be back. A little bit of normalcy in the midst of so many things that hadn't been normal for so long. "Honestly, I'm a little nervous," she whispered to him. "It's been a while…not sure I'll get my old rhythm back."

"Smoke inhalation coming in…times three, ETA ten minutes," Emoline shouted. "One critical, two stable."

"You're going to be fine," James whispered, his lips practically brushing her ear. "It's like riding a bicycle. You may not have been on one in a while, but once you get back on…"

She felt the tingle of his lips on her ear. It spread down her neck, down her arms, down to her toes. "Running an emergency is like riding a bicycle?" she asked, fighting not to visibly shiver.

"OK, so maybe the analogy was a little off, but you know what I mean."

"Yes," she whispered. "I do. And thank you for having that confidence in me."

"I know who you are. And usually I might say something like, if you need me, you know where I am. But I don't have to say that, Fallon, because you *won't* need me."

That wasn't true. She'd needed him from the first moment she'd laid eyes on him. That would never change. For her, James was everything, and her need for him was so close to the surface it was nearly touchable.

"Burn coming in, ETA twenty minutes. They're telling me it's minor," Emoline called out.

Fallon drew in a deep breath. Smiled at James, reached out and gave his hand a squeeze. "I'm glad you're here tonight," she said, then turned to the group. "OK, I need two of you at the door to keep it clear…" She gave the instructions, volunteers scurried to obey, and within mere minutes the emergency room was ready. A short time later, while she was awaiting the arrival of Gabby Ranard, who was going to be doctor in charge, her dear old friend Edith Weston staggered into the emergency room on her own, looking ashen, confused. "Don't feel good…called a taxi…" The rest of her words were garbled as Fallon rushed forward to grab her when the old woman started to pitch forward.

One of the volunteers was there right away with a wheelchair, helping Edith into it. Fallon assessed her pupils immediately, took a pulse after that. "Edith, can you tell me what happened?"

Edith looked up at her, flashed confusion. "I think I

may have had a slight stroke, dear. When the fire started, I was gathering up my photo albums, hurrying too much, then…" She shook her head. "I don't remember." Edith Weston lived at the lodge. Was one of White Elk's grand matriarchs.

"We're going to get you comfortable, Edith. Are you in any pain?"

The woman shook her head. "Just embarrassed that I'm taking up your time when you have so much to do."

Fallon patted her hand. "Truth is, Edith, I'd rather have you taking up my time than anyone else."

"I'm still sorry about my timing," Edith managed. She reached out and took hold of Fallon's hand. "But my home is burning down now, so I guess this is as good a place for me as any."

Edith was showing such courage in the face of adversity. It was something Fallon wished for herself, but her time for that kind of courage had passed, and she'd proved herself lacking. "Did you get your photo albums?" Fallon asked. "Before you had to leave, were you able to find them?"

"Most of them. The important ones. One of the firefighters put them aside for me, promised he'd bring them to the hospital for me later. Those are my memories, Fallon. Good and bad, memories are the things we can hold dear when everything else is gone."

"Well, I'll make sure they get to your room. And, Edith, if you need anything…*anything*…please let me know." Edith was like the grandmother she'd never had. The one who'd baked her cookies over the years, and listened to her when everything had been falling apart. Edith had come to sit with her in the rehabilitation hospital, the only person she'd asked to be there while fighting for her life at first, then fighting to keep her baby. She hadn't included Gabby or Dinah, hadn't included James. But she'd turned to Edith because she'd needed the comfort of a mother or grandmother. Someone who'd seen life and known its pain. Someone whose sympathy was expressed in her eyes, and by the way she'd held Fallon's hand in the roughest hours. Her other friends would have cried, their eyes would have been sad. But what Edith had given her had been poised composure at a time when that's what she'd needed more than anything. "But right now we need to get you into bed and make sure you're as comfortable as possible. Then get a doctor in to see you."

Edith looked up at Fallon and there were no lies to be told in the eyes of either woman. "I worry about you, Fallon. When I knew *he* was here… You're not making it right between you two yet, are you? You haven't told him the things he has a right to know?"

"And hurt him?"

"Pain is part of life, my dear. Once in a while it makes us grow stronger. Often, when it's shared with those we love, we become better for it."

"I made bad choices, Edith. You know that. You were there, telling me to do the right thing. And I wasn't listening to you."

"But it's never too late to do the right thing, dear. Never too late."

Down the hall, James watched the exchange between the two women. While he couldn't hear what they were saying, he saw the tender, caring way Fallon responded to the woman in the wheelchair, and he wanted to punch the wall in frustration. Tomorrow, when this was over, she would go right back to being the way she'd been all these months, withdrawn, hesitant. At least, with him. And it was so wrong. Yet he wasn't sure he knew how to get through to her…not in the way that mattered. As more nurses showed up to work, and a few more doctors came in as well, all of them glad to take instruction from Fallon, all of them depending on her to make the emergency room work the way it should, James knew, more than ever, that he couldn't give up on Fallon. He wasn't sure he could fix *their* relationship, wasn't sure they could ever get back to the place they'd been before she'd been injured. But he was sure that Fallon needed this hospital and, more than that, this hospital needed Fallon.

So did he. But would they work things out between them? Would he get her back? Because Fallon had changed in ways he didn't understand, ways she wouldn't share with him. It scared him, because he wasn't sure what to do any more. Wasn't sure he'd ever be let back in.

CHAPTER FIVE

By all estimations, James still had a few minutes before the first patients would arrive…enough time to dash down to the pediatrics ward to check on Tyler. So he let Fallon know where to find him and hurried down the hall to his room.

"Tyler," James said, entering the ward. "Are you feeling better?"

The boy was sitting cross-legged in the middle of the bed with a game controller in his hand. His attention was totally fixed on a game…something with colorful little animals scurrying in and out of little holes in the ground. He didn't so much as blink when James entered the room. But, then, James was used to that reaction. Understood it, didn't like it but was braced for it.

"Looks like a fun game," James continued, grappling for words as the level of discomfort started to germinate. Funny how he was always so good with other people's children, yet with his own… "Are you winning?"

Tyler shot him a dark scowl, as if James should know that. Wasn't a great response, but it was a response.

"I've never really played any video games before, but I wouldn't mind trying. Can that one be played by two people?"

"I don't want to play with anyone," Tyler said, his tiny

voice defiant. As if he wanted to prove that point, he scooted to the far edge of the bed, as far away from James as he could possibly get.

James chose not to react. Instead, he sat down next to the bed, stretched out his long legs, and relaxed back into the chair. "Why don't you show me how to play," he said, "in case I ever want to try it? Tell me what to do, show me where all those animals are supposed to go." He didn't have time for this, but he couldn't just walk away from Tyler and leave him here alone in such a defensive mood.

Tyler cast a suspicious glance at James out of the corner of his eye, but didn't refuse. Good step, James decided. Small one, but one that seemed headed in the right direction.

"You have to get the red bunnies in the biggest holes with their mommies…that's where they live. And the green squirrels up in the trees 'cause that's where they live with their mommies. And the baby bears have to go in the caves with their mommies so they're safe for the night, 'cause if you don't get them in before the moon comes out, they have to stay outside. But if you do get them all in before the moon, the moon comes out faster next time. And their houses move around."

"Is it bad if they have to stay out all night?" James asked, impressed by Tyler's command of the game.

"They get cold, and scared."

That wasn't in the game, of course, but for James the simple explanation proved what he'd suspected…Tyler was bright. And much more aware of his surroundings than he let on. "Would the mommies miss them if they had to stay out all night?"

A flash of hurt crossed Tyler's face, coming and going so fast that if James hadn't been watching for a reaction he would have missed it. "The mommies don't care," he said. "They have other little boys…bunnies and squirrels and baby bears to take care of."

"But would they miss their mommies?"

Tyler didn't answer that one. Rather, he turned his full attention to the game, clicking the controls like a child possessed. Soon he would have to have that serious talk with Tyler. The child deserved to know. "Look, I've got to get back to work. You do know what I do, don't you?"

Tyler shrugged.

Not to be daunted, James persisted. "I take care of sick people."

"Am I sick?" Tyler asked, keeping his gaze steady on the television screen even though, for the moment, he'd stopped playing. "Is that why my mommy always brings me to you? 'Cause I'm sick, and you're a doctor?"

It didn't get easier for the child. Or for James. "No, you're not sick. Except for your cuts and scrapes, you're in very good health. And remember last time we were together, when I told you I was your dad?"

"Donnie was my dad, too. But not any more. I like doctors better than dads!"

It was so hard, not telling him he wanted full custody. But what happened if he told Tyler, and Tyler counted on that, then the courts didn't comply? What happened if Shelly took him back yet again? "Look, Tyler, I've got to work now, but I'll check on you later. And, Tyler…" He handed the boy a slip of paper with his cellphone number written on it. "If you need to talk to me, call. You do know how to use a phone, don't you?"

Tyler didn't answer, but he did put the paper under his pillow. Then he scooted back to the middle of the bed, resumed his cross-legged position, and totally blocked James out.

"I'll be back when I can, Tyler," James said on his way out the door. But as usual Tyler didn't respond. All he did was turn up the volume of the game and click away on the control as fast as his little fingers would move.

Everything that could be made ready had been by the time the first patients began to be wheeled into the emergency department. Three burns cases went straight to James and a couple of smoke inhalations were assigned to Gabby, as well as a sprained ankle…someone falling down the stairs, trying to escape. "You OK?" Fallon asked, poking her head into the makeshift burn unit. James was busy with the worst of his patients, getting oxygen started on the man, a belligerent patient who was fighting James every step of the way. Dave Ellis was busy treating minor burns on the other two, who turned out to be kitchen workers at the lodge, while Catie, the volunteer, was setting up the supplies being called for by both Dave and James.

Immediately Fallon rushed into the room to help subdue the patient, who calmed down immediately when he saw who she was. She gave James a quick acknowledgment then pulled the IV set-up to the bedside. "You'll be fine, Mr. Chambers. You've got some serious burns to your chest, but once I can get the IV in, we'll get some pain medicine going and you'll feel much better."

"I've heard how bad burns can be, Miss O'Gara," the man managed from behind his oxygen mask.

"They can be, and I won't lie to you. Your chest and left shoulder look fairly involved, but it's a relatively small area. We're going to treat you here then send you to a burn unit in Salt Lake City, and you're going to be fine."

"Thank you," he whispered, fighting back tears.

She glanced over at James, who was busy cooling down the burns with saline. "Mr. Chambers is the caretaker at the lodge," she explained, as she squeezed the frightened man's hand. "His granddaughter is going to be a nurse."

"Like Miss O'Gara," the man said. "She helped Allison with her application to nursing school, let her work part time at the hospital after school, and even gave her a personal recommendation."

"Because she deserved it." Fallon deflected the direction of the conversation with a blush. "Look, I'll check back in on you before you go," she told him, then turned her attention on James. "Are you good here? I'd like to check in on Edith, if you don't need me..."

"Go," he said. "We're good."

Fallon was halfway to the hall when James caught up with her. "Are you OK?" he asked, taking hold of her arm to stop her. "You're running circles around everybody here."

"It's what I do..."

"Maybe it's what you do, but I'm concerned about you. It's going to be a long night, and you haven't done this for a while."

She bristled immediately. "You think I can't?"

"Oh, I'm sure you can. But you worry me."

"Well, I'm not yours to worry about, am I?" she said, jerking her arm away from him.

"That's not going to stop me from worrying, Fallon. One minute you don't ever want to step foot in the emergency department again, and the next you're working like a woman possessed. I understand the dynamics here. Everybody depends on you...the staff, the volunteers, even the patients. But what about you? Who do you depend on, especially when everything's going crazy the way it is?"

"I depend on me," she whispered. "Look, I appreciate your concern, but I got along fine before..." Before the accident, before James. Before so many things in her life had changed in ways she hated.

"Before me?" he asked.

"Yes," she said, trying to be defiant about it. But there was no defiance in her. "This is what I've always done, it's who I am." Rather, who she'd once been, and who she wanted to be again. Right now, she was play-acting her way through it, but someday, maybe...

"Not who you are, Fallon," he said, raising his hand to brush her cheek. "It's only a small part of you. There's so much more. So many things I'm not sure you even see."

For an instant she didn't flinch, it was as if she'd forgotten she was supposed to. Then, suddenly, she did. Flinched, pulled back. Cleared her throat to throw off the tension. "Look, Emoline will call for transport when you're ready to send Mr. Chambers to the burn unit. And I need to—"

"Don't overdo it, Fallon. That's all I'm saying. If you need help, you know where I am. Just ask me, will you?"

Just ask... So hard to do, because she wanted to separate from James, not draw closer or become more dependent. Except her heart wanted to meld so badly with his...

"Edith," she said, stepping into the quiet room a minute or two later. It was well away from all the activity, its window with a lovely view of the Older Sister. Safety for a moment. Away from James. "How are you feeling?" she asked, pulling up a chair to the old lady's bedside.

"I know you have more important things to do than sit with me," the woman said.

"There's nothing more important than sitting here with you for a few moments. And if anybody needs me, they know where I am."

"It's so good to see you working again. It's not too much for you, is it?"

"They need me, and I'm doing fine."

"Or you need them. Because you do need this, Fallon." Edith turned her head to the window. "It's a lovely sight," she said, "and I think it's true what they say about the Three Sisters protecting everyone in their shadows. I've lived a blessed life here. Wouldn't have changed a thing about it."

"It's an amazing place," Fallon agreed. "I missed it when I wasn't here." Wanted to get home. Ached to get home. "It was good to get back."

"Good to have you back," Edith choked out. "But you don't look happy, dear."

"I'm fine," she said. "It's been difficult, but I'm getting better."

"No, I don't think you are. Fine is OK, happy is better. You need to be happy again. The way you used to be. You don't smile now, and I miss that."

If only it was that simple. "I'm building up to…well, my old life, I suppose."

"You're blocking it out," Edith argued, then smiled. "Stubbornness. Good when you use it wisely, bad when you use it against yourself. And that's what you're doing, you know. You're denying what you want. Denying *that* you want."

"Can I get you something to drink, Edith? Some tea, or juice?"

"Ignoring it won't make it go away, Fallon."

"Where were you all those years when I needed a mother?"

Edith laughed. "You still need a mother, dear. We all do sometimes. And mothers come in so many forms, don't they?" She turned her head to the window. "Isn't it beautiful? I want to see the view while I still can." She drew in a wistful breath. "You need to see the whole view, Fallon. That's where you'll find your happiness." Her eyes started to flutter shut. "I promise, that's where you'll find it, *when* you want it badly enough."

Fallon pulled the sheet over Edith's shoulder and gave her a gentle kiss on the cheek. "It used to be a lovely view, Edith. But I can't bear looking at it any more."

"Stubborn," Edith whispered, although her eyes were closed. "That's all it is."

The hallway wall outside Edith's door turned out to be a great support as Fallon leaned heavily against it for a moment, thinking about the woman's words. *You need to see the whole view, Fallon. That's where you'll find your happiness.* The whole view...whatever that was. She wasn't sure she would want to see it even if she knew what it was.

Shutting her eyes, Fallon rubbed her head, bracing herself to go back to the emergency department. It was a stressful, busy night. She wanted it to be over, wanted the morning to dawn bright and sunny, wanted everything to be right. But she knew better. Practical experience was always the best teacher. And usually the harshest.

Harsh... She peeked into Tyler's room on her way back to Emergency. Harsh shouldn't have any place in the life of a child but sadly it did all too often. Poor Tyler was only at the beginning of what was going to be harsh in his world, and she wasn't sure there was any way around it. James would help him, though. He'd be an amazing father... *was* an amazing father. Someone who deserved to be an amazing father to other children. "You OK?" she asked from the doorway. Tyler was sitting on the bed, playing a video game.

"Fine," he said, his voice so quiet she barely heard him.

"You winning?"

He shrugged.

"Look, we're really busy in Emergency right now. But how about I come see you later, when things slow down?"

He shrugged again, and Fallon turned to leave. But before she had stepped away from the door, Tyler spoke up.

"Why?" he asked.

"Why what?"

"Why are you busy?"

"There was a big fire tonight at one of the buildings up on the mountain. If anybody gets hurt, we have to take care of them."

"I didn't do it!" he said, dropping his game controller and scurrying for the shelter of his blankets. "I didn't start the fire."

Fallon's cellphone took that particular moment to jingle. She glanced at the number...the emergency desk. "Hello," she said.

"It's about to break loose down here," Emoline Putters said. "They've been trickling in, nothing we couldn't manage, but one of the beams in the lodge came down, and we have four firefighters injured, as well as three of the hotel personnel. Don't know the extent of the injuries, but Eric is coming in with them. ETA ten minutes or less."

"I'm on my way." She clicked off, torn between hurrying to the ER and staying here a minute or two, trying to comfort the little boy who'd crawled all the way under his covers now. Not even his head was showing. "Look, Tyler," she said, "I know you didn't start that fire. It was an accident in the kitchen. The grease got too hot and when that happens it can cause a fire."

"Really?" he said, still covered.

"Really. No one meant it to happen, and we know you didn't start it."

"That's why he doesn't want me," he said.

"Who?"

"My first dad...Donnie."

"Because of a fire?"

He didn't say anything, but she saw the blanket bob up and down and took that for a yes.

"Did you start a fire at your house?"

"He said so, but I didn't do it."

"What kind of fire?"

"In his chair. He was sleeping and it just caught on fire."

"In Donnie's chair," she said, just to be sure.

The blankets bobbed up and down again.

"And Donnie said you started the fire in his chair?"

"Said it was my fault 'cause I didn't get it. I was supposed to get it when he went to sleep, and I forgot."

"What, Tyler? What were you suppose to get?"

"His cigarette," he said, snuffling. "I always had to get his cigarette."

Fallon drew in a furious breath, trying to keep her voice calm for Tyler's sake. "So he'd go to sleep while he was smoking and it was your job to take the lit cigarette from him when he did?"

"Uh-huh."

Fallon's phone rang before she could respond. She glanced at the number. It was Emoline Putters, getting impatient, she guessed. "Look, Tyler, we know the fire up at the lodge wasn't your fault. Nobody's blaming you." While she truly wanted to comfort Tyler over what Donnie had done to him, and tell him that it wasn't his fault, that Donnie shouldn't have done that, it wasn't her place. Like

Edith had said, everybody needed a mother sometimes, but she wasn't Tyler's mother, and she had to remember that. Had to remember that the mothering instinct she felt toward him was because he was her son's brother. *But Tyler was not hers.* He belonged to James, and this was something James would have to deal with. "Look, I'll be back in a while, Tyler, and maybe you can show me how to play that game."

He poked his head out from under the covers. "I'll beat you," he warned.

She smiled. "I'm sure you will."

On her way back to the ER, she thought about the many ways she'd like to throttle that Donnie character, and every which way seemed too kind. A man like that deserved...

"From the look on your face, I'd say you're about to tie someone up with surgical tape," James said. He was bandaging the hands of the cook who'd tried dousing the grease fire with water. Not a good move. The fire had leapt from the pan. Luckily, the cook had managed to jump back far enough that his injuries weren't serious.

She went to the sink to scrub her hands. "Surgical tape's too good. I want something that'll hurt more coming off."

"Not for me, I hope," he teased.

"For Donnie."

"Donnie? As in...?"

"The man who *isn't* Tyler's father! Tyler thinks he'll be accused of starting the fire at the lodge," she said, trying to keep her temper in check, even though she was so angry she was almost shaking.

"I don't understand."

"I mentioned that we had to take care of people from the fire and he said he didn't start it. Because of the way he reacted, I asked him if he'd ever started a fire at his house, and he said his dad accused him of it. It seems one of Tyler's *chores* was to pull a burning cigarette from Donnie's lips if Donnie dozed off. Apparently once Tyler didn't do it and Donnie's chair caught on fire."

"Damn," James muttered, as he rolled gauze over the fleshy part of the cook's palm.

"I hated to leave him but we've got several people coming in at the same time and…"

"I understand," James said, through gritted teeth.

"He's fine, James. For now, he's fine."

"Plucking lit cigarette butts from the lips of his step-father… A mother who allows that…" He looked up at the ceiling, clearly trying to grapple with his emotions. "Nothing about him is fine, Fallon. The kind of life he has to live with his mother… The thing is, I should be there to help him, right now when he's afraid he'll be accused of starting the fire. But I'm not there, like I wasn't there when *you* needed me."

She stiffened. "Don't turn this into something about me! I told you I understood, James. Tyler needed you then, and you had to be with him. *He* needed you, and I was fine. And I'm pretty sure Tyler understands why you're not there now," she said, even though she knew James was right. Tyler needed his father…his real father. Right now. "Once Eric gets back, maybe you can go to him."

Maybe turned out to be a fantasy when seven patients rolled through the door, one after the other. Not only had Eric come in with them, so had Neil. "Fallon," Eric called, from down the hall. "I'll need you in room three. Get me an oxygen set-up and an IV."

"Fallon," Neil yelled, from the other end of the hall, "get respiratory therapy in here, stat."

"Fallon, we need bandages down here in exam two,

and can you check the vitals on the patient in exam one...
he claims he has high blood pressure, and I'm afraid the
stress of all this might be too much for him." That from
Gabby.

And so went the next two hours, with Fallon running
from place to place, being all things to everyone. In a spare
moment James watched her. Simply leaned against the hall
wall for ten seconds and observed—his first time ever to
see what she did so well—and it took only a moment to
understand why everybody in the hospital praised her so
highly. Fallon was amazing. Absolutely everybody here
on every medical level depended on Fallon to do, well,
pretty much everything. And she did, without ever missing
a beat. She responded to the doctors, took time to comfort
the patients, directed the volunteers and nursing staff. Yes,
she was truly amazing. And if he hadn't fallen in love with
her all those months ago, he'd have fallen head over heels
in love tonight.

Damn, he wanted to make things right with her. He
wasn't sure how, wasn't even sure what, but there had to
be a way. But he had to make things right for Tyler, too.
And that thought overwhelmed him. Fallon...Tyler... How
was he going to do it? How was he going to be everything
both of them needed?

"I think you're good to go see Tyler," she said as she
rushed by him. "No more burns coming in, and word from
the scene is that there are no more casualties. So I'd say
now is as good a time as any to get out of here."

He reached out and caught her arm. Stopped her and,
surprisingly, she didn't yank away from him, as he'd expected her to do. In fact, she looked grateful for the momentary break. "You need to slow down," he said.

"I will."

"Now. You look...exhausted."

"And I feel exhausted, but it's almost over. All the serious injuries have been treated, and as soon as we get the barrage of minor injures taken care of, I'm going to take a break."

"How about I go check on Tyler for a minute then come back and take over Triage for you while you go put your feet up for a while? It's showing on you, Fallon. It's been months since you've worked this hard physically, and I'm worried."

"I appreciate that. And you're right. I *am* out of shape."

"Then for once you'll listen to someone else?"

Stubborn was what Edith had called her. She wore that with some amount of pride but sometimes it did get in the way. "I'll listen. But just this once, and don't get used to it."

James chuckled. "You do have your red-headed ways, don't you? I think one of the first things I liked about you was that stubborn streak. At least, some of it."

"I prefer to think of it as independent, not stubborn."

He chuckled again. "Like I said…" This was the old Fallon, and it was so nice to have her back. Even if only for a moment. "Look, let me get out of your way, go see Tyler. Then I'll be right back. OK? You're not going to go back on your word, are you?"

"No. Unless someone needs me."

No one needs you like I do, he thought. Then he spun away before he said the words aloud. But Fallon reached out, grabbed hold of his hand, and pulled him back to her.

"I know it's not the way you want it to be between us, James. And I know this is hard on you. But someday you'll realize that what we're doing now is the way it has to be. And in the meantime…" She stood on tiptoe and brushed a light kiss on his cheek. "Thank you. Thank you for caring about me, thank you for helping me and, most of all thank you for letting me be part of Tyler's life. He's an amazing little boy. So go. If he's awake, tell him I'm anxious for my first lesson."

"Lesson?"

"Video game. He's going to teach me how to play."

"Are we talking about *my* Tyler? The little boy who breaks things? *That's* the Tyler who offered to teach you how to play?"

"One and the same. We had a talk earlier, have a little bet going that he'll beat me."

James blinked hard. "Amazing. I can't even get him to talk to me, and here he's offering to play games with you? How'd you do that, Fallon?" He was surprised and, admittedly, a little hurt at the same time. Tyler wanting to teach Fallon was a good thing, but it would have been nice if Tyler had made the same offer to him. Of course, Fallon was Fallon, and everybody responded to her that way. He had. So why should Tyler be the exception?

She tossed James a sassy wink. "I'll never tell." This time she was the one who spun away from him.

As it turned out, Tyler was sound asleep when James finally got back to his room. So he stayed but a moment, pulled the covers up over him, gave him a light kiss on the forehead then returned to Fallon. When he found her, she was carrying a stack of IV set-ups to the central supply area. He took them from her then she was off to take a break. Like a whirlwind, James thought. Damn, he loved that whirlwind.

"You OK?" James asked.

She was studying the choices of soft drinks in the vending machine, trying to decide between the orange and the strawberry. She'd been standing and staring blankly at them for the past several minutes, almost too numb to think. "I'm fine. Just ready to call it a night and go home. Everybody has been seen, we've transported a few people to Salt Lake City, most of the volunteers have left. So, after a sugar boost from one of these cans, I'm out of here."

"And your friend Edith?"

"Good. Giving me hell for being so stubborn. But good. I'm going to make arrangements to send her to her sister in Florida for a few weeks. Edith needs some warm weather and sunshine, I think. She asked me to come along and be her private duty nurse." An intriguing idea, and a tempting one. But she'd had to turn it down because, well... she wasn't sure. Somehow she just couldn't bring herself to leave White Elk. Funny thing was, just a few days ago she'd have probably jumped at the chance to get away for a while. Now she couldn't. "All expenses paid. Beachfront cottage. Amazing restaurants. A dream come true."

"And?"

"And I turned it down. Arranged for Jessica Walthers to go in my place. She's a retired nurse, widowed. I thought the warm weather would do her some good."

"It wouldn't do you any good?" James asked, the corners of his mouth turning up.

Fallon looked away. "I have a job now."

"But Gabby's not in a big hurry. Besides, most of what you're doing to get her hospital set up could probably be done from a warm, sunny beach in Florida."

"I don't fly any more. Edith is going to fly."

"Take a train and meet her there. I'll bet it would be a nice, relaxing ride across country."

"So how's Tyler?" she asked, turning back to the drinks machine, trying to change the subject, trying to ignore what James was hoping to get her to admit—that she was staying because of him, because of Tyler. "Last time I looked in on him he was busy playing his game. Doing really well with it, too. He taught me a couple of things, then turned around and beat me. And had the audacity to laugh at me."

"I've never seen him laugh."

"I'm sorry, James. I never…"

"Don't be sorry. It's good he's comfortable with you. God knows, he's not with me. But if it's not me, I'm glad it's you, Fallon. I trust you with my son."

His words were like a sharp knife through her heart. Words that were meant well and turned into bitter, deep pain. "I, um…I want to go home," she said. "Get some sleep." Get away from James. Get away from the reminders.

"Then I'll drive you. And if you don't want me there, I'll come back and sleep in one of the on-call rooms… won't even try and persuade you to let me stay."

"I can drive myself."

"You're exhausted."

That, she was. And this was an argument she wasn't going to win because she was in no condition to drive.

"How about this? I'll take you home, and when we get there you can decide what you want to do with me? Fair enough?"

"I'm not going to send you away. But…"

"But you're still not easy with the decision of having me stay there…not when Tyler's not there."

"Maybe a little. But he'll be there in a day or so. And I want him to be comfortable, to be settled. And with Christmas coming…"

He shushed her with a finger to her lips. "One day at a time, Fallon. And on this day I'm taking you home to sleep. When you wake up, we'll decide what happens from there. OK?"

She nodded her agreement. He was so easy to give in to. And that was the problem. She wanted to give in. With James, she always wanted to give in.

Fallon slept the whole way home and, to be honest, she didn't remember getting out of the car and walking into her house. Surely, the brisk winter wind or the falling snow would have woken her up, but her first recollection when she finally opened her eyes was of her sofa. She was under the patchwork quilt she kept on the back of it, all comfy and safe. She was still tired, and a little achy from over-exertion. Most of all, though, she was really wishing the morning light wasn't peeking in through the living-room curtains because she wasn't ready to start the day.

"I didn't look when I undressed you," James said.

He handed her a mug of coffee, but she refused it. Instead, she peeked under the covers to find, much to her relief, that she was still dressed. No snow boots, no socks, but otherwise decent.

"You thought I'd strip you naked?" he teased.

"I don't know what you'd do." Finally, she snatched the mug from him and took a sip.

"Actually, what I did was carry you in from the truck."

"No, you didn't," she said, forcing herself to sit up.

"Well, somebody did. And I'm the only one here." He stepped back then grinned at her. "You've put on a couple pounds, Fallon. And I've got the sore muscles to prove it."

"I have not," she argued, realizing he was just trying to get a rise out of her.

"If that's how you want to argue this thing, that's fine with me."

"You!" she said, tossing a throw pillow at him. 'You always did like to goad me into things."

"Or out of things…like your clothes, if I recall. But that didn't take much goading, did it? In fact, I remember a few times when you—"

She thrust out her hand to stop him. Just like that, the light moment between them was over and all the bad things were weighing her down again. "Not the past, James. I don't want to talk about the past."

"Was it that bad for you, Fallon? Because I thought you were happy…we were happy together."

They had been. She had been. But that had been a different life. One to which neither of them could ever return. And the way this conversation was turning into those memories—that was the reason she couldn't be around him. It was too painful.

Fallon cleared her throat. "Is…um…is Tyler going to be released today?"

The expression on James's face shifted almost instantly, going from warm and caring to reserved. "Eric wanted to run another set of tests this morning…a fasting blood sugar in case his mood swings are coming from an onset of diabetes, but he'll release Tyler after lunch if nothing shows up. Under the present circumstances, I don't think we should come back here to stay. You need more rest, and—"

"We can get along, James. You can bring Tyler back here, and the three of us can get along."

"The three of us, maybe, but what about the two of us?" James sighed deeply, audibly. "I don't know any more, Fallon. One minute you and I are doing fine, then the next…" He walked away from her, went to the kitchen door, and stopped, but didn't turn back around. "Tyler responds to you. That's a good thing and I'd like to see if you can draw out more in him than I've been able to. I think he might warm up to the maternal instinct in you, and you do have that toward Tyler. It's pretty obvious. But this animosity between you and me…"

She was afraid of that, afraid that denying her maternal instinct wasn't enough. But what could she do? She was a mother without her baby, and he was a little boy without a real mother. Those were situations she couldn't change, situations that were causing what James was seeing. But it was temporary. Once James and Tyler found another place to live… "Not animosity, James. I don't have *any* bad feelings toward you. And for what it's worth, I want you to stay. I just don't want you and me to live in the past because we can't get that back."

He finally turned around. "Then why do I feel like I never lost it, Fallon? Because I still have the same feelings for you. Still have the same reactions whenever we're together."

"You'll move on. Once your relationship is more settled with Tyler, you *will* move on."

"The way you have? Because I hope to God that doesn't happen to me. I loved what we had, what we were. And I don't want to lose it or, worse, pretend it never existed."

"It existed," she said, praying the tears wouldn't come. But she could feel them, stinging in the backs of her eyes. "It existed then it was gone." But not forgotten. Never, ever forgotten.

But now it was a shadow. One that broke her heart.

CHAPTER SIX

"Basically, he's healthy. Couldn't find a thing wrong with him except his blood sugar was a little off. But that could be stress working on him. I'd like to test him again in six months, after his life has settled down, and see what we get then. In the meantime, just make sure he gets a healthy diet, and you'll be fine." Eric sat the chart down on the desk. "And maybe I should prescribe the same for you, James. Because you're looking really stressed out."

"I am. I'll admit it. I'm living with Fallon, still in love with her and pretty much facing her brick walls every time I turn around. And I have a son who barely speaks to me, who's destructive, who may get yanked away from me at any minute if, or when, his mother decides she wants him again. I'd say that's stress."

Eric shook his head. "Anything I can do, James. Just name it, and I'll try my best."

"Do you know a good local lawyer? My last lawyer… well, let's just say that he went off to seek his fame and fortune chasing ambulances, which leaves me high and dry. And I really do need to file for custody before Shelly does whatever it is Shelly intends to do next."

"Actually, I have a great attorney—Jason Greene. Say the word, and I'll make a call."

James didn't even hesitate. "Make the call. I'm ready

for the battle, and I hope that the way Shelly has abandoned Tyler with me three times in six months counts for something. This attorney, Jason Greene, has to be good enough to make it count for something, because I want Tyler all the way. Full, permanent custody, with limited visitation from his mother and none from the stepfather of his."

Eric patted him on the back. "Jason's good enough. I'll call him this morning, see if he can get you in right away. He has a chronic upset stomach, a symptom of his profession, and he's had a few spur-of-the-moment appointments with me, so now it's payback time."

"You know, the longer I stay in White Elk, the more I like it. I think the lifestyle could be addictive. The people here sure are."

"That's why we're expanding our medical facilities. Once people stay here for a while, they never leave. It's what happened to me. Neil convinced me to come, give it a try. Now I own a hospital, I have a wife, I've just bought a new house." Eric smiled the smile of a contented man. "What can I say? Life in White Elk is good. I hope that happens for you soon, too."

"So do I, for Tyler. I think I'd like to raise him here. Look, I've got to make rounds in the pediatric ward. If Jason Greene agrees to take me on as a client, tell him I'll free myself up to meet him at his earliest convenience."

Jason Greene's earliest convenience turned out to be late afternoon and it was amazing how much better James felt after the appointment was set. For the first time in days he allowed himself to feel a little hopeful that this situation could work out for the both of them…him and Tyler. Father and son. Father and son and…Fallon. No! He wouldn't allow himself to think that. Not when he was more than willing to meet her in the middle, but the closer he got to that middle, the more she backed away. Right now, it was up to Fallon. Her steps to make. Her choices. Yet, he hoped...dear God, he really hoped...

"Ready to go home?" he asked Tyler, just as the lunch tray was being carried from his room. James noticed that Tyler hadn't eaten a bite. He'd also been told that Tyler had refused breakfast.

Tyler shrugged.

"Dr. Ramsey said you're good to go."

Tyler's reaction was to clutch the video game control tight to his chest. "Don't want to," he said. Not the words James wanted to hear, but at least Tyler was finally speaking. "Why not?" he asked.

"'Cause Fallon doesn't have games."

"I thought you liked Fallon."

Tyler shrugged.

"I'm pretty sure she likes you, even though you broke her shelves." He was sure Tyler liked Fallon, so this resistance came as a surprise. "And she's fixed up a room for you."

He shrugged again.

"And I think she wants to make a snowman with you."

He shrugged once more, but this time something about the snowman had, apparently, sparked his interest. "A little one?" Tyler asked.

"Not too little. One at least as big as you are."

"Or as big as you?"

Finally, his son was responding. "Well, I suppose you could make a snowman as big as me, but it might fall over."

"Head's too big," Tyler said shyly. Then giggled.

"What?" That was the first time he'd heard Tyler

giggle, or even seen him smile. It was a surprise that gave him hope.

"Head's too big, that's why it'll fall over."

"How about you make one, and I'll make one and we'll see which one won't fall over."

"Can Fallon make one, too?"

"Of course she can. But maybe we should keep a little secret from her."

Tyler eyes widened. "What?" he asked, almost whispering it.

"Maybe if we don't tell her that a big head is the reason it'll fall over, then she'll make the biggest head and hers will fall over first."

Tyler giggled again, but didn't answer. James could see the mischief dancing in his eyes for a moment. It was a good sign. After all these months it was a very good sign. "Let's get out of here, OK?"

Surprisingly, Tyler latched right on to James's hand. To casual observers in the hospital hallway who didn't know any better, they looked like a perfectly normal father and son.

"I'm so glad," Fallon said, resisting the urge to throw her arms around James's neck. It was her natural reaction, but she had to stop doing that, and after her last hug she'd reaffirmed her resolve. Shored it up, braced it with steel, braced it with steel again for an extra layer. "And Jason Greene's really good." They were speaking in hushed tones so Tyler wouldn't overhear. "Tyler needs to be in your custody no matter what, and the sooner the better. It scares me to death when I think that Shelly might come back here and get him. Especially after what he told me about how Donnie used to make him take the lit cigarettes from his mouth. That's a horrible thing to do to a child and I don't know how any mother would tolerate that."

"A good mother wouldn't," James said. "But who ever said Shelly was a good mother?"

"Well, it's started, James. And that's good. Tyler really needs to feel safe and secure, and Jason will be amazing. He has five children of his own, loves kids. He won't let Shelly get away with anything." Her gaze went to Tyler, who was sitting by himself, staring out the window. "Maybe I could watch Tyler for you during your appointment? I'm finished working for the day, so it wouldn't be a problem." There she was, getting involved again. One layer of steel slipping away and she was doing nothing to stop it. If she had any sense, she'd run upstairs, hide behind her locked door, and not come out.

"Actually, I wanted to take him with me. I need to find more ways to be with him when I'm not working. But you could come along, I know he'd love that. And maybe we could have dinner at Catie's Overlook afterwards."

It was a nice offer, but too cozy. She simply wasn't ready for anything like that. "Sorry, but I have dinner plans," she dodged. Dinner for one, whatever she could grab from her fridge. "But you and Tyler go, and enjoy yourselves. Tell Catie to give Tyler a piece of her extra-special chocolate cake." She said that purposely loud so Tyler *would* hear.

Tyler twisted ever so slightly to look at Fallon, fighting hard not to show too much interest in that chocolate cake but losing the battle the way most little boys would at the mention of something so yummy.

She tossed a knowing smile at James. "You know which one I'm talking about…three layers, all kinds of chocolate frosting?" With her hands, she gestured something that was a good three times the size of any cake Catie offered, and Tyler's eyes widened to twice their size. "The one that comes with a huge scoop of vanilla ice cream."

That was more than any child could take. Tyler finally turned the whole way around to face James. "Can I have chocolate ice cream instead?"

"If you're very polite when you ask Catie, and say please and thank you."

"I want Fallon to come, too," Tyler said. "So she won't find out while we're gone."

Fallon sensed a little conspiracy going on between father and son. "What don't you want me to find out?" she asked.

"Our secret."

Fallon winked at James then immediately looked back at Tyler. "You have a secret?"

He nodded, and kept a very serious face.

"Will you tell me your secret?"

Tyler shook his head then looked to James for approval. James gave him the thumbs-up sign, and nodded. "If I tell, then it's not a secret," Tyler explained very seriously to Fallon.

"But is it about me?" she asked.

This time Tyler merely shrugged. But he was trying to fight back a smile. And, oh, how she wanted to see that smile.

"So, if it's about me, should I know what it is?"

Tyler rolled his eyes up to James for help with this answer. And James answered. "But if you know what it is, then it's no fun any more."

"So, it's a fun secret?" Her question was directed at Tyler, who nodded his head. "But is it fun for you, or for me?"

"Me," he admitted. "And…him." He nodded toward James.

"Then what you're telling me is that it's the two of you against me?"

Both James and Tyler nodded. And when Fallon saw that, her eyes nearly filled with tears. They were so much alike. Looked alike. Acted alike. Same mannerisms. Same mischievous sparkle in their eyes. "OK, if that's the way you're going to be, then I might just have to come with you and eat all of Catie's chocolate cake before you have a chance to order some."

"It's about the snowman's big head," Tyler blurted quickly. "It makes the snowman fall over. Now can I have the cake?"

Fallon turned away abruptly. "This is so good," she whispered to James. "He's an amazing little boy," she continued, swiping away a tear threatening to slip down her cheek.

"Is Fallon crying?" Tyler asked James.

"Looks like she is."

"Am not," she denied.

"I'm sorry," Tyler said, slipping his hand into her. "I didn't mean to make you cry."

One tear turned into a waterfall, and she excused herself from the room before Tyler felt any worse. Right now she was just so darned happy for no reason she could understand that her cry was going to take a good half-dozen tissues.

"Happy tears," James reassured Tyler. "Women do that."

"Women," Tyler said, mimicking James's tone of voice. "They just do that."

James had to clear his throat and refocus, because he was about to do that, too.

* * *

The appointment with Jason Greene was short. Fifteen minutes was all it took then James was back in the waiting room, where Fallon was busy watching Tyler play with a video game. She'd decided to come with them, but only because Tyler had braved the stairs, knocked on her door, and asked her. "He said it's promising." James put on his jacket. "But there's a lot of research to do first. He thinks, though, that if everything is as I think it is, it could go my way because Shelly is establishing a clear pattern of behavior." A heavy sigh escaped him. "He warned me that it could be a long, expensive fight if she doesn't want to surrender custody, because oftentimes parents like Shelly who don't want their children will put up the fight anyway, for appearances or financial gain."

"And?"

"Let the fight begin, if that's what happens. It's not about the money and Jason said he's going to make sure it's not about what Shelly wants since she's proving she *doesn't* want Tyler. I'm actually conservatively optimistic about this, Fallon. Jason said I shouldn't start celebrating yet, but I feel like celebrating, anyway."

"Small celebration," she said, smiling.

His looked over at Tyler, who was so engrossed in some kind of virtual reality he hadn't even noticed James standing there. "I see video games in my future."

"Then be prepared to take a beating because he's good. And I'm not just saying he's good for a five-year-old. He's good for anyone."

"With all the bad things that have gone on around him, he's really struggling to be a normal little boy, isn't he? The kids I see in my practice are just like him…fixed on the games, paying no attention to the adults. Creating their own little worlds."

"He needs to be normal, James. Needs it all the time, not just when he's with you."

"Well, no matter what else is going on with Tyler, Jason's going to file for emergency temporary custody first thing tomorrow morning. He thinks I'll have a pretty good chance of having it granted this time, and that having temporary custody gives me a much stronger position when we get to the hearing for full custody. Besides, it's a good safeguard for Tyler. If Shelly does come back, I won't have to give him to her. She'll actually have to hire a lawyer and go to court to get him back as long as the temporary custody is in force."

Tyler glanced up at the mention of his name, clearly torn between what was being said about him and staying involved in the race between to two cars on the game screen. His car was winning. "What's good for me?" he asked, then immediately switched his attention back to the game.

"Staying with me without going anywhere else for a while."

With those words spoken, Tyler crashed his car and the game was over. He held onto the game controler for a little while, and the frown on his face clearly indicated he was thinking about what James had said. Finally, when he'd processed it, satisfied he understood, he looked up. "Like back to my mom and my old dad?"

"In a way," James hedged. "You OK with that, Tyler?"

Tyler responded with his typical shrug then stood up. "Are we still going to live with Fallon?"

"For a while, if she doesn't mind."

He shrugged that one off too. Gave a wistful glance over his shoulder at the video game set-up then headed for the door. "It's going to be boring," he muttered. "She doesn't have games."

Fallon bit back a laugh at that comment, and if the expression on James's face could have screamed anything, it would have screamed, *God, help me!* He held out his hand for Tyler, though, and for the second time Tyler took hold.

Fallon, bringing up the rear as they walked to the parking lot, brushed away a tear once more.

The walk to Catie's Overlook was pleasant. White Elk looked like Christmas now. Old-fashioned streetlamps were decorated with pine boughs and red ribbons, merchants' windows were strung with lights. The Christmas-tree festival was under way, where each little shop owner purchased a well-grown live tree, set it in front of his or her shop and sponsored the decorating. In other words, anyone who wanted could pay to decorate one of these trees, and the proceeds would go to charity, which, this year, was the pediatric ward at the hospital. And, more specifically, a program in the planning stages at present that would help children with juvenile diabetes. It was a good deed in that the cause was worthy but also a good deed in giving White Elk an authentic Christmas charm. With a nice dusting of snow covering everything, it was a fairyland. Beautiful. And if Fallon had been in a Christmas mood this year, this would have made her feel even more in the mood.

But she wasn't. Christmas just didn't mean anything now, the way it had never meant much when she'd been a child. Back then her Christmases had been filled more with sadness than anything else, because she had always been the child who hadn't belonged, the one who'd been staying with a distant relative, the child who hadn't fitted in. Usually the gifts she'd got had been last minute or thoughtless. Sometimes she hadn't got a gift…nobody had thought to buy one for the little girl who hadn't really belonged there. And to be honest, she didn't remember ever spending Christmas with the same people. One year she'd be packed off to distant cousin Flora, the next she'd end up with Great-Aunt Henrietta. And so her Christmases went. No fond memories.

But not for Tyler, if she had anything to do with it. If his Christmas memories from the past were bad, this would be the year they would be good. This year, and every year after, she hoped. Because now Tyler was in White Elk with his dad. And Christmas was about the little boy whose face was pressed to the toy-store window, looking at the toy train set he saw there and the box of building blocks. Being just like every other little boy at this time of the year. Like her little boy would have been… "I was thinking about a Christmas tree," she said, before the sad thoughts had time to take hold. "Do you think we should get a little one?"

Tyler rolled his eyes, but didn't offer an opinion.

"Maybe, instead of having a tree at home, we could sponsor one of the charity trees and decorate that?"

Tyler shook his head this time, and actually looked up at James, as if asking him to intercede here.

James looked at Fallon, winked. "Maybe we don't need a tree. I haven't had one since I lived at home with my parents, and I don't miss it. Instead of a tree, maybe we could buy a potted plant and hang a few glass balls on it. That would look like Christmas, wouldn't it?"

"But I want a *real* Christmas tree," Tyler cried. "A great big one! With lots of lights."

Was that the kind of tree he'd had with his mother and Donnie, or was that another of his wishes? Maybe one that had never come true. Fallon wondered if Tyler had ever had nice Christmases, or had they been miserable, like the ones she'd had when she'd been young? "You might have to help me move furniture so we can get a big one in the house."

Tyler nodded eagerly. "And throw some of it away if there's not room for the tree."

Fallon laughed. Well, the child was enthusiastic about something. And the way his eyes sparkled…he was James. Easy to love. "I think we'll manage without throwing away my furniture," she said. "And, Tyler, we're going to have to buy new decorations. I've always had a little tree and I don't have enough to decorate a big tree. So, will you be in charge of picking out the decorations?"

He hesitated for a moment, didn't respond as eagerly as she'd expected. Then he reverted back to his usual behavior. He shrugged, and totally zoned out of all the Christmas decorations strung up everywhere as they continued their walk to Catie's. The reaction of a child who'd built up hopes before then had them destroyed.

It was a delicate balance and she and James were going to have to be careful because, now that she'd started Christmas for Tyler, she didn't want to ruin it for him, too.

Pulling her scarf up tighter around her face to fight off the chilly air whipping around her, Fallon dropped back and walked behind James and Tyler, and twice, when James glanced over his shoulder at her, she feigned fascination with something in a shop window. Maybe she shouldn't have gotten involved. Because she was becoming almost as excited about Christmas as Tyler had been for a little while, and that wasn't good. She was used to living without the hopes and promises now, and here she was, building a few around something she couldn't have. And she really did want a Christmas tree…a big one. With lots of lights.

"He went right to sleep," James said, dropping down onto the couch next to Fallon, keeping his proper distance from her, of course. "I sat with him about five minutes, thought he might ask some questions about why he was going to keep on living with me for a little while, or maybe talk about the Christmas tree, but he just turned over on his side and went to sleep. It was a big day for him. I think we actually wore him out."

"He's had a turbulent life so far. He copes by acting out or by not acting at all. Probably the only two reactions in his young repertoire. And as far as the Christmas tree goes, I have an idea he's learned not to count on anything. If you don't count on it, you don't end up being disappointed." She raised her mug of hot chocolate to her lips, but paused before she took a sip. "It's not a mistake, is it, giving him this big Christmas?"

He laughed. "Giving a child a big Christmas? I think it's absolutely the best thing we can do for him. Tyler needs something to look forward to in his life. I don't think he's ever really had that."

"You, too," she added. "You need something to look forward to."

"And what about you? What do you need, Fallon?"

"Nothing. I never had good Christmases when I was growing up, and I don't need them now."

"I'm not talking about Christmas, specifically. What do you need in life, Fallon? There was a time I thought I knew, but maybe I was wrong. I mean, we talked about having a large family. You wanted a big house for all those children we were going to have. You didn't want to quit work because you were totally devoted to the idea that a woman is capable of doing everything she wants. But now I don't know if that's what you need in your life, and I want to know. It bothers me that I don't. Or that I might have been wrong all along."

She bristled. "This isn't about me. I invited you to live here because it was supposed to be about Tyler. *Only Tyler.* And I don't want you to make this about something it's not."

He held up his hand to stop her. "Whoa, there. You really do have a way about turning a nice, innocent conversation into something adversarial, don't you?"

"It wasn't innocent, James. When you made it about me, it was anything *but* innocent. You know you were trying to manipulate me, trying to take advantage of the moment to pry into something that's none of your business any more."

"What if that's what I was doing? I'm not admitting it, but for the sake of the argument, what if I did try to make it about you? Is that really so bad?"

"It is when I laid down the ground rules about you staying here."

"Fallon! For God's sake. We've made love. I've seen that little heart-shaped birthmark on your back. Doesn't that give me some rights?"

"No," she snapped. "That was then. This is…this is another time, another life. And you know my terms, James. If you can't live with them, I won't kick you out, but I'll take a room at the lodge until you and Tyler can make better arrangements."

"But aren't you the one who keeps stepping over the line? Be honest with yourself, Fallon. Aren't you the one who keeps getting involved?"

"With Tyler. I'm getting involved with Tyler."

"But getting involved with Tyler is getting involved with me."

That much was true. And she'd have to try harder to stop it. "I think I can separate the two of you."

"I don't believe that! Sometimes when I see the way you look at him, there's such longing. And I remember that look, Fallon. Used to see it when we talked about our future. Talked about the children we wanted to have and the life we wanted to build for them."

"You're wrong, but go ahead and believe whatever you want. I really don't care!"

James ran a frustrated hand through his hair. "OK, that little heart on your back aside, we had something good going on between us. I messed up after your accident, but I thought we could put that behind us and move on from there. Hoped we could, anyway."

"We can. I'm *not* angry that you had to choose Tyler over me. That's what you should have done…what you should always do. But, James, that was so long ago, and I've been through so much. I can't be *that* Fallon any more. She's gone. She's not coming back."

"She's not that far away, Fallon," he said gently. "I see her all the time, when she's not trying to be so… guarded."

Unfortunately, that was the problem. She couldn't hide from James. Couldn't hide anything. "Not guarded, James. Just not the same. And that's what you've got to understand. So back to your original question… What do I want? I want the best Christmas ever for Tyler. I want him to be with someone who cares enough to help him build some hopes."

"The way you do?" he asked gently.

"The way *you* do," she replied.

"Like a real family," James said. "A real family for Christmas."

"For Tyler," she reminded him "Like a real family *for Tyler*, for Christmas." To think of it in any other way hurt too much.

"Then tell me what happens when Tyler starts loving the mother in this little Christmas family, and she eventually walks away from him?"

"Are you talking about you, or Tyler?" she asked, pushing herself off the couch. "Because if we want to help Tyler, we've got to get over this. *You've* got to get over it." *She* had to get over it.

"As in getting over *you*? Is that what you mean?"

"Something like that."

He shook his head. "You know what, Fallon? Your friends have given you a lot of slack because of the accident. They've done everything you wanted them to do because they loved you, even if what you wanted essentially pushed them away, maybe even hurt them. I don't know why you keep pushing people away, and I don't want to argue about it. But I'm not giving you that same slack. You can't tell me to get over you and expect that I'll just do it because you want me to. It doesn't work that way. Not when I love you. And I do love you. So, no, I'm not getting over you. Like I've said, already, and I'll keep saying, I'll respect the distance you want…the boundaries you've built up around yourself. But you can't tell me how I have to feel about you. You don't have that right." He stood, too. "Look, I'm going for a walk, to clear my head. I'll be back in half an hour." Then he threw on his jacket and walked out the front door. More like strode out the front door, with every harsh footstep she heard on the hardwood floor a testament to exactly what he was feeling.

In a small way she was flattered. In an even bigger way she was scared. Not because he'd told her off. But because he'd been right. About everything. Except him being right about everything still didn't make things right in her life. Because nothing there was right, and she still didn't believe it could be right ever again. Not without James…and Tyler. Not without James Allen Galbraith, Junior. But that's the way it was, whether or not James Allen Galbraith, Senior, liked it or not.

Three hours of tossing and turning, and she was barely asleep when the first crash startled her awake. The second one sent her over the edge of the bed and scurrying to pull on her bathrobe. The third crash propelled her out her bedroom door and straight to the top of the stairs, where she looked down and saw James, dressed in boxer shorts and a T-shirt running for the kitchen. He didn't look like he'd had much sleep either.

Fallon padded down the stairs, wondering if her bare feet would be safe, considering what she expected to find in the wake of Tyler's tirade, and fell into step behind James who, she had to admit, looked downright sexy first thing in the morning. Sexy and, right this moment, ready to explode.

"Tyler," he called on his way through the kitchen door. "What are you doing?"

Fallon, who was so close behind him she could practically smell his aftershave, bumped right into the back of him when he stopped dead in his tracks. She braved a peek around James, expecting the worst, only to see Tyler standing there amid a clutter of pots and pans all over the floor, along with spilled silverware and practically every utensil she'd had in the drawer. But on the counter were three bowls, filled to the top with breakfast cereal and overflowing with milk, which was dripping down into the open, and empty, utensil drawer. Along with the cereal were three slices of bread smeared from crust to crust with strawberry jam…jam that was likewise slathered across a good portion of the counter top. And there were three poured glasses of orange juice, with a fair measure of juice trickling down the front of the cabinet.

It was a spectacular mess to behold, and Tyler was standing in the middle of that mess, grinning from ear to ear—his first real grin. He'd fixed them breakfast.

"It looks delicious," she said quite brightly as she stepped away from James and pulled a kitchen stool over to the breakfast counter. As delicious as any breakfast could look at three in the morning, given the disheveled condition of her kitchen.

James chuckled. "Looks like the best breakfast I've ever had at this time of the day." He followed Fallon's cue and pulled up a kitchen stool for himself then one for Tyler. And the three of them sat down together and ate breakfast in the middle of a mess that was going to require about an hour's worth of cleaning and showers for everybody. "So, why'd you do such a nice thing for us?" James asked, choosing careful words as he picked up the piece of bread that nearly collapsed under the weight of the jam on it.

"Wanted to," Tyler replied.

"And I, for one, am glad to have another cook in the house," Fallon chimed in. Where she was sitting, a little stream of juice once flowing in one direction had redirected itself and was fast closing in on her. Rather than cleaning it, she scooted over, which brushed her right into James. Either he didn't notice or he was the best impostor in the world, because he simply plopped his piece of jammed-up bread into his mouth and didn't so much as flinch over the fact that Fallon was nearly draped over his lap.

"Can we go find a Christmas tree after breakfast?" Tyler asked shyly.

James and Fallon looked at each other then smiled. "Can we take a little nap first?" Fallon asked. "Get rested up so we can have lots of energy to find the biggest one?"

Naturally, Tyler looked disappointed. He'd had a plan, but now it was being put off. In his mind, having it put off was the same as not having it happen at all, and Fallon couldn't stand that. "As soon as it's light. There's a Christmas-tree farm about twenty miles from here, and we can go pick out the perfect one as soon as we can see everything they have. OK, Tyler? They won't let us pick out a tree if it's not light out, so it'll be up to you to come tell us when it's light. Can you do that?" The child *needed* to know that what he wanted mattered.

Tyler shrugged. But James didn't let him get away with being noncommittal.

"It's up to you, Tyler. OK, or not?"

"OK," he said tentatively.

"Well then," Fallon said, standing, ready to go back upstairs and leave the mess to James, who already sensed it would be his job to clean it up, "I'm going to go back to bed, and dream about Christmas trees. And I'm leaving the scrubbing of the kitchen up to you two." With that, she walked over to Tyler and gave him a kiss on the forehead.

"Him, too," Tyler said. "He needs a kiss, too."

"Yes, I do," James prodded. "I need a kiss, too."

"Right here," Tyler said, pointing to the spot on his forehead she'd kissed him.

James mimicked that. "Right here, and remember, it's about Tyler."

She sighed heavily, narrowed her eyes in protest as she approached James. Then aimed for his forehead, but got intercepted when he tilted his head back enough that her kiss caught him on the lips. And lingered a while. Long enough that she relaxed into the kiss, and James relaxed into the kiss, and they both totally forgot about Tyler for a moment. Then...

"Can I go move the furniture to make room for the tree?"

Both James and Fallon turned their heads toward the little boy at the same time, and answered in unison, "No!" Ten seconds later, Fallon was on her way back to her bedroom, her face flushed, her breaths short, her pulse racing. She needed a door. A big, heavy door to shut and lock. One for her heart, too. And a good place to throw away the key.

CHAPTER SEVEN

"It's a huge decision," Fallon said, smiling. They'd been looking at trees for almost an hour, after being the first ones lined up to get into the Christmas-tree farm. Now, after searching row after row of greenery that all looked pretty much the same to her, give or take a few scrawny exceptions, Tyler was still in decision mode, taking his job seriously. In fact, he was very methodical in the way he went about scrutinizing the various trees and tying scraps of fabric on the ones he was keeping under consideration. James was busy marking their location on a map provided by the owners of the tree farm.

"And I'm going to be late for work if he doesn't hurry up," James said, as he plotted the tenth tree.

"You've still got an hour before you have to go, and according to Tyler's calculation that's at least a dozen more trees." She grinned. "But isn't this fun?" Actually, it was. She'd never seen so many Christmas trees, didn't know that places like this existed. Her tree was stored in a small box in her attic. Fresh trees, with the luscious pine scent, were practically a novel concept for her, and she was in love with the idea of having a fresh tree in her home.

"And this farm has a good five hundred more acres of trees which, by *my* calculations, will take us about three more days to look at." He grinned back. "Think they'll let us camp here tonight?"

Fallon laughed. "If you think this is taking a long time, wait until we go to the Christmas store in town and he gets to pick out the ornaments. I predict at least two days there, and I'm pretty sure *they* won't allow camping."

James moaned then plotted yet another tree Tyler had tied a piece of white cloth on. "Seriously, we've got to bring an end to this if I'm going to have to chop it down then get it tied to the car and hauled back to your house."

"And remove all the markers on all the trees Tyler tagged."

James moaned once more. "Why do I have the feeling this is getting out of control?"

"That's what raising a child is about," she said. "Everything getting out of control. However, you're supposed to look like you're in control even when you're not, and when you're not you're supposed to act like you are so the child won't find out. Because if he does figure it out, he'll take control of you *and* the situation. So it's all about perceptions. If the child perceives you to be in control, even if you aren't, you're fine."

"And that flawed logic is exactly the reason I wanted to have ten or twelve children with you. You're such a good advocate."

Even though he'd meant nothing by those words, they did sting, and reflexively Fallon stepped away from James. She didn't mean to be so sensitive, didn't want to spend the rest of her life overreacting to perfectly innocent words, but she couldn't escape her reaction. It simply happened.

"Damn," he muttered. "I didn't mean to say that."

"It's fine," she said, stepping even farther away from him. One slow step at a time, with only her footprints in the snow to remind her how close she and James had been standing to each other. "Look, I have another suggestion. They'll dig the tree out for us and deliver it. We can put it in the house, keep it alive then plant it somewhere later. A tree Tyler will be able to keep as a reminder of his first Christmas with you."

"I'm sorry, Fallon. I really didn't mean to—"

She thrust out her hand to stop him. "I *said* I'm fine. Let's just leave it at that. OK?"

"But we'd talked about having children, Fallon. I remember telling you what a great mother you'd make. It was that day—"

"I remember the day," she snapped. Remembered it vividly. On a hike in the mountains, they'd run into a dozen little boy scouts. Cute, vivacious, having the time of their lives looking for a good campsite to spend the night. She and James had fallen in with the boys, hiked a couple of miles with them and she hadn't been sure she was going to be able to pull James away when it came time to part, he'd been having so much fun. That's the first time she'd thought she might wants lots and lots of children with him. They hadn't been engaged to be married, and most people would have said they were too new in their relationship to be thinking about children. But she was thinking about it anyway. And again, later, when James had mentioned wanting their very own little scout troop. He'd proposed a dozen children, which hadn't been serious. But she'd watched him in his element, seen his true heart with those children. So they'd talked a little that night. Tossed out funny names like Mortimer, Aloysius and Shadrach. Then settled on James, Junior.

Perfect thoughts for perfect days. And now those thoughts were all sad. "We talked about a lot of things, but that was a long time ago. And we were different people then."

"No," he said gently, "we *weren't* different people. You may think we were, *or you were*, but those same two people are standing right here, being awkward with each other for no reason. And I'd built some hopes and dreams around *us*. Counted on us being together. The only difference between me then and now is that back then I had something I wanted so badly I ached for it, and I thought I was going to get it. I still ache for it Fallon, but the change in me is that I don't know if I will get it. You tell me I won't, but I'm not ready to believe it yet."

"Believe it, James." She glanced out at Tyler, who seemed to have settled on *the tree*. At least, the jumping up and down and excitement he was showing over a particularly bushy one seemed to indicate he had. Long needles, a beautiful bluish-green, and with some artful trimming just about the right size, it seemed to be a perfect tree. "Counting on too much can get you hurt," she said.

"Or it can lead to everything you've ever wanted. I'm not ready to give up."

"I'm sorry it's turned out the way it has." Sorry for James, sorry for herself.

"It hasn't turned out any way yet, Fallon."

He stepped up to her, and ran his thumb down her cheek, a gentle stroke she remembered and loved. "Don't," she whispered. "We shouldn't have yesterday, and we can't…not again."

"Don't what?" he asked, tracing his thumb along the contour of her jaw then moving his touch ever so slightly underneath. "Don't do this?" He tilted her head up and kissed her on the lips. Tiny butterfly kisses that caused her to shiver. "Is that what you don't want me to do because you always enjoyed that, didn't you?"

Fallon willed herself to speak, willed herself to break free of his spell, but she couldn't.

"Or is this what you don't want?" He pressed his lips harder to hers this time. Parted her lips with his tongue and met her tongue in an instant fury.

Her hands snaked around his neck and her fingers inched upwards, entwining in his hair, massaging his scalp. Bodies pressed tighter, and even through the bulk of their jackets she could feel his erection pressing against her pelvis. She pushed into him, deepened the kiss, groaned.

But then he pulled back. "Is that what you don't want, Fallon? Because from this side of the kiss, I felt you kissing me back."

She wanted to be the one who took a step back now, but there was nothing in her that forced her to move. She could barely breathe. Barely focus. Barely think. Because James was right. She was kissing him back. And more. Just like always, this was where it had started with them. A simple kiss was never simple. A fond embrace was always filled with the expectation of so much more. "What I used to enjoy has nothing to do with the way things are now," she finally managed to choke out.

"Used to enjoy, Fallon? There were two people in that kiss, and both of them were enjoying it. So, the way things are now is that you're resisting me. For whatever reason, and I wish to God you'd be honest with me about it, you're resisting me."

She braced herself to the next part of the round. "And what would you have had me do when you kissed me? Slap you in front of your son? He's looking at us right now, you know that, don't you? Do you really want me to put on a spectacle for him, because I can do it."

James stepped back, blew out an exasperated breath. "Why has it become such a battle between us? I love you, I'm pretty sure you still love me. So shouldn't we be able

to find something in there that's simple? A place where
we can start from that and rebuild what we had, or what
we were trying to have, before your accident?"

"Nothing's ever simple, James. If there's one thing
I learned when I was a child, that's it. Nothing is ever
simple, and there's no point in pretending that it can
be." She pulled up her scarf. "I think Tyler has found his
tree, so I'm going to go make arrangements to have it
delivered."

James didn't respond, but the look on his face, as he
turned to go after Tyler said it all. She'd slapped him without raising her hand. Maybe that was a good thing. Maybe
now he'd leave her alone. Or alone long enough to get
her armor up again. This time, though, she'd have to put
on the whole armor rather than the bits and pieces she'd
donned before in the hope that was enough. Because it
was clear it wasn't enough. Which meant she now had to
gird herself to go the distance because if she didn't, she'd
end up hurting the person she loved most in the world.
Her armor…it was to protect James. Not her. She'd faced
the facts…*her facts*…months ago. They might be living
as a family now, but it was only for show because Tyler
needed the solidarity for a time. As soon as James was
able to find a place for the two of them, she'd put an end
to it once, and for ever.

That's the only way it could be because of what she'd
done. This was for James. Only for James.

Eight hours into his shift and he was restless. He wanted
to go home. "Home," he muttered, on his way down to
exam three to treat a two-year-old with sniffles. "Like
I've got a home."

"You need a place to stay?" Emoline Putters asked, as
he passed by her desk. "Because I've got a big old house

up on Ridgeview Road just sitting empty. Too big for me now that my husband is gone, and I hated rattling around in there all by myself, so I took an apartment closer to the hospital, and haven't gotten around to doing anything with the house. But it's got all my furniture, and it's in good shape, if you want to rent it. Or even buy it."

It wasn't what he wanted to hear, because he didn't want to move out of Fallon's cabin. It was too small for the three of them, though. And the tension building up...

"Big yard, too, for that boy of yours. Part of it's fenced in. Did that when my own children were young. The back of the property backs up to several acres of woods leading up into the foothills a piece. Nice place for a boy to go tromping around with his dad. Had a lot of good years in that house, and now it's time to let another family enjoy it."

Another family...his family of two. "Sounds perfect, Emoline. I'd like to take a look. Might take me a couple days to find a hole in my schedule, though. We're getting into the cold and flu season, and the clinic's pretty backed up right now." One step. That's all it was. He was going to look at a house. One step, but it was a big one.

"Sure. Stop by my desk later, and I'll give you the keys. You can go take a look when you're ready."

"How long has it been empty?"

Emoline Putters, usually prickly and irascible, drew in a deep breath, and at the end of it there was sadness on her face. A sadness that told James so much about her. She'd loved deeply, and hadn't gotten over the loss of that love. "Going on to five years now. Ed Lester, the head of hospital maintenance, goes up every couple of weeks and looks after it for me because I haven't been able to do anything about it. But I think you'd be good there, and it's time for that old house to see some new life."

Impulsively, James gave the woman a hug and, surprisingly, she didn't stiffen under his embrace, as he'd expected from her. It occurred to him that she wasn't prickly and irascible as much as she was lonely, and trying to hide it. She'd mellowed, though. Found the right time, and the right reason, and mellowed, the way he hoped Fallon would. "I appreciate the offer," he said. "And I'll get up there as soon as I can."

"Where you need to get is down to exam three. They've been waiting too long for you, and there's no excuse to keep a sick child waiting all this time."

She cleared her throat, thrust the patient chart at him and marched away, all prickly again. Except James knew better about Emoline. Just the way he knew better about Fallon. It did make him wonder, though, why Fallon was set on imitating Emoline Putters…being all prickly and irascible. Emoline, as it turned out, had a side to her he hadn't known. So was there a side to Fallon he'd never seen? Something he didn't know, or she didn't want him to know?

"We'll go just as soon as I make one more phone call," Fallon promised. Tyler had been having a fit all morning. He wanted to bring the tree inside, he wanted to move the furniture. He really wanted to go buy decorations, and he'd been very loud about that. Loud about being bored. Loud about not having a video game to play with. Loud… And she was getting a headache, because everything she'd planned for her day had gone bust. Each and every time she'd picked up the phone, he'd knocked something off the shelf. When she'd picked up her catalogs to peruse the pages for various obstetric exam tables, he'd started stomping around the house so loudly she hadn't been able to concentrate. Hours of this, and she was at her wit's end.

She understood that he was bored. She honestly did feel badly about that because there was nothing here for a five-year-old to do. No toys, no children to play with. No nothing! And to top it off, she couldn't even allow him to go outside and play in the snow because her yard wasn't fenced and she didn't have time to watch him. As little as he'd slept last night, and as early as he'd gotten up this morning, she'd thought he'd be ready for a nice, long nap. But when she'd suggested it, he'd put his hands over his ears then started yelling.

The final straw was a preliminary interview for the post of chief of nursing. She was trying to prequalify a candidate by phone, so the woman wouldn't have to make the long trip there before Fallon was able to check her credentials and get recommendations. In the middle of the ten-minute interview Tyler had unplugged the phone. Actually, not unplugged it so much as ripped it from the wall. So now she needed a service call to repair the damage, and she was reduced to using her cellphone, which had marginal reception out here.

"I don't want to wait," Tyler said sullenly. "You promised to take me, and I want to go now!"

"I know I promised, but—"

"Nobody ever does what they say," he grumbled.

That caught her attention. And she wondered if Tyler might be reacting from some of the tension between her and James. It was certainly a possibility. He'd built up a few hopes, and with the way she and James were getting along now saw the possibility that he'd be let down yet again. "Who never does what they say?"

"Everybody. They promise me I can stay this time then I can't. And they promise me they'll quit yelling, but they never do."

His home. He was talking about his home…his other

home with his mother. So much insight in so few words. And now she felt terrible, because she knew, for certain, that Tyler was feeling that same kind of insecurity here. While she and James had been saying this was about Tyler, they'd turned it into something about them and Tyler was watching from the sidelines. "Well, I don't break my promises, Tyler. Occasionally it takes me a while to get to them, but I always do. Here's the thing. Sometimes I'm not sure what a boy your age needs to be doing. I never had any little brothers, don't have any little boys of my own…so once in a while someone has to tell me. But not by yelling, and stomping around the house."

"How?" he asked.

"By telling me. Just say, *Fallon, I need something to do.*"

He thought about it for a moment and she could see the concentration in his eyes as he analyzed all sides of what she'd just told him. He was so much like James. The more she got to know Tyler, the more she saw the similarities.

"Fallon, I need something to do," Tyler finally said. He didn't sound sure of himself. It was like he was trying out the concept to see if it worked, to see if she kept her word.

"Tyler, I just happen to have something for you to do."

His eyes lit up. "You do?"

"I think you need to go sledding. And, as luck would have it, I have an old sled in the storage shed out back."

"What's that?" he asked, still cautious.

"You've never heard of a sled?"

He shook his head.

"It's better than a video game. Actually, it's almost like a video game, only instead of you pushing the buttons that make the game do different things, you're the one who's doing everything."

The look on Tyler's face showed marginal interest, mixed with healthy skepticism.

"Want me to prove it to you?"

He shrugged. Still didn't believe she was about to make good on her promise. Poor child. He was too use to being let down and it just made her ache for him. "It's up to you, Tyler. If you want something to do, this is all I've got right now."

"I'll go sledding," he said, much too reserved for a five-year-old on the verge of an adventure.

"Good choice." Fallon reached out to pat him on the back, but he jerked away. "So, do you have any boots?"

He shook his head.

"Mittens, scarf, hat?"

No again.

"Then I'd say we run to town and buy you some sledding clothes. Is that OK with you?"

Twenty minutes later they were barely inside the mercantile when Dinah Ramsey and her twin daughters Paige and Pippa practically pounced on them. Dinah immediately ran to Fallon and pulled her into her arms. "Are you OK?" she whispered. "You look like you've seen a ghost."

"Tension. It's not so good between James and me, and I'm worried about Tyler. I think what James and I are going through is affecting him."

"And he reminds you of your own little boy?"

"My own little boy never drew a breath!" she said, stiffening.

"Your child is your child, Fallon. You and James should have grieved together."

Fallon turned her head, blinked back the tears.

"Sometimes when I watch Tyler I think that he could have been mine. And it hurts so bad."

"But isn't this something you and James should be going through together?"

"What I did to him…"

"Fallon, you were fighting for your own life from all the injuries. And fighting to keep your baby at the same time. You were confused, and no one could blame you for your decisions. I mean, I can't even begin to imagine what you experienced, what you were thinking. And I'm sure if James knew…"

"That's the thing. He should have known. It wouldn't have made a difference in the way things turned out, but he had a son he didn't know about. And I've seen how hurt he was by what Shelly did to him. So how could I put him through that again, especially when *our* son didn't survive?"

"I think you're underestimating him."

"I think I'm protecting him."

"But does James really need protection, Fallon? Think about it."

"That's practically *all* I think about, and I'm…"

"Scared to death?" Dinah asked. "Afraid that if you tell James he had a son who died, James will quit loving you?"

"I don't know, Dinah. I really don't know."

"Well, the one thing I know is that our children are getting impatient." They glanced at the trio, Tyler, Pippa and Paige, who were glaring back at them.

"I promised Tyler we'd go sledding, and he's used to having promises broken."

"Well, I have a fantastic idea. I'm going to take the girls sledding out on Porter's Bluff. It's a mild little hill, perfect for younger children. How about I take Tyler with us? He

seems to be getting along well with them and maybe…"
Dinah hesitated.

"It will do him good to get away from me?"

"Maybe it will give you and James some time to talk. Alone."

It made sense, but the only thing was, she was scared to death of time alone with James. Of course, she could shut her office door and work. That, if nothing else, was the incentive she needed to let Dinah take Tyler for a while. "He throws tantrums," she warned.

"Eric's told me."

"And breaks things."

Dinah nodded, then laughed. "And the twins will out-number him two to one. I think we'll manage."

"Let me ask him, then." She watched Tyler and the girls for a moment, and saw a little boy who was just like any other little boy his age should be. Boasting to the girls, showing off for them, happy, carefree. Tyler desperately needed a normal life, one he could count on. So did she.

"Tyler," she said, bending down next to him, "would you like to go sledding with Paige and Pippa? Mrs. Ramsey has offered to take you with them, but I wanted to ask you, as I'd promised to take you, too."

He glanced at the girls then back at Fallon. "I'll go with them. They have three different kinds of sleds, including a round one, which they say goes faster than a regular one, and all you have is a regular one."

From the child who'd never heard of sledding to the one who was a five-year-old expert. The transformation was amazing, and Fallon was pleased with her decision.

She was still smiling about it two hours later when James wandered in, surprised not to find Tyler there. "Two very pretty young girls had their sway. He chose them over me, and Dinah called a few minutes ago to say that they're all going out for pizza later, so it looks like the old folks are left home, alone for the evening."

"What you're telling me is that he's on a date with twins? Isn't that every grown man's fantasy?"

"He's quite the ladies' man. I mean, he perked right up for them, put on his best manners, puffed out his chest, did some bragging. You know, the typical thing all men do when they're around pretty girls."

"Well, how about I put on my best manners, puff out my chest, and take you up to Pine Ridge for dinner? Not a date. Just two people in need of a meal."

It was tempting. It had been so long since she'd had a real night out...probably her last night out with James all those months ago. Admittedly, getting out more these past days was feeling so good. But this?

"We could sit at separate tables," he said, grinning. "Me at one, you at the one behind it with your back to me."

"I'm not *that* bad," she said, laughing.

"You're doing a lot for me, Fallon, and taking you to dinner is the least I can do to show you how much I appreciate everything."

"We do need to talk about some things, because I think Tyler is picking up on our tension. Maybe we can figure out how to make it better for him." She turned to the picture window, her back purposely to him. When she faced him, when she looked into his eyes, she couldn't resist. And she had to keep her head about this.

"I wish you wouldn't turn away from me, Fallon."

He stepped up so close behind her she could feel the sparky little prickles on her flesh he always caused when he was so close. She remembered that feeling, savored it. *Wanted it.* But being alone with James was too difficult and, as much as she didn't want to go out with him, she didn't want to stay in with him even more. "Let me call Angela," she said in response.

"Angela?"

"Angela Blanchard. She's the executive chef. There's a certain table…"

James stepped back. "I know. In the corner, facing a wall, behind a potted palm. Something that would never be construed as romantic."

She spun to face him, saw a rare flash of anger cross his face. As much as she hated seeing it, she was glad. Perhaps, at least, James was beginning to realize that there was no relationship between them other than friendship. "Actually, that would be a nice table, except I don't think they have one in that spot. I was going to ask for the one near the fireplace, away from the window. I'm still not ready to face that view yet. It overlooks the Middle Sister where…" Where everything about her life had changed.

The hard lines on his face softened. "I didn't know. Would you rather we simply stay in?"

Staying in came with more peril than going out. Either way, she'd have to cope with something she didn't want to. Staying here with James and risking the overtones of that, or facing a view of the thing she wasn't sure she could ever look at again?

Why was it that lately her life had been reduced to choosing between the lesser of two things she didn't want? For her, one choice held the promise of mortal terror, while the other choice promised an agony like nothing she'd felt throughout her entire ordeal. Either way, she couldn't win. But neither could James, and that's what bothered her most.

CHAPTER EIGHT

FALLON chose dinner at the restaurant. James figured that for her the choice was the lesser all of her perceived evils. And now, thirty minutes later, they were seated at a comfortable table for two in front of the massive stone fireplace in what was unquestionably White Elk's most romantic restaurant. The music playing in the background was a soft, sexy jazz, the chef's special *du soir* was a Chateaubriand for two, and the compliments of the chef was a bottle of champagne. If there could have been anything else spelling out a cozy, romantic evening, he wasn't sure what it was. Until…a bouquet of roses arrived at the table. From Angela, not from him. But the look on Fallon's face when they arrived was so close to panic that he almost wished he hadn't suggested this. *Almost.* Because, honestly, it was nice being out with her this way. And he hoped that somewhere during the evening she would loosen up and enjoy herself. Fallon was so tight, so full of stress and, if anything, as the days rolled by, it seemed to be getting worse.

"Are you nervous with me right now?" James asked. He knew she was. Anyone looking at her could see it—the way she clasped her hands so tightly, the way she frowned. But she'd have been nervous spending the evening alone with him in the cabin, too. Or nervous if they'd gone to have pizza. Or if she'd spent her evening locked in her office and he'd spent his shut behind the door in the den. Truth was, any close proximity to him, whether it was across the table, the next room, or the next block over, and she would be nervous. He did that to her now. He hated it that he did that. Wanted to change it. But so far he was failing miserably.

"No. Well…maybe, a little."

Her head was tilted down and he desperately wanted her to hold her head high, to look at him eye to eye the way she used to. But she was afraid to, and he'd seen that fear in her. That's what he didn't understand, couldn't figure out. They had differences, that much was painfully obvious. But this fear he kept sensing? What did she think she had to fear from him? It put him on edge. Made him nervous because he had to choose careful words, had to look at her carefully, had to adopt careful gestures. And he was also nervous for fear he'd slip. It was an onerous task and he hated always having to be on his guard with her. Hurting Fallon in any way, though…he wouldn't do it. Which meant that if he wanted her company, he'd have to continue being careful. "It's just dinner, Fallon. Two people eating together. No pressure from me, I promise."

"It's a *candlelit* dinner, James. With champagne. And have you listened to the music in the background? If that's not meant to seduce some man's lady love into bed this evening, I don't know what is."

"I'm not trying to seduce you, if that what you think I'm doing."

"Aren't you?" she asked pointedly.

"If you could see the way you look right now, with your arms folded across your chest, your shoulders so rigid, sitting on the edge of the chair, looking like you're ready to run at the first little provocation…believe me, even the most insensitive of men would pick up *those* clues. And I have picked them up, so you don't have to worry. I'm only here to eat."

"If I make your evening so miserable, why do you want to spend it with me?"

"Because I'm hoping that at some point during the evening you'll relax. We used to have a good time together, even when the intention was not to run home and make love. And I want that again for us. Even if we can't be one of the romantic couples, I'd like to be one of the friendly couples. Or at least make people believe you can tolerate my company for a few hours."

"You know I can tolerate your company, James," she whispered.

"Sometimes I don't know that any more," he said, wishing they could move on past this. That wasn't going to happen, though. Not tonight. No time in the foreseeable future either. "I mean, I know what we had at first happened like a tornado—fast, with so much passion. In retrospect, maybe it was too intense for something so new. I honestly don't know, because I was just so into falling in love with you that I didn't see anything else. But that's just the way we came together, Fallon. Right or wrong, that's what we did to each other. Now I wish—"

"That we hadn't?" she interrupted.

"No, I'll never wish that. But I do wish I'd found a better way to handle things after you were injured. Because maybe if I had, we might not be at this point now." He shook his head. "And I can't figure out why you're always resisting me, Fallon. If I thought that by backing off a few weeks, or even a few months, things would be better at the end of it, I would. But I know that if I do back off, you'll slip away altogether."

"That's what I want to do, James. What I've been telling you all along."

"Is it really, Fallon? Because one minute you're telling me to leave you alone, and the next you're falling into my arms. Oh, I know you're fighting it when you do. I can see it, feel it. But you do fall. Which makes me wonder why you push yourself away then fall right back."

"We have this attraction level," she started to explain, then stopped. "I won't deny that because we both know it's there. But why isn't it enough that when I tell you that what's in the past is in the past, you won't believe me? That when I say I don't want to get involved with you again, you keep pushing me?"

"Because you haven't put the past in the past, Fallon. I don't even know why I believe that, but I do. Something there happened. Maybe it was when I had to choose Tyler over you, maybe it wasn't. But there's something in the past, and I just don't understand what it is, because I truly believe that you would never hold my decision to be with Tyler against me. That's not the kind of person you are."

"I don't hold it against you, never have. But there's nothing to understand," she said. "Nothing at all."

"Fallon, I just want…" He stopped. This was pointless. She looked miserable, he felt totally drained. And all he'd wanted was a nice evening out. Nice dinner, nice conversation. And look what he'd turned it into. "Do you remember that night we went to Ming's? You ordered the dumplings, I ordered the scallops, and we both got…"

"Chicken nuggets," she said, the smile creeping back to her face. "Mine in a clear broth, yours in a lemon sauce. And Ming kept insisting we had what we'd ordered. And the rice was…"

"Crunchy."

"Ming said it was supposed to be crunchy."

"I was on call. It was the only place close to the hospital. I mean, this was our first date. I'd have loved taking you out to a nice restaurant, but…"

"But duty called, and you left me sitting there alone, with Ming watching over me like a hawk, getting insulted when I slowed down my eating. And the food was horrible. It tasted like dirty dishwater, not that I've ever tasted dirty dishwater. But if I had, I think that's what Ming's food tasted like."

James laughed. "I did come back, though."

"An hour later. I sat there one whole hour, and Ming got so worried that I was alone he sent his teenage nephew over to keep me company…a kid who was plugged into his music, who spent most of that hour drumming rhythms on the table and droning the words to whatever he was listening to. It wasn't the best first date I've ever had."

"But the most original. And I did make it up to you the next night, when I wasn't on call." He'd cooked, they'd stayed in, listened to good music, danced, watched the dawn come up together, surprised that the night had escaped them so quickly. A night like he'd hoped for tonight. But he'd been wrong, and maybe it *was* time to quit pushing her. Maybe it *was* time to simply stand back and see what happened. For the life of him, though, he wasn't sure he could. Wasn't sure he knew how.

"That was a nice night," she agreed.

The night he'd known he loved her. Oh, he'd thought that at first sight, had been pretty sure of it after she'd been so good about the awful debacle at Ming's. But on their second night he'd known for sure, and hadn't even been surprised how hard he'd fallen, and how fast. Because it was Fallon and she was…everything.

Later, when he'd dropped her off at the bus station to send her back to White Elk, it had felt like someone was kicking him in the gut. Seeing her step up on the bus, her hesitant little stop on the top step, turning around and smiling at him…her face in the window as the bus had pulled away… Damn, he loved her. Loved her then, loved her more now, even though she was fighting him. Because she still was everything. And he missed her so badly, even when she was sitting right across the table from him, he ached. There was such a distance now. "Would you dance with me, Fallon?" he asked impulsively. "Nothing intended but a dance." Truth was, he wanted her in his arms, needed her there, needed to close that distance. Any way would do.

He didn't expect her to say yes, though. For a moment he wished he hadn't asked inasmuch as he didn't know if he could bear the rejection. Yet when he looked at her for an answer, she smiled, nodded.

"Just one," she said. "*Only* a dance. Nothing else."

He wasn't sure why, but he knew the heavens were smiling on him as he led her to the dance floor and a fairly brisk tune turned into a mellow, slow one. She didn't meld easily into his arms, and at first he could feel every tense muscle in her body fighting against him. Her dance flow was stiff, her breathing shallow in his ear. But she felt good in his arms. And that's all he concentrated on for the next three minutes as the song played on, and the two of them, in an embrace, swayed to its rhythm.

About halfway through, Fallon began to relax into him. Her sway to the music mellowed. Her head dropped to his shoulder, a sigh escaped her lips, and for a moment they were the couple they'd been at the beginning. No cares, no worries. Simply two people falling in love and enjoying the moment.

It was a song and a mood that could have gone on much longer. For ever. But all too soon it was over, and he was leading her off the dance floor, grateful for one dance and quite aware he should not push his luck and ask for another.

"That was nice," she said, but the stiffness returned to her voice the instant she sat back down. "I enjoyed it, thank you."

It was a formal thank-you, not an easy one. And that's when he knew that it was time to step away. For good? He didn't know. Didn't want it to be. But he didn't want to burn all his bridges now, and he was afraid he was getting close to that. So, yes, it was time to move on, and hope that space would be the healer, or at least the eye-opener. Pray that when she opened her eyes she'd see him standing there, waiting for her, wanting her. Because the alternative scared him…opening her eyes and being glad he was gone. "Look, Fallon, I have some news. I thought about waiting until later, but…" He shrugged, a gesture reminiscent of Tyler's. "I may have found a place for Tyler and me to live. It was offered, I have the keys so I can look at it whenever I want."

"Really?" She nearly choked with surprise.

"Even if I take the place, Tyler needs some balance for the holidays, so I wouldn't do anything until after New Year. And if we leave, you'll get your life back. I know we've been disruptive, and you've hated it. So this way—"

"I haven't hated it," she interrupted. "And it's only been a few days. I thought…" She paused, seemed to re-think what she was about to say then forced a smile. "I hope Tyler will find some children to play with. He needs them."

For an instant she'd seemed like she wanted to stop them leaving. At least, that's what he'd been hoping for. But Fallon, true to who she was now, simply built the wall a little higher around herself, and stayed there through the dinner's main course and halfway through the dessert. Stiff conversation, and very little of it, took up the space between them. Until a commotion at one of the tables near the window caught their attention.

Fallon whirled around to look, knew immediately what it was. So did James, who launched himself from his chair without a thought. Like well-trained sprinters, they were across the room in a second, with James going into action first and Fallon doing what she always did, what she was born to do—taking control of the situation. "Please, everybody, move back. We need some room here."

She looked down at the man who was sprawled on the floor, and gasped. Walt Graham. Former obstetrician at the hospital, someone she knew well. "Aspirating?" she asked James.

He shook his head gravely. "Don't think so."

Bracing herself for the worst, Fallon flagged over a man she recognized. "We're in a white pick-up truck, parked in the last row." She bent, grabbed the keys from James's pants pockets then tossed them to the man. "There's a medical bag behind the seat. We need it urgently."

The man didn't question her. Didn't even blink. He simply turned and ran from the restaurant as Fallon pushed the line of observers even farther back from Walt. For his sake, she didn't want them witnessing this. He deserved his privacy, and dignity. And there was nothing dignified about collapsing in public this way.

"What do you need?" Angela Blanchard called, running up to her.

"More privacy?"

"I can do that. Anything else?" Angela, sister of Dinah Ramsey, looked down at Walt and gasped. In the early days of her pregnancy he'd been her doctor. "Did he choke on the food?" she asked.

Fallon leaned over, whispered, "I don't think so. James is trying to figure it out, and so far all I've done is manage to get the crowd pushed back. Call Eric, tell him we need transport up here. Helicopter, if he or Neil can manage it. Ambulance, if not. Tell him it's Walt."

"It's that serious?" Angela asked, on the verge of tears.

"He's not conscious, but James hasn't started CPR, so that's a good thing."

Angela nodded, turned and ran to her staff. Within seconds the guests of the restaurant were being moved even further back, while Angela was making arrangements to have Walt taken to the hospital.

Fallon dropped to her knees alongside James. "Walt," she whispered. "It's Fallon. Don't worry, I'm here to take care of you." Her fingers went automatically to his pulse. Weak, but there.

"What?" she asked James, who was trying to assess Walt's pupils without the proper equipment.

"Diabetic coma, I'm guessing. I can smell it on his breath, that fruitiness."

"I've sent someone for your medical bag. It'll be here in a minute. And I've arranged to have him transported to the hospital."

"Already?"

She shrugged. "It's what I do."

"So, you know this guy? Do you know anything about his medical history?"

"He's a part-time doctor at the hospital. Retired, mostly. But he'll come back when we need him, if we can find him. And as far as I know, he's very healthy. At least, that's what I'm assuming as he's spent the better part of the last half-year hiking around in the mountains."

"This is Walter Graham?" James asked, unbuttoning Walt's shirt. "I've heard about him."

"He's Santa Claus."

"What?"

"On the Christmas train. He's Santa Claus. That's probably why he's back in town. The train starts running in few days, and it has to have Santa Claus on it. Walt's been Santa for twenty-five years now."

"Your bag," a winded man said, running up behind them. He looked down at Walt. "He delivered all three of my children. Is he going to be OK?"

"We're trying," Fallon said, more for Walt than the man. "We're really trying." But trying wasn't good enough, and if this did turn out to be a diabetic problem he needed to be in an intensive care unit, with drugs they wouldn't have out in the field. Question was, would they be quick enough to save his life?

While James listened to Walt's chest, Fallon took a blood-pressure reading. Choked in surprise. Took it again. "Walt," she gasped, even though the man clearly could not hear her. "Did you know you're hypertensive?"

"What is it?" James asked.

"Two-twenty over one-sixty."

James let out a small whistle. "I don't suppose you'd know if he was being treated for it?"

"Knowing Walt, he wasn't. He's as stubborn as they come. Good at demanding things from his patients and nagging at them until they do it, but apparently not so good when it comes to taking care of himself."

"Well, it goes with his condition. Not unusual in diabetes, especially if he's not been treated."

"Look, James, you stay here. I'm going out to the parking lot and see if I can see anybody coming…an ambulance, a helicopter." It was much too soon, she knew, but she couldn't just kneel here doing nothing. "I'll be right back." She stood, and practically ran over a wall of a man standing behind her. Handsome man, sun-bronzed complexion, dark brown hair. A real breath-taker for some lucky woman. "Sorry," she said, stepping around him.

"I'm a doctor," he said, his voice almost a whisper. "If you need some help here."

She pointed to James. "Dr. Galbraith there might need you. Check with him, and I'll be right back." She wondered who the doctor was. Didn't think he was on staff at the hospital. Pretty sure he didn't live in White Elk. Probably one of the many here on holiday, and she was glad he was there to assist James, if necessary. Because she needed to be in the parking lot, ready to direct the rescue crew the minute they arrived. Ready to expedite that end of the emergency.

On her way out the door, her phone rang. Dinah Ramsey, according to caller ID. "Eric said his ETA is less than five minutes," she said breathlessly. "Neil's gone to Emergency to get things set up. Is it true, that it might be a diabetic coma?"

"James thinks so. And hypertensive as a collateral condition. His wife took good care of him all those years, then when she died he went to pieces in more ways than one." The loss of true love was something she understood.

Lights in the sky, followed by the whir of the engine caught her attention. Caused her heart to pound harder, her breaths to strangle in her throat. No matter how hard she tried to keep herself calm, it didn't always happen. "I think…" Deep breath. "I think I see him. Is Eric flying?" She made herself focus on how she *was not* going up in that helicopter, willed her heart to stop its galloping, demanded her breathing go back to normal.

"That's his helicopter. He finally took the plunge and he's trying it out before the hospital makes the purchase. Look, Fallon, tell James that Tyler is fine with me and the girls. We've had pizza, and I've got them all settled in, watching a movie. As I have an idea this is going to be a late one, why don't you let him stay here tonight? That way you and James won't have to worry about him."

The way Dinah talked, it was almost as if she and James were parents and Tyler was their child. It was a nice image, just not the real one. "I'll let James know. And if he wants to do anything different, I'll have him call you. Gotta go." She ran to the edge of the parking lot and watched the helicopter land in a field at the end of it. Before she could run to greet its pilot, Eric had jumped out and was halfway across the grass, running as fast as he could, carrying an armload of supplies. "More in the chopper," he yelled as he passed Fallon. "Grab the stretcher if you can."

She grabbed the stretcher, a lightweight frame, and a bag full of miscellaneous supplies and ran right back to the lodge, where Eric was already hooking Walt up to a heart monitor, James was readying an oxygen set-up, and the unknown doctor was taking vital signs. As soon as she got there, she wiggled her way in next to James to begin the IV prep.

"He's coming round," James said, as Walt started fighting the oxygen mask, thrashing about, trying to strike out at his rescuers.

"Walt," Fallon said in her sternest voice. "Listen to me. We're trying to help you. Please don't fight us."

Walt opened his eyes, but they didn't focus.

"Do you understand? We're trying to help you."

His eyes moved slowly until they locked on Fallon, and

whether or not he understood her words was anybody's guess, but once he saw her, he settled right down.

"I'm afraid he's going to start thrashing again once I stick him to get the IV in," she whispered to James.

The other doctor responded. "How about I do that while you keep talking to him? He seems to calm down when he hears your voice, so hold his other hand, make sure he keeps his mask on."

"As soon as you get the IV started, we're going to take him down to the hospital," Eric said. "Mark can ride with me, and you two can get back to doing whatever you were doing." He smiled. "A date, wasn't it?"

"Dinner," Fallon corrected him. "That's what we were doing. Just *dinner*. And wouldn't you rather have someone you know with you on the transport…James." She wouldn't fly, wasn't sure she ever could again, but James would. And after being in his arms, after that one dance, she was ready to get some space from him.

"Mark Anderson," the other doctor said by way of introduction. "And Eric knows me. He and I…and Neil Ranard were colleagues back in California." He held down Walt's arm while James located the vein and sank the IV. Within seconds the bag was hooked up, and all three men were in the process of getting Walt strapped to the stretcher. Once that deed was done, James, Eric and Mark rushed him out the door, leaving Fallon standing in the middle of the dining room alone as all the diners still stood off to the side, watching.

"You OK?" Angela asked, rushing to Fallon's side as she prepared to leave.

"Sure. Tired, but OK."

"That was amazing, what you and James did. I admire all of you…my sister, Eric. I mean, I come here and cook every night, and you…you do something that counts."

"Cooking counts," Fallon said, suddenly realizing she was on the verge of total exhaustion. "Without the cooks of the world, those of us who burn water would starve."

"Who was the other doctor?" Angela asked. "I haven't seen him before."

Fallon tried to remember his name. "Rick. Or, Mark. I think I heard him say he was from California, but I was talking to Walt at the time, trying to reassure him."

"He's going to be OK, isn't he? I mean, I was thinking that if you and James hadn't been here when he collapsed…"

As the helicopter lifted off, and she watched it makes its way skyward, Fallon's head went light and she took a staggering step backwards. "I think I need to go home," she said. "I'll call you as soon as I hear anything about Walt."

"Can I drive you?"

"I think James is waiting for me. At the truck. He was going to help get Walt loaded into the helicopter then come and get me. But thanks." The two exchanged hugs, and as Fallon was about to pull away from Angela, James stepped up behind her.

"James *is* waiting for you. And he's taking you straight home and putting you to bed." Angela took that as the hint to leave them alone as James slid his arm around Fallon's waist to support her. Never had anything felt so good. At any other time she would have struggled to stand on her own, but this was the second time James had practically carried her home, and this was the second time she had been willing to let him do it.

"Tyler's with Dinah and the twins. Spending the night, if that's OK with you."

As the two of them strolled across the parking lot to the truck, she leaned into him more and more, until he was practically holding up her full weight. "Eric mentioned that. I told him it was fine with me. Look, Fallon, I think maybe I should carry you."

"No, I'll make it…" As long as he was there to help her. "I don't have my full stamina back and I think my little adrenalin surge has worn off. But I can walk to the truck."

Which she did. And she even walked into the cabin on her own. But made it only as far as the couch, where she collapsed, promising herself she'd rest a minute or two before she climbed the stairs to her bedroom. She had to get up those stairs because she was feeling too vulnerable, too cozy. She wanted to shut a door between them. Wanted to put up a physical barrier that would block out everything she was fighting to give in to. She and James together, upstairs. Weak thoughts attributed to a tired body. Something she had to remember. "Thanks for dinner," she said, as she pushed herself up off the couch. "I'm sorry it didn't turn out better."

"Well, except for the first half-hour when you were so nervous, and the last half hour when Walt collapsed, it wasn't all that bad."

Fallon laughed. "Always the optimist, aren't you? Seeing the glass half-full, not half-empty."

"But it is half-full. Although I'll admit, when I asked you to dance, I was pretty sure it was going to be empty."

"But I danced."

"That, you did. And I'm wondering why."

She looked up at him, sighed. Attempted a smile. "Because you wanted to. I'm not an ogre, James. I do want to be your friend, if we can find a way to work that out."

"Friend? That's all?" He shook his head, sucked in a frustrated breath and let it out slowly. "I can't keep doing this, Fallon. Can't keep hoping. It's getting more and more exhausting for me. And right now the only thing on my mind is how much I want to carry you up those stairs, which is why I'm going to leave. I've decided to buy Emoline Putters's house sight unseen. Maybe move in as soon as the day after Christmas. Because I need to get out of here. Need to get Tyler out of here and leave you to whatever it is you want to be left to."

The words she'd been wanting to hear. But hearing them didn't make her feel any better. If anything, she felt worse. Afraid. Alone. She couldn't let him see that, though, or he wouldn't leave. So she braved up, squared her shoulders, forced a smile. "You're right. That's what you need to do. It'll be best for everyone."

"And that's it?"

"What else should there be, James? This was never a permanent arrangement. You were always going to leave, and now it's official." Her brave front was slipping, but she didn't want him to see that. "So, in the meantime, if you hear anything about Walt, let me know. Yell it from the bottom of the stairs, though. I don't want you coming up."

"Be honest with me, Fallon. Is that because if I did get to the top, you wouldn't send me back down?"

She couldn't lie to him. Dear God, she wished she could. That would make it easier. But she couldn't. "If you climbed those stairs, I wouldn't send you back down." She turned away and started walking upstairs, wondering, for a moment, if they could have just one night…one more night. Make it simple, be clear about it. Wake up in each other's arms for one last time. Say the final goodbye to the part of their lives that desperately needed closure, and start a new chapter, separately. Her list of reasons sounded good to a weary mind. So why not? James would understand what it was about and maybe it would help him move on. Help her move on.

She could do this. And it didn't mean she was giving in. It meant that she was finally putting it to rest. Closure. Yes, that was it. She was seeking closure. Of course, there was the real possibility that in the morning, when her head was clear, she'd regret her decision, and see her list for what it was…a pathetic attempt to live in the past, to hang onto a part of that past she couldn't have now. She turned to invite him up, but he was already gone. And she didn't go after him.

"He's doing well. Grumpy, but otherwise in remarkably good condition for what he suffered last night."

"Huh?" Fallon looked up at James through a hazy stupor. She hadn't slept at all last night. She'd tossed and turned, paced, fixed herself hot milk, read a magazine, gone over files for the new hospital, and admonished herself for what she'd almost done every second her head hadn't been full of something else. She would have slept with him. Made love, and quite possibly would have been making love again right this very minute. So this morning she wasn't up to facing him. More than that, she wasn't up to facing herself.

"Walt Graham. He's grumpy…"

"He was always grumpy," she said, twisting away from James. He was standing over her, she was sitting at the breakfast bar, pretending to eat a carton of yogurt. There was no way she could twist far enough away from him to forget what she'd wanted to do. "Gentle soul inside, grumpy on the outside."

"He wants to be Santa. Says he'll check himself out of the hospital and do what he wants to do."

Fallon managed a laugh, in spite of her glum mood.

"And that's what he'll do, if there's any way he can get himself into his Santa suit and hoist himself up on that train."

"That's what Eric said, too. We had coffee together a while ago, and he said Walt could bellow all he wanted, but he was grounded this year."

"You had coffee with Eric?"

"And Neil and Gabby, and the rest of the doctors. Staff meeting, actually. Bright and early. We talked about expanding the hospital by another new staff member."

She hadn't known, hadn't heard him leave. And here her thoughts had been full of sweet morning love. Well, now, if she didn't just feel like an idiot! Glad, though, that James hadn't been privy to the tumultuous thoughts that had kept her awake all night.

"And I stopped by the Ramseys' to see Tyler for a few minutes. He was busy making snow angels. He said he still wants to build a snowman with you, and do all that Christmas shopping you promised him. And he doesn't want you forgetting that." James chuckled. "He's enjoying the attention of two lovely ladies, though. I've been told Paige and Pippa have both declared their undying love for him, and they don't want him going home, *ever*. But my little Casanova took me aside and told me he wants to come back here with you."

Suddenly, her bad mood melted away. "He does?" she asked, finally mellow enough to look him straight in the eye. "Are you sure?"

"He likes you, Fallon. Like father, like son."

"Are you on duty, or can you come with us to build that snowman?"

"On for the morning, off for the rest of the day."

"Then how about Tyler and I go shopping for ornaments, and after you're home we start on the snowman and maybe drag the tree into the house. He's really anxious to put it up, you know."

His face darkened. "I have an emergency hearing this afternoon. My attorney got the temporary custody papers filed, and the judge wants to hear the case immediately."

"That's fast!"

He nodded. "I'm not sure what to make of it, but he wants Tyler there with me. So maybe we can get to the snowman or the tree afterwards."

It was all beginning to happen. James getting custody of Tyler. Tyler and James starting their new life together. She was happy for them. Truly happy for them. But sad for herself because she already felt left out. It's what she wanted, but she didn't have to like it, didn't have to like the feeling it left her with. Still, she was glad for James because he did deserve some happiness.

And her…getting what she wanted ached so bad she wanted to curl up in a tight, little ball and stay that way. She missed James and he wasn't even gone. So, how was she to survive this? How was she to make it through the next days without giving herself away to him? Because the tears welling behind her eyes right now would surely give her away. And she couldn't let him see that. Not now, not ever.

CHAPTER NINE

"AND you have no knowledge of her whereabouts?" Judge Stanley asked James.

"She may live in Arizona or New Mexico. But Tyler doesn't know, and as she didn't leave me any forwarding information, I don't know either. My attorney and I are working on that, though. And I've had an investigator looking for her for a while."

"But the blood tests match? And the DNA?" He shuffled through a stack of papers, looking through a tiny pair of reading glasses that balanced precariously on the end of his nose.

"No doubts," James said. "He's my son."

The judge nodded without looking up. "And you dated the mother for how long?"

This was beginning to make him nervous. "A few weeks. Not seriously, though."

He glanced up at James. "Seriously enough to conceive a son." Then he returned to his papers.

Bad sign. Really bad sign. He wished he could have asked Fallon to come and stand with him. Even though Jason Greene was with him, he felt alone. Tyler was sitting in the judge's office, under the watchful eye of a court clerk, and here he was, doing something he'd never even considered would happen to him. He was asking the judge to take the first legal steps in granting him sole custody of his son. It was good, but he missed Fallon being involved. It wasn't her fight, though. And he knew he had to get used to not having her around because, as of an hour ago, he'd agreed to buy Emoline's house. Which meant he was doing what Fallon wanted all along...moving on.

So why involve her in this, when in a few more days she wouldn't be involved in anything in his life? He did hope, though, that she'd stay involved with Tyler. Tyler loved her.

"Seriously enough to conceive a son," he said back to the judge.

"What happens when you get to a permanent custody hearing and the boy's mother fights you?"

"I fight her back. After all, I'm not the one who keeps abandoning our son. I'd say that's a pretty good argument."

The judge looked up again, but this time took off his glasses. "What you're asking to do here, Doctor, is the start of something with a very serious consequence. You realize that, don't you?"

"What I realize is my son needs a stable life. I can give that to him, but his mother cannot. If she wants visitation rights, we can work that out because I think it's important that Tyler has a relationship with his mother. But I'll do everything in my power, spend every cent I have if that's what it takes, to make sure he spends the rest of his childhood with me."

"Well, according to the court report, he's a difficult child...behavioral problems of some undiagnosed sort," the judge continued. "I know you're a pediatrician, well aware of what adjustments might have to be made for the boy. But are you prepared to deal with that every day until the permanent custody is established and, perhaps, for the duration of his childhood, if that's the way it works out? Deal with it as a father?"

"It's the *father* in me who wants to take care of his son. The *father* who loves that little boy more than life itself, and wants to give him the kind of home he deserves. That's who you see right now, and I'm fully prepared to deal with his problems. Although once he has someone he can count on, once he knows he's not going to be abandoned every few months, his behavioral issues will disappear. And that's the pediatrician speaking as a professional."

Outside, in the corridor, Fallon shut the door to the hearing room and dropped down onto the wooden bench there in the hall. OK, so she really didn't need to be here, had promised herself that she wouldn't come. But she had anyway. And she'd been listening to the arguments and discussions for the past twenty minutes, standing there with the door opened barely a crack, ready to spring in and testify on James's behalf, if he needed it. But he didn't need it, and the tears streaming down her cheeks were the proof of that. Tyler was on the verge of a new life now, and she was so happy for the both of them. If only she could have been part of that arrangement.

"Why didn't you come in?" He'd known she was there. Had seen her peeking in.

Fallon, still facing her car, with her key in the door, sucked in a sharp breath. "I didn't know if you wanted me there. And I didn't want to intrude."

He took her by the shoulder and spun her around. "There's no place in my life I don't want you, Fallon. But I don't know how to get you back in my life the way I want you." With the snowflakes brushing her face as they fluttered to the ground, and her eyes so wide and questioning, she was the most beautiful woman he'd ever seen. So much so she nearly took his breath away. "And I didn't ask you to testify for me because…." He brushed a snowflake off her cheek. Wanted to kiss her so badly it stung. "Because it's so difficult, Fallon. Wanting you, knowing I can't have you."

"But I would have testified. If you'd asked I would have."

"I know you would, but this distance between us…it shows. People can see it, see the tension. And I was afraid the judge might wonder why the woman Tyler and I are living with would appear so standoffish. So I couldn't risk it." Mentally, he braced himself not to step forward, not to cross that invisible barrier she had up around herself. "Sometimes, Fallon, it's not about you. I'm sorry, but I was afraid you could hurt my chances."

Tears immediately sprang to her eyes. "You're right," she said, turning back to the car. "It's not about me."

Damn, he hated himself. Hated this situation. Hated it that he couldn't risk pulling her into his arms to shield her from the world she feared. "I'm sorry," he whispered, his voice nearly breaking with agony. "I didn't mean to hurt you."

Still facing the car, she said, "I know you didn't. I'm the one who hurts you, the one who should be apologizing."

What kind of man would let the woman he loved hurt so badly and simply stand there and watch it? The worst kind. The answer sat bitterly in his heart. *The worst kind.* He was at breaking point. "Fallon," he said, his voice turning rough. "Turn around, look at me."

She didn't. So he stepped around and physically wedged himself between her and the car door, and when she started to back away from him, he took hold of her arm, stopped her. Then, when she started to pull back the way he knew she would do, started to tilt her head toward the ground, he stopped her. Placed his hand under her chin and tipped her face toward his, fully expecting her to pull away, to literally run away.

But, she didn't, and that surprised him. Fallon stood there, meeting him eye to eye, and allowed him everything he needed for the first moments. But it wasn't enough. He knew that, so did she. Then as if some gusty mountain wind blew her right into his arms, she was there, her arms snaked around his neck, her body pressed so close to his he felt every one of her curves, even through her bulky winter clothing. It didn't take but a second for him to respond to the need tearing at him, right there in the public parking lot of the White Elk Town Hall, so aroused he couldn't think straight. It didn't take but another second for his lips to claim hers…hard, demanding. They'd always been vigorous in their passion, and this kiss was no exception. But it was *her* tongue forcing its way into his mouth now, *her* tongue exploring the warm, sensitive contours, *her* tongue causing him to groan like no man had a right to groan in a public place.

Had the chill wind not been blowing swirls of snow around their ankles, he would have thought he was hallucinating. But as the cold crept up his leg and joined with the fire she was igniting in him, he was snapped into the realization that he couldn't do this. This time he was the one who had to pull away because if he didn't, Fallon would retreat and, perhaps, this time she might never come back because he was, indeed, moving on. Besides, what he wanted from her was so much more than a feverish kiss in a wintry parking lot. So he broke loose, pulled back, hated doing it. Dear God, he hated doing it. But what choice did he have? It wasn't the little campaigns he wanted to win with her.

"I…I shouldn't have done that," she stammered, raising her hand to her lips.

Already they were red and swollen from the encounter. And so inviting it was all he could do to keep himself from claiming them once more. "You're right," he said, backing away from her. "We shouldn't have. Look, I've got to go back inside and get Tyler. Why don't we meet at the mercantile and do that shopping you've been promising him then we can go put up the tree?" Unless she didn't want them in her house any more. That was the question that hung in the air between them for the next moment.

"What we did shouldn't ruin his holiday," she said. "I know you're getting ready to move, but I think you should stay until after Christmas so he can have some sense of belonging. It's only for a few more days, and…" She paused, grappled for the right words. "And we won't do that again. For Tyler's sake, we can't. Agreed?"

"Agreed," he said. Agreed, but not sorry about what he'd done.

Fallon forced a difficult smile. "Good. Then I'll meet you at the mercantile in a while."

Which she did. Fighting with herself every step of the way. Why had she kissed him like that? And there was no mistaking what had happened. He'd approached and she'd taken full advantage. Like a woman possessed. Well, it was a good thing they'd be gone after the holidays because it was clear that the best intentions meant nothing. Where James was concerned, the only way to deal with him the way she needed to was to completely remove him from her life. Otherwise… She cringed, thinking about what tagged along on the end of that otherwise. She was so close to the edge and ready to topple. Make no mistake, she was the one standing right there, ready to give herself the shove that would send her plummeting. And all it would take was such a little shove.

"The star goes at the top," she said, handing it up to James, who was balanced precariously on a wobbly stepladder. Tyler was busy below, hanging the several dozen ornaments he'd chosen. No theme to this tree other than fun. Tyler definitely showed a preference for cartoon-character ornaments, while her taste ran more to snowmen and Santas and angels. James didn't have a preference, so he concentrated on the lights and chose strands of all different colors, lights that twinkled. All in all, it was turning out to be a rather amazing mix of gaiety, and after the first hour of stringing up decorations, the trio put the project on pause long enough to take advantage of the fresh snow outside, where James instructed Fallon and Tyler in the fine art of snowman-building.

Naturally, they all had their own variations on a theme, Fallon making more of a snow princess, adorned in an old sequined shawl she hadn't worn in years, while Tyler definitely went for something more in his own image and size. James, on the other hand, had a secret project going, and insisted that Fallon and Tyler were not to come around to the south end of the cabin until he called them.

"Think we should sneak around there and see if we can have a peek?" she whispered to Tyler.

"Maybe he'll get mad at me," Tyler said, on the verge of turning sullen after a long afternoon filled with so many fun things.

Poor child. He deserved time to be carefree, time to be a little boy who didn't have such deep worries on his mind. "Why would that make him angry?" she asked.

"I have to do what he says. That's the way it is."

"What happens if you don't? What do you think he might do?"

Big tears started to roll down Tyler's face. "Make me go live with someone else."

"Like your mother made you come live with James when you didn't know him?"

He nodded.

"Do you want to stay here?"

He nodded again.

"Well, your dad…*James* wants you to stay here."

"Do you, too?"

"Of course I do. I want us to be best friends."

"You're not going to be my mom?"

This was getting too complicated. And she truly didn't know what to say because Tyler would see just how broken up she was about this, and she didn't want him to feel like it was his fault that he and James would be moving out. Thankfully, James interrupted at just the right moment.

"You two about ready for the big unveiling?" James shouted from the other side of the house.

She held out her hand to take Tyler's, and he grabbed hold and clung like she was his lifeline. "Remember how big heads on snowmen are what makes them fall over?"

"Un-huh."

"Think this one will have a big head?"

The answer to that awaited them just around the corner, where James had constructed a large snowman, with a huge head. One he was fighting to keep on top.

"It's going to fall!" Tyler squealed, breaking away from Fallon and running straight to James. Actually, more like straight into James. Which sent James falling backwards, causing one huge snowman head to fall on top of both of them.

"Want me to show you how to make a better one?" Tyler asked innocently, as he poked his head out of the snow.

A better snowman, a better life...Tyler had so many things to show them, if either of them were open enough to learn the lessons of a child.

"That's what he said?"

Fallon nodded. Settling into the couch, with a mug of hot chocolate in hand, she tucked her feet up under herself and stared at the Christmas tree. It was a mess, and it was also the most beautiful tree she'd ever seen. "He wanted to know if I was going to be his mom."

"And you said?"

"Nothing. I didn't know what to say. I think it's pretty clear he doesn't want to go back to his real mom, though. Probably not even for visitation, if the court decided to allow that."

James shut his eyes, dropped his head back against the chair. "It's always going to be in his mind, isn't it? Even if he never goes back to her, if he stays here with me until he's an adult, and lives a normal life, he's never going to get over what she's done to him."

"But you can help him deal with it. It's not easy, but you can teach him to be a strong little boy. And, James, he'll learn to trust you. Once he's certain of consistency in his life, something he knows he can count on, he'll trust you."

"Did anybody ever help you learn to deal with it?"

She shook her head, too close to tears to speak.

"Talk to me, Fallon. Tell me what I need to know, what you need to say. It's driving me crazy. I see it there, see it in your eyes, and don't understand it. And I want to."

"What I need to say? Like, I was thrown away just like Tyler was? To be honest, James, that's all there is to say.

It hurts, and you never stop wondering why the ones who should love you the most don't." She drew in a ragged breath, swiped away a tear. "But you can help him get past that. And that's what he needs the most. Someone fighting for him, someone who loves him so much he'll never give up."

"The way I love you, Fallon. The way I won't give up, even though you keep trying to push me away?"

She thrust out her hand to stop him. "Don't, James. I keep telling you, over and over, that I can't deal with it any more."

"Why?" he asked. "You owe me that much. Tell me why, Fallon. The truth… I deserve to know what's keeping us apart. Because, I can't, for the life of me, figure it out, and I want to. And I won't move on until I know."

She laid her hands across her belly, could almost feel the barrenness under her fingertips. There was no fight left in her any more. James was right. "I guess you do deserve that closure, don't you?" She drew in a deep breath, braced herself. Felt surprisingly calm about it. Now that the moment had arrived, it seemed surreal, finally knowing that this would end it…end the relationship, end them, end the dreams. Permanently. But she loved this man more than anything she'd ever known, and she owed him this one, final truth. "I suppose the simple answer would be that one of my surgeries was a hysterectomy. I can't have children. Can't give you all those children we'd planned on having."

He arched his eyebrows in surprise, but didn't get overly emotional. "And you didn't tell me?"

"No. Because I…because I…" The words were so difficult to find. She'd rehearsed them a million times all these months, known exactly what she would say when the time came. But now she couldn't find them. "I was afraid, I suppose."

"A hysterectomy doesn't matter, Fallon. We can deal with that! If we want children, we can adopt. Or concentrate on raising the one I hope we're about to get custody of."

"I know that, and for a while that's what I told myself. Tell James about the hysterectomy and leave it at that. But the hysterectomy is the simple part, James. It's what came before." She wouldn't look at him for this. Couldn't look at what she knew she would see on his face. "Before we… before the plane crash…I discovered I was pregnant."

"Oh, my God!" he whispered. The emotion was rising now. He wasn't holding it back. "Fallon, I don't…don't know what to say…" Anguished words. So much pain in them already. The pain she'd never wanted to cause.

"It's not what you need to say, James. It's what I need to say, what I've needed to say for such a long time, and couldn't. I knew about my pregnancy for a few weeks before the plane crash, and I kept it to myself. You were under so much stress at the time with your job, and I wanted to find the perfect time to tell you. I had these visions of what that perfect time would be like, but you were struggling so much, always on edge, that I kept putting it off, telling myself I'd tell you tomorrow, or the day after that. But it never seemed like the right time. I should have just come right out and told you, but in the back of my mind I saw something so nice. Not like what happened with my mother, who never even knew who my father was.

"Also, I was nervous because we really hadn't been together very long. We'd had a couple of intense months and I knew we had deep feelings, but I think I was afraid that we might be mistaking physical passion for the real

thing. Whatever the case, I kept it to myself, always thinking that we had tomorrow. And I'm so sorry I did."

"So am I. I would have liked knowing. Liked to experience it with you. But I do understand your confusion."

She turned her head to look at him. "See, that's the
thing. Maybe you think you understand right now, but
what happens after it's sunk in, after you're not in shock?
After you've had time to think about what I did…to you.
James, I don't want you being so nice to me. I don't deserve
it. Don't want it!"

"You want me to be angry because you miscarried in
the plane crash? It wasn't your fault, Fallon! You're right, I
may be angry after I've absorbed that you weren't ready to
tell me, but I'd never blame you for how it turned out."

"The thing is, James, I didn't miscarry. I came through
the crash, badly injured, with my pregnancy intact.
Had so many surgeries afterwards. The surgeries, the
anesthesia…"

"No," he choked. "I don't understand. You didn't miscarry and you still didn't tell me?"

Now she saw the anger. It was awful, she hated it, but
this was the way it had to be. And every time he looked
at her, she'd be the reminder of something bad, something
filled with indescribable pain. The secret he couldn't forgive. "How could I? I was fighting to stay alive, fighting
to keep my baby alive, and you…"

"I was busy with Tyler." With this his anger turned to
agony. "I thought you were strong enough, took you for
granted, and I wasn't there the way you needed me to
be."

"Tyler needed you. I always understood that. You'd told
me he was going through a hard time. And he was…was
my baby's brother. I couldn't let you divide yourself!

"And, James, I really thought that I would tell you about

our baby when my physical condition improved, when you weren't fighting so many battles. But nothing got better. I had so many complications, and I knew that if you found out what I was going through, you'd be with me, stay with me, never leave my side. You couldn't do that, though. Don't you see? I couldn't take you away from Tyler. He wasn't part of me but he was part of you…part of our child. And I was a mother too. A mother fighting to save her baby…a mother with a baby inside her who needed her to fight for him the way you needed to fight for Tyler. That's the way it had to be, James. You had to take care of Tyler, not me."

"What happened?" he choked, his voice so hoarse the words barely came out. "To the…to our baby?"

"I had our baby…stillbirth. I was just over six months along."

"Six months?" he gasped. "You were six months along and didn't tell me? How could you do that, Fallon? I had the right to know."

"You did. I always knew that, and felt so guilty. But the longer I didn't tell you, the more I didn't know how. And my lawyer… He checked in on you, told me about your situation with Tyler. You had him, he was taken away. Then you got him again… And I was so…so confused. So hurt." She drew in a steadying breath. "For the longest time I had this fantasy that our baby would be fine. That one day I'd call you to come visit us, and I'd introduce you to him. In retrospect, I know I was kidding myself about the outcome, because I did know how bad the situation was. But I'd fantasize that I'd get to the end of the pregnancy, give birth, then…

"But the other part of me, the pragmatist, knew that you were in such a dark place, and it hurt me. I truly didn't want to burden you with more, and I'd convinced myself that not telling you was protecting you from even more pain.

"Then when my mind started to clear up, I felt so… guilty. Knew I should have told you even then. But it was too late. The doctor told me the odds of my baby surviving were overwhelmingly slim, and that my odds of survival were almost none if I somehow managed to go to term, or even close to it. Still, I wasn't going to abort my baby, no matter what. I had to fight for him, and that's why I left. Why I wouldn't tell you where I was. Because if you knew…"

"You should have told me, Fallon. If your life was at risk…"

She shook her head, almost violently. "See, that's what I knew you'd say. That's what I knew I'd have to fight, and I just couldn't fight anything else. You would have won, James. You would have connected with the nurse in me, and won. I always knew that, and that's why I didn't take your calls, wouldn't let you come see me. I couldn't let you win because if you won, if you'd have convinced me to save myself and not our baby… But in the end, none of it mattered. I lost our baby anyway. And when he died I just couldn't face you. Because I know how wrong I'd been, leaving you out. You deserved to know him, to be part of him for that short time…"

"He?" James choked.

"We had a little boy." She swiped at the tears rolling down her cheeks. "And when they let me hold him, that's when I knew it was too late. That there was no going back. I cheated you of your son. You didn't get to hold him, James. You didn't get to…"

James swiped at his own tears. "Fallon, I'm so…" His words broke off. He sucked in a sharp breath. "I wouldn't have hated you. Couldn't have…"

"I hated myself, James. Don't you see? All these months I've hated myself, because I wasn't strong enough to keep him alive. Because I wasn't strong enough to tell you and fight the fight to keep our baby, if that's what I had to do. It was just easier to be alone. But you deserved better. Then, and now. I've watched you with Tyler. You're such a good father. A great father, and you love being a father. You need all those children, James. And I can't be the one to give them to you. Couldn't even be the one to give you *our* son."

"Did he have a name, Fallon? Our son, did he have a name?"

She nodded. But her lips only formed the words as her voice failed her. "James Allen Galbraith, Junior."

He didn't say anything for a while. Just sat in the chair across from her and stared out the window, for which she was grateful, because she didn't want to be in his arms, didn't want to feel the pain that would surely radiate from him, pain she had caused. So they sat in silence, for half an hour, or an hour…she didn't know. Time passed and she was too numb to feel it. But finally James cleared his throat, squared his shoulders. He stood. And she knew that once he walked out of the room, he might never come back. At least, not emotionally.

It's what she deserved. What she'd known all along would happen. But being right about it didn't make her feel any better, didn't bring her any relief.

She couldn't watch him go, however. So she shut her eyes, blocked it all out. Held her breath until she heard the door close behind him.

But it didn't close. Yet she waited. Dear God, she waited for ever, then finally opened her eyes, only to find James kneeling in front of her, the pain on his face so acute she wasn't sure either of them could get through this.

"I'm sorry," he whispered. "Fallon, I'm so sorry. What you did... I don't blame you for anything. How could I?"

"But you should. And in time you will. You should have known about the baby at the beginning so you could have celebrated the happy days with me, and at the end mourned the loss. You should have held him in your arms the way I did, and stood next to me at the grave when I... when I buried him. It was your right... He was *your* son and I took that away from you." She reached out tenderly to brush a tear from his cheek. "I was so confused..."

He took hold of her hand and kissed it. "I know you were. But, Fallon, I do understand that you did what you thought was right for me, and for Tyler. How could I ever be angry about that?"

"Don't you understand, James? I'm the one who's angry. I thought you might be, tried to convince myself you would be, but in my heart of hearts I always knew you'd forgive me. But I'm the one who's angry. So damned angry."

"At me?"

She shook her head. "At me. For not being strong enough. See, I didn't *ever* want to tell you. At first I thought that I'd never tell you, and that maybe we could get back together and simply go on. You'd never have to know. But after a while I knew that I couldn't go through with that because I can't lie to you, and not telling you the truth was lying. But I didn't want you to suffer the pain I had. Or suffer even more pain because I hadn't included you. Yet I knew that I was bound to tell you everything if we stayed together long enough, and I didn't want to hurt you. So I've been trying to push you away, James. Not because I hated you but because I loved you. But I couldn't do it. I was too...weak."

"You're not weak, Fallon. You're the strongest person

I've ever known. And what you perceive as weakness is truly strength."

"Then I hate being strong." She sniffled. "And all this time when you've said you made a mess of things…it was always me. I knew that, and I kept on letting you think it was you because I was still trying to find a way to keep my secret. I was right about one thing, though. When I told you that you don't need me, you don't. Now that you know the truth, you can move on. Start over."

"How the hell can you tell me what I need, Fallon? How the hell can you tell me to move on when you know it's breaking my heart? Everything you're telling me is breaking my heart. You are breaking my heart. But I still love you, and I don't want to walk away."

"Do you honestly think you could look at me every day for the rest of our lives and not think about what I did to you? You'll think about it for a while…days, months, years. Convince yourself that you're not angry. But then one morning, out of the blue, you'll wake up, look at me, and finally realize you hate me. And every time you'll look at me you'll remember what I did…and I can't bear that. Can't even look in a mirror at myself and not think about what I did, so how can I expect you to simply think it will go away? Right now, it's so raw, you don't know…but I've lived with it. I do know. That's why you and Tyler… You have each other and you can get on with your lives, and in time you'll both forget…"

"We'll forget you? Is that what you think? Tyler loves you, I love you, and you really believe that we'll just get over you because you tell us to?"

"Because you need to," she said, her voice breaking. "You need to, for both your sakes."

"You don't know a damn thing about what I need. Not a damn thing." He shut his eyes, trying to rein in the emotion. It wasn't sinking in yet. Oh, he understood the words. Every last, ugly one of them. And he even understood why Fallon had made the choices she had. He couldn't even begin to imagine what she'd gone through all those months, and the pain of realizing how she'd gone through it alone was nearly as bad as the pain of losing his son. So maybe she was right. Maybe in time, when it all made more sense, his feelings, his reactions would change.

But hating Fallon?

That would never happen. "It wouldn't be hate I'd have, waking up with you on that morning, Fallon. I might be angry, might want to put my fist through the wall…hell, if your walls weren't made of logs I'd put a fist through one right now. But these are things we can work through. Maybe get counseling…get it right away."

"I can't trust that, James. I can't trust…anything."

"Not even me?"

"I do trust you. That's the thing. You're the best person I've even known. The most noble. Someone who deserves a life with someone *they* can trust. And can you really say, right now, that you do trust me? Completely? Is trust your initial reaction toward me after everything I've told you?"

It wasn't. To be honest, there were so many emotions in him right now, he didn't know what he was feeling. "I need some time…"

"All the time in the world," she said, almost sounding relieved. "Because I don't have the heart to ever find out that you stopped loving me one day, and started hating me."

"I never knew you thought so little of me, Fallon," he snapped, rising from the couch.

"I don't think so little of you. But I do trust human

nature. It always comes through." And, finally, it was over. She'd pushed him away.

"You're wrong, Fallon. Dead wrong. I love you. That's all this is. I love you. But I can't do this right now." He stormed out, got to the den door, then turned around and went back to the living room. "And just so you'll know, I still love you. But you know what? I don't think you love me. You couldn't. Or else you'd have included me in this decision…not the one about our baby, but the one about ending our relationship. Because true love's about inclusion, not exclusion. And you talk about people turning their backs…about how you thought I'd turn my back on you eventually. Well, you're the one who turned your back. Not me. You."

"That's not fair! I'm doing this for you."

"Don't!" He ran an angry hand through his hair. "Pushing away someone who loves you, someone you love… You've fooled yourself into thinking you're doing this for me when, in reality, it's for you because it's the easy way out. Without me, you won't have to deal with your guilt. Not over what you did to me. But especially not over losing our baby. And that's the real guilt here, Fallon. The real anger." His voice softened. "Our baby died and you don't know what to do about it. Push me away, and you push that away from you, too. And, sweetheart, we really should be pulling together now. Now's the time we should be depending on each other to get us through it, except you won't let yourself depend on anybody, will you? And that gets to the heart of the matter. You can't let yourself depend on someone else." He shut his eyes, drew in an agonized breath. "Look, I love you, Fallon, and that's not going to change. But I love Tyler, and he needs me. I'm sorry I couldn't be the one you trusted enough to help make you whole again, but my son needs that from me now."

"And you should give it to him," she said.

"I'll give it to you, too. If you'll let me. But you have to be the one to ask, because I've done everything I can do, and I've run out of ideas. I want to marry you, want you to be Tyler's mother, but the next move is yours, Fallon. I have to fight the battles for my son, and I'll fight the battles for you…for us, too, but I have to know you'll be fighting with me, not against me. And here's the thing. It's OK to depend on someone else. I don't think you realize that, don't think you've ever allowed yourself to do it. And I'm not criticizing you for that, because I think you learned at a very young age that you couldn't depend on anyone. Tyler's learned the same thing but I'm going to teach him differently. I'm going to show him that some people will let him down, but most will not. You depend on someone, they let you down, it breaks your heart, and that's all he knows right now. All you know. Because of that you grew up strong. So strong that you became the one everybody else depended on. Then somewhere along the line you perceived any weakness in yourself as something that would let the people who depend on you down. They take you for granted…I took you for granted. But the one who takes you the most for granted is you, because you have to keep yourself at a respectable distance, especially when deep down you just want to lean on someone else for a little while. But here's the thing, Fallon. We all need to depend on others at one time or another. Hell. That's all I've been doing since Tyler came into my life."

He paused for a moment, watched her for something, anything. Saw the barriers up all around her, didn't know how to bring them down. And realized it wasn't up to him. Couldn't be up to him. Fallon had to want it. Fallon had to do it. Until she did, this was where they would stay. On that sad note, he walked over to her, bent, kissed her tenderly on forehead then straightened. "You're afraid to reach out, Fallon. Because what if you did and no one was there…like no one was there when you were a little girl? That's what this is about. Somewhere, some time, you've convinced yourself it's easier to do it alone. You stand out there by yourself as this larger-than-life woman who doesn't need anybody, someone who can handle everything by herself. But you're still that little girl who got pushed away, and you've convinced yourself that if you do it all alone, no one will hurt you. But you're hurt. And you're wrong. You can't do this alone. You shouldn't do this alone because what you've gone through… Our son died, Fallon. You didn't kill him. It wasn't your fault. No one should ever have to face something like that alone, and I'm sorry you didn't know that."

James drew in a deep breath, wanting her to respond, to say something, anything. But she wouldn't. He knew that. Knew from the expression in her eyes she was shutting him out again. And now there were no more words. It truly was up to Fallon. "I love you," he said. "I've done so many things the wrong way, so have you. But I'd never wake up some morning, look at you, and hate you. That's not what you're running away from, Fallon. And not why you're pushing me away either. I'm sorry for the choices we've both made, but there would never be a morning in my life that I wouldn't wake up knowing I loved you more than life. I trust that in myself. And I only hope you find some way to trust it in me, too. And in yourself. But if you can't…"

James withdrew to the den and shut the door, leaving Fallon alone, next to the Christmas tree. Looking up at the star on the top. "What have I done?" she whispered, pulling the blanket up to her chin, then rolling into a ball in the cushions. "What have I done?"

CHAPTER TEN

THE evening settled in bright and clear for the inaugural journey of the Christmas train, and a light dusting of snow throughout the day had made the whole event even more perfect for all the children lined up, anxiously waiting to board. For Fallon, it meant nothing, as she'd turned down numerous invitations to take the first ride. But for Tyler, and his new best friends Paige and Pippa, the all-day anticipation had been almost as bad as waiting for Christmas itself to arrive.

"Why can't she come?" Tyler whined, as he and James moved through the line to climb the steps to the train car. The train consisted of a circa 1928 steam locomotive, two cars and a bright red caboose. All restored to period, with a few exceptions meant to occupy the interests of children. Additions such as twinkling lights, music piped through the entire train and a refreshment stand specializing in hot chocolate and sugar cookies. Santa's huge throne-like chair, too. Elevated on a platform, painted in glitzy gold. For two weeks, a child's fantasy come true.

"She has other plans," James said stiffly. She was going to sit at home and order tongue depressors, or thermometers, or accomplish some other equally dull task. That's all she'd done for the past week…work. Since their talk, she'd avoided him as much as she could, choosing instead to spend any time they might have had together with her head buried in a catalog. Oh, she was wonderful with Tyler. They'd gone Christmas shopping, gone to the Ramseys' to bake Christmas cookies, gone sledding. All of it when he was working, of course. Then, when he came home, she retreated to her catalogs. That had been their sole existence for seven long, stressful days. But he'd never once thought that she wouldn't come with them for a ride on the Christmas train.

Then, a little over an hour ago, she'd begged off, saying she had work to do. Tyler's response had been to turn sullen, then knock over and break a lamp. Sometimes it seemed like they were taking two steps forward, one step back. And this latest setback with the boy was definitely that one step back. In another week, after Christmas, the backward steps they were going to have to face would be insurmountable, he was afraid. But what choice did he have? Fallon didn't want him. Even after everything that had been said between them, she hadn't budged. But Tyler desperately needed him, which made his course clear.

It took an hour to board everyone, get them seated in close proximity to Santa, who was, after arguments and promises, Walt Graham, on his best behavior. New diet, being overseen and cooked by Catie, owner of Catie's Overlook. Promises to take his medications, being overseen by Neil, Eric and Gabby. Promises to exercise more, being overseen on daily walks with Pippa and Paige Ramsey. All part of the bargain to be Santa. "Ho, ho, ho!" he yelled as the train finally pulled away from the station and dozens of children sat on the edges of their seats, waiting to be called to visit Santa.

"I wish Fallon had come," Gabby said, handing her son, Bryce, to his dad while she made herself comfy on the seat by propping a pillow behind her back. "She's been working like crazy, and we're really not going to be doing much toward opening the hospital until after my baby arrives. She's been so stressed out lately, and I think this would have been good for her."

"Any excuse," James muttered, sounding as bitter as he felt. It was sinking in, all of it. And, yes, he did hurt. Badly. But he was also angry, and not about the decisions Fallon had made those months ago. He was angry for the ones she was making now...the ones that kept him from helping her get through this. That kept her from helping him get through this. They needed to be doing this together, dealing with it, healing, holding onto each other through the pain, but every day she seemed to pull away from him more and more. "If it hadn't been work, it would have been something else."

"Sounds like the two of you aren't doing very well right now."

"Actually, there's no such thing as the two of us. Ask Fallon. She'll be the first to tell you that we've gone our separate ways. It's what she's wanted all along and it finally happened. She got her way." She'd won, but they'd both lost.

Gabby exchanged wary glances with Dinah, who was sitting directly across from her. "I thought she'd been doing better lately," Dinah ventured. "I mean, the only times I've seen her these past several days she's been with Tyler. And she looks totally happy. They have a good time together, and I don't think she's faking that."

"She'll do anything in the world for Tyler." Just not for Tyler's dad, he thought.

"Well, give it time," Gabby consoled. "I'm sure things will work out. Fallon's come a long way in just these past weeks. After what she's been through, it's pretty amazing, when you come to think about it."

"Well, what I *don't* have is time. Being a single dad is taking up every spare minute I have. I'm either working or taking care of Tyler, which isn't a complaint. But it's a fact of life for me now, and while I'd rather be doing everything with Fallon, she's not budging." He didn't know if her friends knew, or even suspected, the reason, and it wasn't up to him to tell them.

"But you're still going after full custody of Tyler, aren't you?" Dinah asked.

"It's in the works. My investigator finally located Shelly, so the legal papers were served and now we're waiting to see if the court gets a response from her." He'd wanted to celebrate that next step with Fallon, but she'd turned him down. Told him to celebrate with his son.

"And?" Dinah pushed.

"Nothing, so far. The judge has given her another week to respond then we're moving forward with or without her." With or without Fallon, too. Truth was, he was happy about almost everything. Not having Fallon part of his happiness with Tyler dampened the mood, but didn't ruin it. He wasn't going to let that happen. However, this should have been the best time of his life, and in ways it was. Still, part of him was holding back. He knew that, and couldn't get past it because hoping for Fallon to change her mind was dragging him down. Nonetheless, this was about Tyler, now. Meaning he had to move on and hope Fallon followed someday. Or, learn to live without her if she didn't.

"Well, if there's anything Eric and I can do to help you, please don't hesitate to ask. Our daughters are infatuated with your son…" She pointed to the seat across the aisle where the three of them had their faces plastered to the glass, looking at all the magical Christmas decorations outside. Lights formed in images of ice skaters, and palaces, and dinosaurs.

Dinosaurs… Just like Matty Brower had promised. It was time to shake off the glum mood and enjoy the ride with his son. "I appreciate the offer, but so far Tyler and I are doing fine. He's still up and down with the behavioral issues, but even those seem to be evening out." Evening out like Fallon had said they would. Damn, he wished she'd come on this trip. If ever anybody needed a flashing red Christmas dinosaur to brighten her life, it was Fallon.

She couldn't wrap her mind around tongue depressors. Not today, not any more. The job was nice to have, it gave her a sense of purpose, but it was also filling her with such longing to return to nursing. This evening, she was particularly restless. She'd wanted to go on the Christmas train but, truly, she didn't belong there. It was for the children, and their parents or grandparents. She wasn't a parent. She didn't have a child, didn't want to sit on a train full of parents who had their children. It would have hurt so much. More than that, she would be losing Tyler, soon. And James. So much loss for her Christmas, she just couldn't put on the act tonight. Not even for Tyler's sake. This was the way it was meant to be but she'd never counted on it hurting so much. Never counted on feeling so empty.

Well, she'd made her choices. The ones in the past, the ones now. *Her choices.* That's what she'd have to keep telling herself. Because James…what he'd said. She did want to believe that, did want, with all her heart, to trust that. "But it's what you wanted," she reminded herself as she stared at the Christmas tree, trying to forget. Yet she couldn't. Because the harder she tried, the more she thought about James, about the things he'd said. There'd been times these past days when she'd been on the verge of convincing herself that he was totally wrong about everything, telling her she was afraid to let someone help her, that she found it easier to be alone than have someone there to help her. At those times she almost believed he had been lashing out at her because he'd been hurt. Then she'd think about James, remember the reasons she'd fallen in love with him so quickly, so deeply, and realize that he never lashed out unfairly at anyone. And that he had deep, thoughtful perception. When she let herself remember that, the thoughts that always followed were how he was right. Right about everything. Then her gut would knot, knowing how wrong she'd been.

But making it right? It scared her to death. She didn't know how. Didn't want to feel the excruciating pain again.

So tonight she was alone, staring at the tree. A beautiful tree. Tyler had been adding ornaments daily, some he'd bought, others he'd made. She loved these days with him, wanted more. Hoped that James would allow her some visitations, too. In fact, she was positioning a few of Tyler's hand-made ornaments front and center when the phone rang. It was Emoline Putters, in a panic.

"Don't know what to do," she cried. "We've got Dr. McGinnis on call, and she can't leave the hospital…"

"Slow down," Fallon said. "Take a deep breath. Start at the beginning."

Emoline's deep breath was audible over the phone. "It's the train," she finally said. Then paused.

In that pause, a million bad scenarios passed through Fallon's mind. She held her breath, trying not to leap ahead, trying hard to hold to the moment. "What about the train?" she asked the older woman.

"They turned the bend at Hubbard's Creek, started up

the incline there. You know how it gets steep for a while then levels off before it gets steep again. They got to the part that levels off, and…"

Fallon shut her eyes, pictured the terrain. Steep rock face to the right, a small shoulder to the left then a drop-off into the river. Most of the ride was on even ground, but this was one of two places where the lay of the land was a little dicey. Probably not so much for a modern locomotive, but for the antiquated Christmas train…

"Anyway, they started up the second incline…"

She pictured that incline. Not too steep, but steep enough to slow down the train.

"Avalanche off Daphne's Pointe. Hit part of the train. Buried it."

Emoline's voice trailed off. Or maybe it was Fallon's mind, already on course for something else. "Did it stay on the tracks?" she asked pointedly. "Did the train stay on the tracks?" Worst case scenario, it had been shoved off the tracks and toppled over the edge. Maybe all the way down into the river.

"Don't know," Emoline said. "It just happened a minute ago. I called you first."

"Any communication from anyone on the train?" Unlikely, due to all the mountains.

"Not so far."

"Is the train completely covered with snow, or is any of it visible?"

"Don't know anything yet. Except we need you here. Need you to be in charge. You're the only one, Fallon…"

She didn't even hesitate when she responded. Because, yes, James was right. People depended on her. "Put out all the normal calls. Get all the rescue crews we have mobilized, call everyone who's not on shift back to the hospital.

I'm on my way." For the next ten minutes, trying to keep her mind on the road as she maneuvered through all the icy turns and curves, she caught her thoughts drifting off to James, and Tyler. They were on that train! Trapped, maybe hurt. Maybe… "Dear God," she whispered, forcing her concentration back on the road. "Take care of them. Please, take care of them."

The lights were out, and the little pot-bellied stove at the rear of the train car had long since been extinguished for fear that fumes could back up into the train car, cause carbon monoxide poisoning without proper ventilation. There was no way of knowing if this was the only car trapped or if the entire train had been buried. Naturally, his cellphone didn't work, but James kept trying for a signal anyway. Punching in Fallon's number, over and over. Finding some comfort in knowing that even though she wasn't answering, she was out there, somewhere. Or maybe it was simply that the glow from his phone was reassuring. Presently it, along with the glows from other phones, was the only thing that kept them from sitting in pitch blackness.

"When can we get off?" Tyler whined.

"In a while," he answered. Same answer for the last hour. Same answer all the parents were giving their children.

"But I'm cold. And I want some hot chocolate."

Me too, James thought as he pulled Tyler closer to him, fully prepared to have Tyler push him away. Which was what he always did when he was grumpy. But this time he wasn't pushing away. If anything, he seemed to be clinging harder and harder. "When we get off the train, you can have a gallon of hot chocolate. Two gallons, if you can hold that much."

"What's a gallon?" Tyler asked.

Paige and Pippa, sitting on the other side of the aisle with their parents, both giggled. "It's like what the milk comes in," their united voices rang out. "That's a gallon."

"Is it?" Tyler asked James.

"The ladies are right," James responded, once again flipping open his cellphone. Still no bars. Still no contact. But a little light was good and he dialed her number anyway.

Once again, nothing connected, so he settled back into his seat, staring into that light for a few moments. By now the rescue operation would have been called. Of course, all those in charge of mountain rescue were right here on the train with him. But that didn't bother him so much because by now Fallon would be in charge. And here he was, depending on that strength in her he'd come so close to criticizing.

"I need to get up and have a look at the scene," Fallon told Jess Weldon, one of the locals, who owned a helicopter. "Need to see what we're dealing with before we do anything." It was dark, no one had any idea as to the extent of the damage. But she couldn't put any kind of plan into action until she made the proper assessments and that, it seemed, was what everybody expected her to do.

"It's waiting for you," Jess said. "Any time you're ready."

"I know," she said, fighting against the panic welling up in her. She was perfectly content to never fly again. Walking, driving, taking a bus…all fine and dandy. But not lifting up off the ground. "Is there a road up there?"

"There is, but it will take you an hour, if you can even get through. It's probably not been cleared since the last hard snow, and I'm betting you'll probably come across a tree or two down on the road."

"So flying's the only way," she said, not to Jess but to convince herself.

"Unless you want to waste half the night, it is."

"Then all I have to do is…" Her hands started shaking. "Is get into the helicopter, fasten myself in, and…" And think of James and Tyler. And all her friends. They were counting on her now. Everybody in White Elk was counting on her, and here she was, working on a good case of nausea. She shut her eyes for a moment, trying to steady her unraveling nerves, but in the darkness behind her eyes she could see James and Tyler very clearly. "All I have to do is get in," she said resolutely. And that's exactly what she did. She marched to the helicopter, climbed into the seat, fastened herself in, and folded her hands in her lap as it lifted off into the darknight. Forcing herself to breathe. Forcing herself to concentrate on what had to be done.

Five minutes later, five minutes that felt like an eternity to Fallon, Jess was hovering over Daphne's Pointe, shining his spotlight down on the train. Or what should have been a train. The old locomotive and the first two cars were not visible at all, and only the tail end of the caboose could be seen. Those who'd been riding in the caboose were standing on the tracks, waving. Somehow the caboose had separated from the rest of the train and they'd managed to get out safely. That was a blessing.

The second blessing came when she saw that the rest of the train was on the tracks. Good news she radioed immediately to the hospital.

"Can I have a look at the side of the rock?" she asked after she was sure that the entire train was still upright. "Because what concerns me is that if we bring in crews to dig out the train, we might put them at risk from another avalanche."

"First avalanche we've had in these parts for fifty years," Jess said, bringing the helicopter round to a better spot. Once there, he turned his spotlight on the side of the mountain looming directly above the train. "Damned shame it had to happen just as the Christmas train was passing through."

While she wasn't an engineer, Fallon didn't rule out the possibility that the train was the reason the snow had broken loose and plummeted off the mountain. They'd had unseasonably warm weather, followed by several snowfalls, then warm weather, followed by snow again. The constant changing, plus the vibration of the train, seemed as good an explanation as any for what had happened. Only thing was, any more activity was likely to set off another avalanche, cover the train even more than it already was. And already Fallon was worried about the amount of oxygen inside the train cars. She had no reason to think that there would have been injuries as a result, but every fiber of her being screamed of suffocation because the train looked sealed shut inside a white mountain!

"I need an engineer who can figure out if the rest of the mountain's going to come down on us when we begin the rescue," she shouted to the group of people loitering in the hospital hall, waiting for instructions on what to do. "And I need someone who can tell me about the train car...what kind of timeline we're talking about on the oxygen situation."

Emoline stood off to the side, her hands jittery, her eyes full of tears as she took hasty notes.

"I want the best climbers we can find in White Elk, and notify the forestry service to respond, and I need..."

Strength. Dear God, she needed strength. There were so many people to rescue. If only James were here to help her through this. "Also call the avalanche center and tell them we need all the help that we can get, that we may have up to a hundred people trapped in those cars.

"How long's it been?" she asked Emoline.

"Just over an hour. Jackie Peterson called it in. He was watching the train from the opposite ridge. Saw it happen."

"Well, the good news is, we've got some people out on the tracks—they got out of the caboose. We need to get them out of there as fast as we can."

"I'll do that," said one of the volunteers, Mark Anderson.

She remembered him from the restaurant.

"I'll go with him," George Fitzhenry volunteered. "And take my crew." He was one of the senior members of the White Elk Mountain Rescue Team. "I'll also see about getting a bulldozer loaded up and transported down there. Maybe get another one coming in from the opposite side." He flipped open his phone and started dialing. "The back-up engine for the Christmas train should be available, so I'll have somebody go get it ready."

"They won't have much time," Mark Anderson whispered in her ear. "A few hours. But without fresh oxygen, and with all the carbon dioxide they're exhaling while they're sealed in…"

"It's going to take a miracle, isn't it?"

"I prefer to believe in skill," he said, quite rigidly. "Let the believers have their miracles. I'll rely on my skills."

"Then I hope you've got some mighty good skills because, at the end of the day, when they run out, we'll all be praying for a miracle. And that will include you too, Mark."

In the course of the next two minutes Fallon ordered out the rescue team's emergency lights, and put out a general call through White Elk that if anyone had any kind of generator-based lighting, or kerosene or propane lighting, they needed it. She wasn't sure yet how to get it to the scene, but she knew that this was a rescue that had to have as much light on it as they could muster. Daylight would have been good. Unfortunately, they didn't have it. But she depended on the people here to do what was necessary. She *depended* on them… "James," she whispered. "You were right about everything.

"I'll be working from the field," she told Emoline, as she did a mental check. "There are enough people here, in the hospital, to handle whatever comes in. And I'd feel better on the scene, directing operations from there." She'd feel closer to James and Tyler.

"You handle what you have to, any way you have to," Emoline said, batting away a tear. "We know you'll take care of this. You're the only one…"

An ominous distinction. One she didn't want, yet one she couldn't refuse. James was on that car. And Tyler. People she loved. People she didn't want to spend the rest of her life without. She'd already suffered so much loss, and the most excruciating pain…the one she feared most… was the loss of even more. She knew that now. And while every available avalanche expert and rescue team in the area converged on White Elk, she couldn't put aside the fact that she loved James and Tyler with all her heart and she'd made a huge mistake, turning away from them. *She did need them.* They would make her whole again. All these months, pushing people away, pushing James away… it had always been about her. Her fears, her denials, her pain. Not about James. Now she had to tell him. He had to know she'd been wrong, and he'd been right all along.

And all the time she'd wasted, trying to find ways to push him away… "We've got to get them, Emoline. That's all there is to it. We've got to get them." When they did, all she wanted was to collapse into James's arms and lean on him for a while…for ever.

At the two-hour point, Fallon went back out to the field. She needed to see the scene again. Needed to see if anything had changed, needed to direct all the people now coming in to help. So she turned over hospital preparation to half the handful of doctors who'd come in, and took the other half of them with her. Along with more than a hundred other volunteers. She wasn't sure what she would do with all that many people but if the train was declared stable enough, she'd have every one of them digging by hand, if that's what it took.

"Don't give up, James," she whispered, running through the parking lot on her way back to the helicopter. "I can do this. I know I can do this." If ever there was a time she needed to believe in herself, to trust herself, this was it.

At the three-hour point, Fallon received the news she'd been waiting for. "We think it's an isolated incident, Miss O'Gara," Ben Lawson from the avalanche center told her. "My engineers are up top and don't see anything that looks like it's going to come down. The snow load that broke loose is fairly light, so we should be able to move it off pretty quickly once we get the equipment out here. I do need to advise you that it will be a safer job for the rescuers if we wait until daylight. I commend all the people here for the way they're trying to light up the area, but it's not good enough, and I can't recommend a night-time rescue. It's too risky."

She glanced across the canyon at all the lights lit up on the opposite ridge. It looked festive, like White Elk had joined together, bringing every light they could find, just to have a party. Not to rescue the Christmas train and all its passengers. "They're going to run out of oxygen," she said gravely.

"They should make it until morning."

"Should?"

"It's hard to calculate."

"Well, *should* isn't good enough."

"Maybe not for you, but it's still not advisable to start some kind of haphazard rescue. It puts the rescuers at as big a risk as the people trapped in the train. And in all probability, like I said, the oxygen should hold out until we can get to them."

"And like I said, *in all probability* isn't good enough, Mr. Lawson." The tough decision was about to weigh down on her. She could already feel it pressing on her shoulders, feel all the people depending on her now crowding in. "I have to have a guarantee. A one hundred percent promise that if we don't go in tonight, every single person on board will come out fine and dandy in the morning when we finally do get to them. Can you give me that?"

He shook his head. "You need to know all the variables. That's all I'm telling you."

"And I appreciate that, but the only variable you need to know is that those people trapped in the train have to be rescued *now*. Not tomorrow. And it's my decision to make." She understood the risks both ways, but she also understood all those variables he talked about. And the one variable he didn't know was the volunteers…she knew them, trained them, worked with them, trusted them. Depended on them. More than that, they trusted her. It was a variable Ben Lawson couldn't even fathom. "My decision is that we're going to do it *now*."

* * *

"So, what's the status?" she asked George Fitzhenry.

"We got fifteen people off the tracks, and they're on their way back to the station. Walking. Cold. Shaken up. But glad to be alive. And, no injuries."

"That's good. What about the bulldozer?"

"We're in some luck there. We're about thirty minutes out, having one brought in from White Elk, and Aspen Grove is sending one up from their end of the tracks. It's got an ETA of about an hour. They're also sending in volunteers with it."

She glanced up at the helicopter overhead. Jess was back up again, hovering, keeping watch. His engine was loud. Could James hear it? Would he know that was her trying to rescue him? "Radio Jess for me. Tell him to set down in the meadow, that I need to go up top again and have another look for myself."

"At what?"

"The safety of going over the edge. We need people on top of the train. It's all well and good to dig from both ends, but we've got to get the top cleared so we can get some windows open. Ben Lawson said it looks stable to his people, but it has to look stable to me before I send anybody over the edge. And, George, I want you up there with me. By rights, you're the lead on this operation and I need your expertise on this."

"Maybe by rights, but I think I'd be barking orders at a crowd that's waiting for your orders, Fallon. They listen to me, but they depend on you, and that's the difference. But I'll go up with you. Give me five minutes to secure my team down here. OK?"

Five minutes where she wanted to dig at the snow with her fingers.

"When are they going to turn on the lights?"

James looked at the cellphone display. Four hours now,

and nothing. He'd expected…no, he'd hoped for..some-thing. A tap from outside, an errant cellphone message getting through. Anything. But they'd been sitting in the dark for four long hours, getting colder as well as running out of oxygen. Neil had managed to find a rescue tank in a supply closet and had it on hand for Gabby, who was too close to her due date to suffer any kind of oxygen deprivation. Other than that, all they could do was sit and wait, and not panic. Panic sped up oxygen consumption. Theoretically, they could exist here for days, if they had oxygen to breathe. They were safe, no injuries, no one suffering any real ills. And there was plenty of cold hot chocolate and cookies to dole out in moderation over the course of several days.

"I know she's working on it," Eric said from across the aisle, where he was huddled with his wife and daughters.

"She's got good instincts," Neil added. "She'll get this figured out."

But in time? James wanted to believe that Fallon could pull out a miracle, but even Fallon had her limitations. "You knew I wanted to marry her, didn't you?" he said into the dark, knowing all his friends were listening. Somehow, talking about Fallon brought her closer. Made him, and probably everybody else, feel more confident. Most especially made him believe with all his heart that Fallon would pull out the miracle. That she *was* the miracle. "That's why I originally applied for the job here, to be closer to her. She's stubborn, you know. I knew it was going to take some work." It still *would* take some work. And once they got off this train…

In the dark, as the silent agreement spread over them, everyone chuckled at their own recollections of Fallon's stubbornness.

"Haven't given up, though," James continued. "I thought I was going to, that it was time for me to move on with my life. Fallon has this idea that she's better off alone, but she's wrong about that. So once she gets us out of this, I'm going to start all over and this time do what it takes to convince her that she's wrong about that and I'm right." And he *was* right. Fallon needed him, and Tyler. She knew it, and she denied it, and she fought it because she was afraid they'd leave her, like her mother had. Like her baby had. What she'd done during those months when she'd been clinging to a futile pregnancy… He couldn't fault her for that because he would have been fighting to save *her* while she'd braved the fight to keep her baby. That's the Fallon he loved. But *that* Fallon wouldn't have given in to him, wouldn't have ever thought that *she* came first, not as long as her baby was still alive inside her. Not as long as she was holding onto hope. That, too, was the Fallon he loved. She'd done the only thing she could do, and hated herself for it. But now it was time to find a way to help her, to make her feel safe again, to convince her that the people who loved her wouldn't leave her. That he wouldn't leave her. When she understood that, her true healing would begin. And as hard as she would fight to push him away, he was prepared to fight even harder to stay.

"What are you right about?" Tyler asked.

"That the three of us should be a family." He'd sworn not to tell Tyler until the custody arrangement was in place, but he couldn't wait any longer. Fallon had waited too long to tell him what he should have known and they were both reeling from the devastation that had caused. He wasn't going to wait any longer to tell Tyler because Tyler did have the right to know he was wanted, that he was being fought for. The way Fallon would know as soon as he could tell her. "I'm working very hard right now to have you come live with me for ever. All the time, in that new house I'm buying for us."

"The great big one on the hill?" he asked.

"The great big house on the hill. Would you like to live there?"

Tyler didn't answer, but James felt his usual shrug. And smiled. That was as good as a yes.

From across the aisle, Dinah strangled back a sob. "That's so…nice," she said.

"We'll help you," Gabby said from behind him. "Whatever it takes, let us know."

It would take a change of heart from Fallon. And that was solely up to him to achieve. But it was nice knowing his friends were on his side.

Ben Lawson was right about the condition of the snow above the train, and it was such a relief. "It looks like most of the snow rolled off," Fallon said, aiming her light down the cliff. "And I think we can get down on top of that train."

"I've got eight strong climbers, all of them ready to go," George Fitzhenry said, clicking on his walkie-talkie. "Give us an hour, and we'll be down there."

"I want to go, too," Fallon told him.

"That's a long way down, Fallon. I know you're a strong climber, but are you up to it? I mean, it couldn't have been easy going up in the helicopter the way you did. I'm concerned that once you get to the edge of the cliff…"

"I can do this, George," she said. "Everything important in my life is in that train, and I have to go down there. And I'm going to be first, because I don't want a lot of weight on top of the cars until I've evaluated them. So, what, maybe send two people per car at first?"

"We can do that," George said. "But we're going to have to get some lights up here before anybody goes over the edge."

"That's the easy part," Fallon said, waving for Jess Weldon. "Jess," she said. "One hour. Get as many working lights up on Daphne's Pointe as you can.

"That other doc at the hospital…his name's Anderson. Mark Anderson…"

"What about him?"

"He just radioed me. Said he's a licensed helicopter pilot. Wants to know if we can use him."

"Eric has a helicopter…"

"It'll speed things up, having us both bringing up lights."

And speed was what she needed. "Tell him to do it. Also, I don't want any of the lights on the opposite ridge moved. We need them there as much as we need them up here."

"White Elk's bulldozer is five minutes out," George informed her.

"Then I guess I need to figure out what they'll do." She trotted after Jess Weldon, leaving George on the peak as she went back to the plateau below that was the marshaling area for everything taking place. After a fast consult with the engineers, it was agreed that the first task would be to get the caboose off the track. Dig it out, pull it away. While that was being done, engineers and experienced mountain rescuers were evaluating the stability of the train itself on the tracks. Best scenario was that is was fully upright, not tilting or skew in any way.

With things squared away there, Fallon was back to the helicopter. It was hard to believe that only a few hours ago an entire army couldn't have dragged her into one, and now there was no fear. It was what she had to do.

No thoughts to do otherwise. And this time, when Jess dropped her off up top, her next task was to get the climbers ready to go down. She being one of the climbers. No fear, again because when she allowed herself a moment to fix on the faces of James and Tyler there wasn't a question in her mind. Or her heart.

"What kind of casualties are you expecting?" one of the climbers asked her.

She wasn't thinking in terms of casualties. Sure, she'd alerted several hospitals in Salt Lake City to be on stand-by. And she'd arranged for a dozen ambulances to come in from all the surrounding villages and towns. But she wasn't expecting casualties. Didn't have room for that scenario in her mind.

"None," she said. Either everyone would survive with little to no injury. Or everyone would... But she couldn't say that out loud. If she lost James and Tyler...that was a tragedy from which she'd never recover. It put everything into place in her life. In that instant she'd heard about the train, she'd known...everything. "I'm not expecting any casualties," she said, praying it was true.

Tyler stirred against James's side. "I hear Santa," Tyler said.

It was the first thing anybody had said for nearly half an hour. People were uncomfortable and cold. Children were restless, adults were finally giving in to fear. People in the train car had talked at first and the mood had become quite jovial. Eventually, the talk died down to whispers, reverted to couples and families saying the things that needed to be said in their last hours. People were trying to make their peace.

Which was what he had to do with Tyler, James decided, now that Tyler was awake again. No more secrets.

Not ever. "When your mother brought you to me, I didn't know you were my son, Tyler. She'd never told me."

"Donnie used to be my dad."

"But not your real dad. He was your dad because he was married to your mom. But I was always your *real* dad, from the minute you were born. And I would have been there, Tyler. If I'd known you were my son, I would have always been there."

"Why didn't you know?"

Such a hard question. One he had to get right, so he thought for a moment. "I think your mother just forgot to tell me," he finally said. Someday, when Tyler was older, he'd understand. For now, this was enough. "Like the way you sometimes forget things."

"Oh," he said, totally accepting, then snuggled a little closer. "Well, I don't think Santa forgot, because I think he's coming to get us now."

The optimism of a child. It made him proud, and broke his heart for the things he'd missed, and the things he might never have now. He cleared his throat, swallowed back the emotion boiling up inside him. Now it was time to ask because he had to know, had to hear it from Tyler. "Do you want me for your dad?" he asked, a huge lump in his throat almost choking the words. "Do you want to stay here and live with me all the time now?"

"Sure."

It was a matter-of-fact *sure*, not an excited one, not an emotional one. But for James it was the single best word he'd ever heard in his lifetime, because Tyler had just accepted him. Now, if only Fallon would.

"And can I have Fallon for my new mom?" Tyler asked.

Across the aisle and behind him, the strangled sobs

from Gabby and Dinah rang out in the dark. "I'm working on it, Tyler. I'm really working on it."

"Good, and maybe I can help you, Dad." The word *dad* came so easily from him. Like maybe he'd practiced it, or been prepared for it? "Can you hear Santa *now*?" Tyler continued.

As James swiped at the tears streaming down his face, glad he was sitting in total darkness, he almost believed he, too, heard Santa. Then suddenly the train rocked... People inside gasped, several of the women sobbed. Fear of the unknown, that's what it was. They were frightened by the unknown. But he knew what the unknown was and, for sure, it wasn't Santa. It was the woman he loved.

Nothing could have stopped her from going over the edge when the time came. No person on earth, not even her own fear. In fact, she didn't even think about the height, or how she would be practically dangling in mid-air from the top of a mountain cliff when the OK was given to proceed. She simply lowered herself down, keeping her mind focused on the task ahead. The old Fallon was back, and Fallon was glad to embrace her. The fit was perfect, it felt good. Felt great.

Fallon was holding onto the ropes for dear life. It had been so many hours now, she'd lost track. But they were so close she could almost feel James's presence. "How should we proceed?" she asked George Fitzhenry.

"I think what we need to do is clear a section all the way across the train top and move it down the side. Get a window exposed, break it open. Each of the cars, and the engine. Once we do that, the rest won't matter. It'll probably take a while to get everybody out. And if we do have any serious injuries inside, or if Gabby chooses now to have that baby, we can deal with the rescue."

Progress in getting the area cleared took longer than Fallon expected because they had to take care not to cause too much rocking to the train. Digging out the snow, little by little, took an interminably long time. But finally a window was exposed.

"I can't see anything," she told George. She was trying to see inside. Suspended in the air, swaying with the mountain winds that were picking up as the night grew later and longer. But all she could see was blackness.

"Take the hatchet, and knock it out," George called to her. "Knock on the window a few times so people will move away, then break it."

Which was exactly what she did. One hatchet, one hard whack, and the window shattered into shards. Fallon didn't even wait for all the pieces to land before she screamed, "James! Tyler! I love you! Can you hear me? I love you! Nothing else matters. I want to marry you. *Both of you*. I want to marry you!"

"See," Tyler told his dad. "I told you I heard Santa."

"The best Santa I've ever heard," James whispered.

All around him, the people in the train car broke into spontaneous applause, not for the rescue but for James and Fallon.

It took nearly twelve more hours to get everyone safely home and pull the train off the tracks. The total casualty count—zero. People were cold, hungry, achy, but that was all. Days later, on Christmas Eve, most of White Elk gathered in the town square to sing carols and celebrate a miracle.

As for Fallon, she'd spent the past few days huddled under a blanket on the couch in front of the fireplace, barely taking her eyes off the people she loved most in the world. Clinging to them, and happy to do so.

People stopped by the house at all hours of the day and night. They brought food and gifts, or simply came for a short visit, and they were invited in. Welcomed. And when she thought about how things could have turned out so badly, and how many of her dearest friends would have been affected…well, she'd never take her friendships for granted again. She was a lucky woman because the people of White Elk were true friends. One of the best gifts of her Christmas was coming to understand the meaning of true friendship. The best gift of all, though, had arrived in the form of a letter from the court stating that Tyler's mother was relinquishing all custody, unconditionally. Maybe that was the only way Shelly knew how to show that she loved her son. Or maybe it was simply about convenience.

"We could always adopt," she whispered to James, as they were making plans for their future. Part of those plans being Emoline Putters's house. A place to start over, a place to heal *together*. And that would take time, and more pain. They understood that. But together it was something they could face. Together it was something they would work through and find a deeper meaning in their love. Fallon accepted that with all her heart. Because she trusted James. Because she depended on James.

"Or be grateful for the family we have," James said. "Because the three of us are pretty awesome together." They were watching Tyler contemplate all the gifts under the Christmas tree. "I don't need to have a dozen children to make me happy, Fallon. I know that's what you thought, maybe even what I thought. But sitting in that train all those hours, I had a lot of time to think. And what I came to realize was that with Tyler, and you, I have everything in the world I need to make me happy. Everything I want. And telling you that I wanted a dozen children was… arrogant."

"You're not arrogant," she said.

"Well, maybe not arrogant so much as unrealistic. But there's something about being stuck on a freezing train and slowly running out of oxygen that really grounds you. Really makes you take a hard look at your life. I wanted you before, Fallon. Have never stopped loving you, and won't stop loving you, no matter what kind of fears you have about that. We'll work through the past. There's still a lot of emotion there, a lot of pain, but we have time to make it better."

"I know," she said.

"Do you really?"

"I had a lot of time to think in those hours, too. And the one thing that kept coming back to me was you. I know you, James. Know your heart. You were right. It *was* me I was running away from, not you. Everything hurt so bad that I just didn't know what to do. I was so...confused. Lost."

"But I've found you, Fallon."

"And I want to stay found."

He tightened his hold on her, and she sighed contentedly. "I'm still stubborn. That's not going to change."

"I'm counting on it."

"And Tyler? Have you talked to him about...us?"

"Actually, he's the one who talked to me. Asked if you were going to be his new mom. In his matter-of-fact way, of course."

"With a shrug?" she asked.

"Only the way Tyler can shrug. One little gesture and my whole life fell into place."

"Poor James." Fallon laughed. "Treated with indifference the way most children treat their parents."

"A cruel dose of reality. And the best one I can think of."

"But look how happy he is now. That's all that counts,

you know. We have him, we'll take care of him, and we'll get him through whatever problems he'll have because of his past. The three of us…three's so much better than one." Nothing about Tyler's past was going to change. But that part of his life was over. Like so much of her past life had finally been put behind her. She was wanted now. Someone…two someones…finally, truly wanted Fallon O'Gara. And Fallon O'Gara finally, truly, knew that. "Want to build a snowman?" she asked her men.

James moaned, Tyler groaned.

"OK," she conceded, "let's play a game. I know it's not Christmas yet, but I'm pretty sure there's a game system under the tree. Santa dropped it off early so he wouldn't have to carry it around when he goes out later tonight, so…"

Tyler ran out from behind the tree, where he'd been organizing the packages. "Which one?" he squealed.

"The red one. But be careful you don't…" Words of caution on deaf ears. Tyler dove after the package, effectively knocking the tree flat on the floor, with him underneath.

"You OK?" James called, jumping up to rescue him.

"I found it. And it's just what Santa promised me."

Laughing, Fallon joined James, and both of them simply stared down at the mess. "We could just leave it," she said, snaking her hand around his waist. "Maybe if Santa stops by again he'll clean it up for us."

James bent to whisper in her ear. "I think Santa has something entirely different in mind for his next visit tonight. If we can ever get Tyler to go to bed. And somebody invites Santa upstairs."

"Santa's invited." They'd slept together, *all three of them*, for the past days. Mostly because she didn't want either of her men out of her sight, not even for a little while. But now it was time to move on. She knew that, understood it in profound ways. "Then I think we need to get that game set up and wear him out." She glanced anxiously at the stairs. It had been too long. It was time to rectify that. "Fast!"

"Are you sure, Fallon? I'm a patient man. I can wait."

"But I'm not a patient woman, and I can't. No more wasting precious time, James. Not ever again."

"Well, in that case…"

She expected a kiss, but what she got was a tug into the heart of the Christmas tree mess, first to retrieve their son, second to get his game. Time was being wasted and she did, indeed, have something to celebrate tonight. "I'm going in," James said, dropping to his hands and knees, blowing her a kiss then smiling. "Wish me luck."

Laughing, she tossed him an air kiss. "In case you don't come out, I love you. I always have. Always will."

"I know," James said, crawling partially underneath the tree then latching onto Tyler's hand. "I always knew you loved me. No matter what happened, I knew that, Fallon. And I've always loved you. I didn't always go about it the right way, but my feelings have never changed."

From James's lips to her heart. It was the best Christmas gift—ever!

You need to see the whole view, Fallon. That's where you'll find your happiness. Such wise words from Edith Weston. She did see the whole view now. It was a beautiful view. Perfect. And it was truly where she *had* found her happiness.

EMERGENCY: SINGLE DAD, MOTHER NEEDED

LAURA IDING

PROLOGUE

JT STOOD outside in the cemetery between his Uncle
Gabe and his grandma. The man wearing all black
except for a white collar was talking about what a wonderful person his mom had been and how much she'd
be missed. He dug the toe of his shoe into the soft earth,
sad because he already missed his mom. He had been
waiting and waiting at Uncle Gabe's for her to pick him
up. But she hadn't come.

Uncle Gabe said JT was going to live with him now.
He was glad 'cos he liked Uncle Gabe but he still
thought maybe his mom might come. They told him his
mom was up in heaven but he didn't know why they had
to put her in the ground first. Maybe she'd be so good
in heaven that God would send her back down to earth
to be with him.

Grandma was crying. JT felt bad. He'd cried when
they'd first told him how his mom had got hurt but now
he couldn't cry anymore. There was a heavy rock sitting
on his chest, but he couldn't cry.

He tipped his head back, looking up at the tops of the

trees near the gravesite. Was his mom already up there, looking down at them? Uncle Gabe had explained all about how heaven worked. Uncle Gabe said that his mom would always be there for him, watching over him like an angel. JT wished she didn't have to be an angel.

He wanted her to come back and be his mom.

Something small moved near the gravestones. It looked like a baby kitty, except the face had dark circles around the eyes. Not a kitty, but a baby raccoon. He watched the way the baby raccoon moved one way and then the other, as if it might be confused.

When the man in black stopped talking, the grown-ups came over to talk to Uncle Gabe and Grandma. JT ducked away when no one was looking. When he got close to the gravestone he discovered the baby raccoon on the ground was shaking as if it were scared.

Maybe Uncle Gabe would let him keep the baby raccoon as a pet? JT crossed over but the baby raccoon tried to get away, hiding in the grass. He quickly caught it in his hands, but it nipped at his finger. Surprised at the sharp pain, he let it go.

JT sucked the small drop of blood off his finger and watched the baby raccoon run away. Maybe it was too young to be a pet. He thought it must be a boy raccoon, lost and missing his raccoon family.

Just like he missed his mom.

CHAPTER ONE

One month later...

DR. HOLLY DAVIDSON hadn't even hung up her coat on the back of her office door when her pager chirped. First day on the job as the pediatric infectious disease specialist at the Children's Medical Center and she was more than a little nervous. She glanced at the text message: *Stat ID consult needed in ED.*

Okay. She blew out a breath. Guess she didn't have to worry about keeping busy. Trying to ignore her sudden anxiety, Holly tossed her purse into the bottom desk drawer and then quickly headed down the hall toward the elevators.

Several people nodded or smiled at her as she passed them. The anonymity of working with a sea of faceless strangers was a welcome blessing after the speculative looks and abruptly dropped conversations she'd endured for the year after her divorce.

She jabbed the elevator button with more force than was necessary. Well, now things would be different.

She'd come home to Minneapolis, Minnesota after five and a half years to make a fresh start, and to keep an eye on her ailing mother.

Keeping her chin up, Holly entered the busy arena of the ED. A couple of residents hovered around the central nurses' station, laughing and talking with the nurses. She wanted to warn them not to mix business with pleasure, but doubted her wise advice would be welcome.

"Excuse me, I'm Dr. Davidson. Which patient needs an ID consult?" she asked the unit clerk seated like a queen on her throne at the center of the main desk.

"Just a minute," the woman muttered, before picking up the constantly ringing phone. "Emergency Department, this is Susan. May I put you on hold for a moment? Thank you." Susan didn't seem at all frazzled as she glanced up at the list of patients. "ID consult? Mark Kennedy in room twelve."

"Thanks." Holly let Susan go back to her incessant phone calls and walked over to the computer terminal near room twelve, one of the many isolation rooms they had in the ED. She needed to get a little more information about her patient before she examined him.

She logged into the system, relieved her brand-new passwords worked without a hitch, and quickly entered Mark Kennedy's name to access his current medical record information. He was a fourteen-year-old who'd just entered his freshman year at a boarding school. He'd been brought in for nausea, vomiting, severe headache and stiff neck, complaints he'd had for the past two to three days.

Bacterial meningitis? Or the less severe viral meningitis? She hoped the poor kid had the less serious type
but was afraid it was more likely he had bacterial meningitis, given his history of being a freshman in boarding
school. They needed a lumbar puncture to make a de-
finitive diagnosis. Had one been done? She scrolled
down to read the notes, seeing there was a notation
about the LP being performed. The name of the ED at-
tending physician, Dr. Gabriel Martin, registered just as
a deep male voice behind her said her name.

"Holly?"

Her heart leaped at the familiar sound of Gabe's
voice. She had to brace herself before turning to face
him, knowing the smile on her lips couldn't possibly be
reflected in her eyes. "Hello, Gabe. How are you?"

The shock on his face didn't make her feel any better.
"You're back?"

"Yes. I moved home a few weeks ago. My mother has
some kidney failure as a result of her diabetes."

"I'm sorry to hear that."

They stared at each other for a long moment, the
awkwardness painful. Hard to believe they had once
been friends. A friendship she'd helped to ruin, long before Gabe had walked out as the best man on her
wedding day.

"It's good to see you." His statement was polite but
the reserved apprehension on his face said just the opposite. "Welcome home."

"Thanks." She hadn't been prepared to see Gabe
again, assuming he'd moved on with his life and his

career. Since he was still here at the Children's Medical Center, his career obviously hadn't changed. On a personal level, though, she suspected they were both very different from the carefree residents they had once been. She swallowed hard and looked over toward the isolation room. "Is Mark Kennedy your patient?"

"Yes." Gabe appeared grateful to get things back on a professional note. "He's a fourteen-year-old boy who just moved into a boarding school dormitory six weeks ago. His symptoms are pointing to bacterial meningitis."

She nodded. "I agree, although we need to isolate whether the source is Neisseria or Streptococcus. I'm leaning toward the latter, since it's often the cause of dormitory-related infections. Do you have the results of his lumbar puncture yet?"

"No." Gabe glanced at the computer terminal, which still displayed Mark's information on the screen. "When I reviewed his history and examined him, I requested he be placed in isolation. Several of the nurses may have been exposed, though. If he does have bacterial meningitis, they'll need prophylactic treatment."

"Of course. You'll need treatment, too." She turned toward the isolation cart, opened a drawer and pulled out a face mask, gown and gloves. "Have you started him on antibiotics yet?"

"No. I thought I'd wait for your recommendation first. Especially as I don't know the type of bacterial infection we're fighting."

"Start him on broad-spectrum antibiotics," Holly advised, trying not to notice Gabe hadn't changed much.

Tall, with dark brown hair, bright blue eyes and broad shoulders, he had a rugged attractiveness that she'd always been drawn to. Maybe there were a few more wrinkles around his eyes, but otherwise he looked good. Too good. Distracted, she focused on the situation at hand. "Mark has already had symptoms for almost three days. I'm worried he's going to take a turn for the worse if we don't get a jump on this."

Gabe nodded, agreeing with her recommendations. "I'll get the antibiotics ordered right away."

"Great." Once all her protective gear was in place, Holly stepped into the patient's room, leaving Gabe to enter the antibiotic order in the computer.

"Hi, Mark. Mrs. Kennedy." She felt bad for the patient and his family, and could empathize with how it must feel to end up with an infectious disease. "My name is Dr. Holly Davidson. I'm the infectious disease specialist here."

"Yes, Dr. Martin told me he was calling in a special- ist." Mark's mom looked upset, her eyes red as if she'd been crying. "Is my son going to be all right?"

"I hope so. We're going to start treating him imme- diately." She approached the bed, shifting her attention to the patient. Gently, she placed a hand on his arm. "Mark? Can you hear me?"

The boy was very lethargic as he opened his eyes and slowly turned his head toward her. "Yeah," he whispered.

Her stomach clenched. The poor boy was much worse than she'd originally thought. There was no in- dication in the record that he was this out of it, so maybe his neuro status had only just started to deteriorate. "Mark, we're going to need to start an IV in your arm to give you antibiotics." As she spoke, his eyes slid closed and he didn't respond. She hid a flash of panic. "Mark? Are you all right?"

"Yeah." He answered without opening his eyes.

She felt for his pulse, reassured herself that it was beating steadily beneath her fingers. She turned toward his mother. "Mrs. Kennedy, Mark seems to be getting worse. I'm worried the infection is affecting his brain."

Mrs. Kennedy's eyes widened in alarm. "What does that mean?"

"Just that the sooner we can start the antibiotics, the better." As she finished speaking, a nurse came into the room carrying IV supplies. As she finished her exam, the nurse prepared to place the IV catheter into the antecubital vein in Mark's arm.

"Mrs. Kennedy, I'm worried about you and your family. If this is a bacterial infection, as we suspect, it's highly contagious. You'll need to wear a face mask to help protect yourself from getting sick."

The woman paled. "Contagious? What about the rest of my family?"

"I'm afraid they may need treatment, too." Holly made her tone as reassuring as possible. "The good news is we can treat all of you so you won't get sick. How many siblings does Mark have?"

"Two younger sisters. They're only five and seven, children from my second marriage."

"All right, we'll make sure everyone gets the medication they need. And we'll probably need to tell the school too. His roommates may also need antibiotics."

The nurse placed the IV in Mark's left arm, the boy barely flinching as she slid the needle into his vein. Once the IV was running, Holly hurried out and grabbed more protective gear for Mark's mother, helping her to put the items on.

The mask was the most important piece, and Holly reiterated the need to keep the face mask on at all times.

Gabe walked into the room, carrying the mini-bag of IV antibiotics. The nurse took the bag from his hands and hung it on the IV pole, reprogramming the pump accordingly.

"Please, take a look at him. I think his mental status is much worse," she said in a low tone.

Gabe approached Mark, calling his name just as she had earlier. After a quick exam, concern shadowed his eyes. "He needs to be intubated." He glanced at the nurse. "Melanie, will you grab the intubation bin?" He turned toward Mark's mother. "Mrs. Kennedy, I need to put a breathing tube into Mark's throat to protect his airway. He's so lethargic I'm afraid he's going to stop breathing. I've already made arrangements for him to be transferred to the PICU."

Watching Gabe in action, Holly had to admit he was impressive. Especially the way he took the time to explain everything to Mark's mother. Emergency medicine wasn't her specialty and she stepped back to stay out of the way and to give him the space he needed to take care of Mark, but Gabe stopped her. "Holly, wait. I'll need your help."

"Of course." Her earlier anxiety returned as she walked back toward the bed, watching Gabe set up his equipment with deft fingers. She placed a reassuring hand on Mark's arm, hoping and praying that somewhere deep down he'd feel her touch. "Mark, we're going to place a breathing tube in your throat. It will be uncomfortable for a few minutes, but then your breathing will be much better." Mark didn't indicate that he'd heard her but that didn't mean much. He might not be able to make his muscles obey his commands.

"Help me position his head. With his stiff neck, I'm going to have trouble getting his head tilted to the correct angle."

She understood Gabe's dilemma, and moved over to help. The nurse sat next to Mark's mother, who'd started to cry. Holly wanted to cry right along with her but focused instead on helping Gabe place the lifesaving breathing tube in Mark's throat. Gabe's face was close to hers, the worry in his eyes contagious.

"A little more," Gabe said urgently, as he tried to slide the breathing tube down. "I can't quite get it."

Mark's neck muscles resisted the movement as she struggled to tilt his chin toward the ceiling. She met Gabe's eyes over his face mask. "I can't move his head back any more without hurting him."

Gabe nodded. "All right, then, we need a paralytic. There's some succinylcholine in a vial on the table. Give him a milligram and see if that helps."

Holly's hands were shaking as she tried to draw up the medication. She hadn't been this involved in an emergency situation since she'd been a resident. The medication would help relax Mark's muscles, but it would also stop him from doing any breathing on his own. She injected the medication and shot an apprehensive glance at Gabe. "How long before it works?"

"Not long." He met her gaze, as he gave Mark several deep breaths, using the ambu-bag. "Are you ready?"

She nodded. After the third big breath, Gabe set the mask and ambu-bag aside and she helped tilt Mark's head back to the correct angle. This time she was able to give Gabe the extension he needed. He slid the breathing tube into place, and pulled out the stylet. "Hurry. Hand me the ambu-bag."

After disconnecting the face mask from the end, she handed him the bag. He clipped a small device to the end of the endotracheal tube before connecting the ambu-bag, giving several deep breaths. The end-tital carbon-dioxide detector turned yellow, showing the tube was in the correct place. "Listen for bilateral breath sounds, just to make sure," he told her.

She tucked her stethoscope into her ears and listened as he gave more breaths. She nodded and folded the stethoscope back in her pocket with a sigh of relief. "Sounds good."

"Melanie, call for a portable chest X ray," Gabe directed. "And get a ventilator in here."

"We have the breathing tube in place, Mrs. Kennedy. Mark's breath sounds are good. I know this is scary, but Mark is better off now with this breathing tube in place." Holly did her best to reassure her.

"We'll give him some sedation too, so he doesn't fight against the breathing tube," Gabe added.

"Thank you," Mrs. Kennedy whispered.

Holly was glad to help. She reached over to hold the ET tube while Gabe secured it in place. "Nice job," she said in a low tone. Gabe's quick action had helped to save Mark's life.

His eyebrows rose in surprise and his gaze warmed, lingered on hers. "Thanks."

For a moment the years faded away, the easy camaraderie they'd once shared returning as if it had never left. She'd missed him, she realized with a shock. She'd missed Gabe's friendship.

And more? No. What was she thinking? Taking a quick step back, Holly decided it was time to leave.

"I'll check on the LP results," she murmured, before leaving the room. Glancing back over her shoulder, she saw Gabe was watching her with a speculative glance.

Her stomach tightened as she let the door close behind her and began stripping off her protective gear. She and Gabe had grown close in those months up until her wedding. But that had been nearly six years ago.

She'd learned two hard lessons since then. Men couldn't be trusted and never, ever mix personal relationships with professional ones.

Unfortunately, Gabe lost on both counts.

Gabe instructed the respiratory therapist on the vent settings he wanted Mark to be placed on and spent a few minutes reassuring Mark's mother that they were doing everything possible for her son. He took the time to make sure Mark was comfortable and that his vitals were stable before he left the room. While stripping off his protective gear, he glanced around the ED arena, disappointed to realize Holly was gone.

He opened Mark's electronic medical record and read her note. She recommended changing the antibiotics now that the LP results were back, confirming streptococcal meningitis. She went on to recommend prophylaxis to any exposed staff and for all of Mark's immediate family.

He finished arranging for Mark's transfer to the PICU, and then followed up with the nursing staff who'd been exposed to Mark before he'd been placed in protective isolation. He wrote prescriptions for Mrs. Kennedy's family and one for himself.

Once he was caught up with his work, he went over to the unit clerk. "Will you page Dr. Holly Richards for me again?"

Susan, the unit clerk, frowned at him. "Holly who? You mean the infectious disease doctor? Dr. Davidson?"

Davidson? She'd changed her name from Richards to Davidson? Had she been wearing a wedding ring? He didn't think so. The truth hit him like a brick between the eyes. Holly must have divorced Tom, taking back her maiden name.

Guilt burned the lining of his stomach as he realized her divorce might be a part of the reason she'd returned home. He furrowed his fingers through his hair, not entirely surprised by the news.

Damn. It wasn't too hard to figure out what had happened. He'd bet his life savings Tom had cheated on her. The jerk.

Guilt swelled again, nearly choking him. He should have handled things differently. Why had he believed Tom when he'd claimed he'd changed? Tom had always been too much of a womanizer, and Gabe suspected Tom hadn't changed, even after Tom had asked Holly to marry him. But he hadn't had any proof, just the deep niggling suspicion that wouldn't go away.

On the day of Holly and Tom's wedding, he'd noticed Tom flirting with Gwen, Holly's maid of honor, and confronted him. They'd argued bitterly. Tom had sworn he'd given up other women, promising he'd gotten them out of his system once and for all. Gabe hadn't believed him, telling Tom how Holly deserved better. Tom had turned the tables on him, accusing Gabe of wanting to cause trouble as he desired Holly for himself.

The accusation had been painfully true. More true than he'd wanted to admit.

He'd known the wedding was a mistake, but had figured there wasn't anything he could do about it. But as the hour had grown closer, he'd realized he couldn't stay. Couldn't stand next to Tom at the altar as his best man, watching Holly marry a guy who didn't deserve her love. So he'd handed the rings to one of the other groomsmen and left the church. In some perverse way he'd hoped Holly would get the message and do the same.

But he'd learned later that she hadn't walked away.

The wedding had gone ahead as planned. She and Tom had moved to Phoenix, Arizona shortly after the wedding, so Tom could take a position as medical director of a large surgical intensive care unit while Holly had taken a critical care fellowship position.

Only now she was back, as Holly Davidson rather than Holly Richards. And she was an infectious disease specialist, not a critical care intensivist.

"Did someone page?" Holly asked, walking back into the arena. She'd come from another room, and he felt foolish for interrupting her while she was seeing another patient.

"I did." He hated this feeling of unease between them. "When you're finished, will you give me a call? I'd like to talk to you."

"I'm ready. I just need to write my note." She was looking at him with a puzzled expression, as if she couldn't quite figure out what he wanted to discuss. No surprise, since he wasn't sure what he was going to say to her once they were alone either.

Regret, mingled with guilt, continued to weigh on his shoulders. He couldn't help feeling her divorce was his fault. Especially since he suspected Tom's infidelity might have started before the wedding. Maybe he could have prevented her from marrying Tom if he'd really tried.

"I'll wait." Luckily, the ED wasn't too busy. He'd seen and written orders on all the patients who'd been brought back so far. Mark was the only serious case needing his attention.

Holly strode to the closest computer and signed in.

His gaze roamed over her familiar features. She was more beautiful than ever. Her shoulder-length dark hair framed a heart-shaped face. Her dark brown eyes were always warm and smiling.

"Has Mark taken a turn for the worse?" she asked, logging off the computer.

"No, I just sent him to the PICU." He took Holly's arm and steered her toward the physician lounge, grateful to find it empty. "And I changed his antibiotics, as you suggested."

"Good. I'll go up to visit him in the PICU later. I'm still very worried about him, I hope he turns around with the antibiotics soon." She glanced around at the empty lounge, then back up at him. "So what's up?"

He hesitated. There was so much he should say, but part of the problem was that he should have told her his suspicions a long time ago, even without proof to back up his claim. Yet just like all those years ago, the words seemed to stick in his throat.

She sighed and jammed her hands into the pockets of her lab coat. "You don't have to do this," she said slowly. "I already know why you left the church the day of my wedding."

His mouth dropped open in surprise. Had Tom told her about their fight? If so, he'd no doubt left out key details. "You do?"

She nodded, finally bringing her gaze to his. "It was my fault. Because of the night I ruined everything by almost kissing you."

CHAPTER TWO

THERE. She'd said it. Boldly brought up the night she'd crossed the line, ruining their friendship, forever.

After admitting the truth, Holly felt as if a huge weight had rolled off her shoulders. It was good to have everything out in the open between them. At first she'd been so angry at Gabe for walking out on her wedding, until she'd realized it had been her own fault.

Looking back, she realized she should have taken her subtle feelings toward Gabe, and his subsequent leaving of the church, as a sign. Especially after the horribly public and painful way her marriage had ended. Still, wasn't it always easier to look back after the fact, to realize what you should have done?

"Holly, it wasn't your fault at all."

He was just saying that to be nice. The night she'd almost kissed him, he had been the one who'd pulled back, who'd stopped her from making a terrible mistake. She hadn't even had a good reason, the situation hadn't started out as anything more than two friends going to check out a band for her wedding. Tom had been called into surgery, so Gabe had gone with her instead. They'd crashed the wedding, had a few drinks and danced, deciding then and there to hire the band. She'd only intended to thank him for coming along. But the moment she'd looked up into his dark eyes the atmosphere had changed. Suddenly she'd wanted to kiss him. Had actually leaned toward him, until he'd pulled back, making her realize what she'd almost done.

Afterwards, she'd been horrified at her near miss. And, right or wrong, she hadn't said anything to Tom. What could she say? That she'd almost kissed his best friend? She hadn't, but being tempted even for a second was bad enough. She'd tried to brush the whole episode off as a foolish mistake, a result of too much wine, but that moment in time had bothered her long afterwards.

"When did you divorce Tom?" he asked.

Her eyes widened. Good grief, had the news of her divorce traveled all the way across the country? A note of panic laced her tone. "What makes you think I divorced him?"

For a moment he looked taken aback by her question. "Because you're using Davidson, your maiden name."

She let out an exasperated huff, realizing she'd overreacted. Thank heavens the gossip mill hadn't reached this far. She didn't want Gabe to know the gory details. "Not all women take their husband's name," she pointed out. After the divorce she'd wished she hadn't, as changing her medical license in both the state of Minnesota and the state of Arizona had been a pain. "But you're right. Tom and I split up almost two years ago."

"I'm sorry," he murmured.

He was? She ignored the tiny pang of disappointment. "So am I. But I'm over it now." She didn't care about Tom anymore. Any feelings she'd had for him had been wiped out by his betrayal.

But she didn't think she'd ever get over losing her daughter. The familiar wave of grief tightened her stomach. She'd wanted children so badly, had been so thrilled to become pregnant. Looking down into her daughter's sweet, tiny face and knowing she'd been too young to survive had been heart-wrenching.

She'd never forget Kayla. Lost in the sorrowful memories, she belatedly realized Gabe was staring at her. With an effort she tucked her daughter back into a protected corner of her heart and glanced around. "I, uh, need to get back to work."

"Wait." He held out his arm, stopping her from brushing past him. "I'm sorry, Holly. You have every right to be angry with me."

"I'm not," she protested. His fingers were warm against her arm and she must be pathetic and desperate to wish he'd haul her close. She needed to get a grip on her emotions and keep a polite distance between them. "Honest." She stuck out her hand. "Friends?"

He stared at her outstretched hand for so long she feared he wasn't going to take it, but then his large hand engulfed hers, easing her inner tension. "Of course, Holly. I'll always be your friend."

"Good." One could never have too many friends, right? She missed her friend Lisa from Phoenix, but somehow suspected Gabe wasn't going to be able to fill that role. She shook his hand firmly, before stepping back. Nothing good would come of rehashing the past. Moving forward was what was important. Taking this position at the Children's Medical Center was a huge step forward in her career. Now that she was here, she wanted to do a good job.

And if that meant working with Gabe on a professional level, then fine. No problem.

"Gabe?" One of the nurses poked her head into the lounge. "There's a call for you. It's JT," she added when he looked as if he would brush her off.

He nodded and turned away. "I have to take this, Holly. Excuse me." Without waiting for a response, he strode out to the closest phone.

Curiosity compelled her to follow him, shamelessly listening to his end of the phone call. "JT? What's wrong?" He paused. "Another nightmare? Hey, it's all right, buddy. I understand. I'm glad you called, see? I'm here at work. Everything is fine. I love you, JT."

Holly sucked in a harsh breath, shock rippling all the way down her body to the soles of her feet. From the tone of his voice and the brief reassuring conversation it was easy to deduce JT was a young child.

His son. Gabe must have a son.

Which meant he was likely married, too.

A stab of disappointment pierced her heart, stealing her breath.

"Maybe you'd better let me talk to Marybeth, okay?"

Gabe said in a cajoling tone. "Don't worry, I promise I'll run home to see you during my lunch-break."

Holly turned away, feeling slightly sick. Why she was bothered by the fact that Gabe had a son and a wife, she had no idea. He certainly deserved to be happy. But she couldn't help feeling as if the rug had been pulled out from beneath her.

Maybe because Gabe had a family.

And she didn't.

For a moment she remembered the excitement of being pregnant, the thrill of carrying a tiny life in her womb.

But she'd lost her small daughter. And in almost the same moment had lost her husband.

No, a family wasn't in her future.

She must have been standing in a daze because suddenly Gabe was back. "I didn't mean to ditch you like that, but when JT has nightmares, he needs to talk to me right away."

"Sure, I understand. Congrats." She pushed the word through her constricted throat, trying not to dwell on the painful past. "On your marriage and your son."

"I'm not married," he said, a slight edge to his tone. "Marybeth is JT's babysitter."

He wasn't married? Skeptical, she found herself wondering if he was really telling the truth, but then remembered how he'd referred to Marybeth by name. He hadn't said maybe JT should let him talk to *Mom*, he'd said maybe JT should let him talk to *Marybeth*. The difference eased the tension in her chest.

"Sounds like you have your hands full," she murmured. She wondered where JT's mother was. Had Gabe gotten a divorce too? Did they share custody?

"Yeah, a bit." He shrugged, although his expression was still troubled. "I'd ask you out for dinner, but I can't leave JT home alone and his babysitter takes night classes."

Dinner? As much as she was tempted, she knew seeing Gabe outside work was just asking for trouble. The last thing she needed was to be seen with one of her colleagues outside work. Still, it sounded as if he might need some help. And she was more curious than she had a right to be about JT's mother. "It's okay, but if you need help with JT, let me know."

He flashed a lopsided smile. "Thanks. But I think I have everything under control."

Of course he did. Gabe was always strong, and extremely competent. The way he'd taken control with Mark proved that. "See you later, then."

"Take care, Holly."

She turned away, heading back to her office where she'd left the list of patients she was scheduled to see.

The list was long, but that was all right. Better to keep busy than to wallow in the mistakes of the past.

Or to wish for something she could never have.

After he found someone to cover over his lunch-break, Gabe rushed home, knowing he didn't have a lot of time. "Hey, JT, how are you?"

"Uncle Gabe!" The five-year-old threw himself into Gabe's arms. "I missed you," he mumbled against his shoulder.

Gabe closed his eyes, holding the little boy close. The poor kid had been through so much, yet he couldn't keep leaving work every day either. "I missed you too, sport." He hugged JT tight, then eased back to look into the boy's eyes. "You had the bad dream again?"

JT nodded. "Wild animals came out of the woods and tried to bite me."

Gabe didn't understand this sudden fear of wild animals that JT seemed to have. But he suspected the real underlying factor was losing his mother. And worrying if he was going to lose Gabe too. "Last night, before you went to bed, I explained how I had to work today. Remember?"

JT's lower lip trembled, his blue eyes wide. "I know, but when I had the nightmare, I forgot."

"It's okay." He couldn't be mad at the poor kid, after everything he'd been through. When his sister, Claire, had been killed in a car crash, he'd taken custody of JT. His mother, who'd recently moved to Florida and remarried, had offered to move back to help out in raising her grandson, but he'd declined her generous offer. After all these years, his mother deserved to be happy.

So he'd taken JT because there wasn't anyone else. And he'd even gone as far as to apply for formal adoption. He'd managed to get things moving the week after Claire's death but now they were waiting on DNA tests from the two men who, according to his sister's diary, may be JT's biological father. Despite the security he'd tried to give his nephew, JT had a deep fear of losing Gabe in the same abrupt way JT had lost his mom.

He'd hoped the boy's nightmares would fade over time, but so far no luck. Of course, it had only been four weeks since the funeral.

"Everything all right?" he asked Marybeth, JT's babysitter. The girl was a young college student who watched JT during the day and took a graduate class two evenings a week, on Mondays and Wednesdays. He was lucky to have her, especially when she'd established a great rapport with his nephew.

"Fine," she reassured him. "JT is always better once he talks to you."

Crisis averted, at least for the moment. "Do you think he's okay to attend his pre-school this afternoon?"

"Sure. I think he'll have fun."

"Okay, then. I'll pick him up on my way home."

"Let me know if you run into trouble, I don't start class until six o'clock."

"I will." The few times he'd had to work late Marybeth had been more than willing to pick JT up after pre-school. He turned back toward JT. "I'm going back to work now, but I'll pick you up at four. You know how to tell the time, don't you?"

JT nodded with enthusiasm. "Yep. When the big hand is on the twelve and the little hand is on the four." He hopped from one foot to the other, his earlier fears seemingly forgotten. "Me and Jeremy are going to play swords this afternoon."

"Be careful." Why did boys always want to play with weapons? Gabe figured he must have done the same thing at JT's age, but it was amazing how almost anything he gave the boy to play with ended up as a sword, a knife or a gun, no matter how hard he tried to discourage it. Maybe JT could use the sword to kill the wild animals in his dreams. He pressed a kiss on the top of JT's head. "All right, then. I'll see you later, buddy."

"Bye, Uncle Gabe." JT's face was relaxed and smiling, making him feel better about going back to work. As he strode to his car, he noticed he'd barely have time to wolf down a quick sandwich before seeing patients. But the potential indigestion from eating too fast was worth taking the time to calm JT's fears.

Too bad he hadn't been able to ask Holly out for dinner, but leaving JT wasn't an option. The boy's emotional status was still too fragile. Would probably be too fragile for a long time to come.

Yet after meeting Holly again that morning, he couldn't get her out of his mind. Interesting how she'd assumed he'd left because of the moment he'd sensed she'd been about to kiss him when in reality it had been his own response he'd run from. She couldn't know how close he'd come to crossing the line that night, too. Stepping back from her had been one of the hardest things he'd ever had to do.

Tom had been right during their argument on his wedding day. He *had* wanted Holly for himself. But that was then, and things had changed. He wasn't just a single guy anymore, he had JT to think about now. The boy needed a home, stability. Besides, he wasn't still hung up on Holly.

He'd moved on with his life, had been engaged to

marry Jennifer before Claire had died. Their engagement had been broken off when he'd discovered that she hadn't been at all willing to take JT in as their adopted son. She'd kept arguing that they needed to find JT's real father, something he was trying to do. His plan all along, even once they found JT's biological father, was to fight for sole custody of JT.

Forced to make a choice between Jennifer and JT, his young nephew had won hands down. And if the reality of living with a young boy day in and day out was overwhelming, he'd have to learn to deal with it.

He caught a glimpse of Holly leaving the ED and his pulse kicked up in awareness. He took a deep breath, trying to ignore his body's reaction, telling himself it was only physical because he hadn't been with a woman since Jennifer had walked out on him.

There were more important things to worry about than the last time he'd gone out with a woman. Right now, JT had to come first.

With everything that had happened in the past, he knew better than anyone that he and Holly could never be more than friends.

Holly spent the rest of the afternoon trying to keep her mind off Gabe and figuring out how to balance the stat calls with the scheduled patients she needed to see. At three-thirty, her mother called to let her know she was finished with dialysis. Holly had just finished seeing her last patient, so she readily agreed to drive her mother home.

The outpatient dialysis unit wasn't far from Children's Medical Center, so it didn't take her long to get there. She tucked her mother into the passenger seat, and then headed to her mother's house.

Hemodialysis treatments usually left her mother feeling exhausted, but that didn't stop her from asking questions. "How was your first day at work?"

"Pretty good. Busy," Holly answered as she negotiated rush-hour traffic. She cast her mother a quick glance. "I really like my job. I have many interesting cases."

"I'm glad." Her mother smiled faintly, her face pale. "I hope I didn't take you away from anything important."

She thought of Mark, the young boy whose condition was still so tenuous. "No, you didn't. Although I do have a very sick young man in the PICU."

"I'm sure you'll help make him better." Despite her mother's reassuring tone, deep lines of fatigue bracketed her mouth. For a moment Holly felt a flash of resentment toward her father. Her father had been Dr. Kendall Davidson, the chief of neurosurgery and he'd died several years ago after a long night of surgery. Her parents had divorced when she'd still been in high school, a traumatic event when she'd discovered her father had been cheating on her mother. When his young lover had become pregnant, he'd filed for divorce.

She'd made peace with her past, except for rare moments like this, when resentment still burned. How ironic that by marrying Tom she'd made the same mistake her mother had.

Tom had seemed to want the same things she did, a

loving home and family. Children in particular were important to her, she hadn't wanted to put her kids through a painful divorce like she'd experienced.

After Kayla was stillborn, Holly had known there wasn't anything left of her marriage to save. Wisely, Tom hadn't bothered to put up a fight. To his credit, he'd made the divorce proceedings as painless as possible.

Pushing the memory aside, she pulled into her mother's driveway and brought the car to a halt. After getting sick, her mother had finally given up her mausoleum of a house to move into the much smaller, more practical home located closer to the hospital. So close she could easily take a care-van to her dialysis appointments. Holly hurried around to open the car door. "Here, let me help you."

Her mother leaned heavily on her arm as Holly guided her inside. After she'd got her mother settled on the sofa, covered in a warm, wool blanket, she went into the kitchen and threw together a light meal of scrambled eggs and toast, carrying everything out on a tray.

"Thanks, Holly." Her mother's grateful tone made her feel guilty for leaving during those years she'd been married to Tom. It was good that she'd come back home. Obviously her mother needed her.

"You're welcome." She leaned over to give her mother a gentle hug. "Is there anything else you need before I go?"

"No, thanks, dear."

"All right, then. Call my cell if you need me." Holly let herself out of the house, wondering if the time would come that her mother might need more full-time care. If so, she'd do her best to take care of her.

Family was important, even if her father and Tom hadn't thought so.

Her pager went off and she paused in the driveway to glance at the display. The message wasn't from work, as she'd expected, but rather from Gabe.

Please, call me when you have a minute, Gabe. He'd left his number on the text message too.

Was he still at work? Had something happened to Mark? With a frown, she flipped open her cellphone and dialed his number.

"Hello?"

"Gabe? It's Holly. What's wrong?"

"I picked up JT from his pre-school and something just doesn't seem right. He's running a low-grade fever and has chills." Gabe sounded uncertain, not at all like his usual self. "I don't think it's serious, but I could use a second, unbiased opinion." He paused and then added, "If you're not too busy."

She hesitated for the barest fraction of a second before she realized she was allowing her personal need to stay away from him to interfere with taking care of a sick child.

How could she turn him down? After all, she'd offered her help. "Of course I'm not too busy. I'll be right there."

CHAPTER THREE

HOLLY wasn't sure what to expect when she arrived at Gabe's house. Luckily, his directions had been easy to follow, but when he opened the door before she had a chance to knock, it was clear his usual calm composure had deserted him. He wore a haggard expression and his brown hair stood on end, as if he'd raked his fingers through it non-stop for the past few hours.

"Thanks for coming over." Gabe stepped back to allow her to come in. "I'm pretty sure JT just has a virus, but I want to make sure I'm not missing something, like strep. I've peered down his throat so many times I'm starting to doubt myself."

"That's because you're thinking like a parent, not like a doctor." She'd seen plenty of stressed parents and those with medical backgrounds weren't any different.

"Yeah, maybe." He sighed and scrubbed a hand over his jaw. "I know I'm probably overreacting, but this is the first time JT's been sick."

"The first time, ever?" She was taken aback by the news, considering the boy was five years old. Most kids at least had the occasional ear infection or bout of flu before the age of five. "I'm surprised."

She barely had time to notice the warm, welcoming earth tones of his living room before he dragged her down the hall to his son's room. "I'd like you to take a look at him. My first instinct was to treat him with a pain med and wait to see how he does overnight, but he's been so listless I've started to doubt my objectivity. Be honest. Tell me if you think I should take him into the clinic."

"All right." Odd, it wasn't at all like Gabe to doubt himself. He was after all board certified in emergency medicine. Taking care of sick kids was his specialty.

But, then again, she'd made similar mistakes with horrible consequences. Assuming her cramping pains during her pregnancy had been from stress and not from placenta previa, a condition where the placenta broke away from the wall of the uterus prematurely. She'd downplayed her situation and had lost her daughter as a result.

Even if she had gone to seek help earlier, there really hadn't been a chance of saving the baby, not at only twenty-five weeks gestation. Still, her medical knowledge hadn't helped her then.

Gabe's might not be helping him now either.

He pushed open the door to a small, cozy bedroom. "JT? Hey, buddy, this is Dr. Holly. I've asked her to take a look at you."

"Hi, JT." She approached the boy, who was curled up on the bed.

"Hi." His dark blue eyes, so much like Gabe's, stared up at her. "I don't feel so good."

"So I hear." She sat on the edge of his bed, noticing his face was flushed. She offered a reassuring smile. "Does anything hurt you?"

"My head hurts."

"Hmm. How about your throat?" She felt his forehead, noting he was indeed running a slight fever but not one that was dangerously high. She trailed her fingers down to his throat. No swollen glands from what she could tell. "Can you open wide for me?"

Obediently he opened his mouth. "Ah-h-h."

Using her penlight, she peered down his throat. No sign of any infection at all, from what she could see. Although maybe it was too early to tell. "Great job. How about your tummy? Does that hurt?" She gently palpated JT's abdomen, and he didn't wince, neither did she find any enlargement of his liver.

"No, just my head. The lights are too bright."

Hmm. Strange that he would have photosensitivity. She spent another minute or so examining him, but didn't find anything seriously wrong. His pupils were equal and reactive. Yet, like Gabe, she sensed something just wasn't quite right. She glanced back at Gabe, who hovered over her shoulder. "You treated his fever?"

"Yeah, I gave him a dose of pediatric pain med right before you came over."

"Good." JT closed his eyes, either because the light was too bright or he was simply tired and falling asleep.

"He was fine at noon when I came home for lunch," Gabe muttered. "Suddenly I pick him up from his pre-school class and he's running a fever and not acting at all like his usual self."

"I'm sure it's just a virus," she assured him.

"So you don't think I need to take him in?" Gabe asked.

She hesitated for a moment, and then shook her head. "No, I think I'd wait and watch him. If his headache persists tomorrow, though, I'd take him in. Kids do get headaches with fevers." She rested her palm against JT's flushed cheek for a moment, thinking how young and innocent he looked.

JT's eyelids fluttered open. "You're pretty," he murmured.

His sweet expression tugged at her heart. It was no secret where the boy had gotten his charm. "Thank you."

She glanced up to find Gabe watching her intently.

"JT obviously has good taste," he murmured in a low tone.

Raising a brow, she didn't try to come up with a response. Since JT was starting to doze off, she gently stood and tiptoed out of the room. Gabe followed her, softly closing JT's door behind him.

By mutual consent, they moved into the living room so they wouldn't wake him. Gabe's expression held chagrin. "I suppose you think I'm an idiot for calling you over."

"Not at all." Holly subtly looked for pictures of JT's mother, but didn't find any. "I'm sure it's not easy being a single parent."

"No, it's not." Gabe dropped onto the sofa with a sigh. "I don't know what got into me, but suddenly I was staring down at him, thinking the worst. And then I thought of how stupid I'd look if I took him in for nothing. But if you hadn't answered your page, I probably would have risked it."

"Hey, it's all right. I really don't mind." She sat in the matching love seat across from him. "I know it's none of my business, but where is JT's mother?"

Gabe stared at his hands for a long minute, before lifting his head, his eyes dark with pain. "She died in a car crash less than five weeks ago."

"How awful," she murmured, thinking it was a good thing JT had someone like Gabe as his father.

"Yeah, it's been a little rough, more so for JT." Gabe abruptly stood. "Are you hungry? I made some spaghetti for dinner but JT wasn't hungry. The least I can do is feed you for your trouble."

His abrupt change of subject caught her off guard, but hearing that JT's mother had died so recently she supposed she couldn't blame him for not wanting to talk about it.

Gabe headed for the kitchen, leaving her little choice but to follow him. She knew being here with him was like tempting fate to repeat itself, but the spicy garlic and oregano scents drew her forward.

"Have a seat." Gabe waved at the small, oak kitchen table. "This will only take a few minutes to warm up."

Her stomach chose that moment to rumble loud enough for Gabe to hear. Leaving now that he knew she was famished would be too obvious, so she sat. "Guess I am a bit hungry after all," she admitted with a sheepish smile.

Gabe flashed a grin and opened his fridge. "Let's see, I really wish I had a bottle of fine Italian wine to offer you, but it seems all I have at the moment are two of JT's favorites, grape juice or milk. Take your pick."

She laughed. "Gosh, tough decision. I'll choose milk."

"Milk it is." He pulled out the container and filled up a large glass, setting it in front of her. "The pasta should be done in a few minutes. At least I have home-made garlic bread."

The butter and garlic scent was already filling the kitchen, mingling with the zesty spaghetti sauce. "Smells delicious. I had no idea you could cook."

"Pure necessity for two bachelors living on their own." Gabe stirred the sauce and then pulled out two plates. He dished out the pasta and sauce, adding a large chunk of fresh garlic bread to each serving.

Her mouth was watering as he set down her plate and then sat across from her. He lifted his milk glass and touched the rim to hers in a quick toast. "Thanks, Holly. I appreciate you coming to my rescue."

She rolled her eyes in exasperation before taking a sip of her milk, suddenly glad they weren't drinking anything stronger. The last time she'd shared a few drinks with Gabe she'd foolishly attempted to kiss him. "You and JT would have been fine. The worst thing that might have happened is that you'd have taken JT to the clinic for nothing more than a virus."

"Maybe," he conceded, his gaze holding hers. "But it was still nice to have someone else to talk to."

The poignant sadness lurking in his eyes made her wonder if Gabe was still in love with JT's mother. He'd claimed he wasn't married, but did that mean they were divorced? Or was he a widower of only a month? If so, all the more reason to keep her distance from him emotionally. Gabe was in no position to start a relationship, even if she was willing to risk one.

Which she wasn't.

"Eat," he urged.

The sooner she ate, the sooner she could leave. She dug in, nearly closing her eyes in ecstasy when the taste of the tangy tomato sauce exploded in her mouth. "Mmm. This is divine."

"Glad you like it." Gabe grinned, and instantly the flash of sorrow was gone. "It's an old family recipe from my mother's side. She's a great Italian cook."

She widened her eyes in surprise. "I didn't know your mother was Italian."

"Absolutely." Gabe gestured with his fork. "Her maiden name is Fanelli. She's living with her new husband down in Florida."

"And your dad?" she asked, before she could think.

His expression closed. "He's been out of the picture for a long time."

"I'm sorry." She reached for his hand, realizing she'd touched a nerve. Yet it was a bit surprising to realize she and Gabe had something in common. Apparently neither of them had been close to their fathers.

He held her hand in his for a long minute. Her heart thudded in her chest as the light-hearted mood turned into something more serious.

"Uncle Gabe?" JT's plaintive cry broke the moment. "My tummy hurts."

"Uh-oh, maybe he's going to throw up." Gabe jumped up from his seat at the table. "I'll be right back."

Confused, she sat back in her seat, staring after Gabe as he disappeared down the hall to JT's room.

Uncle Gabe? She'd assumed JT must be his son, but obviously the boy was really his nephew. Still, he was caring for JT, so he must have custody. She knew she should admire the close bond they shared, but couldn't help feeling resentful.

Somehow it didn't seem fair, that Gabe had the joy of love and caring for JT while she'd lost her daughter.

Gabe sat beside JT but the boy didn't vomit. The bed was damp, though, so he helped JT change his pajamas and then stripped the sheets off the bed, replacing them with a spare set from the hallway closet.

"Hey, buddy, maybe you should try to eat. Your tummy might hurt because you're hungry." Gabe tried not to wince at the mountain of laundry growing larger by the minute. It seemed as if he had constantly been doing laundry since JT had moved in. Not that he was complaining, but in the battle between him and the washing-machine, he rarely emerged the winner. "I can make you some chicken noodle soup, your favorite."

"No, I don't think so." JT scrunched down into the covers, blinking owlishly against the light. "Is the pretty lady still here?"

"Dr. Holly?" Unable to squelch a flash of guilt, he settled on the edge of JT's bed. Since taking custody of his nephew, Gabe had never invited a woman over. Until

now. Logically, he knew JT was too young to understand the potential implications, but he intended to set
a good example for the boy, anyway. "Yes, she's still
here. Why, did you want to ask her something? Does
your throat hurt now?"

"No." JT shook his head. "But I like her. She seems
nice."

"She is nice." Oh, boy. They were treading on dangerous ground here. Gabe tried to think of a way to
prevent JT from getting the wrong idea. "She's a good
doctor. She often takes care of sick kids, just like you."

"Oh." He could see the wheels turning in JT's mind. In
a disappointed tone the boy asked, "She's a real doctor?"

"Yep. She's a real doctor, just like me. We work
together at the hospital."

JT bit his lower lip, his gaze wistful. "Do you think
she'd come back and visit once I'm better?"

She would, he knew, if only for JT's sake, but the
knowledge made Gabe hesitate. He'd give anything to
help JT deal with his nightmares. At the same time he
wasn't willing to start something he couldn't finish. "I
don't know, she's pretty busy. Why don't you get some
sleep, hmm?"

JT nodded, pulling his green and yellow stuffed dinosaur close, the one Claire had given him. The toy had
been his constant companion over the past few weeks.
Gabe brushed a kiss over JT's forehead before getting
up to leave.

"G'night, Uncle Gabe," he whispered.

"Goodnight, JT."

Outside JT's room, he leaned back against the door and stared at the ceiling. JT was seeking a mother substitute because he missed his mother. As JT's grandmother lived in Florida he didn't get to see her that often. Obviously, JT approved of Holly.

He couldn't blame the kid. He did, too.

Blowing out a heavy breath, Gabe dropped his head and rubbed the back of his neck. There was no way to explain to JT that bringing a woman into the mix was the wrong idea. He knew from experience that not all women were willing to raise someone else's son.

Heck, he was struggling a little with the reality of being a parent and he already loved his nephew.

It would be better for both of them if he and JT stuck it out alone. Maybe he should move to Florida? JT's grandmother could fill the motherly role.

Using Holly wasn't an option.

Strengthening his resolve, he hustled back to the kitchen, where he'd left Holly. When he walked in, the first thing he noticed was that she'd cleaned up his entire kitchen. Very nice, considering he wasn't exactly a neat cook.

"You didn't have to clean up," he protested.

She lifted a shoulder, avoiding his gaze. "It's all right."

He hesitated, realizing Holly was upset. Was she upset that he'd put JT first, rushing off to take care of his needs? No, he couldn't believe Holly was that much like Jennifer. She looked more upset than angry.

"What's wrong?" he asked, as she carefully folded his dish towel and hung it on the drying rack.

Holly turned to face him, her eyes full of reproach. "Why didn't you tell me JT was your nephew?"

Damn, he'd forgotten. He hadn't wanted to push JT to call him Dad, not when he'd known him all along as Uncle Gabe. "JT is Claire's son."

His sister's name caused her expression to soften. "Oh no, Claire? Claire is the one who'd died in a car crash?"

Holly had only met Claire once, so it wasn't too surprising that she hadn't jumped to the right conclusion right away. If he was honest, he'd admit he hadn't tried very hard to clarify the truth either. "Yes. I took custody of JT the same day."

"I'm sorry." Remorse filled her face. But then she frowned, her expression more hurt than puzzled. "But, Gabe, why didn't you tell me? You must have known that I'd assume JT was biologically your son."

The hurt in her eyes made him want to cross over to her, but after the conversation he'd had with JT he forced himself to stay where he was. One brief visit and JT was already wondering if the "pretty lady" would come back again. He never should have called her over here. Getting close to Holly wasn't an option. "Maybe I should have told you. I've petitioned the court to formally adopt him."

"What about JT's biological father? Doesn't he want custody?" she asked.

"No." His answer was evasive and he knew it. JT's biological father was the last subject Gabe wanted to talk about—it was one complication he refused to discuss, especially with Holly. Not until he had the DNA results back. He didn't want to hurt her unnecessarily. "Right now, I'm the only family JT has, besides his grandmother. I can't just let him go to some stranger."

"I understand." Holly's gaze warmed, her earlier pique forgotten. "I admire you, Gabe. It takes a special man to step up in a crisis. I think you'll be a great father."

"I hope so." He wished he could be so sure, especially considering he hadn't had a good role model. Balancing the effort of raising JT and work wasn't easy. In fact, days like today he wondered if he was cut out for the job.

Holly's willingness to come over helped, though. And her kind words touched a place in his heart he thought he'd closed off a long time ago. He missed the closeness they'd once shared. The night they'd danced together, during the wedding they'd crashed to see a band, was permanently etched on his memory.

"Hey," she said, bringing him back to the matter at hand as she smiled gently. "You'll be fine."

He nodded, glad she hadn't reacted negatively, the way Jennifer had. Except for that brief moment when she must have assumed he'd lied to her on purpose. But Holly's appreciation was almost harder to take. Desperate for distance, he edged toward the front door. "Thanks again for coming out, and for cleaning up my messy kitchen."

"You cooked. Besides, I needed something to do." Holly caught his hint, picking up her purse and following him through the living room. At the front door, though, she paused and glanced up at him, her citrus scent wreaking havoc with his brain. "Gabe?"

He braced his arm against the doorjamb, trying not to let her sensual scent overwhelm his common sense. "Yeah?"

"I'm sorry. I was upset, partially because I thought you lied to me about JT on purpose."

His fingers curled into a fist to keep from tucking her hair behind her ear, tipping her face up to his. "I didn't mean to."

"I know. It's just that I've been lied to a lot in the past." Her earnest gaze held his. "Thinking you had lied to me too…" She let her voice trail off.

For a long moment he stared down at her. Tom's infidelity had done more damage than he'd realized, to her self-confidence and her self-esteem. "Holly, you deserve better. Don't sell yourself short. Ever."

Her sad smile ripped at his heart. "I'll try."

She moved as if to open the door. He didn't make a conscious decision to stop her, but he must have because suddenly she was in his arms, her soft curves pressed against his hardness, her mouth sweet yet passionate beneath his.

CHAPTER FOUR

Lost in wonderful, myriad sensations, Holly reveled in the kiss. Until a tiny corner of logic deep in the recesses of her mind forced her to realize what she was doing.

As much as she wanted to kiss him, heavens, she loved kissing him, Gabe was wrong for her. Starting something on a personal level with him would only end badly. For her. Bringing her hand up to the center of his chest, she gave a weak push. He reacted instantly, breaking off the kiss and taking a quick step back, stumbling, nearly falling in his haste to get away.

She felt lost without his arms supporting her. Missed his warmth, his heady desire. Trying to gather her reeling senses, she whispered, "We can't do this."

"No." Gabe surprised her by agreeing, as he blew out a heavy breath and scrubbed a hand over his jaw. "We can't. I'm sorry."

Sorry he'd kissed her? Or sorry it had been the wrong time and place for both of them? She should be glad she was the one who had been strong enough to end the insanity but instead she only felt cold. Bereft.

Every neuron in her body tingled from the effects of his kiss. That a simple kiss could affect her so deeply, knocking her off balance in a way Tom's kisses never had, frightened her.

"I have to go." Blindly, she turned and headed for the door.

"Holly." Gabe's voice stopped her. Steeling herself against a strong desire to throw herself back into his arms, she glanced over her shoulder at him. "If things were different, I'd ask you to stay."

Her knees wobbled as a fresh wave of desire curled in her belly. She wanted to deny how much she wanted him, but she couldn't lie. Not about this. "If things were different, I might."

For the longest moment they stared at each other. But Holly knew standing there and wishing for things to be other than what they were was absolutely useless. So she turned and continued outside, heading to her car.

She could feel Gabe's gaze on her back, but she didn't turn to look. Heaven knew, she didn't want to see the same longing she was feeling reflected in his eyes.

Coming out to help him with JT had been a mistake.

Somehow, some way she needed to forget those brief moments of pure heaven she'd spent in Gabe's arms.

Holly was relieved she didn't get called down to the ED again the next day. Avoiding Gabe would help re-establish her equilibrium. Maybe if she was lucky, she wouldn't have to see Gabe the rest of the week.

On Thursday afternoon she went up to check on Mark. His mother was alone, seated at his bedside in the PICU.

"Good afternoon, Mrs. Kennedy." She flashed a warm smile. "How are you holding up?"

Her response was a wan smile. "I'm fine. It's Mark I'm worried about."

Placing a hand on the boy's arm, Holly gazed down at him, feeling helpless. The antibiotics should be fighting the infection by now. His neuro status should be starting to improve.

But it wasn't.

"Mark?" She tucked her hand around his. "Can you hear me? Squeeze my hand."

Nothing. She bit her lip and tried again. "Mark, wiggle your toes. Come on, show me how you can wiggle your toes."

Still no response. She pressed her thumb into the back of his hand and he pulled away from the slightly painful stimulus. At least that much of a response, withdrawal from pain, was a little encouraging.

"He's not getting any better," Mrs. Kennedy said in a low voice. "And it's all my fault."

What? Holly left Mark's side and crossed over to his mother, crouching in front of her to take the woman's hand. "Mrs. Kennedy, don't blame yourself. It's not your fault Mark contracted a bacterial infection."

But the woman was shaking her head. "I'm the one who agreed to send him to boarding school. It was my husband's idea. He thought the structure of a military boarding school would be good for Mark, but in reality

I think maybe he just wanted my son out of his hair." Her voice broke and she tugged her hand from Holly's grasp and buried her face in her hands, sobbing quietly.

Knowing very well how easy it was to wallow in guilt, Holly put her arm around the woman's shoulders and hugged her. "It's not your fault. There are plenty of kids who go to boarding schools every year, and they all don't get meningitis." She didn't add the fact that bacterial meningitis was more common in dormitories and there was a vaccination against it. The poor woman felt bad enough. "And do you know how tough it is to raise teenagers these days? I have to say, your husband might have had the right idea, putting him in a structured school right from the beginning. A good friend of mine had so much trouble with her teenage son she often wished she'd done something like that right from freshman year."

Mrs. Kennedy sniffled and raised her tear-streaked eyes. "Really?"

"Yes, really." Plucking a box of tissues off the counter, Holly handed them to her. "Please, don't feel guilty. Mark needs you to be strong. There's still a chance he can pull through this. Hang in there with him, okay?"

She blew her nose and nodded. "I will."

"Does your husband come to visit Mark?" Holly asked, trying to get a feel for the family dynamics. She hadn't been lying about her friend's troubles with her son, but there may have been a grain of truth to what Mrs. Kennedy had described. It could be that her husband had wanted her son from her first marriage out of the way.

"He wanted to, but I wouldn't let him." Mrs. Kennedy sniffled again. "Maybe structure is good for teenage boys but I still think he just wanted to get rid of Mark."

Mark's illness could easily drive a wedge in the family. "Mrs. Kennedy, your marriage isn't any of my business and I'm not trying to pry, but it's at times like this when you need to come together as a family. Do you love your husband?"

Wordlessly, she nodded.

"Well, then, don't hold this against him. Blaming him or yourself isn't going to help Mark at this point." Holly didn't want to see this family fall apart. If Mark did pull through, he'd need both his parents' help and support. She was a firm believer that kids deserved an intact family, she'd often wished she'd had one. "My advice is that you let your husband visit Mark. He should be here with you, or at least relieve you so you can spend time with your other children. You need to lean on each other, get all the support you can."

Mrs. Kennedy's eyes filled with cautious hope. "Do you really think so?"

"Yes. I do." She reached over and gave the woman another hug before rising to her feet. "I'm going to talk to Mark's critical care physician, see if there's anything else we can do. Take care of yourself, all right?"

She nodded. "Thank you."

"You're welcome." Holly left the room, wiping at her eyes, which were starting to brim with tears. She felt so bad for Mrs. Kennedy and for Mark. What a difficult situation.

After conversing with the critical care physician in charge of Mark's care, they agreed to reduce his sedation to see if they could get him to be more responsive. Holly had also insisted on another CT scan of his head. She wondered if he was suffering from an increase in brain tissue swelling.

Trying not to dwell on the seriousness of Mark's situation, Holly continued the rest of her rounds. She was just finishing a consult note on a young girl with a fever of unknown origin when her pager went off.

She read the text, her heart sinking. The call was from the ED. Full of trepidation, she finished her note requesting an MRI brain scan and then called the ED. No reason to worry, there was a good chance Gabe wasn't working today. "This is Dr. Davidson from Infectious Diseases. Did someone page?"

"Holly?" Gabe's familiar voice echoed in her ear. "I need your help. We have a serious situation down here."

"What is it?" She straightened in her seat, alarmed by his grave tone.

"I have three Hmong children all showing signs of active tuberculosis."

"Active TB? Are you sure?" Her heart sank in her chest. Active tuberculosis was rare, except in certain patient populations. This was serious, especially if the Hmong children had been exposed by an infected adult.

"I'm sure." Gabe's tone was grim. "They all have fevers and a cough, two of the older ones tested positive on their PPD skin test, but the youngest is only four and came up negative. We've had chest X rays done and are treating them aggressively, even the youngest one. But there are about twenty family members packed in the waiting room and it's likely one of the adults is the primary source of the infection."

Dear God. Hmong families tended to stick together, everyone showing up at the hospital when one loved one was ill. And they often lived together too, many people crammed into small residences. Fertile ground for fostering infection. The possibility of a sick adult spreading tuberculosis to more children here at the hospital was horrifying. Having three infected children was bad enough. "Do whatever you can to isolate the family. I'll be right there."

Gabe had never been in such a volatile situation before. The implications of extensive TB exposure was overwhelming. Even now he could see there were at least fifteen to twenty other people in the ED waiting room, and if any of them had been close to the source of infection, they would need treatment.

After donning a face mask, he ushered the family into a large conference room where he could at least shut the door. It didn't have negative pressure, as dictated by hospital code, but it was better than nothing.

"My name is Dr. Martin and I'm afraid the three girls you brought in, MeeKa, BaoKa, and YiKa, all have tuberculosis. Tuberculosis is a very serious and very contagious lung infection." He scanned the room. In the center of the group, his gaze rested on the oldest member of the family, the grandfather, whose pale skin, sunken eyes, and deep rattling cough triggered his internal alarms. "Sir?" He approached the elder. "How long have you had that cough?"

A woman stepped up. "Excuse me, Tou Yang doesn't speak any English. I can tell you my father has been feeling bad for a long time, many weeks. Tou Yang has refused to go to the hospital to see a doctor, though."

The Hmong were a very patriarchal society, so he understood how it might be that no one in the family dared to go against the grandfather's wishes. With a sinking heart he realized they'd have to force the man into treatment in order to preserve the health of the community.

Where was Holly? He glanced at his watch. Despite the kiss that had shattered his piece of mind, he was anxious for her help. He really could use her expertise.

"Gabe?" As if he'd conjured her by will alone, Holly stepped into the room, wearing a tight-fitting face mask just like his. "I've been in touch with health department officials—they're on their way."

Thank heavens.

Holly swept her gaze over the group. "Do they understand they will all need to be evaluated for treatment?" she asked in a low tone.

He shook his head. "Not yet. Although I believe the grandfather is the original source."

Holly stepped forward. "I think Dr. Martin explained how the three girls you brought in all have tuberculosis. We believe your grandfather has passed the lung infection to the children. I'm afraid this means you have all been exposed as well. Each of you will need to be evaluated for treatment."

Those who understood English gasped and several translated to the family members who didn't. Gabe watched the shocked reaction go through the group and knew with a sinking certainty they didn't understand the bigger issue. Treatment for active TB wasn't as easy as taking a pill for a week. The drugs were highly toxic, with many possible side effects, and the usual treatment regimen lasted a full nine months.

The family asked lots of questions. Between them, he and Holly answered them the best they could. Once they had generally calmed the family's fears, Gabe and Holly left.

Outside the conference room, he tugged his face mask off and scrubbed a hand across his jaw. "Now what?" he asked.

Holly stripped her mask off too, taking a deep breath. The masks were very restrictive. "We keep them here until the public health officials arrive. At least most of the family members appeared to be in pretty good health."

Gabe nodded. "I think I'd better give the ED at Minneapolis Medical Center a heads-up. The kids can be evaluated here, but the rest of the family will need to be taken to the Center."

"Good idea. And what about the people who were in the waiting room when they came in? How on earth are we going to identify them?"

He'd had the same concern. "They all have to register when they come in, so we can pull the list of all the people who registered within fifteen minutes of the Yang family, and maybe fifteen minutes afterwards, to capture them all. If the family had pretty much kept the grandfather surrounded, we probably don't have to do much more than TB skin tests on the rest of the people who were in the waiting room."

"All right, let's get that list."

He led the way back to the arena, already feeling much calmer about the situation. How was it that Holly's presence helped him to relax? She'd had the same effect on him last night, dealing with JT's sore throat.

"Dr. Martin? You have a call on line two. Something about being late to get home?"

Damn, how could he have forgotten JT? Appalled with himself, he grabbed the phone and punched the button to connect. "Marybeth, I'm so sorry."

"It's all right, I don't have major plans for this evening." He was so lucky to have someone as understanding as Marybeth helping to watch JT. And it was Thursday, a day she didn't have class. "But JT was worried, so I figured I'd give you a call."

"I understand. Put him on the phone." After a few seconds, he heard JT's voice come on the line. "Hey, buddy, I'm sorry I got stuck here at work. We have lots of sick kids here who need my help."

"When are you coming home?" JT asked in a plaintive tone.

Good question. One he wasn't sure he had an answer

for. He shouldn't have forgotten about picking him up in the first place. And now, as much as he wanted to be there for JT, he couldn't just walk away from this mess. "I'll be home by six o'clock, okay? Marybeth is going to make you dinner but I promise I'll be home right afterwards."

"Okay. Tell the sick kids to get better."

Gabe had to laugh at the child's logic. If only it were that easy. "I will. See you soon, JT."

He hung up the phone and turned, bumping right into Holly.

"Gabe, I can stay and handle things here." Her compassionate gaze confirmed she'd overheard his conversation with JT. "You should go home."

For a heartbeat he imagined what his life would be like if he had someone like Holly to help him with JT. A wife to come home to, a true partner rather than a college-student babysitter.

As quickly as the tempting thought formed, he pushed it away. JT was fragile enough—the boy didn't need any more complications in his life.

Losing his head and kissing Holly had proved she was a major complication and more.

"I'm staying. But thanks." He forced himself to step away, more tempted to share his burdens with her than he wanted to admit. "Let's get this resolved, shall we?"

Holly admired Gabe's dedication, especially as the torn expression in his eyes when speaking to JT showed how much he really wanted to be home. Since he didn't take up her offer to cover for him, she left him to take care of the girls while she met with the public health department officials to deal with the rest of the Yang family.

Luckily, the health department agreed with her assessment and, as Gabe had anticipated, got the entire group of adults moved over to a secure location at Minneapolis Regional Medical Center, located adjacent to Children's. Despite his wishes, the grandfather would need to be admitted immediately.

When she had that problem solved, she decided she should check on the three girls, who were the most sick. As she entered the isolation room she found Gabe was already there, holding the youngest girl, YiKa, who was only four years old, against his chest. The tender expression in his eyes squeezed her heart, stopping her in her tracks.

The poignant picture was enough to steal her breath. He was so caring, so compassionate. She could easily see him cradling his daughter the same way.

He was a wonderful father.

JT was very lucky to have him.

She wanted to leave, to wipe this compelling vision from her mind. Gabe was clearly the father she'd wanted Tom to be. But instead of being there for her, when the cramping pains of her placenta breaking away from her uterus had started, Tom had been with some other woman. He'd betrayed her in more ways than one.

Squaring her shoulders, she fought the sudden urge

to cry. The last thing she wanted was Gabe to see how much his presence affected her.

There was no point in longing for something she could never have.

CHAPTER FIVE

HOLLY kept herself occupied with work, the tuberculosis situation consuming most of her time. Thankfully
she didn't have to interact with Gabe much, especially
once the three girls were admitted up on the fifth-floor
general medical unit.

So far the girls were tolerating their treatment well,
but it was also very early. Most of the side effects of the
medication hit after about a week or so. She'd heard
from the public health department that there were two
other adults, aside from Tou Yang, who also had active
TB, but the rest of the family only needed outpatient
prophylactic treatment.

A part of her wanted to tell Gabe the news, yet
another part of her wondered if she was simply looking
for an excuse to see him again. There was really no
reason to go down to the ED. She didn't really even
know his work schedule. In the end she decided that if
she happened to run into him, she'd let him know the
outcome of the Yang family. For all she knew, he might
have heard the news from some other source.

On Friday evening she gratefully wrapped up her first week of work. Mark Kennedy was finally starting to wake up, the infection having been beaten by the antibiotics. Looking back, she wanted to laugh at her initial nervousness. Five days and she already felt like an integral part of the team.

Her first week had been full of challenging cases, what with the meningitis and active tuberculosis.

In less than a week she'd also broken her cardinal rule by kissing Gabe.

She sighed and reached for her purse, knowing she needed to get over this strange obsession with him. He was a friend, nothing more.

Her cellphone rang. She recognized the number and realized the caller was her friend, Lisa Waltrip, from Phoenix, Arizona.

"Hey, Lisa, how are you?"

"Great. Hey, guess where I am?"

Holly frowned. "Um, Phoenix?"

"No, silly." Lisa laughed. "I'm here in Minneapolis. How would you like to get together for dinner?"

"I'd love to!" Holly was thrilled her friend had come to visit. "Where are you staying?"

"At some hotel across from the airport." There was a slight pause. "Ok, I can see a restaurant from my window—a Mexican place called Chili's. Are you in the mood for a margarita?"

Holly laughed. Spending time with her friend was just what she needed. "Absolutely. Would it be all right if I met you there, say, in about an hour?"

"It's a date."

Holly hurried out of the hospital before her pager could go off and keep her from meeting Lisa. On the ride home she called her mother to check on how she was doing. Friday was another dialysis day and because she'd been so tied up with the TB cases, she hadn't been able to give her mother a ride home.

Her mother sounded tired as usual after her treatments, but her spirits were good.

"I'm meeting a friend from Phoenix for dinner. Do you want me to stop by afterwards on my way home?" Holly asked, feeling a little guilty for going out at all.

"Oh, no. Georgia is stopping by. Don't worry about me. Just go out and have fun."

Georgia was her mother's youngest sister. Holly was glad her mother wouldn't be all alone tonight. "All right, but call if you need me."

She ended the call as she pulled into her driveway. Dashing into the house, she quickly changed into a comfy pair of jeans and a royal blue sweater that made the most of her creamy skin and dark hair. For a moment she wished Gabe could see her like that, but then just as quickly pushed the thought aside. What on earth was she thinking? Spending time with Lisa was supposed to help her forget about Gabe, not bring him to the forefront of her mind.

Annoyed with herself, she headed back out to meet Lisa. The traffic was backed up, so she arrived a few minutes late. Standing at the hostess desk, she scanned the restaurant and found Lisa sitting at a table in the middle of the room. She hurried over.

"Lisa! It's so good to see you."

Lisa stood to return her hug and it was then that Holly noticed her friend was pregnant.

Very pregnant.

"Surprise!" Lisa's laughter bubbled out as she stared at Holly's dumbfounded expression.

"Oh. My. Goodness." Holly felt the blood draining from her face and fought to keep her shock from showing in her eyes. She forced a smile. "Congrats." Belatedly she gave Lisa another tight, enthusiastic hug. "When are you due?"

"In two months, just before New Year." Lisa beamed as they took their respective seats. Her pregnancy obviously agreed with her. "I'm ready any time, though."

Holly was happy for Lisa, truly. But at the same time she couldn't deny a twinge of envy. Beneath the cover of the table her hand went to her own stomach, as if seeking the familiar bulge, the reassuring sensation of the baby moving. She'd been thrilled to be pregnant, just like Lisa was, but hadn't made it to her seventh month.

Kayla. Sweet, innocent Kayla. She still had a picture of her daughter, the tiny pink dress they'd put on her and the footprint in clay they'd made, all courtesy of the caring, compassionate nurses in the neonatal ICU.

"Holly?" It took a moment to realize Lisa was talking to her.

"I'm sorry, I was daydreaming for a minute there. What did you say?"

Lisa's smile faded. "You're upset, aren't you?"

"No." Her denial was a little too quick. "Of course not,

Lisa. I'm very happy for you. Honest. Tell me every-thing. What did Ben say when you told him the news?"

"Holly, it's okay. I understand." Lisa reached across the table to give her hand a squeeze. "I know you're happy for me, but that doesn't mean you don't miss your daughter."

Her throat tightened and she nodded. "Yes, I'll al-ways miss Kayla. But now is not the time for you to think about pregnancy horror stories." Like hers. "Seri-ously, tell me everything. I know I haven't seen you in about five months, but I didn't even realize you guys were trying to have a baby."

Lisa stared at her for a long moment, and then went into a detailed explanation of the events—how they hadn't really been trying, but had gone on a weekend getaway and had forgotten protection. "I think Ben planned it all along, but I guess I won't complain," Lisa finished with a broad smile. "Having a baby is a perfect way to start the new year."

Holly tried not to think about how she'd lost her baby right before Valentine's Day. Holidays didn't always hold good memories. At least Valentine's Day was nothing special, especially when you were single.

The waitress came and took their order. Lisa requested a non-alcoholic margarita, and Holly did the same.

Her mood was volatile enough, without adding alcohol to the mix. Lisa described how she was really in town for a work-related presentation, but soon the conversation turned back to her baby.

Holly didn't try to stop her from discussing her pregnancy. After all, she remembered what it was like to have a baby be the center of your world. Soon, though, the topic of conversation turned to the people they'd both worked with.

"Kris has been nothing but a pain in the butt ever since…" Lisa's voice trailed off.

"Ever since what?" Holly asked. Kris had been one of the nurses in the ICU who had been extremely annoying to most of the physicians at one time or another. The woman was young but had the personality of a scorpion and always thought she was right, even when she wasn't.

"Never mind." Lisa picked up her drink and took a huge gulp, avoiding her friend's gaze. "It's not important."

Suddenly she knew. "Kris is dating Tom, isn't she?"

Lisa sighed and hung her head. "Holly, I'm sorry. I wasn't going to bring it up."

"It's all right." Holly picked up her water, wishing it was full of whiskey. "My marriage to Tom is over."

"True. And, really, Kris is such a witch, she deserves him. She should know better than to marry a guy like Tom, especially knowing his reputation."

Holly carefully set her water glass down. Little had she known Tom's reputation had been common knowledge long before she'd discovered his infidelity. And because she'd been blind to the truth, her reputation had suffered too. It was one of the things she regretted most.

She was fiercely glad she wasn't still in Phoenix, especially now that she knew there was a chance Tom might get married again. If she thought the whispers and stares had been bad then, they'd be a million times worse now. She couldn't bear the thought of people talking about her behind her back.

Holly managed to get through the rest of the meal, but the jeering voices in the back of her mind followed her all the way home.

Poor Holly. Losing her baby and her husband in the same day. How tragic. Too bad she didn't figure out Tom was cheating on her before she got pregnant.

Now she has nothing.

By Saturday Gabe was relieved to see that JT seemed better. His headache was gone but the boy was still more tired than normal. JT had a Cub Scout field trip planned at a local dairy farm and the boy had been very excited, waiting very impatiently for this day to come.

Gabe struggled with a feeling of strange desolation as he waved at JT, watching him ride off in a large vehicle with a group of five other boys, all from the same pre-school class. Was he a bad parent because he hadn't volunteered to chaperone? Being a guardian to JT was more complicated than he'd imagined. Once again he wondered if he should move to Florida with JT. Staying here in Minneapolis, where JT's life could have almost the same routine as before Claire's death, had seemed to be the best option. So why was he doubting his decision now?

There was plenty to do around the house but, rather than be happy to have the time to himself to get things done, he couldn't escape the feeling he should be spending more time with JT. Originally, he'd been scheduled to work this Saturday but then a colleague had needed to switch weekends so he'd ended up being off. Maybe he should have added his name to the chaperone list for this trip, even if it had been at the last minute.

Deciding he was doing his best at being a guardian for JT, he picked up the gallon of blue paint JT had picked out for his room and headed down the hall to the bedroom. He quickly pulled all the furniture away from the walls and into the center of the room, then went to work. Slathering paint on the walls was a mindless job, which was good in a way yet he couldn't stop his mind from drifting to Holly, wondering how she was spending her weekend.

She wasn't working the weekend, because he'd checked.

If he was interested in seeing Holly on a personal level, this would be a perfect opportunity, considering JT would be gone for most of the day. What would she say if he asked her out for lunch?

The selfish part of him, the part that relived her kiss over and over each night in his dreams, wanted to see her again, even though he knew that starting something with Holly was the last thing JT needed. JT would latch on to Holly, or any other woman he chose to date, because of how much he missed his mother. Yet at the same time, if things didn't work out, his nephew would be the one to suffer. Logically Gabe understood the dynamics, the reasons he'd made the firm decision to avoid relationships, but that didn't stop him from thinking about the possibilities of seeing Holly anyway.

Once the Yang girls had been admitted to the general floor he hadn't seen Holly at all. He'd missed working with her.

He enjoyed being with Holly, no matter what they were doing. He'd felt that way years earlier, before she'd married Tom, and somehow the passing of time hadn't changed a thing. If anything, the desire to be with her only seemed to have grown stronger. Especially since their kiss.

Because she was free, no longer engaged to his friend.

But now he was the one with responsibilities. An emotional young boy, suffering from nightmares and reeling from the recent loss of his mother. A boy who desperately needed a parent to hold on to.

Painting JT's room didn't take long, and as he cleaned off the bright blue paint rollers, he inwardly debated whether he should call Holly or not. Was he being selfish if he stole a little time for himself?

He called Holly's cellphone and was disappointed when she didn't pick up, the call going directly to her voice mail. He left a brief message before hanging up, trying to be relieved to know the decision had been taken out of his hands.

Then he remembered how Holly had mentioned her sick mother, suffering from diabetes and renal failure. Knowing Holly, she was likely over there now, taking care of things.

Her mother didn't live far away—he remembered

being there prior to Holly's wedding—so he drove past, just to see if his suspicions were correct.

They were. Holly was outside, wearing a bright red jacket, her dark hair falling freely to her shoulders, her cheeks pink from the wind as she raked leaves around the base of a large maple tree. He pulled up in front of the house, thinking she was fighting a losing battle because the wind kept blowing the leaves away from her pile. He climbed out of his car, intending to help.

"Hi, Gabe." She seemed surprised to see him, but leaned on her rake as if glad for the break. "How are you? Is everything all right with JT?"

"Yes, he's fine." He gently tugged the rake from her hands and picked up the chore where she'd left off, sweeping all the leaves into a large pile. "JT's on a Cub Scout trip to the dairy farm."

"Great. That must mean he's feeling better."

"He is." Gabe tried to block the wind with his body, but dozens of leaves danced along the yard regardless. He grimaced, reaching out with the rake again. "I don't think we're going to get them all."

"No, probably not." Holly glanced around, propping her hands on her slim hips. She was so beautiful, with her eyes sparkling in the crisp fall air, she took his breath away. "Guess this means we have no choice."

"No choice?" He didn't understand.

"No choice but to jump." She let out a laugh and in a carefree movement that reminded him of JT plopped into the large pile of leaves. Still giggling, she picked up a pile of leaves and threw them at him.

The smell of the earth, intermingled with the crunching of the dried leaves, took him back to his own childhood. When he and his sister, Claire, had spent hours playing in the leaves in their front yard beneath twin oak trees.

"Hey," he protested lightly, grinning at her antics. Unwilling to be left out of the fun, he tossed the rake aside and jumped in beside her.

When she let out a startled cry and rolled into him, he put his arms out to help protect her. Laughing when their limbs became tangled, her efforts to get free only brought them closer. When she ended up in his arms, practically on top of him, he realized his mistake. Or his good fortune.

Her laughter faded as she gazed down at him, unaware or uncaring how leaf fragments clung to her hair. His chest tightened and he knew this was exactly what he'd wanted. Why he'd come to find her.

"Holly," he murmured, reaching up to thread his fingers through her hair and slowly easing her head down until her lips met his.

This time their kiss was even more explosive, his senses reeling as Holly's breasts pressed against his chest. Gabe growled low in his throat and deepened the kiss, exploring her sweet depths the way he'd wanted to before. Unlike the last time, Holly didn't resist.

Closer. He wanted more, wanted to feel every inch of her body against him, so he rolled, switching places so he was on top, the leaves providing a soft cushion from the damp ground. He kissed her again and again, barely pausing to breathe, desperately wishing he could make the barrier of their clothes disappear.

"Gabe." Holly moaned his name when he trailed a string of kisses to the soft spot beneath her ear. When he scraped his teeth against her skin, she gasped and writhed beneath him.

He wanted to take her home. Now. To his bedroom.

A car drove by and the driver beeped the horn twice, breaking the moment. He glanced up in time to see the teenage boy behind the wheel flashing a leering grin and a thumbs-up sign.

He wanted to laugh, but Holly stiffened beneath him and suddenly gave a Herculean push against his chest. He moved aside and she scrambled to her feet.

"What's wrong?" he asked, moving much more slowly, thanks to his almost painful arousal.

"I— We— Anyone could have seen us." Holly was brushing leaves off her clothes, tugging the hem of her jacket down. "I have to go."

"Go?" Call him slow, but he didn't understand what in the world had her so upset. "Go where? I thought…?"

"You thought wrong. This shouldn't have happened." Her about-face, changing from the woman who'd shivered and moaned in his arms to the woman glaring at him as if he'd committed some horrible crime, confused the hell out of him. She turned and headed toward the house.

"Holly, wait a minute." He tried to stop her, but she ignored him, disappearing inside her mother's house and closing the door behind her with a decisive and final click.

CHAPTER SIX

MORTIFIED, Holly leaned against the closed door, covering her burning cheeks with her hands. What had she been thinking to roll around in the leaves, kissing Gabe? Had she completely lost her mind? And what if someone from work had driven by, instead of some teenager? She could already hear the whispers if anyone had seen them together.

She knew comparing the past to the present wasn't fair. The gossip that had surrounded her after Tom had been different. Tom had cheated on her while they'd been married. And she'd been pregnant.

Technically, she and Gabe were free to see whomever they wanted. What they did on their off time should be none of anyone else's business.

Too bad that wasn't the way things worked, especially in hospitals where the employee grapevine was more reliable and saw more traffic than the biweekly administrative newsletter.

The last thing she wanted was for her private life to be in the public spotlight. When she started dating again, she intended to find someone who had nothing to do with her work, preferably not connected with the field of medicine at all. She'd envisioned a lawyer or a banker. Not another doctor. Not Gabe. He was all wrong for her.

"Holly, did you get the leaves raked?" her mother called from the kitchen where she was making a batch of Holly's favorite chocolate-chip cookies.

"Ah, no, it was too windy." Taking several deep breaths, she tried to relax her racing heart, wishing she could dunk her head in a bucket of cold water to douse the flames Gabe had ignited with a mere kiss. Just because she'd temporarily lost her mind, it didn't mean her mother needed to know. She strove for a light tone. "Do you need help with the cookies?"

"Sure, although I'm almost finished."

Shaking off the devastating effects of Gabe's kiss wasn't easy. Hiding her trembling hands in a sink full of sudsy water to wash dishes helped.

But even as she chatted with her mother, she couldn't get Gabe out of her mind.

Especially knowing that if she hadn't pulled away when that kid had honked his horn at them, the chances were high that they wouldn't have stopped except maybe to move somewhere more private.

And there was a tiny, traitorous part of her that wished they had.

At the end of the afternoon Holly took the cookies home with her, as her mother was diabetic and couldn't eat them anyway. On the way back to her house she stopped at the grocery store, not in the mood to cook but needing something she could throw together for dinner.

Since a salad sounded good, she headed to the fresh produce section and bumped her cart into a guy coming the opposite way.

"I'm so sorry!" she exclaimed.

"My pleasure." The guy was about her age, and very attractive with a wide smile and dark, wavy hair. The blatant approval in his eyes as they focused on her face couldn't be missed, yet she wasn't able to summon an ounce of interest.

He may have been a banker, or a stockbroker, or a lawyer, but it didn't matter. Because he wasn't Gabe. The realization knocked her back a step. "Excuse me." She wheeled her cart around him and crossed straight to the spinach.

The gorgeous man took her brush-off with a casual shrug and headed off in the opposite direction. Rattled, she gathered her salad ingredients and went through the checkout line, feeling slightly sick. Maybe she'd eaten too many of her mother's cookies.

At home, the nauseous feeling in her stomach persisted.

Because as much as she didn't want to be involved with Gabe, or with anyone she worked with, it was obviously too late.

She wasn't attracted to anyone else.

Gabe couldn't stop thinking about Holly, wishing things could have ended differently.

He'd just finished putting the chicken in the oven when JT came home. The child seemed exhausted, maybe some lingering effects of the virus he'd had. He wasn't too tired to give Gabe a big hug. Gabe returned the embrace, telling himself this was all that mattered.

He'd figure out how to be a good father somehow. Maybe he and JT could figure it out together.

"Did you have a good time?" he asked.

"Yeah. It was so cool!" JT was tired, yet he'd clearly had fun as he described everything he'd seen at the farm. "We saw cows, horses, chickens, but no pigs." JT looked perplexed. "The farmer said he didn't have any pigs."

"Bummer." Gabe suppressed a grin.

"We watched the farmer milk the cows, but the milk was gross." JT wrinkled his nose. "It was warm. Yuck."

Gabe had to laugh. "We only keep milk in the fridge so it doesn't spoil."

"And then we saw a baby cow, he was so cute."

"Calf," Gabe corrected.

"Yeah, a calf. Then me and Kyle climbed all the way up to the top of the loft. There was lots of straw up there and it made us sneeze."

Gabe only listened to JT with half an ear because he was distracted by thoughts of Holly.

This had been the second time she'd pushed him away. You'd think he'd get the message she wasn't interested.

Except she'd kissed him back. Had urgently pressed against him in a way that couldn't be mistaken for anything but interest.

Until the car driver had beeped his horn.

"Is supper ready?" JT peered at the oven. "I'm hungry."

"Almost." Gabe focused on finishing his dinner preparations, including mashing the potatoes and cooking the broccoli, JT's favorite vegetable because he liked the way they looked like little trees.

JT continued to talk about his trip, more about the antics in the car on the ride up than anything else. After dinner was bathtime.

JT splashed in the tub and Gabe sat on the lowered seat of the commode, thinking about the long, lonely night ahead of him. JT was already yawning, the adventures of his day catching up with him. No doubt he'd be asleep well before his usual eight o'clock bedtime.

He noticed JT kept dropping the soap. At first he thought the boy was just too tired to get a grip on the slippery bar, but then he noticed JT eventually picked it up with his left hand.

But the boy was right-handed.

"Is there something wrong with your hand?" he asked, wrapping a large bath sheet around the boy's damp body.

"No. It just feels tingly."

Tingly? Gabe frowned, wondering why on earth JT's right hand would be tingly. Was this some sort of leftover symptom from the virus he'd had? Maybe he should take the boy in to the pediatrician for a good work-up.

Tucking JT in a few minutes later, he sat on the edge of JT's bed. "I'm glad you had fun today."

"Me, too." JT smiled, his eyelids starting to droop. "Did you talk to the pretty lady yet?"

Holly? "Uh, sort of."

"Is she coming over?" JT blinked, trying to stay awake.

"Soon." Gabe felt bad about lying, but he couldn't invite Holly over. Could he? He pressed a kiss on JT's forehead and the boy's arms came up around his neck in a fierce hug. He returned the gesture, hoping that applying for adoption was the right decision, for both of them. "Good night, buddy."

"G'night, Uncle Gabe."

He returned to the living room and stared at the blank TV. He didn't want to watch some brainless show or outdated movie.

He wanted to see Holly. Damn it, there had to have been something more going on this afternoon. She had been as emotionally involved in their embrace as he'd been.

Fishing his cellphone out of his pocket, he dialed Marybeth's phone number. If she was busy, fine. At least he'd tried.

"Marybeth? It's Gabe. Hey, are you doing anything tonight?"

"Well, it is a Saturday," she said in a wry tone, and his heart plummeted.

"I understand." Of course she was busy. What college student wasn't busy on a Saturday night?

"But you're lucky I broke up with my boyfriend a couple of weeks ago so I'm not doing anything but studying."

He pumped his fist in the air and mouthed a silent, "yes." Continuing aloud, he said, "Really? You seriously don't mind?"

"No, I don't mind. I'll come over and watch JT. I can study there just as easily."

"Thanks." Grateful, he hung up and then sprang into action.

He was going to Holly's house to talk to her. And he wasn't leaving until he had answers.

Holly took the pink box off her dresser and carried it into the living room. Lifting the cover, she stared at the meager yet precious contents.

Kayla's picture was on top, her daughter's face relaxed and at peace. If you didn't look too closely, you could almost believe she was asleep.

Carefully, she lifted out the pink dress, knowing that she really needed to preserve the fabric in a protective sealed container but unwilling to pack it away just yet. Touching the silky fabric helped her to remember Kayla's birth. Lastly, she lifted out the pink clay footprint, with Kayla's name and birth date incised along the top.

Kayla Marie Richards. She traced the letters of her daughter's name with her index finger, feeling sad. Born February fourteenth, died February fourteenth.

Tears pricked her eyelids and she brushed them away with an impatient hand. She needed to stop wallowing in the past. She loved her daughter, missed her very much, but there wasn't anything she could do to bring her back. Kayla would always live in her heart.

And maybe it was time she started thinking about a future.

She could admit now that she'd overreacted that afternoon with Gabe. She'd taken the opportunity to run because she was starting to care too much.

Kissing Kayla's picture, she packed everything back into the pink box and carried it back to her room. Instead of setting it on the top of her dresser, where she'd always kept it close at hand, Holly took it to her closet and chose the highest shelf, one she could barely reach, and pushed the box way back so it was out of view.

Satisfied, she closed the closet door, wishing it was as easy to close away her past.

Her heart leaped when her cellphone rang. Racing to the living room, where she'd left it, she picked it up and opened it without even looking. "Hello?"

"Holly? It's Tom."

Tom? As in her ex-husband? Shocked, she couldn't imagine why he was calling, they'd only exchanged a dozen words, all very polite and civilized, in the two years since their divorce. "Is there something wrong?" she asked, thinking it had to be serious, like his mother was ill or dying, for him to call.

"No, but I'm trying to get in touch with Gabe. Have you seen him?"

All the air left her lungs. Did Tom have some sort of latent psychic ability to know she'd spent a portion of the afternoon rolling in the leaves with Gabe? "Why do you think I know where Gabe is?"

"Holly, it's a simple question." Tom's tone was irritated. "If you don't know where he is, just tell me."

"I don't know where he is." Holly was still having trouble comprehending how Tom and Gabe must have kept in touch all this time. And wasn't it interesting how Gabe hadn't mentioned a word? "Did you try him at home?"

"Yes. Never mind, I'll just leave him a message. Sorry to bother you." He hung up.

Her doorbell rang, and with a frown she glanced at the clock. It wasn't that late, only eight-thirty, but she still glanced through the window, surprised for the second time that day to see Gabe.

She opened the door, not feeling very gracious. "What are you doing here? Where's JT?"

"Hi, Holly. May I come in?"

Sensing he wasn't about to leave without talking to her, she opened the door. "Is this about Tom? Because he just called here, looking for you."

"Tom?" Gabe's frown was genuinely puzzled. "Called for me? Why?"

"I don't know." She closed the door behind him. "Are you telling me you guys haven't kept in touch?"

"No. I've only spoken to him a couple of times out of pure necessity." Gabe took a seat on her sofa. "I walked out on the wedding, remember? We argued. We haven't exactly been on friendly terms."

"I see." Maybe she shouldn't have doubted Gabe. Knowing Tom, he probably wanted some sort of favor. Why she'd been blind to her ex-husband's selfish tendencies she had no idea. Feeling awkward, she stared at Gabe. Why was he there? "Do you want something to drink? I have a bottle of wine chilling in the fridge."

"Really?" Gabe brightened. "That would be great."

Still somewhat confused by Gabe's presence at her house this late, she went into the kitchen for the wine. Gabe took it from her fingers. "Do you have a corkscrew?"

What was it with men needing to be in charge even of something as simple as opening a bottle of wine? Suppressing a sigh, she opened the drawer and handed him a corkscrew, then went to another cupboard for the wineglasses. Gabe deftly opened the wine and she waited while he poured.

"Cheers." He lifted his glass and she had to smile when she remembered how they'd done this same thing at his house with milk.

"Holly." Gabe's expression turned serious. "I'm sorry about this afternoon."

"You are?" Her left eyebrow arched skeptically.

He stared at her for a minute. "No, not really." At her look of astonishment, he went on, "I mean, I'm not sorry I kissed you. Dammit, I've done nothing but dream about kissing you. But something happened—one minute you were in my arms, the next you were running as far from me as you could possibly get. I'm sorry for whatever I did to make you run."

"You didn't do anything." Holly carefully set her wineglass on the counter. How could she explain what she wasn't sure she understood herself? "It's me, Gabe. I don't want to get involved with anyone from work."

He was silent for a moment. "So you're telling me if I worked at some other hospital in the city, things would be different?"

Spoken so bluntly, her reasoning did sound ridiculous. They both specialized in pediatrics, and there was only one children's hospital in the Twin Cities area. But feelings and emotions weren't always logical. She lifted a shoulder. "I guess. Yes, things might be different."

"So it was the driver honking at us that freaked you out."

His persistence was annoying but he deserved the truth. "Look, Gabe, I've had enough of gossip to last me the rest of my life."

"Gossip?" He took another sip of wine, gazing at her over the rim. "Because of Tom?"

She sucked in a harsh breath when he nailed the truth.

His eyes filled with compassion. He set his own glass aside and crossed over to her. "Holly, I'm sorry. What happened?"

She didn't want to tell him, but then realized if she did explain all the gory details, he'd understand why her request wasn't unreasonable. "I was pregnant, about twenty-five weeks along, when the cramping pains started. At first I thought it was just that I needed to rest, but they got worse. I was at work, so I found myself a wheelchair and called Tom's cellphone."

Gabe's hands were suddenly holding hers, tightly.

"He didn't answer, and didn't answer. So I called my doctor and she came running over to push me up to the labor and delivery area. My friend Lisa was with me, too. I kept calling Tom, leaving frantic messages as I knew he wasn't scheduled to do surgery that day. As it happens, there is a whole suite of on-call rooms along the hallway leading to the elevators to go up to L and D. I could hear a cellphone ringing from one of the rooms and suddenly the door opened, and Tom was telling a completely naked, tiny blonde female OB resident how he had to leave."

Gabe's hands tightened on hers, and he swore under his breath.

"Looking back, the expression on his face when he saw me sitting there in the hall outside the call room was pretty comical. But then the pains got bad, really bad, and I was rushed past Tom into the delivery room. My daughter was stillborn. At twenty-five weeks, Kayla Marie was too young to live."

CHAPTER SEVEN

GABE couldn't believe Tom had been so cruel, so callous as to blatantly have had an affair where he worked. Where they'd both worked. And hearing Holly's story made his suspicions about Tom's infidelity prior to his marriage to Holly all the more damning. He knew he should probably tell her his suspicions yet at the same time there was no sense in hurting her any more. Not until he had proof. She'd been through enough pain.

No wonder she'd freaked out when the car driver had honked his horn at them. Tom's affair had been so public, he could easily imagine the extensive gossip she'd endured.

Especially after giving birth to a stillborn baby.

"I'm so sorry you lost your daughter." He couldn't imagine anything worse than losing a child. Especially now that he had JT. "Kayla Marie is a beautiful name."

"She was beautiful." Holly's smile was sad. "But you know what? I grieved more for her than I did for the end of my marriage."

"You had every right to be angry." Gabe found

himself growing more furious by the minute. What in the hell had Tom been thinking? Not only had Tom broken his vows, he hadn't been there for Holly when she'd needed him most.

"Discovering how Tom was having sex with a colleague while I was losing my baby made me vow to never get involved with anyone where I worked ever again."

The anguish underlining her tone tugged at his heart. He understood her logic but didn't like the way she seemed to almost blame herself for what had happened. She deserved better. "Holly, remember how I walked out on your wedding?" When she nodded, he continued, "I had a huge fight with Tom that day, and the fight was about you."

"Me?" Her eyes widened.

"I told him he didn't deserve you. And in turn he accused me of wanting you for myself." He stared into the bottom of his wineglass for a moment, wishing more than anything he'd told her his suspicions before, even without proof. Finally he dragged his gaze up to hers. "He was right. I did want you for myself. I barely held back from kissing you that night we danced, so don't for a moment think I wasn't tempted because I was." His voice dropped to a husky note. "And I always thought you were too good for him."

A tremulous smile played across her mouth. "Thanks."

"You're welcome." He set his own glass aside and approached her, reaching out to tuck a strand of her dark hair behind her ear. Her skin was silky soft. "I guess what I'm trying to say is that I still want you. More than

I did six years ago. But things with JT…" He frowned, reluctant to tell her everything. "Are complicated."

"I see." Although the puzzled expression shadowing her eyes belied her words. "Did you wait until JT was asleep before leaving him with a babysitter?"

"Yeah." He automatically checked his cellphone to make sure Marybeth hadn't called.

"And you came by this afternoon while he was gone on his trip to the farm," Holly said slowly.

He stared at her for a moment. Okay, he could see the pattern for himself, he didn't need Holly to point out the obvious. *Did you talk to the pretty lady? Is she going to come over?* Damn.

"Try to understand. JT's been through a lot these past few weeks. After losing his mom, he's going to be looking for another woman to take her place." He spread his hands wide in a helpless gesture. "I don't want him to get hurt."

The wounded expression in her eyes made him feel like a heel. "And you think I would?"

"No." What could he say to make her understand? Heck, being alone with Holly was making him doubt his own logic. "I was seeing a woman fairly seriously when Claire died. But Jennifer wasn't happy when I brought JT home to live with me. And she didn't want to continue our relationship once she knew I was serious about adopting him."

Holly sucked in a harsh breath. "Why?"

He lifted a shoulder. "She didn't want a ready-made family. But you know what's funny? Like you, I think

I grieved for JT's loss far more than the ending of my relationship. JT was with me. He and I agreed to stick together. Nothing else mattered."

"She was an idiot." Holly's stout declaration made him smile. "She didn't deserve you either."

"JT asked about you tonight as I was tucking him into bed."

A ghost of a smile tugged at her lips. "He's sweet."

"He wants to know if you'll come for dinner." He reached for her hand, knowing he was standing too close to the edge but unable to back away from the cliff. So he took a leap of faith and jumped. "Will you?"

She bit her lip, hesitation in her eyes. "Are you sure?"

"I'm sure." And he was. Sure that he wanted to spend more time with Holly.

"Then I'd love to."

"Tomorrow night?" Tomorrow was Sunday, he'd have plenty of time to run to the grocery store for whatever he needed.

She nodded. "Gabe, I'd never hurt JT."

"I know." He couldn't resist tugging on her hand until she moved closer. Wrapping his free arm around her waist, he pulled her toward him, bending his head to find her mouth with his.

She melted against him and he deepened the kiss, reveling in the heady feeling of having Holly in his arms. He could easily get addicted to holding her, kissing her. For long moments he was lost in the sweet taste of her. As much as he wanted to push for more, to lift her in his arms and find her bedroom, he knew it was too soon.

Breathing heavily, he broke off the kiss, resting his forehead against hers. "Holly, tell me to go home." *Ask me to stay.*

"Go home." But her tone lacked conviction and she curled a fist into his shirt, as if she couldn't bear to completely let go. "What if JT has another nightmare? He'll panic if you're not there."

She was right. As much as he didn't want to leave, he knew she was right. And her concern for JT touched his heart. Holly was nothing like Jennifer. Hope swelled in his chest. This could work.

"Tomorrow night," he reminded her in a hoarse tone, willing his heart rate to return to normal. "Come early."

"All right."

He wanted to kiss her again, but forced himself to let go, to take a step back while he still could. She reluctantly let go of his shirt, smoothing out the wrinkles, and it took every bit of willpower he possessed not to haul her close and kiss her again. "Good night, Holly."

"Good night."

Leaving wasn't easy. Yet even as he drove home, congratulating himself on being smart, Gabe acknowledged he'd taken a big risk in asking her to come for dinner. Imagining JT's reaction was easy. The boy would make more out of the evening than he should.

Taking a deep breath, he let it out slowly. Everything would be fine. He'd just have to explain to JT that he and Holly were just friends.

Yeah. He snorted loudly. Sure. Just friends.

A friend with whom he wanted very badly to make love.

* * *

Holly agonized over whether or not she was doing the right thing, agreeing to have dinner with Gabe and JT.

Gabe's concern for JT was humbling. As much as she resented being lumped in with the woman who'd been stupid enough to leave him when he'd provided his nephew with a loving home, she also understood Gabe's caution was part of what made him a good father.

How could she fault him for that?

Her experience with her own father and with Tom had forced her to believe that most men were extremely selfish. Selfish when it came to sacrificing their family for their own needs.

So far, Gabe's actions proved he was anything but selfish. She admired his dedication to JT.

Gabe had let her know that dinner would be ready at five-thirty in the evening. Earlier than she normally ate but she understood the time would suit JT. Just another example of how Gabe put JT's needs first. At three-thirty, she headed over to Gabe's house, with a container brimming with her mother's home-made chocolate-chip cookies.

"Hi," Gabe's gaze was warm, approving as he opened the door to invite her in.

"Hi." She handed him the container of cookies. "I brought dessert, my mother's home-made chocolate-chip cookies."

"Excellent." Gabe's face lit up. "JT's favorite."

"Is she here?" Holly heard JT ask, seconds before he came dashing across the room. "Hi, Dr. Holly!" He threw his arms around her waist in an exuberant hug.

His enthusiasm dispelled her fears. "Hi, JT." She bent over to return his embrace, poignantly aware of how much she'd lost when Kayla had died. "Hey, you look much better than the last time I saw you."

JT nodded and stepped back. Then he grasped her hand, tugging her farther into the room. "Do you wanna see my new truck?"

"I'd love to." She willingly followed him over to where he'd left a shiny black pick-up truck. Clutching a remote-control device in his small hands, he made the truck spin in a circle and race off down the hall. She laughed. "That's awesome."

"Can I get you something to drink?" Gabe asked.

When she glanced over at him, she noticed a guarded expression in his eyes. Her smile faded. Did he regret inviting her over? "Water would be fine."

"I bought some wine and soft drinks, if you'd prefer."

What she preferred was the grape juice and milk he'd offered her last time. At the very least she preferred a smile. But Gabe wasn't smiling. "Maybe later."

"Look, Dr. Holly, watch this." JT moved the levers on his remote control and the truck spun around again with such force the momentum made it flip over and over several times before smacking into the wall.

"JT, remember I told you to be careful of hitting the walls," Gabe warned.

JT seemed oblivious, more worried about his truck than the wall as he hurried over. Anxiety laced his tone. "Uncle Gabe, I think it's broken!"

"Bring it here." Gabe was calm, reassuring as he sat

on the edge of the sofa while JT ran over with the truck. As their two heads bent over the toy, Holly was aware of how perfect they looked together. No one seeing how Gabe interacted with JT would doubt he was the boy's father in every way that counted.

Ridiculous tears pricked at her eyes and she quickly blinked them away.

The woman who'd walked out on Gabe had to be as selfish as Tom had been. What difference did it make that she wasn't JT's biological mother? He was a precious child, a child any woman could love. Maybe raising children wasn't easy but any woman would be lucky to have Gabe as a partner, as a father for their children.

Wait a minute. The realization made her take a hasty step back, secretly glad Gabe was preoccupied with patiently trying to help JT fix his truck. She didn't want a relationship with Gabe, did she?

The image of the three of them together filled her mind. Her knees felt weak. Yes, she did.

The enormity of what she longed for immediately made her wonder if there was a way to keep their relationship a secret at work. She wouldn't want anyone to know. They would need to figure out how to hide their attraction for each other.

Because she was very much attracted to him. Her intense response to his kisses only reinforced that she had no resistance to him. If Gabe hadn't been the one to stop last night in her kitchen, to break off the kiss and to walk away, she knew exactly what would have happened. They would have made love.

Every cell in her body ached to make love with him.

"There, it's all fixed," Gabe was saying to JT. "Now, remember what I said, don't hit the walls."

"Okay." Relieved, JT came back to Holly. "Da—er—Uncle Gabe fixed it, see?"

Had JT almost called Gabe Daddy? She noticed Gabe freeze in the act of heading toward the kitchen, his expression a mixture of alarm and pleasure when he glanced back toward JT.

"I see." She forced herself to focus her attention on JT. "He's good at fixing things, I bet."

"He had to fix the clothes washer too," JT confided. "But he said a naughty word. Davy at school said that same word and the teacher called his mom." JT's eyes were wide. "Davy got in big trouble."

She suppressed a smile. "I'm sure he did."

Gabe came back with her water. "I can't say anything with Mr. Big Ears around," he muttered under his breath, having overheard JT's story about Davy.

No kidding. She gratefully accepted the water, taking a long sip.

"I hope you like Mexican food," he said, ushering her toward the sofa. "Because JT wanted enchiladas."

"Whatever you make is fine." Holly was pretty sure she wasn't going to be able to eat much anyway. Being here with Gabe and with JT, as if they were a family, was wreaking havoc with her nerves.

What was she doing here?

Could she trust Gabe not to hurt her?

The way he trusted her not to hurt JT?

She thought she'd be able to relax as the evening went on, but instead she became more and more aware of Gabe.

His earlier aloofness faded. Now he was ultraattentive, touching her constantly. A hand against her back as he asked her if she wanted anything more to drink. The briefest squeeze of her hand as he drew her into the kitchen when dinner was ready.

The barely suppressed heat in his eyes as he watched her across the table.

She drank her wine, even though she knew she didn't need the stimulant. Was Gabe sending her a silent message? Did he want her to stay once JT went to bed?

Or was her imagination only playing out her own secret desires?

JT seemed to be a well-adjusted little boy, considering how traumatized he must have been when he'd lost his mother. Obviously, living with Gabe over these past few weeks was exactly what he'd needed.

The three of them played games after dinner. JT's favorite was a board game where one player could bump another player off the board, sending them back to the starting place.

JT enjoyed himself, but he was also a very bloodthirsty player. He bumped both Gabe and Holly off the board as often as possible. When he won, Holly lifted her hands in surrender, deeming him the expert.

When it was time for JT to get ready for bed, he asked if Dr. Holly could tuck him in, too.

Gabe's guarded expression was back as they both

took turns to sit on the edge of JT's bed and give him a hug and a kiss before going to sleep.

They obviously needed to have a talk. But when they returned to the living room, the phone rang. She froze, hoping the caller wasn't Tom. She didn't want the mistakes of her past to taint the possibility of the future. Especially now that she'd had a tiny taste of how wonderful the future could be.

As soon as Gabe answered, though, she knew the caller wasn't Tom. Especially when Gabe asked, "Are you sure you're all right?"

There was another long pause, then he responded, "Don't worry about a thing. I'll figure something out. You just take care of yourself, understand? And let me know if you need anything."

"What's wrong?" she asked when he finally hung up.

His expression was full of concern and he raked his hand through his hair. "That was Marybeth, JT's babysitter. She's in the emergency department over at Minneapolis's Medical Center and needs surgery for an emergency appendectomy."

"Oh, Gabe." Holly understood why he was so upset. "What are you going to do? Are you supposed to work tomorrow?"

"Yes." He sighed. "I'll have to start making phone calls to get someone to cover my shift. And then I'll need to hire a new sitter until Marybeth recovers from her surgery."

If she had been qualified to cover his shift, she would have offered. But she could help Gabe in another way. "I'll stay here tomorrow."

"You?" He frowned. "Thanks, but if one of us is going to call off work, it should be me. He's my responsibility."

"Gabe, I'm scheduled to work next weekend, so I'm off tomorrow."

"You are?" Hope filled his eyes. He came toward her until he was standing so close his male, musky scent clouded her brain, teasing her senses. "Are you sure you wouldn't mind?"

"I don't mind." And she didn't. Watching JT wouldn't be a hardship.

"Holly, I have to be at work early, by seven in the morning." Reaching up, he cradled her shoulders in his hands. "It might be easier for you to spend the night here."

CHAPTER EIGHT

SPEND the night? Had he lost his mind? Had he really just asked her to spend the night?

"I don't know if that's a good idea." The uncertainty in her eyes should have given him the perfect opportunity to back off. So he did. Sort of.

"You can take my bed. I'll sleep on the couch," he said, knowing full well he'd much rather share the bed.

With her.

All night.

Guilt free, as this was really for JT.

"Gabe." Holly's voice was soft, as if afraid she'd wake JT. "You and I both know what will happen if I stay."

He hoped so. He really hoped so. No—wait—that was the wrong answer. Wrong, wrong, wrong. He couldn't spend the night making love to Holly while JT slept blissfully in the next room down the hall.

As much as he wanted to, and he really, really wanted to, it wouldn't be right to let Holly stay.

"Okay, you're right. I don't know what I was thinking." Cool logic finally overrode his libido. He

took a deep breath and let it out slowly. She couldn't
stay and that was the end of it. "Will you give me a
minute to let JT know about Marybeth? I don't want him
to be shocked to find you here in the morning."

"Sure."

He walked back down the hall to JT's room. The boy
was asleep, but Gabe shook his shoulder and woke him
up enough to let him know Marybeth was sick so Dr.
Holly would stay with him the next day. JT mumbled
something that sounded like "That's good," before he
rolled over and went back to sleep.

When he returned to the living room, he was disappointed to find Holly standing near the front door with
her coat and her purse, ready to leave.

Because he'd pushed. Too fast.

"Thanks for dinner, Gabe."

Don't go! "You're welcome to come back, any time."

She let out a sigh of exasperation. "You need to make
up your mind about what you really want. One minute
you're looking at me as if you're not at all happy that
JT wants me to tuck him in and the next you're asking
me to spend the night."

He swallowed hard, disconcerted that the inner war
he'd waged had been so obvious. He knew what he
wanted. Holly. In his arms. In his bed.

But unfortunately he suspected that JT wanted
something too. A mother. And he couldn't start something with a woman just because JT needed a mother.
Holly wouldn't hurt JT on purpose but there were no
guarantees. Anything could happen. Especially given

the very complicated events surrounding JT's adoption. What if his worst fears were correct? How would he explain to Holly?

If he was right about JT's biological father, he'd lose Holly forever.

He was playing with fire by continuing to see her, but couldn't seem to help himself.

"I know what I want," he admitted. "But you're right, I am worried about how this will affect JT. I think we'd better take things slowly."

Slowly was going to kill him.

She stared at him for a long moment and then nodded. "All right. I'll research some nanny services tomorrow if you'd like." She hooked her purse over her shoulder.

He couldn't let her do that. She was already doing enough by staying here on her day off. JT was his problem, not hers.

"No, I'll do it." The more he thought about his situation, the more he realized he needed to call his mother. He'd avoided taking advantage of her because she'd experienced a difficult life with his father. Now that she'd found and married Hank, she was deliriously happy.

He didn't want to impose on her, but he needed help, at least for a few weeks. This wasn't the best time to bring a new nanny into the picture. JT needed stability. Structure.

Holly left after promising to return at six-thirty the following morning.

Gabe stared out the window, watching her drive away, hoping he wasn't being selfish to take advantage of Holly's generosity.

Finding Holly here the following morning was going to feel to JT as if she'd stayed the night.

Scrubbing his hands over his face, he wished he could erase the image of Holly in his bed. He had to stop torturing himself.

Using Holly as a surrogate mother for JT wasn't smart. He needed to ask his mother to fly up to Minnesota, as soon as possible.

Holly didn't sleep well and it was all Gabe's fault. His ridiculous suggestion to stay the night kept echoing over and over in her head.

When she finally dragged herself out of bed next morning, she had dark circles under her eyes, betraying her restlessness.

After doing her best to hide the effects of her long night, she headed over to Gabe's house. Luckily her normally cheerful nature eroded her crankiness, with a little help from Mother Nature as the sun peeked over the horizon, the sky glowing in glorious pink and orange hues. Sunrises, especially in late fall, were breathtakingly beautiful.

Going over to Gabe's to watch JT was simply helping out a friend. She would do the same for Lisa if she were here. She wasn't getting in over her head.

She parked off to the side in Gabe's driveway, leaving lots of room for him to back out of his garage. She couldn't help shooting a wary glance over her shoulder to make sure no one was watching as she walked up to his front door.

As soon as the thought formed, she became annoyed

with herself. Why did she care what Gabe's neighbors thought? She was here to watch his nephew, nothing more.

Gabe responded quickly to her knock. "Good morning," he said in that sexy, low voice of his. "Thanks again for coming over. I really appreciate it."

"No problem." She hadn't made any firm plans for her day off. Her mother could get a ride to dialysis. Sniffing the air, she homed in on the marvelous aroma of coffee. "Is that coffee?"

Gabe's husky laugh sent tingles down her spine. "Yes. Come on, I'll pour you a cup before I leave."

Sharing coffee in Gabe's kitchen was strangely intimate. She tried to get things back on track. "Anything in particular I need to know about JT?" she asked, sipping the flavorful brew and hoping the caffeine would hit her bloodstream fast.

"Not really." Gabe looked comfortable wearing his dark green scrubs as he leaned against the kitchen counter. "I called my mother last night. She's going to catch the first flight from Fort Meyers, Florida to Minneapolis today so you won't need to worry about wasting any more of your days off."

Spending time with JT wasn't a waste but she thought she understood what he was really saying. He didn't want JT to become too attached to her. Trying to ignore the tiny flash of hurt, she nodded. "Let me know if you need me to pick her up at the airport."

"I will." Gabe set his empty coffee-mug aside and pushed away from the counter. "Don't hesitate to call if you need anything."

Holly followed him to the door and he hesitated for a moment, as if he were going to kiss her goodbye. He didn't, but smiled crookedly as he murmured, "Thanks again, Holly. I owe you one."

Maybe, if she were the type to keep score. But she wasn't. "Have a good day. Don't worry about a thing. We'll be fine."

Gabe hadn't been gone for thirty minutes when JT cried out from his bedroom. Anxious, Holly hurried in.

"JT? What's wrong?"

JT was staring at her blankly, as if he was still half-asleep. She crossed over to sit on the edge of the bed, hesitant to approach too quickly.

"JT, do you remember me? Dr. Holly? I'm here because Marybeth got sick."

His expression cleared. "I remember."

Good, she thought with relief. "Are you all right? Did you have a nightmare?"

JT nodded and moved closer. She wrapped her arm around his shoulders and cuddled him close.

"I have lots of nightmares about wild animals. They bite."

Wild animals? She frowned, wondering what kind of wild animals JT was afraid of. "Yes, I know. But there aren't many wild animals around here."

"I saw a raccoon at the cemetery and my teacher at school says they're wild animals." JT seemed content to stay by her side. "I miss my mom. Sometimes, when I first wake up in the morning, I don't know where I am. And I get worried when I don't see Uncle Gabe," he confided.

She could certainly understand why the boy would have nightmares about wild animals and being abandoned. "I talked to your Uncle Gabe this morning before he went to work at the hospital. If you want to call and talk to him, I'm sure he won't mind."

JT didn't answer right away. "No, I'm okay here with you," he said finally.

Pleased that she'd been able to reassure him, she sat with him for a few more minutes. "Are you hungry? What would you like for breakfast?"

He shrugged against her. "Pancakes?"

"No problem." At least pancakes were easy. She was glad he hadn't asked for something more complicated.

"You smell good, like my mom," he said in a wistful tone.

She caught her breath at his admission, glancing down at his dark blond head tucked against her. The poor kid had been through the wringer these past few weeks.

Maybe Gabe was right to protect his son so fiercely.

And she was wrong. Sitting here with JT cuddled against her, she realized she was already in way over her head.

As the morning wore on, Holly grew more and more concerned about JT. She'd made him pancakes for breakfast, but he ate only a few bites. He also didn't want to play outside, but asked if he could lie on the sofa to watch movies. Halfway through the first one, he fell asleep.

JT's lethargy and poor appetite bothered her. After a brief internal debate, she called Gabe.

"Holly? What's wrong?"

"Sorry to bother you but I think JT's sick again." Holly went on to describe the boy's symptoms. "Remember last time you asked me if he needed to be seen? Well, I think this time he definitely needs to be seen."

Gabe didn't argue. "Actually, I was thinking the same thing. He just didn't seem himself all weekend. I called his pediatrician first thing this morning and have an appointment for tomorrow, but I'll see if I can't get him in today."

Relieved he was with her on this, she added, "I think that's best. Maybe it's nothing but the fact he hasn't been feeling well for a while makes me think there might be something more serious going on."

"I'll call you back." Gabe hung up.

Holly watched JT sleeping on the sofa. He moved restlessly at times, as if he wasn't comfortable. Should she move him to his bed? No, she'd wait to hear from Gabe first.

He called back just a few minutes later. "I have an appointment for him this afternoon at two. I also found someone to cover the rest of my shift. I'm going to pick up my mother from the airport and then head over to get JT."

"We'll be waiting."

Either the airport wasn't busy or Gabe broke speed records getting there and back because he arrived home in just over an hour. Gabe's mother was a plump, petite woman who wore her gray hair short and when she smiled she looked just like Gabe.

"Holly, this is my mother, Isabella Brown. Mom, this is a friend of mine, Holly Davidson."

"Nice to meet you," Holly murmured.

"It's a pleasure to meet you, too." The speculation in Isabella's eyes was hard to ignore. "And where's my grandson?"

"JT?" Holly called. The boy came out of the bedroom, smiling when he saw his grandmother. Still, he didn't run across the room to greet his grandmother with a hug. She cast a worried glance at Gabe. "He's been sleeping a lot and didn't eat much for breakfast or lunch."

Gabe frowned. "Thanks for letting me know."

Watching JT with his grandmother made her realize Gabe had been right to bring his mother up from Florida. Maybe it was best for JT to have his grandmother close by, rather than her.

Sensing she wasn't needed anymore, she took a step back. "I'd better go."

"Thanks again, Holly." Gabe walked her to the door.

"You're welcome." She couldn't help one last glance at JT contentedly seated beside his grandmother. "Will you let me know what the pediatrician says?"

"Absolutely." Gabe gazed down at her. "Actually, depending on what's wrong with JT, I was hoping maybe we could get together later."

He was? A warm glow of pleasure wrapped around her heart. "I'd like that."

"I'll call you." Gabe's low husky voice sent a ripple of tingling awareness down her spine.

Holly couldn't deny she wanted to spend time with

Gabe. Yet it was a little disconcerting to realize Gabe
wanted to see her alone, without JT.

She hadn't imagined the banked desire in his eyes.
And she couldn't help but anticipate what the evening
might bring.

Gabe and his mother took JT to the pediatrician's office.
The pediatrician was Dr. Cameron Feeney, a good
doctor who Gabe knew fairly well from the Children's
Medical Center.

"Gabe, I don't know what to tell you," Cameron said
after he'd examined JT. "There are many possibilities.
He could have a simple virus. Or a not-so-simple disease
such as Guillain-Barré syndrome. I'd like to do a lumbar
puncture here to check his spinal fluid, and then refer
you to a neurologist."

"He doesn't need to be admitted to the hospital?"

"No, I don't think so. Other than being tired, he
seems fine. You could give him a protein drink in his
favorite flavor until his appetite improves."

Gabe nodded, hoping JT didn't have anything more
than a virus. The possibility of Guillain-Barré syndrome,
a disease affecting the nerves of the muscles, causing
weakness, had lurked in the back of his own mind, too.
The lumbar puncture was rough, but JT was a trouper,
getting through the procedure without too much crying.

His mother had cried with JT and afterward declared
they needed to stop for ice cream as JT had been so
brave. JT polished off his entire ice-cream cone, which
made Gabe feel better.

That evening, once JT was asleep and his mother was settled in the guest bedroom, she found him in the kitchen.

"Did you call Holly?"

He raised a brow at her. "Matchmaking, Mom?"

"Maybe." His mother propped her hands on her hips. "What's wrong with a mother wanting to see her son happy?"

He had to admit he'd been thinking about Holly all day. Only concern over JT had taken his mind off her. "JT's sick. I should probably stay home."

"JT's fine. You have an appointment to see the neurologist in a few days. Besides, I heard you tell Holly you'd call her."

Suppressing a sigh, he remembered why he hadn't wanted his mother's help with JT. She meant well, but her dogged persistence drove him crazy.

Still, he had promised. "Okay, fine. I'll call her."

Gabe called Holly's cellphone, pleasantly surprised when she picked up after the first ring. "Hi, Gabe. How's JT?"

"He's fine. The pediatrician did an LP and didn't see any obvious signs of infection. He wants me to take him to see a neurologist."

"A virus? Guillain-Barré?" Holly guessed.

"Maybe." He hoped not, but knew it was a possibility. Guillain-Barré certainly wasn't fatal, but it was a progressive disease that often got worse before it got better. Patients usually recovered fully.

Thank heavens his mother was here to help.

"Are you in the mood for some company?" he asked, trying not to betray how badly he wanted to see her.

There was a pause and his heart dropped.

"Yes. I'd love some company," she finally said.

He sighed in relief. "Great. I was hoping you hadn't changed your mind."

The sound of her laugh reassured him. "No way. I've been waiting for you to call."

She'd been waiting for him. The thought sent a shaft of desire straight to his groin. "I'm on my way."

He hung up the phone and barely said goodbye to his mother before dashing out to his car.

There was no reason for Holly to wait any longer.

Holly flung clothes out of her closet, trying to find something classy yet sexy to wear.

Why didn't she own a single item of clothing that made her feel sexy without being too obvious? Finally settling on a V-necked ruby-red sweater and a pair of black jeans, she barely had time to hide the mess in her closet when the doorbell rang.

Taking a deep breath to calm her jagged nerves, Holly swiped her damp palms down the sides of her jeans and forced herself to walk slowly to the door. When she saw Gabe standing there, looking anxious, her nervousness faded.

She opened the door with a shy smile. "Hi."

"Hi." Holding a slender brown paper bag in the crook of his arm, Gabe stepped inside, bringing a cool gust of autumn air. "I brought wine."

"Great." She took the bottle of wine so he could shrug out of his leather jacket. Wearing black jeans and a white shirt, open at the throat, he looked wonderful.

She must have been gawking because he smiled as he reached for the wine. "I think I remember where your corkscrew is."

Following him to the kitchen, she remembered the last time he'd arrived on her doorstep, just a few nights ago. Back then she'd been running from her feelings.

She wasn't running from them tonight.

The air crackled with tension as Gabe opened the wine and poured two glasses. Carrying them both in one hand, he drew her to the sofa, urging her to sit before handing her one of the glasses.

"Here's to us," he offered as a toast. "To the beginning of something special."

Something special? Her throat went dry and she couldn't speak as she took a sip of the fruity red wine. Did that mean what she thought it meant?

"Holly." Gabe reached up to cradle her cheek in the palm of his hand. "You're so beautiful. I thought of you all day."

She wanted to tell him to stop, that he didn't have to say nice things because she already wanted him. More than she'd ever wanted any man.

Even Tom. Especially Tom.

"Gabe," she murmured, not sure of how to tell him, to express what she really wanted. And then she didn't have to. Because he read her mind, taking her wineglass from her fingers and drawing her into his arms for a deep kiss.

Yes. This was what she wanted. Gabe's warm strength surrounding her, his mouth taking possession of hers. Reaching up she entwined her arms around his neck, pulling him closer against her. In a deft movement he lifted her up, pressing her back against the couch so she was stretched out beneath him.

She reveled in the hard length of him pressing against her. He was strength and tenderness wrapped in one desirable male package. Gabe raised his head, his eyes desperate with need as he gazed down at her.

"Holly, please, tell me you want this as much as I do." His husky admission only fueled her passion. No man had ever looked at her with such desire.

"Yes, Gabe. I want this as much as you do." She swallowed hard and admitted, "Maybe more."

CHAPTER NINE

GABE stared at her for a long moment. He was almost afraid to believe he'd heard right.

"Please, be sure," he murmured hoarsely. Every muscle in his body was taut with need. Never in his life had he wanted a woman as much as he wanted Holly.

Her smile was seductive, sensual and she reached up to thread her fingers through his hair. "I'm sure. Kiss me, Gabe."

Gladly. He'd kiss her all day, every day, given the chance. Holding his weight off her with one arm, he leaned down to cover her mouth with his.

Her sofa didn't provide a lot of room, but as far as he was concerned they weren't in a hurry either. He kissed her slowly but deeply, enjoying the wine-tinged taste of her mouth and the feel of her soft breasts pressed against him. He wanted to strip their clothing away, to see every creamy inch of her skin, but he held himself in control.

Barely.

Holly tugged on his shirt, sliding her hands underneath the fabric, her hands cool against his fevered skin.

Shifting his weight off her as much as he could, he
trailed a path of kisses to her throat. And then as far
down as her V-necked sweater would let him go.

"My bedroom," she gasped, as he nudged the fabric
aside and found the upper curve of her breast.

"In a minute," he whispered, pushing her sweater up
and out of the way. He took a moment to admire the way
her breasts looked in the lacy blue bra before making
quick work of the front clasp.

A guy had to like expensive lingerie. Some things
were worth any price.

Gently peeling the bra away, he freed her breasts.
Annoyed with his own shirt, he ripped it off and then
gathered her close, enjoying the feeling of her softness
against him.

Holly ran her fingers over his back, making him
shiver. He loved the way she touched him, full of awe
and wonder.

"Did you say something about your bedroom?" he
asked, lightly brushing a kiss over her mouth.

"Did I?" Her eyes were glazed with passion. "Oh,
yes, down the hall."

Down the hall seemed like miles, yet as much as he
didn't want to move he knew Holly deserved to be
comfortable.

He wanted this night to be special for her. JT was in
good hands with his grandmother. He didn't want to feel
guilty for stealing these few hours alone.

Tonight was for Holly. And for him.

Peeling himself away from her, he held on to one of

her hands as he stood, bringing her up beside him, unwilling to let her go, even for a moment. He didn't bother trying to find his discarded shirt but led the way down the hall, figuring out which bedroom was hers by a process of elimination.

He didn't flip on the light switch as he entered the room, wanting to see her but not willing to make her feel self-conscious.

It took a few seconds for his eyes to adjust to the darkness. There was a little bit of light shining through the doorway, enough that he could make out the large bed in the center of the room. He paused at the edge of her bed and turned to face her.

"There's still time to change your mind," he felt obligated to point out, although he hoped and prayed she wouldn't.

She didn't answer, but grasped the hem of her sweater and lifted it up and over her head. Her open bra fell off her slim shoulders to the floor. When she stepped forward and reached for the fly of his jeans, he groaned and tried to hang on to the last vestiges of his control.

Her fingers seemed to spend more time exploring him than getting rid of his clothes. When he couldn't take her exquisite torture a moment longer, he shucked his jeans and boxers in a swift motion, and then reached for her. Lifting her up, he gently placed her on the bed, and then he peeled off her jeans and matching blue bikini underwear.

Damn, she was beautiful. He wished the lights were on so he could explore every inch of her satiny skin, but there wasn't time. Holly was already urgently reaching for him, her deft hands igniting small fires as they touched him everywhere.

"Please, Gabe…"

He couldn't deny her, not when his pleasure depended on hers. He fished in his jeans for protection, and then returned the favor, stroking her skin, kissing her breasts until he could barely think. When she wrapped her legs around his hips he couldn't hold off another moment, but slid deep, branding her as his.

The strong feeling of possessiveness shocked him. As he made love to Holly, drawing out the sensation until they both reached the pinnacle of pleasure, he held her close, burying his face in her hair, knowing things had irrevocably changed.

She belonged to him now. And he wasn't planning to ever let her go.

Holly held on to Gabe's strong shoulders, her face pressed to the hollow of his neck, deeply shaken by the experience they'd shared.

Gabe was a wonderful lover. Unselfish to the core, seeking to satisfy her needs before his own. Even after he shifted to the side, he gathered her close as if unable to bear leaving any space between them.

She closed her eyes, relaxing against him, enjoying the moment for as long as it lasted. He'd probably have to leave soon. She understood he wouldn't be able to stay the night.

JT needed him.

A tiny part of her mind realized Gabe must have felt better about leaving JT with his grandmother than with a babysitter, even someone as responsible as Marybeth.

But what would happen when Marybeth was released by the doctor to return to her babysitting duties and JT's grandmother went home?

The tumultuous thought wouldn't leave her alone, even though she knew she was borrowing trouble.

Best not to worry so much about the future. Gabe had claimed they needed to take things slow. Making love with him hadn't exactly been slowly, but she figured he was really referring to her relationship with JT. That was the part they needed to take slow.

Not this part. The being-with-him-in-her-bed part.

Gabe didn't leave. Several hours later he woke her up, making love to her again, this time languidly exploring her body as if they had all the time in the world.

Eventually, she realized how late it had become. Dawn was just an hour or two away.

She fell asleep again, waking up only when Gabe kissed her. "I have to go to work," he whispered.

"Okay," she murmured groggily.

"I'm going to borrow your shower."

She nodded, yawned and stretched while Gabe disappeared into her bathroom. Her alarm wouldn't go off for another half-hour, but she climbed out of bed anyway, to make Gabe some coffee before he left. Seemed like the least she could do after the wonderful night they'd shared.

She pulled her robe on and padded to the kitchen. Did Gabe eat breakfast? She wasn't sure. Truthfully there was a lot she still didn't know about him.

Although she already knew the important stuff. Like what a great lover he was. And what a wonderful, unselfish father he was to JT. Family was important to him, too.

He'd spent the whole night with her. Somehow she hadn't expected he'd do that, even with his mother at his house, watching over JT.

Gabe walked into the kitchen fully dressed in the clothes he'd worn last night. "Good morning," he said huskily, pulling her close for a kiss.

"Good morning." She was breathless when he finally let her go. As he reached for his mug of coffee, his cellphone rang.

Gabe frowned as he pulled open his phone. "Hi, Mom. What's up?"

His face paled and his expression turned grim as he listened on the other end of the phone. "I'll meet you at the hospital," he said in a terse tone.

The hospital? "Gabe? What's wrong?"

"She called 911 for an ambulance because JT's having seizures. I need to go."

She could only watch as he spun on his heel, grabbed his coat and bolted out the door.

He never should have gone to Holly's house last night.

He never should have left JT alone.

He'd never be a good father.

The self-recriminations echoed over and over in his

mind as he barreled through the streets of Minneapolis, cutting the normally short drive to the hospital in half.

How long had JT been having seizures? All night? His gut clenched with pain. What if JT suffered irreversible neurological damage as a result?

Guilt swelled, choking him. Dear God, JT had to be all right. He just had to be.

Gabe beat the ambulance to the hospital. He paced the center of the ED arena but then belatedly realized he was scheduled to work. Inwardly swearing, he headed off to find Mike Johnson, the physician who'd staffed the ED overnight.

He found Mike sitting in front of one of the bedside computers, finishing his chart documentation, and quickly explained what had happened with JT.

"Hey, it's all right," Mike said in his normal, easy-going manner. "I'll stay and make a few phone calls to find someone to cover your shift."

Gabe was grateful his colleague was so willing to help out. "Thanks." He glanced down, realizing his hands were shaking.

What was taking the ambulance so long to get here? Had something happened to JT on the way? His mind easily painted the worst picture, imagining the paramedic team running a full-blown respiratory and cardiac resuscitation on JT during the trip to the hospital.

Then suddenly he saw JT's name listed on the arena's census board. The doors from the ambulance bay burst open and a team of paramedics wheeled JT in, his mother hurrying alongside.

"What happened on the way?" Gabe asked, gazing down at JT, who appeared to be asleep. No breathing tube had been placed, thank heavens. But clearly the boy wasn't very responsive to his surroundings.

"We gave him a dose of Versed and the seizures stopped. But he's still pretty lethargic. His vital signs are stable, except he's running a fairly high fever—102.8 Fahrenheit."

Had the fever caused the seizure? "Get him on the monitor and then draw a full set of labs, including blood cultures. We also need a chest X ray."

The nursing staff stepped up to take over JT's care from the paramedic team that had brought him in. Gabe stared at JT's peaceful face, wondering what was going on in the boy's small body. A virus of some sort was the obvious answer, but what kind? And if it was Guillain-Barré syndrome, that didn't typically cause seizures or a high fever.

"Get a neurology consult, too," he added, remembering the pediatrician's recommendation. "And I want a CT scan of his head."

Someone tapped him on the arm. "I'm officially taking over as the physician of record here, Gabe."

He glanced down to see Dr. Tara Irwin standing beside him. Mike must have called her to cover his shift. While he was grateful, he was also a little annoyed. His feelings must have shown on his face.

"Don't argue with me, Gabe," she warned.

At her determined expression, his annoyance faded. He stepped back, knowing Tara was absolutely right.

He couldn't be calm and rational, not when JT's life was at stake.

Especially when they didn't even know what was wrong with him.

He listened as Tara confirmed most of his orders and added a few of her own, including an infectious disease consult. JT woke up, crying a little when a nurse drew blood.

"Shh, it's okay, buddy." Gabe pulled a chair close to JT's bed, taking his hand. "I'm here. I love you, JT."

Shortly after they finished the procedure, JT fell asleep again. Gabe tried not to panic at the extent of his lethargy, as it was normal after a seizure.

As the staff hurried to complete the orders, his mother came up to stand beside him. "Are you all right?" she asked.

"Fine." His words were clipped and he realized he was coming across as angry. And he was mad, but at himself, not at his mother. He'd made the decision to leave JT in her care while he went to Holly's. This was his fault and no one else's. "Sorry, I'm just worried about him."

"I know." His mother laid a hand on his shoulder. "But stop beating yourself up, Gabe. JT was fine last night, I checked on him before I went to bed. This morning I heard him cry out as if he was having a nightmare so I hurried into his room. His body started to convulse, on the right side especially, so I quickly called 911 and then called you."

Gabe closed his eyes, relieved to know JT hadn't been seizing all night.

"Thanks for telling me," he said finally. Maybe she was right, and nothing would have changed even if he had been there. Was it so wrong to take some time for himself? He didn't really think so yet, no matter how illogical, he couldn't get past the feeling he'd let JT down.

Maybe he wasn't cut out to be a father.

"Dr. Martin?" One of the nurses poked her head into the room. "Radiology called to tell us they're ready for JT. We're going to take him over for his CT scan now."

"All right." Gabe stood and moved back, so the transport team of the nurse and the radiology aide could disconnect JT from the heart monitor. Gabe watched, bereft, as they wheeled his son away.

"Are you hungry?" his mother asked.

He shook his head, knowing he couldn't eat. "Go ahead, though. I'll just wait here for JT to get back." CT scans of the head didn't take long.

His mother seemed to hesitate, but then nodded. "All right, I'll be back in a little while."

He sat back in the chair, cradling his head in his hands. JT had to be all right. They'd figure out what was wrong with him and they'd treat him. He'd be fine.

He had to believe JT would be fine.

"Gabe?"

He raised his head at the sound of Holly's voice. She stood in the doorway, as if unsure of her welcome.

For a moment he longed to go to her, to take her into his arms, drawing comfort. But he couldn't move. As much as he knew that none of this was her fault, he couldn't get past how he'd selfishly gone over to her house, leaving JT home alone with his grandmother.

"Where's JT?" she asked, taking another step farther into the room. "How is he?"

"They stopped the seizure but he's still pretty out of it." Gabe strove to keep his tone steady, although inside he felt as if he might shatter into a dozen little pieces. "He's in Radiology for a CT of his head."

"I see." Holly's expression was wary, as if she could sense how he regretted the time they'd spent together. None of this was her fault either. She hadn't asked him to spend the night.

He'd made that decision on his own.

"Thanks for coming to see him," he said.

She licked her lips and glanced away. "Actually, I'm here on consult."

That's right, he remembered Tara requesting an infectious disease consult. He tried to pull his scattered thoughts together. To see Holly as a physician, not as the woman he'd spent the night making love with. "Do you think he could have viral meningitis?" he asked.

Holly shook her head. "I checked the results of the LP they did on JT yesterday—there's no evidence of meningitis."

Gabe sighed, unsure if that was good news. At least if they had a diagnosis they could formulate a treatment plan. "He was running a fever this morning. It could be that the seizure was related to the fever and not to anything neurological."

"Maybe." Holly didn't sound convinced.

Their conversation was interrupted when the nurse brought JT back to his room. Once he was reconnected to the bedside monitor, Holly came forward.

"I'll need to examine him."

Gabe stood back, allowing Holly to do her job. He felt sick all over again when he realized JT was still pretty lethargic. If JT's responsiveness didn't improve, he'd end up getting intubated in order to protect his airway. Remembering Mark's mother's traumatic reaction to watching her son be intubated, he suddenly understood exactly how she'd felt.

Swallowing hard, he watched Holly go through her in-depth exam. When she'd finished, she turned toward him.

"Has JT always been afraid of wild animals?" she asked.

"No." He didn't understand what she was getting at.

She hesitated, then said, "I think we should test him for rabies."

Rabies? Gabe stared at her. "Why? There's no way JT could have been exposed to rabies."

"Yesterday morning, JT told me wild animals bite. Then he said he saw a raccoon at the cemetery, and I'm assuming that was probably during Claire's funeral." When he nodded, she continued, "Four to six weeks is the typical incubation period for rabies. What if he saw a rabid raccoon and it bit him? I don't want to ignore any possibilities."

Gabe had trouble wrapping his mind around the implications. "But he hasn't been given the vaccination for rabies."

Holly didn't say anything. She didn't have to. Once a patient showed clinical signs of rabies, the mortality rate was very high.

The tightness in his chest intensified. If JT had really been exposed to rabies six weeks ago, there was a very good chance he would die.

CHAPTER TEN

HOLLY cradled the phone receiver between her ear and her shoulder, listening to the dreadful music as she waited for the lab tech at the Center for Disease Control to put her in touch with the physician who specialized in rabies. As soon as Gabe had admitted there was a possibility JT had been bitten by a raccoon, she'd called to get their recommendations.

Rabies wasn't very common. Treatment after known rabies contact had become so good there had been little recent research on the subject. Local labs didn't even run tests for rabies. If infection was suspected, the patient was simply treated no matter what any blood tests showed.

"Dr. Davidson? This is Dr. Lois Whitney at the CDC. I was told you have a case of suspected rabies?"

"Yes." Holly explained the potential raccoon bite and then described JT's symptoms. She'd noticed JT's right side was convulsing and he was salivating more than normal, which was one of the symptoms of rabies. In reading up on the disease, she'd discovered some patients had literally drowned in their own secretions.

"Send us some blood and cerebral spinal fluid samples immediately," Dr. Whitney told her. "Put them on dry ice and ship them as fast as possible." Lois Whitney hesitated, and then added, "From what you described, you'd better treat him as if he is positive for rabies."

"I understand." Holly hung up the phone, feeling sick. She'd hoped she'd been wrong about JT having contracted rabies.

Without immediate post-exposure vaccinations, the disease was highly fatal.

She took several deep breaths, trying to hold panic at bay. They had the best medical experts in the country here at the Children's Medical Center. If anyone could get JT through this, they could.

Poor Gabe. She knew how devastated she'd been after losing Kayla. Losing JT would be worse. Much worse.

Stop it. She mentally gave herself a hard shake. They weren't going to lose him.

Somehow they were going to find a way to successfully treat him.

Turning blindly from the desk, she bumped into Dr. Jeff Konen, the neuro specialist assigned to JT's case. He'd come in to examine JT right after she'd broached the possibility of rabies.

"According to the CDC, we need to treat JT Martin as if he has rabies. And we need to get some blood and cerebral spinal fluid samples sent to Atlanta immediately."

The older man blew out a heavy breath. "Okay, so if your theory is correct and he was bitten almost six weeks ago, then the virus has already begun its attack on his central nervous system. The typical rabies vaccine injections are used to prevent the virus from attacking the nervous system. In JT's case, it's too late to prevent that. Which means we have to try to minimize the damage."

The large knot in her stomach tightened. She knew the mechanism of disease as well as he did. This long after the time of infection, there wasn't much that could be done to stop the progression of the virus.

"We need to talk to Gabe, to include him in this discussion," she said firmly. Gabe was a physician as well as being JT's uncle. He'd want to be included in all aspects of JT's care.

Jeff hesitated and nodded, turning toward JT's room. She followed close behind.

While she'd been in touch with the CDC, the nurses had placed JT in isolation. Both she and Jeff donned a face mask, gown and gloves before entering the room.

Gabe wasn't wearing any isolation gear, as if he could care less if he was contaminated by the virus. From her research she knew that person-to-person transmission of the virus was rare. Still, infectious disease literature said that it was better to be safe by placing patients in isolation.

Gabe sat on JT's bed, holding the boy in his arms. His face was pale and drawn, his eyes bleak with grief.

"The CDC would like samples of JT's blood and cerebral spinal fluid," she told him. "They recommended we treat JT as if he's already tested positive for rabies."

Gabe gave a slight nod. She wasn't sure if he was

agreeing to send blood to the CDC or to the proposed treatment plan. Hopefully both.

Jeff stepped forward. "Gabe, I propose we get JT intubated and sent up to the PICU. I think if we paralyze and sedate him, putting him into a barbiturate coma, we'll have a chance to protect his brain while it fights the virus."

Holly raised a brow. The neurologist's proposal was intriguing. And somewhat experimental. Similar treatment plans had been tried but not all of them had been successful. There were so many variables, especially as there were at least eleven different strains of the rabies virus.

When Gabe didn't say anything right away, she spoke up. "Gabe, I've done some research on rabies, and there has been limited success with this approach. I have to agree with Jeff's treatment plan. I'd also add another possibility. Ketamine, a drug used primarily for anesthesia, has been shown to decrease the rabies virus in mice. It hasn't been tested on humans, but if we use a combination of ketamine and Versed to decrease the toxic effects on JT's brain, we may have a chance to beat the virus."

There were no guarantees. As a physician Gabe had to understand that more than anyone. Yet Holly firmly believed that if doctors did not try, they would not succeed. If the chances were high that JT might die, there was no reason not to try this radical treatment option.

Gabe gazed so intently down at JT she wondered if he'd heard anything they'd said. But then he slowly nodded.

"Do whatever you have to do to save my son."

His son. Tears burned the back of her eyes and she had to look away, biting her lip behind the face mask.

Once they had paralyzed and sedated JT, they could ensure he wouldn't feel any more pain or discomfort.

Gabe's suffering, for the son he might never get to formally adopt, would be much harder to bear.

Gabe didn't leave JT's bedside except to eat and to use the bathroom. Eating wasn't exactly high on his priority list. He wasn't hungry but knew he needed to keep up his strength, in order to support JT.

His mother insisted on staying in Minneapolis, despite the fact that he encouraged her to go home to her husband. Clearly he no longer needed her to watch JT while he was at work.

There was no reason for her to sit here with him. JT's recovery would likely take weeks. Maybe even months.

He refused to consider the alternative. The physician part of him understood the risks, but as a parent he chose to ignore them.

JT would pull through this. He'd make sure of it.

The hours merged into days. He lost track of time, sleeping on the parent bed next to JT in the PICU.

He couldn't complain about JT's care. Everyone bent over backward to take excellent care of his son. Within twenty-four hours of sending blood and cerebral spinal fluid samples to Atlanta, the CDC had confirmed the diagnosis of rabies.

Holly had been right after all.

He couldn't hold JT in his lap anymore now that he was intubated and breathing with the help of a ventilator. There were so many tubes and wires in JT he was almost afraid to touch him. All JT's nutrition came through a feeding tube, not to mention myriad IV medications he was receiving. He knew that despite the radical combination of medications Jeff and Holly had ordered for JT, it was possible the treatments might not work.

So he prayed, like he'd never prayed before.

On Friday, his mother came into JT's room with a pile of mail she'd brought from his house. Gabe hadn't been home since meeting JT and his mother at the hospital, and he found it difficult to care about mundane things like phone bills and bank statements.

One of the letters snagged his attention because it was from the DNA lab in the Minnesota State Lab in Minneapolis. He stared at the envelope for a long time. The DNA results declaring the identity of JT's biological father were inside. This was what he'd been waiting for, in order to move forward with JT's adoption.

He almost threw the envelope away. JT's life hung in the balance—what difference did it make who his biological father was?

Except that maybe JT's biological father deserved to know the truth. Especially now that JT was so sick.

Especially when there was a possibility JT might not survive.

He stared at the letter for a long time, struggling with what to do. If the situation were reversed and he'd fathered a child that no one had told him about, he'd want to know the truth.

"Gabe? Are you all right?" his mother asked.

"Yeah, I'm fine." He opened the letter and scanned the results. Rising to his feet, he glanced down at JT, still motionless in the barbiturate coma. He knew what he had to do. "Will you stay here with JT for a few minutes?"

His mother glanced at him in surprise. "Of course I will."

Gabe nodded and left the room, pulling his cellphone out of his pocket. Then he swore when he realized the battery was dead. He hadn't recharged his phone over the past few days.

He turned and headed to the PICU waiting room. There was a phone in there he could use. If the operator would give him an outside line.

He had a long-distance phone call to make.

Holly checked on JT and Gabe as often as her schedule allowed. Sometimes she came and sat with him at the end of the day, but Gabe didn't say much.

She knew he blamed himself for the seriousness of JT's illness. And maybe a small part of him blamed her as well.

What could she say? There were no words to make him feel better. They were doing everything possible to save JT's life.

All they could do was wait.

On Friday evening she headed into the PICU to find Gabe walking out from the waiting room. She was surprised to see him outside the PICU when he'd been practically living at JT's bedside.

"Hey," he greeted her weakly.

"Hi, Gabe." She longed to put her arms around him, to hold him close. Sometimes she wondered if she'd imagined those stolen hours they'd spent together at her house the night before JT had become so sick. The only evidence she had to prove it wasn't her imagination was the fact that her sheets still carried a hint of Gabe's musky scent.

Gabe stared at her for a long moment, before glancing away. "I need to thank you," he said slowly. "If you hadn't brought up the possibility of rabies when you did, it would have been too late."

She hoped it wasn't too late. So far, she knew JT's vital signs were good, but they wouldn't know about his level of brain function until they brought him out of the coma.

"You don't have to thank me. I wish there was more I could do. I care about you, Gabe. I care about both of you."

"I know." At that moment his stoic expression cracked, revealing the vulnerable man beneath. Unable to ignore his pain, she closed the gap between them and wrapped her arms around his waist, determined to offer comfort even if he did push her away.

He didn't.

Instead, his arms came up to crush her close, his face buried in her hair as he murmured, "I can't lose him, Holly. I just can't."

"I know." She battled tears, holding on to him tightly. She wasn't one to offer false hope but in this case they needed to think positively. "You won't. I'll be here for you. We have to believe you won't lose him."

"I've been a lousy father so far," Gabe whispered.

What? She pulled back to look into his eyes. "That's not true. Compared to Tom, you've been wonderful. Stop blaming yourself, Gabe. How could you know JT had been bitten by a raccoon? The bite would have been so small it was barely noticeable. And how could you know that the raccoon carried rabies?"

"I don't know. I just don't want to lose him." The self-reproach in his eyes made her draw him close, give him another tight hug. His grip tightened, too, as if he needed the support as much as she needed to give it.

She held Gabe for a long time, offering him a little of her strength. When he finally lifted his head and loosened his arms, he brushed a light kiss over her mouth, as if offering silent thanks. "I know you're scheduled to work this weekend, but will you stay, at least for a little while?"

Thrilled and humbled that he'd realized he couldn't do this alone without help and support, she nodded. "Of course. I'll stay for as long as you need me."

"Thanks." Gabe took a deep breath and let it out slowly. He offered a crooked smile and held out his hand. "Let's go."

She took his hand and walked with him into the PICU. Their clasped hands drew a couple of curious glances from the PICU nurses but Holly couldn't bring herself to care. What did a few whispers matter in the big scheme of things?

The only thing that mattered was the fact that Gabe and JT needed her. And if she was honest, she needed them too.

Gabe's mother greeted her with a wide smile. She got the distinct impression his mother approved of Holly's new yet tenuous relationship with her son.

That night, Holly stretched out next to Gabe on the narrow parent bed in JT's room. He held her close, her head resting on his shoulder, their embrace cozily intimate despite the fact that they were both fully clothed. Gabe had changed into a pair of comfortable sweats and a T-shirt, while she'd borrowed a pair of scrubs to wear.

Still, Holly was poignantly aware of the message her actions sent to anyone who walked into the room to care for JT.

She and Gabe were a couple. Together they were supporting JT and each other.

She loved him. The shocking realization made her eyes fly open. Her chest felt tight, as if she couldn't breathe.

Love? How could this have happened? For a moment panic swelled as she stared blindly at the tile ceiling. Falling in love usually meant getting married. Having a family. Another child, hers and Gabe's.

Could she have a family of her own? There was a tiny part of her that always thought she'd feel disloyal to Kayla if she had another child.

Yet being here, next to JT's bedside while the boy fought for his life, she slowly realized nothing could be further from the truth.

Having Kayla had taught her to love. Loving one person didn't mean you couldn't love another. JT needed all the love and support he could get.

So did Gabe.

Nothing else mattered.

The next morning, she awoke when Jeff Konen came into the room. Groggily, she swung her legs over the side of the bed, sitting next to Gabe who'd also just woken up. Jeff eyed her presence beside Gabe curiously, but didn't comment.

"How long do we need to keep JT in a coma?" Gabe asked, scrubbing a hand over his face.

"I'm not sure," Jeff admitted. He glanced at Holly. "What do you think?"

Holly blinked and forced herself to focus. "A full week, to be safe."

Jeff nodded. "Yeah, that's what I was thinking too. We'll start tapering off the medications early next week."

"So there's nothing more to do at this point but to wait," Gabe said.

"I'm afraid so," Jeff admitted.

Waiting was difficult. Holly knew where Gabe was coming from. As a physician he was accustomed to action. Not to the wait-and-see approach.

After Jeff left the room, Holly slowly rose to her feet. "I have to get ready for work," she said, wishing she didn't have to leave.

Gabe nodded, watching her as she gathered her things together. It was too late to run home for a change of clothes so she decided to find a call room to shower and change into a fresh set of scrubs. Scrubs paired with a lab coat would have to do.

"Thanks for staying," Gabe said in a low voice.

She gave him another hug, knowing they'd need to talk but that this wasn't the time. Not when JT's fate was still largely unknown. "I'll be back tonight, unless you decide you don't want me here."

Gabe reached up to cup the side of her face. "I do want you here," he murmured, before bending his head down to kiss her.

His kiss was brief but potent. Her senses swam as she momentarily lost herself in his embrace. He broke off the kiss when one of JT's nurses entered the room.

Holly stepped back, feeling a little self-conscious but not to the point where she regretted one second of their embrace. "I'll see you later," she promised, before picking up her clothes and leaving the room.

Holly showered and changed before starting her rounds. Each of the infectious disease doctors had to take turns staffing on the weekends. She didn't mind, but, having had much of her sleep broken during the night with interruptions from the nurses caring for JT, she had to battle her fatigue with several strong cups of coffee.

She came through the PICU to check on JT halfway through the day. Gabe was still there and he greeted her with a smile that warmed her heart. She was amazed that he was holding up as well as he was.

"I'm going to run home after work but then I'll be back," she told him.

"Thanks, Holly. I appreciate it."

She honestly didn't mind. In fact, she finished her rounds on the floors sooner than she'd expected and as there were no new consults called in she was able to leave by three in the afternoon.

She changed into comfortable clothes, debating what to bring back to the hospital with her. Because if Gabe wanted her to spend the night with him again, she would. Gladly.

In the end she decided to bring enough clothes for the rest of the weekend. She had to work on Monday too, but by then they might have started weaning JT from his medications. They couldn't take him out of the coma too quickly, but would need to take their time over several days.

She didn't eat dinner, deciding she'd force Gabe to eat with her, knowing he probably wasn't taking care of himself the way he should. Arriving back at the hospital, she felt self-conscious bringing an overnight bag into the PICU.

Entering JT's room, she halted when she realized Gabe wasn't alone.

Tom was standing there, gazing down at JT. She frowned, trying to figure out why her ex-husband was there. Had Gabe called him, seeking support from his former best friend?

"Holly." Gabe's expression was pained when he saw her standing there. "Come in. Ah—you know Tom of course."

Of course. What she didn't know was what Tom was doing there. Something was wrong, she could feel it in the somber atmosphere in the room. Her stomach twisted painfully. Had JT taken a turn for the worse? "Hi, Tom. Gabe, is something wrong?"

"No, nothing is wrong." Gabe's expression held a note of uncertainty. "I guess I should explain. Holly, you need to know I called Tom because I felt he deserved to be here, to see JT for himself."

She didn't understand. "Deserved to be here?"

"Yes." Gabe's gaze was apologetic. "I hate having to tell you like this but DNA results have confirmed Tom is JT's biological father."

CHAPTER ELEVEN

HOLLY stared at Gabe in horror. Tom? JT's father? From somewhere beside her she heard a nurse gasp, and when she realized they had an audience, her face flamed red with acute embarrassment.

Why did things like this always happen to her when other people were around to witness her humiliation?

Gabe's words ricocheted through her mind, over and over, like a bad dream. Tom Richards was JT's biological father. JT was five years old. Her ex-husband must have had an affair with Claire.

Before their wedding.

She took one step back. Then another. Gabe moved toward her but she held up a hand, warding him off. "Don't."

He halted, his gaze full of compassion. A part of her wanted to go to him for comfort yet at the same time she couldn't get past the fact he'd lied to her. Or at the very least withheld the truth from her.

Had Gabe known about the affair even back then? Had he known about Tom and Claire but had chosen not to say anything to her? Why? For what purpose? To protect Tom?

Even back then she'd thought Gabe had been her friend too, not just Tom's.

Gabe had walked out on the wedding. All these years she'd assumed it had been because of her attempt to kiss him, crossing the line of friendship. But maybe it was really because he'd found out about the affair.

And he hadn't told her.

Unable to tolerate being there a moment longer, she spun on her heel and bolted from the room, nearly barreling into the surprised nurse who stood in the doorway.

Blindly she made her way through the hospital to the parking structure. She found her car, belatedly realizing she'd left her overnight case in JT's room. She climbed into the driver's seat, blinking away her tears.

Gabe had lied to her. She couldn't get past the pain of knowing that she'd given him her trust but he'd still lied to her.

Just like Tom had lied to her.

Only Gabe's betrayal was worse. Much worse.

Because even in this short period of time she'd come to depend on Gabe to keep his word. Tom had often said things but had never followed through on them. But Gabe was different. Or so she'd thought.

She loved JT like a son. And now she had to accept the fact that her ex-husband was JT's biological father. Every time she looked at JT, she'd be reminded about Tom's infidelity.

Infidelity that had begun before the wedding. Infidelity that had lasted throughout their short marriage.

Her stomach lurched and she swallowed hard, fighting nausea, leaning forward to rest her head on the steering wheel. She didn't care about Tom, not anymore, but obviously she didn't have the relationship she'd thought she had with Gabe.

She'd fallen in love with Gabe. With JT.

But Gabe had lied to her.

How could she ever trust him again?

Gabe swore inwardly, as Holly ran from the PICU. Damn, he'd handled that badly. Yet logically he knew he couldn't change the facts.

Tom was JT's father.

And he still planned to adopt JT. But he couldn't blame Holly for being upset and angry. How could she have a relationship with him, knowing that if their relationship progressed to something serious, it was possible she'd help raise her ex-husband's bastard son?

He scrubbed his hands over his face, feeling as if he stood on the edge of a cliff, the ground crumbling beneath his feet.

He needed to step back, to get grounded and focus on what was important.

He may have lost Holly but JT needed him. There was a chance the young boy might not make it. The five-year-old was lying in an ICU bed, his body functioning only with the help of machines. So far, Gabe had held on to hope but until the team of doctors, including Holly, brought JT out of his coma, they wouldn't know if their experimental treatment had worked.

JT could end up with severe brain damage. The little boy he had been might cease to exist.

"Gabe, you know I'll sign the paperwork," Tom said from beside him.

It took him a moment to realize what Tom was talking about. The adoption paperwork they'd been discussing before Holly had walked in. Tom was willing to sign over his custodial rights, enabling Gabe to move forward with the adoption.

This was what he'd planed from the moment he'd learned Claire had died. Until the doubts had started to creep in.

But now he knew he'd do anything for JT. No matter what. He forced himself to nod. "Thanks. I already love JT like a son and he loves me. We're a good team."

They would be a better team with Holly.

He shied away from the painful thought.

Tom shifted to glance back at his son. "You're a better man than I am, Gabe. I don't think I could take care of him like you are. Kids really have a way of tying you down, you know?"

Tom was an idiot. Loving someone didn't tie you down. Love set you free. Love made you happy. But agreeing with Tom seemed rude. Although it was true. Gabe *was* a better man than he was.

"I'm sorry about Holly," Tom added.

Sorry for what? For cheating on her? For abandoning her when she'd needed him most? Gabe reined in his temper with an effort. "Holly deserves better, just like JT does."

"And that means you?" Tom asked, skepticism lacing his tone.

"Yes. Because I love her. A man who cheats on his wife while she's having a miscarriage doesn't know the meaning of the word."

Tom's eyebrows shot up. "So, she told you what happened, huh?" Tom shrugged. "I didn't mean to hurt her. I loved Holly in my own way. I don't know why I ended up seeing other women. I know you won't believe this but I really tried to be faithful. I actually almost told her the truth the night she told me she was pregnant. She was so happy I decided to keep my mouth shut. And then she miscarried."

Gabe's fingers curled into fists. Tom was right, he didn't really believe him. But, either way, it didn't matter. There was no justification for infidelity so he didn't bother to try to think of one. "Just sign the paperwork, will you? That's all I'm asking. I only called because I thought you'd want a chance to see your son." Before he died.

No, JT wasn't going to die. Not if he could help it.

"Sure. I'll sign." Tom took the legal document and signed the bottom by the X before handing it back to Gabe. Staring at Tom's signature, Gabe wondered if JT's illness had contributed to Tom's willingness to let him go. "I honestly hope JT makes it through this. No kid deserves to be this sick."

"He will," Gabe said with conviction.

"And good luck with Holly."

He didn't have a response to that. Because he'd seen the wounded devastation in her eyes. Luck alone wasn't going to help. He wasn't sure anything would.

After Tom had left, Gabe sat beside JT's bedside, cradling the child's hand in his.

Very soon it would be official. He'd become a father and JT would belong to him.

His chest tightened and he bowed his head. If only he hadn't lost Holly in the process.

The next morning Gabe waited for Holly to make rounds. She was too good a doctor to ignore one of her patients.

And JT was still her patient.

Her small overnight case was still sitting where she'd dropped it after discovering the shocking news that Tom was JT's biological father.

Gabe stared down at JT's small peaceful face, the breathing tube still in his lungs to allow the ventilator to do the work of breathing for him.

Waiting like this, not knowing if JT would survive, was so hard.

He already felt like a father. And loving someone, when you were helpless to fix them, was the most difficult thing to endure.

Holly came through at ten-thirty in the morning. Beneath her white lab coat she wore all black. A black turtleneck sweater tucked into trim black pants. Gabe couldn't help but wonder if she was wearing black for a reason, like mourning the end of a relationship that had barely begun.

Her face was pale and dark smudges underscored her brown eyes. Despite her obvious exhaustion, she still looked beautiful to him. He wanted to go to her but forced himself to stay where he was next to JT's bed.

She glanced at the clipboard in her hands. All the medical and nursing documentation was done in the bedside computer system, but Holly must have taken some notes. "We're planning to start tapering off his medications tomorrow morning."

Gabe nodded, understanding that it might take a while for JT to come out of the medication-induced coma. "Holly, I'm sorry you had to find out about Tom like that."

She avoided his gaze, lifting a shoulder in a helpless shrug. "No worse than watching him come out of his naked lover's call room."

He grimaced and jammed his fingers through his hair. "No, I guess not."

"It doesn't matter. I've been over Tom for a long time." Holly's tone was casual, as if she had more important things to worry about.

He doubted anyone could truly be over something like that, but if what she said was true, why was she acting so distant? So upset?

"Will you come back tonight, after your shift? We could go down to the cafeteria for dinner and talk." JT's condition had been relatively stable but Gabe was loath to leave the hospital just yet. He'd only gone home a couple of times to shower and change his clothes.

"No, I don't think so."

The knot deep in his belly tightened. "Why not?"

She let out a small sigh and finally brought her gaze to his. "Gabe, nothing changes the fact you lied to me."

"I didn't lie to you, Holly. I swear I didn't know who JT's biological father was until Friday." When he saw the skepticism in her eyes, he added, "You can see from his chart that JT's full name is John Tomas. Claire called him JT almost from the moment he was born. I found her personal journal after she died. She'd been intimate with two men, John Olsinksi and Tom. She didn't know which man had fathered JT so she christened him with both their names. I contacted both men, asking for DNA paternity tests."

"Why?"

He tried to make her understand. "Because the adoption agency asked if I knew who his biological father was and I explained it was likely to be one of the two men my sister had mentioned in her diary. The adoption agency suggested I get DNA samples to know for sure so that neither one of them could come back later with a parental claim once I adopted him."

"I see." Holly nodded slowly. "But I'm sure you must have known, even back then, that Tom was unfaithful."

"I suspected," he admitted slowly. "I didn't have proof, had never seen him so much as kiss another woman with my own eyes, but I suspected. The way he openly flirted with women, well, it just wasn't right."

Holly didn't respond.

"I'm sorry you were hurt, Holly. If I had known the truth I would have told you. Maybe I should have said something sooner, even without proof. Yet I have to be honest with you. At first I doubted my ability to do this, to be a parent to JT. But now I'm glad JT's father turned out to be a man willing to give up his rights to him." He didn't explain that John Olsinski had mentioned possibly taking custody of JT, if it turned out he was the father.

Now that Tom had signed, there was nothing standing in his way.

"I'm glad JT is going to be your son, Gabe," Holly said finally. "He needs a father like you."

"He needs more than just me," Gabe countered. This had been his worst fear, losing Holly once he knew for sure Tom was JT's father. Fighting to keep his voice steady, he said, "He needs a family."

Holly turned away. "The two of you with your mother, his grandmother, are a family. I'll be back to check on him tomorrow, after we start backing off on his medications."

He didn't want her to leave. Not like this. Not with so much left unsaid between them.

He loved her. He needed to tell her how much he loved her. How much he needed her support to get through this crisis with JT.

How much he needed her to believe in him, when he hadn't believed in himself.

But then he remembered Jennifer's unwillingness to raise JT as her own. Holly had a much better reason to be less than enthusiastic in raising JT as her own. Could he blame her for not wanting to live with the evidence of Tom's infidelity every day?

He didn't try to stop her when she walked away.

* * *

On Monday morning Holly entered the PICU eager to start doing something for JT besides simply waiting. She accessed the computer system and went into JT's chart, only to discover Jeff had beat her to it, having already written orders cutting the doses of his barbiturates, ketamine and Versed infusions in half.

A tiny thrill of anticipation shot through her. She and Jeff had discussed their strategy yesterday. First they'd cut the doses in half, and twelve hours later, if he didn't have any untoward side effects, they'd discontinue the medication completely.

And hopefully JT would start to wake up.

He wouldn't wake up right away, because it would take some time for his body to throw off the effects of the drugs. They'd kept him pretty deep in the coma, knowing he needed time and rest to keep his brain from succumbing to rabies toxicity.

She hoped their solution had worked.

After logging off the computer, she stood and warily approached JT's room. Gabe was there, as usual, seeming to be a permanent fixture at his son's bedside.

At the doorway, she hesitated, bracing herself to see him. Despite everything that had happened, once the initial sharp piercing pain had receded, she'd found herself thinking about him, replaying their conversation over and over again in her head.

There was a part of her that wanted to believe him. Wanted to believe he hadn't lied to her about the past and again now, more recently.

But trust didn't come easily. She knew Gabe and his

sister had been close. She found it hard to believe Claire hadn't confided in him, especially knowing she and Tom were to be married. And no matter what Gabe claimed, she knew he must have suspected that JT was really Tom's child.

She was finding it difficult to get over the fact he hadn't told her the minute he'd discovered the results. She'd spent the whole night with him, curled up beside him on the narrow cot beside JT.

Yet he still hadn't told her.

"Good morning." She kept her greeting polite as she entered the room. "I'm sure you realize by now that Jeff has cut all JT's medication doses in half."

Gabe smiled and nodded. "I wish they were off completely, but I guess we have to wait until later for that."

"Yes." She glanced up at the bedside monitor, frowning a little when she noticed JT's heart rate had jumped up. "How long has his heart rate been up like that?"

Gabe's smile faded. "Must have just happened because ten minutes ago it was hanging in the 118 range."

She tried not to show her worry, although this was exactly one of the problems she and Jeff had feared. That JT's body might react to the withdrawal of the medications. If so, they'd have to back off even more slowly.

"We may have to go back up on his medication," Holly warned. "I think we can give him a little time yet, but if his blood pressure drops, we'll have no choice but to back off."

Even as she spoke, JT's heart rate continued to climb. It started at 132 and pretty soon it was up to 140. When it hit 144 his blood pressure began to drop.

The PICU nurse rushed into the room. "What's wrong? Why is he having trouble?"

"We need to increase the medications again," Holly said. "Instead of cutting them in half, maybe we should have only cut them by a quarter."

The nurse adjusted the various IV pumps, putting the doses back up so that the drop wasn't so drastic.

Gabe didn't seem to notice she was there but continued to sit next to the bed, holding his son's hand. "Hang in there, JT. Please, hang in there. I need you, buddy. Please, come back."

Holly's throat swelled with emotion. No matter who had fathered JT biologically, she knew Gabe was his father in every way that counted.

She stared at the heart monitor, grateful that JT's pulse had stopped climbing. She took a moment, stepping out of the room in order to page Jeff Konen, to fill him in on the latest development. When she returned she was very glad to see that JT's blood pressure had come back up to within normal range.

Breathing a little easier, she watched his heart rate slowly drop. Not quite going all the way to normal, but at least it wasn't as high as it had been earlier. Jeff rushed into the room, staring at the monitor.

"He's better now," Holly said softly.

Jeff glanced at her. "So do we try to go back down on the medications in another six hours?"

She bit her lip, unsure. Each rabies case was so different there were no hard and fast rules.

"Yes," she finally said. "We should at least try.

Maybe he just needs time to allow his system to adjust to the new dose."

"Okay, I'll write the orders." Jeff left the room to find the nearest computer.

Holly pulled up a chair next to Gabe. JT wasn't out of the woods yet. His body might still reject the decreased medication levels.

She wasn't going to leave until she knew JT was stable.

CHAPTER TWELVE

FEELING completely helpless, Gabe watched JT's pulse and blood pressure fluctuate like a yo-yo.

Holly directed the nurse to make even smaller changes in the medication dosing. She hadn't left JT's bedside in hours. Gabe appreciated her dedication and support but was very afraid that at this rate JT wouldn't come out of his coma until Christmas.

If at all.

"Maybe he needs a longer time on the medication," Gabe said finally. "Maybe he's still suffering the effects of the virus and we're waking him up too soon."

"It's possible," Holly agreed, a troubled frown furrowing between her brows. "Although from all the case studies I've reviewed, a week from the onset of seizures should be enough time for the effects to resolve."

Gabe glanced at her. "And how many of those case studies discussed patients who were only five years old?"

"None." Holly let out a heavy sigh. "The youngest child was seven."

And the seven-year-old child had died. He knew

Holly didn't want to say the words but she didn't have to.

He'd reviewed much of the rabies literature himself, having read the same case studies she was referring to. He'd been impressed with the comprehensive treatment plan they'd adopted.

Yet all their attempts might be in vain.

He stared down at JT's tiny face, dwarfed by the breathing tube. How was it possible for one small boy to imbed himself so deeply into his heart in such a short time?

Granted, he'd known JT since his birth. Had tried to give Claire the extra bit of support she'd needed as a single mother. But being there for special events—birthdays and holidays—was as nothing compared to living with him day in and day out.

"JT has always been a climber," he murmured. "When he was just twelve months old I was watching him over at Claire's and I walked into his bedroom because it had been too quiet for too long, which always meant he was up to something. Sure enough, when I walked in I found him at eye level, standing on the top of his dresser. He nearly gave me a heart attack."

"How on earth did he get up there?" Holly asked.

"Used the open dresser drawers as rungs of a ladder." Gabe chuckled at the memory. "I was afraid to yell at him, I didn't want to startle him into falling, so I talked very nicely and quietly."

"He didn't fall, did he?"

"No." He shook his head wryly. "But I broke speed records getting from one side of the room to the other."

Unbidden, the memories kept coming. "Then there was the time he climbed to the top of the neighbor's swing set when he was barely two. And just a week ago he was telling me how he and his buddy climbed up to the loft during their trip to the dairy farm."

"Gabe." Holly put her hand on his arm. "Don't do this. He's going to pull through. I believe in my heart he's going to pull through this."

He momentarily closed his eyes against burning tears. "I hope so. I really hope so. I don't care if he doesn't climb anymore, I still want him to pull through this."

Holly's warm scent enveloped him when she put her arms around his shoulders for a comforting hug. He grabbed her and held on tight, needing her caring comfort more than he needed air to breathe.

She didn't say anything for a long time, simply held him. After what seemed like forever but was probably really only about twenty or thirty minutes, she loosened her grip.

"I need to call Jeff. I think we need a new strategy for JT," she said in a low tone. After instructing the nurse to stop all the medication titrations, she left the room.

Gabe felt Holly's absence like a sore tooth as he watched the monitor over JT's head, relieved to see his heart rate and blood pressure settle down a bit.

He owed her so much. She'd picked up on the rabies diagnosis very quickly, and had been working diligently ever since to save his son. Tom's son.

Her unselfishness was amazing.

* * *

By Wednesday morning Holly thought it was possible Gabe was right, that JT needed more time to allow the virus to work its way through his system.

"I think we should send more samples to the CDC," she told Jeff. "Maybe they can run some virus titers and let us know if we're making headway or not."

"All right," Jeff agreed. "Call your contact at the CDC and let them know we're sending more blood and cerebral spinal fluid samples."

"Sounds good." Holly hung up the phone and then wrote the orders in the computer. She was glad she didn't have to do the lumbar puncture on JT, she didn't think she could maintain her objectivity in order to get the task done.

When she'd finished the orders, she received a page from a number she didn't recognize. Frowning, she picked up the nearest phone.

"Outpatient Dialysis, this is Diane. May I help you?"

"Diane, this is Holly Davidson. Did someone page me?"

"Oh, yes, one of the nurses wanted to talk to you about your mother. Just a minute."

A wave of guilt hit her as Holly realized she hadn't kept in touch with her mother as often as she should have recently. Dealing with JT's illness had consumed a lot of her time.

And battling her feelings for Gabe had kept her preoccupied as well. But none of that was her mother's fault.

What kind of daughter was she?

Apparently not a very good one.

The music abruptly cut off. "Hello, Holly? This is Angie, one of the dialysis nurses. I'm calling to let you know your mother is being transferred to Minneapolis Medical Center. She had a brief episode of cardiac arrest."

A brief episode of *cardiac arrest*? "What happened?"

"Her magnesium levels must have dropped, she went into a rhythm known as *torsades de pointes*, which is a type of V-fib normally treated with a bolus of magnesium. We were able to convert her very easily back into normal sinus rhythm, but felt she should be admitted to the hospital for evaluation."

Holly sucked in a deep breath and let it out slowly. She was very familiar with *torsades* and was grateful the nurses there had recognized the rhythm right away. Treatment was easy if you knew what you were looking at, but all too often *torsades* was missed. Good grief, she could just imagine how frightened her mother must be. "She's doing all right now?"

"Yes, her blood pressure is down a bit but we've given her a little albumin and she's coming up nicely." Dialysis patients couldn't be given very much fluid as their kidneys didn't work the same way a normal person's did.

"Tell her I'll meet her at the hospital," Holly instructed. "And tell her I love her."

"I will."

She made her call to the CDC, which took longer than she'd thought, and then spent another few minutes finishing her note in JT's chart. Afterwards, she went back into the boy's room to find Gabe.

He was right where she left him the day before,

seated in the chair next to JT's bed as if he'd become a permanent fixture in the room. She hesitantly approached the bedside. "Gabe? I just got off the phone with the CDC, and we're going to send more blood and spinal fluid samples from JT to Atlanta to see if he still has high levels of the virus. After those test results return, we'll have a better idea of how to proceed."

Gabe slowly nodded. "All right, that makes sense. Although I hate to see him poked with more needles."

"I know." She understood his concern. "But it's worth it if we can know for sure whether the treatment is working." She hesitated, then added, "I, uh, have to go but I'll try to check back on you later."

Gabe's exhausted, red-rimmed eyes focused on her face. "Is something wrong?"

How amazing that with everything he was going through he could still sense her own anxiety. "My mother is being admitted over at Minneapolis's Medical Center. She's fine," she added hastily, when Gabe's eyes widened in alarm, "but apparently she had a small episode of *torsades*."

"Do you want me to come with you?"

His very sincere offer touched her heart. Why did Gabe always have to be so nice? Even when he'd withheld the truth, she didn't doubt that he'd done it out of concern for her. "You stay here with JT. I'll let you know if something changes and she's not doing well."

Gabe stared at her for a moment before nodding. "If you're sure."

"I'm sure." Holly left, heading over to the large adult

teaching hospital located right next to the Children's Medical Center. As she walked, she thought it was ironic that the one man she'd thought she couldn't trust was the one who'd offered the most support, even when he was in the midst of his own personal crisis.

Maybe she'd judged him too harshly.

"Mom, how are you?" Holly asked, entering the semi-private room her mother occupied in the ED.

"Oh, I'm fine." Her mother's wan smile belied her easy tone. "Guess my heart went a little funny during my dialysis treatment."

"Yes, but it looks like your heart is doing fine now," Holly assured her, eyeing the heart monitor over the bed. Her physician's eye noted the small changes in the heart rhythm that indicated her mother may have suffered a small heart attack. Concerned, she asked, "Has your doctor been in to let you know what's going on?"

"Yes, but I told him to wait for you." Her mother clutched her hand. "Holly, I need to tell you something."

Her mother's urgent tone worried her. "What? What is it?"

"You have to forgive your father."

She frowned. Where had that come from? Had her mother suffered a lack of oxygen to her brain during the episode with her heart? Her father had been dead for eight years, although she remembered her mother saying something very similar during her father's funeral. Not that it had been easy to forgive him, when his much younger wife and daughter had sat in the front pew of the church. "Mom, don't worry about it," she soothed. "I'm fine."

"No, Holly, listen to me." Her mother tightened her grip on Holly's hand. "You haven't forgiven him, not really. Do you think I can't tell? You've been different since you've been home. There's something wrong and I think it's because you're making the same mistake with Tom."

Holly didn't know what to say. She wasn't still hung up on Tom. Gabe's lies had hurt far more.

"Don't you see? Carrying around all that resentment in your heart isn't good for you." Her mother grimaced. "Believe me, I know it's not easy, but loving a person regardless of their strengths and weaknesses will only make you a better person."

Holly bit her lip, trying to understand what her mother was saying. She already thought she was a better person than either her father or Tom—she hadn't violated her wedding vows the way they had. Yet, even as she watched, her mother's agitation made her heart rate accelerate at an alarming rate so she tried to put her feelings aside for her mother's sake.

"All right, Mom. I'll try. I'll do my best to forgive Dad and Tom."

"Don't just try, Holly. Do it. Tell yourself they were good men in their own way. Every person has good and bad traits. You have to learn to forgive them. If you don't I'm afraid you'll never find love."

Holly breathed in sharply. Why would her mother think she was looking for love? There was no way her

mother could have guessed her feelings for Gabe.
Could she?

Was her mother right? Was the resentment she
carried from the past interfering with her ability to move
into the future?

"I will, Mom," Holly said in a firm tone. "I promise
I will. Now, relax, will you? Worrying about me is putting too much stress on your heart."

Her mother relaxed, as if finally believing her.
"Thanks, Holly," she murmured. "I don't want to see
you making the same mistakes I did."

Just then the ED doctor came in and explained that
he was sending her mother over to the cath lab for a
cardiac catheterization. Holly was glad they were doing
the procedure, and within moments her mother had been
wheeled off.

Leaving Holly to wonder just what mistakes her
mother had made in the past.

Despite his worry and fear over JT, Gabe couldn't help
thinking about Holly. She'd come back briefly to
explain how her mother had suffered a small heart attack
and had undergone a procedure in the cath lab to put a
stent in a blocked coronary artery. But that had been yesterday. He hadn't seen her at all today.

He thought about walking over to Minneapolis's
Medical Center to see how her mother was doing, but
didn't like leaving JT alone.

He could call his mother to come and sit with him
for a little while. She came in every day, staying beside

JT so he could get something to eat. She'd refused to go back home to Florida, no matter how many times he'd told her to go.

Deep down he was secretly glad she'd stayed. Both his mother and Holly had given him tremendous support.

Support Holly might need in return. As much as she'd been there for him, he should do the same for her.

If she'd let him. But he wasn't sure she really wanted support from him.

"Hi, Gabe," Holly said, coming into the room as if she'd known he was thinking about her. "How's JT?"

"No change. But how is your mom?" He stood and crossed over to her. "Is she doing all right?"

"She's much better. Normally, they'd send her home after twenty-four hours, but they're going to keep her one more night, to see how she does during dialysis tomorrow."

"Great. That's great, Holly."

"We haven't heard from the CDC yet on JT's blood and spinal fluid," she told him, glancing at her watch. "I'm hoping to hear something this afternoon."

Gabe nodded. He'd been hoping the same thing. "Holly, I want you to know that no matter what happens I appreciate everything you've done for him."

"I— You're welcome. But we're not giving up yet, not by a long shot."

"I know." He was just trying to make her understand how grateful he was that she'd come back to Minneapolis just when he'd needed her most.

Not just for her expertise in treating JT but for himself on a personal level as well. He'd learned a lot sitting here, doing nothing but thinking. There was so much he wanted to say, yet the timing wasn't quite right. First he needed to know JT was on the road to recovery. Then they could talk.

Although he suspected all the talking in the world wasn't going to change the fact that Tom was JT's father. Yet there had to be a way to get through to Holly.

Because he wanted more than a professional relationship with her. He wanted it all.

The only problem was figuring out what Holly wanted.

"Dr. Davidson?" One of the PICU nurses peeked her head into the room. "I have a call for you on line one."

"Excuse me, I'll be right back." Holly hurried away.

Gabe knew the call was probably just Jeff, asking for an update. Jeff and Holly functioned as a pretty cohesive team. Yet he found himself watching Holly out at the nurses' station, talking on the phone with growing impatience.

He forced himself to look away, checking JT's vital signs displayed on the monitor. His pulse and blood pressure seemed much less labile today.

"Gabe?" Holly rushed back into the room, her eyes bright with barely restrained excitement. "JT's samples show that there's only a very minimal level of rabies virus left in his system."

He was almost afraid to ask. "So what does that mean?"

She smiled, her face lighting up the whole room. "It means it's safe to bring him out of the coma."

CHAPTER THIRTEEN

HOLLY wrote the orders to back off on JT's medications, this time at a slower rate than their first attempt. JT's pulse and blood pressure seemed to tolerate the medication changes better so she decided to take those early indicators as a good sign.

"So now we wait and hope for the best," Gabe murmured.

"Yes." She wished there was more she could do, but at the moment they needed JT's body to do the work of clearing out the medication from his bloodstream.

Some things couldn't be rushed.

She glanced at her watch, realizing it was close to the time of her mother's scheduled dialysis treatment. She glanced at Gabe. "I need to go but I'll come back later, all right?"

"Sure." Gabe smiled and for the first time in a long time she saw the hope that filled his eyes. "I'll be here."

She knew he would. Gabe hadn't left JT's bedside for any period of time longer than it took to eat a quick meal or rush home for a shower and change of clothes. He was a great father. She couldn't even believe he had harbored doubts about it before. She was beginning to think he and JT would pull through this.

Heading over to Minneapolis's Medical Center, she found the inpatient dialysis unit. The nurses were just getting her mother hooked up to the dialysis machine.

With nothing to do but wait, her mother's comments echoed over and over in her mind. She was most curious about how her mother seemed to speak from experience.

Holly finally gathered her courage to ask, "Mom, have you ever loved another man besides Dad?"

Her mother was silent for a long moment. "Yes, at least I thought I loved him. But as time went on I ended up ruining the relationship."

Holly was surprised at her mother's frank admission. "How?"

"I kept looking for reasons not to trust him." Her mother's smile was sad. "No one is perfect, Holly. Your father, Tom, they both had trouble being faithful. But they weren't bad men. Perfection doesn't exist, everyone makes mistakes if you're with them long enough. The sooner you can forgive them and move on, the better off you'll be."

"I don't know if I can," Holly confessed softly. Tom's betrayal was so wrapped up in her daughter's death she didn't know how to separate the two.

"Maybe you need to start with forgiving yourself."

Forgiving herself? She stared at her mother, perplexed. "What do you mean?"

"Holly, I've been there. I know how easy it is to blame

yourself for not seeing through the charming veneer to the man beneath." Her mother grimaced. "You have to forgive yourself for marrying the wrong man, and that's not easy to do. You must have thought you were in love with Tom to agree to marry him in the first place."

"Yes." Her mother's words struck a chord. She had wallowed in guilt for making a bad choice, especially after nearly kissing Gabe before the wedding. Maybe if she had been more honest with herself, acknowledging her feelings earlier, she could have avoided her marriage and subsequent divorce.

But that also meant not having had Kayla, even for those brief moments. And no matter how much she considered her marriage to Tom a mistake, she couldn't consider her daughter to be one, too.

"I think I knew Tom was wrong for me even before I married him," she whispered, speaking the truth out loud for the first time in years. "And you're right, I blamed myself for not being strong enough to break things off then."

"Yes. I had a similar experience." Her mother reached over with her good hand, the one not connected to the dialysis machine, to give Holly's a squeeze. "But I couldn't regret my marriage either, because of you. You gave me something to live for. Something to be strong for. I just wished I could have come to terms with my anger and resentment toward your father much quicker."

So she could move on with someone else? "Who was he?" Holly asked, honestly curious. While she'd still been in high school, she hadn't been aware of her mother dating anyone. Not that she'd been very aware of her mother's problems back then, she thought with a pang of guilt.

"His name was Scott Anderson and I met him through a divorce support group a couple of years ago."

A support group. After all these years? She hadn't even realized her mother had been to one. "So what happened? Are you still in touch with him?"

"Not really, not since I've been sick enough to need dialysis." Her mother waved a hand impatiently. "Why are we talking about me? This is supposed to be about you."

Holly could see what had happened, the way her mother had broken off communication with Scott after she'd discovered her renal failure had meant she'd need to go on dialysis. Knowing her mother, she hadn't wanted Scott to consider her a burden.

"Tell you what, Mom. I'll work on forgiving myself and Tom if you get in touch with Scott. Has it occurred to you he might be worried about you, even as a friend?"

Her mother was quiet for a long moment. "Yes, it's occurred to me."

"So?" Holly persisted. "That means you could at least call him, right?"

"Right," her mother sighed. "It's a deal."

"Good." Holly sat back in her seat, satisfied. Maybe it was too late for Scott and her mother, but even if there was nothing left of the relationship other than friendship, that wouldn't be so bad either.

Friends and family were important.

She thought of Gabe, standing watch over JT. The

boy was still clinging to life, like some sort of tiny miracle. Discovering the truth about who JT's biological father was didn't change anything. JT was still more Gabe's son than anyone else's.

Had she done the same thing her mother had?

Had she deliberately looked for a reason not to trust Gabe?

Gabe had always known patience wasn't his area of greatest strength. Forty-eight hours had passed since Holly and Jeff had started decreasing JT's medication. Last night they'd turned everything off completely.

But JT still hadn't woken up.

He stared at his clasped hands dangling between his knees, battling a feeling of impending doom. What if all this treatment had been for nothing? What if JT never woke up from his coma?

Days ago he'd thought he'd be satisfied to know JT was alive, but as he stared down at his son's youthful face he had to admit he'd lied to himself. Because he wanted more than for JT to simply exist with a stable heart rate and a blood pressure.

He wanted JT to recover enough to be aware of his surroundings. To talk. To walk. To climb trees, swing-sets or whatever else he wanted to climb.

To someday go back to school.

He wanted it all. Not necessarily right away, he could be patient for a little while. But he definitely wanted it all. JT's recovery.

And more. He wanted the impossible.

Holly entered JT's room and he dragged his gaze up to meet hers. "Nothing yet?" she asked.

Slowly he shook his head.

She let out a sigh. "Hang in there, Gabe. You know there is so much we don't know about the brain. The good news is that he's been off all his medication since last night. It may just take a while for him to wake up, that's all."

He couldn't make himself smile. "I know. Logically, I know this may take a while. And he might not even recognize anyone when he does wake up. But it's hard. We've been waiting for so long."

"I know." She moved over to JT's bedside to perform a brief neuro exam. "His pupils are equal and reactive to light," she murmured.

He nodded, knowing fully well, as she did, that JT's pupil response didn't mean anything. All it meant was that his brain hadn't totally shut down. "How long before you do an EEG?"

Holly's glance was surprised. "Has Jeff mentioned doing one?" she asked, avoiding a direct answer.

Gabe lifted a shoulder. "No, but I figured it's only a matter of time. Once the meds have cleared his system, there should be no reason for him not to wake up. Unless his brain is having deep, underlying seizure activity that we're not aware of." Some seizures were so deep, so primitive, they didn't show obvious signs and symptoms.

"We'll give him a few days yet," Holly assured him. "I don't think he's having seizures."

"But the only way to know for sure is to do an EEG," Gabe persisted.

"Yes." She reached over to rest her hand lightly on his shoulder. "Give him some time, Gabe. The virus has been a huge stress on his system. Give him time to wake up on his own."

He took a deep breath and let it out slowly. "Okay. You're right, it's still early." It was ridiculous to be so disappointed that JT didn't immediately open his eyes and look at him, fully aware of his surroundings.

"It is early," Holly agreed. "And we already know that most of the virus is no longer in his system."

Gabe didn't answer. Because he'd read the case studies for himself. Most of the patients had died from other complications, not from the virus itself. In JT's case there could be complications from the coma.

He prayed JT wouldn't be another rabies casualty.

On Monday morning, three full days after they'd stopped all JT's medications, Gabe watched as numerous tiny electrodes were glued to JT's scalp. His eyes burned from exhaustion, but still he couldn't look away.

Three days and JT hadn't woken up.

Gabe was certain there was something serious wrong. Jeff and Holly kept saying to give him time—they'd even taken the breathing tube out—but all he could think was that JT must be having deep seizure activity in order to explain why he hadn't come around from the coma.

"There, last one," the tech said cheerfully. She didn't seem to mind that JT didn't respond, she'd gone on to explain what she was doing anyway.

Gabe stared at the young woman with dull eyes. Irrationally, he wanted to yell at her to stop being so perky. Couldn't she tell JT was going to die? Couldn't she see that everything they'd done had been for nothing?

He wished Holly was there. He needed her to stand beside him if he was going to lose JT.

"Hmm," the tech said, as she started up the machine, watching as JT's brain waves were being monitored by the tiny needles. "Interesting."

He wasn't an expert on reading EEGs but he leaned forward to look at the small zig-zag scribbles the numerous needles were making on the wide graph paper anyway. The device looked primitive, something akin to a seismograph measuring earthquake activities. After all these years of modern advances in healthcare, it seemed as if there should be a better, more technical way to measure brain waves.

"What?" he asked. The scribbles on the paper made no sense to him. "Is he having seizures?"

"I'm just the tech," she said primly. "I'm not qualified to make medical judgments."

He clenched his fingers into fists, controlling his temper with an effort. If she wasn't qualified to make medical judgments, why had she even said anything? And what was so interesting? "Where's Jeff Konen?"

The girl had the grace to look guilty. "I don't know, but I can page him if you like."

"Page him," Gabe said between clenched teeth. He wanted to know if JT was having seizures and he wanted to know now.

Seeing the grim expression on his face, the tech hurried away. The machine continued to roll, like a giant lie detector, the needles scribbling on the paper like a kid scraping his nails down a chalkboard.

Gabe was still staring at the paper when the tech returned with Jeff in tow.

"Gabe," Jeff said by way of greeting. Jeff moved over to glance down at the long page of brain waves already documented by the EEG machine. "So far this looks good."

"Good?" Gabe grasped on the positive note. "You mean he's not having seizures?"

"No seizures—at least, not so far," Jeff confirmed. "Typically we run the test for a good hour, though. Now, calm down, all right? You're scaring the tech."

Gabe hunched his shoulders. "She started it," he mumbled, knowing he sounded ridiculous. After weeks of sitting at JT's side, he felt as if he was close to losing it.

JT's hand moved in a jerky motion. Gabe blinked, wondering if his exhausted brain had imagined it. Then JT's hand moved again, this time as if he was trying to raise his hand off the bed.

"JT?" he called, crossing over to JT's bed. He took the boy's small hand in his. JT's hand moved again, another jerky movement, not a hand grasp by any stretch of the imagination. "Jeff, do you think this might be residual seizure activity?"

"No, you have to remember rabies affects the nervous system. His muscles may not move normally for quite a while yet."

Gabe nodded, clinging to JT's hand. The jerky movements stopped. He willed them back.

The tech finished the EEG and quickly disconnected all the electrodes from JT's scalp. The poor kid looked like some sort of mini-rock star with globs of white goop still matted in his hair, which stuck out from his head at odd angles.

"We'll get that gunk out of your hair, JT, don't worry," the nurse said when she came in a few minutes later. "I found some stuff that works really well."

JT turned his head toward the sound of her voice.

Gabe swallowed hard. There was a loud buzzing in his ears and his heart thundered in his chest. He clung to JT's hand as if it were a lifeline.

"JT?" He had to clear the hoarseness from his throat. "Hey, buddy, it's me, Uncle Gabe. I'm here with you, JT. You've been sick but you're getting better." From the corner of his eye he noticed both Holly and Jeff walk into the room as if curious to see if JT would finally wake up. The PICU nurse stood on one side of the bed, while he stayed on the opposite side. "JT, can you open your eyes for me? Can you see me?"

JT's hand jerked in his, and Gabe held his breath, almost afraid to hope. JT's other hand jerked, as did his feet, but the motions weren't synchronized, as if JT was having trouble getting his muscles to obey his commands.

"Take your time, buddy," Gabe said, even though he was sure more waiting would kill him. "We're not going anywhere. We have all the time in the world."

JT opened his eyes, blinked and then closed them again.

"Dim the lights," Gabe said harshly.

Holly crossed over to dim the fluorescent overhead lights.

"There, JT, the lights aren't so bright now," Gabe said in a reassuring tone. "Can you open your eyes for me? Can you look at me, JT?"

JT turned his head toward the sound of Gabe's voice. Gabe felt Holly and Jeff come up to stand on either side of him. He barely glanced at them, having eyes only for JT.

"He's never seen Jeff, so we need to make sure he can differentiate between you," Holly said in a low tone.

Gabe understood what she was saying. They needed to know if JT was really in there, able to recognize his surroundings. Able to recognize *him*.

JT opened his eyes again, and Gabe's hopes plummeted when it seemed at first as if JT was gazing at nothing, not even the pretty PICU nurse standing on the other side of the bed. But then, slowly, the boy moved his gaze toward Gabe.

"Welcome back, JT," Holly said, her voice thick with suppressed tears. "You've been sick, but you're much better now. We've all been worried about you."

JT's gaze moved from Holly to Gabe and then to Jeff, with no moment of recognition from what Gabe could tell. But then JT's gaze came back to focus on Gabe. His mouth moved and he tried to speak.

"Da-ddy?"

Gabe stared at JT, wondering if he'd really heard the

somewhat garbled word right. Holly's tremulous smile convinced him he had.

JT had not only recognized him, he'd called him Daddy.

CHAPTER FOURTEEN

HOLLY'S eyes filled with tears even as her heart soared with excitement. JT had finally awoken from his coma.

JT had called Gabe Daddy.

The treatment to combat his illness had worked.

"JT, I love you, son. I love you so much." Gabe was crying but seemed not to notice as he gathered the boy in his arms. JT tried to talk again as he cuddled against Gabe's chest as if seeking comfort, but much of his speech was garbled, except for one word that was quickly becoming very clear.

Daddy.

"He's awake. Can you believe it? JT's awake," Holly heard one of the PICU nurses say excitedly.

A ripple of celebration went through the whole unit. Several of the staff, nurses and physicians and techs, came to stand at JT's door, some of them smiling, others wiping away tears.

Gabe just continued to hold his son, smoothing a hand down the boy's back. Holly blinked away her tears of happiness. JT had recognized Gabe, though the rest of his recovery would come more slowly. Youth was on his side.

And there was no rush. JT could take all the time he needed to return to his usual self. The boy had his whole life ahead of him.

"We did it," Jeff murmured, a sense of awe in his tone. "I can't believe we got him through this."

"Love is what got him through this," Holly corrected, unable to tear her gaze from the way Gabe cradled JT close.

"Yeah. You're probably right." Jeff was grinning like an idiot. "But we helped a little."

"We helped a little," Holly agreed. She turned away, feeling a little too much like an outsider. Gabe had his son back. There was no doubt in her mind that JT would continue to recover.

Gabe didn't need Holly's help anymore.

She was glad, fiercely glad that JT had pulled through the horrible virus that had wreaked havoc on his small body. She was happy he was stable enough not to need the acute level of care the peds ICU provided.

Still, she left JT's room, feeling as if her professional job was done.

But also feeling that, just like her mother, she'd somehow ruined her chance for personal happiness with JT and Gabe.

Holly continued to keep an eye on JT's progress. The whole hospital did. JT's survival was the main topic of conversation. By the end of the following week JT was talking better but his language skills came back slowly.

"Holly, I've been waiting for you," Gabe said when she showed up at the end of her day. She was busier than usual, thanks in part to being touted by the CDC as one of the experts in treating rabies. Her colleague was a greater expert than she could ever be, but she didn't mind answering questions from other doctors across the country.

"Good news." Gabe's grin was infectious. "JT's being transferred to Rehab in the morning."

"That's wonderful." She smiled at JT. "First rehab, then the next step is going home. I bet you're going to make your rehab nurses chase you down the hall, aren't you?"

"Don't give him any ideas," Gabe warned half under his breath. "He's already faster in his wheelchair than I can keep up with."

"Sorry," she said with a smile. JT's muscles still didn't always work the way he wanted them to, but the good thing about being a kid was that learning to walk again was easier than it would be as an adult. Soon he'd graduate from the wheelchair to leg braces.

Hopefully JT would be back on his feet, climbing the nearest tree.

"You're not going to sign off on JT's care, are you?" Gabe asked.

She nodded. "Yes, actually, I am. Rehab isn't the same as inpatient treatment. Jeff will continue to follow JT's progress in the clinic, but from here on you don't need me." She hoped her tone didn't sound as dejected as she felt.

"I guess that's a good sign in and of itself," Gabe mused.

Oh, boy, she wished she felt the same way. But she'd always known Gabe didn't need her anymore. Not as far as JT's treatment was concerned.

Maybe not as far as anything else was concerned either.

"Actually, that helps because I was hoping you'd have dinner with me," Gabe said, glancing at his watch. "Tonight. If you're not doing anything."

Dinner? Tonight? Deep in the darkest corner of her heart a flicker of hope flared. Still, she hesitated. "Are you sure? I thought… Aren't you spending the nights here, at the hospital?"

"I've been leaving lately," Gabe said slowly. "Needed to make sure the place was ready for when JT comes home."

She knew Gabe hadn't been back to work yet, but suspected he'd need to return soon. Her tiny flare of hope dimmed. Maybe he was going to ask for help with JT. After all, she'd offered.

And at this point she'd probably take whatever she could get.

"Have to pay my bills. Wouldn't be good if the power company shut off my electricity, now, would it?" Gabe joked.

"No, it wouldn't be good to be without electricity." There was no reason to avoid having dinner with him. So much had happened in the weeks since JT was so sick that they had to start somewhere. "I'd love to have dinner with you," she said abruptly.

Gabe's eyes widened in surprise but he grinned. "Great. I, uh, thought we could try Giovani's. According to my mother's expert opinion, it's the only decent Italian place around."

"Perfect." She wasn't about to argue, especially not with an Italian cook like Gabe's mother. "How is she, by the way?"

"She went home, but she promised to return for a while once JT is released from the hospital."

She couldn't help raising a brow. If he had his mother's help, maybe he didn't need hers. "Great."

"And Marybeth is recovering from her surgery. She's been in to visit JT, too." It was as if Gabe had read her mind, putting all her misplaced fears to rest. "Are you ready to leave now? Or do you have more patients to see?"

Suddenly she didn't feel very ready, but she nodded. "No more patients to see. JT's my last one." And it was officially her last visit as JT's infectious disease doctor. She took JT's hand in hers. "Glad to see you're doing so much better, JT."

"Better," he repeated.

She smiled. "Be good to the nurses in Rehab, you hear? The sooner you do what they tell you, the sooner you'll go home, okay?"

This time he simply nodded.

"Bye, JT." She squeezed his hand and let go.

"Bye, Dr. Holly. See you soon." JT's stilted speech, stringing six whole words together in two distinct sentences, sounded like music from the finest symphony. She had absolutely no doubt he'd get the rest of his vocabulary back soon.

"Are you ready to go, then?" Gabe asked, his hand resting on her lower back.

Her stomach fluttered but she forced herself to nod. "Yes. I'm ready."

Gabe finally had Holly all to himself, yet he was already having doubts about his plan. Maybe because he was having trouble figuring her out. Her attitude toward JT seemed the same as it had been before she'd known who his biological father was.

Did that mean she didn't care about Tom's affair with his sister? Or did it mean she was treating JT only as a patient and not as a child she might someday call her own?

He wished he knew what she saw when she looked at his son, but he didn't.

And he wasn't sure how to ask.

He hiked his jeans a little self-consciously as they made their way down the elevator to the lobby level. He'd lost a bit of weight through the time of JT's illness and figured eating a good Italian meal was one way to help pack the carbohydrates back on.

Besides, he had been remiss in not taking Holly out for a proper date sooner.

There were a lot of things he should have done. Not least of which was to tell her how he really felt.

"I'm glad to see you're getting out of the hospital, at least for a little while," Holly commented as he walked her toward his car. "How much longer will you be off work?"

"Just a couple of weeks. JT should be home soon and

then we'll get things back into a normal routine." A normal routine that he knew very well would consist of a lot of physical therapy, speech therapy and a variety of other doctors' appointments.

A fresh wave of doubt hit him. What was he thinking? Maybe he was committed to being JT's father, but what right did he have to ask Holly to share in any of this? They'd only made love that one night, maybe he was crazy to be thinking about a future.

Even if visions of the future were the only thing that had kept him sane over these past few weeks.

"It's amazing that he pulled through, isn't it?" Holly said, settling in the passenger seat of his car.

"Yes." Gabe had to hide his momentary flash of annoyance. For once he didn't want to talk about JT. Call him selfish, but for a brief hour he wanted to talk about something else.

About Holly. About the wonderful feelings that had bloomed between them when they'd made love.

And more than anything he wanted to know if there was anything left between them to build on?

He swallowed hard and concentrated on driving. His mother's opinion proved to be correct—Giovani's was a great place. Once they were seated in a romantic corner, he felt a little of his determination return. He ordered a bottle of wine and took a sip to hide his nervousness.

"Holly," he began, after the waiter had taken their order. "I know it's been a long time since the night I spent at your place, but I still think about those hours with you a lot."

A ghost of a smile played along her mouth. "Me, too. At this point it seems like more a dream."

More of a dream than reality? Not a positive note to move forward with. He frowned, and wondered if he ought to try another approach. "One thing I realized, sitting with JT, is that life is meant to be shared. You were the main reason I was able to keep going, even when JT was at his worst."

"Me?" She toyed with her wineglass. Was she nervous about this, too? "I don't understand."

Gabe scrubbed a hand over his face and decided this beating around the bush was useless. Better to get straight to the point. "I love you. I knew I'd fallen in love with you that first night we spent together. But then JT was so sick I didn't have a chance to tell you how I felt." Since he was being honest, he amended that latter part by adding, "I didn't take the time to tell you how I really felt."

Her mouth opened, and closed, no words coming out. Holly wasn't often speechless.

"But this isn't just about us," he continued slowly. "JT is officially my son. I received approval from the adoption agency this morning. So the real question here is about you, Holly. I guess I need to know if you're ever going to be able to accept JT for who he is."

There was a long moment of silence when his confidence wavered. He understood he was asking for a lot.

"Yes," Holly finally said in a soft but decisive tone. "Gabe, I love JT as much as you do. I could never hold his genes against him, any more than I could have held it against Kayla."

Hope flared, burning brightly in the center of his chest. "But Kayla was your daughter, too."

"I know. But what made her my daughter? Simply giving birth? I don't think so. What makes JT your son?"

Was this a test? He'd hated quizzes in medical school. "Love?" he guessed.

"Love." A tremulous smile curved her lips. "Love is what makes the relationship between a parent and their child special. Just like love is what holds a relationship between a husband and a wife together. With love anything is possible."

The truth shone from her eyes and he considered himself the luckiest man on earth to have found a woman like Holly. He reached for her hand, suddenly wishing he hadn't chosen a public place like Giovani's to talk to her. "Are you sure? Because if not I'll give you time. As much time as you need."

"I'm sure." Holly's smile widened. "I've learned a lot over these past few weeks, too. The biggest thing I've learned is that I probably started falling in love with you a long time ago. The night I almost kissed you."

That was good, wasn't it? He wasn't sure. But then he decided that as he'd come this far, he'd better go all the way. "Does that mean you'll marry me?"

"Yes, Gabe." Her fingers curled tightly around his. "I love you. I'd be honored to marry you."

He didn't have a ring, but somehow he didn't think Holly cared. He rose to his feet and came around to her side of the table, drawing her up, too. Pulling her close, he kissed her. Then, when he could hear the whispers moving through the restaurant behind him, he broke off the kiss and turned to the group and boldly declared, "Holly Davidson has just agreed to be my wife."

It wasn't until a ripple of applause and wolf-whistles surrounded them that he realized what he'd done. Holly hated being in the limelight. She didn't like being the center of gossip.

"Damn. What was I thinking? I'm sorry," he tried to backpedal to undo the damage he might have unwittingly done, turning back to wave at the people in the restaurant, trying to shut them up.

Holly grabbed his arm, laughing. "For heaven's sake, don't be sorry. I'm proud I'm going to be your wife."

Relief flooded him. He hadn't ruined things between them after all. "Good, that's good." Why couldn't he think of something more intelligent to say?

"Gabe." She tugged on his hand until he stepped closer. She lifted her mouth to his, teasing his lips with hers. "After dinner, will you take me home?"

"Yes." That's exactly what he wanted, too. A whole night, all to themselves. "I'll take you home, tonight and forever."

Home had never sounded so good.

EPILOGUE

JT FROWNED when his daddy leaned down to let him look at his new baby brother. He wasn't going to say anything, but he thought there might be something wrong because the baby's face looked all red and wrinkly.

"Isn't he amazing?" his daddy asked.

"Yeah. Amazing." JT didn't quite understand what was so amazing, although it was weird that one minute his new mom's tummy was huge and now it wasn't big anymore but there was a baby.

What he really wanted to know was how that baby got in there in the first place. And were there any more babies in there, ready to come out? If so, maybe he should ask for a sister.

"We thought we'd name him Jeffery, after the doctor who helped make you all better," his new mom said.

"Holly, you were a part of the medical team, too," his dad argued, but when his mom gave him an exasperated look he lifted his hands in the air. "But if that's what you want, Jeffery it is."

Jeffery didn't sound like a bad name. "Hi, Jeffery," he said to the baby.

His dad rested a hand on his shoulder. "How do you think you'll like being a big brother, JT?" his dad asked.

He glanced up at his dad and then over at his mom. They were both looking at him as if they were afraid of what he might say.

The baby didn't look like he'd be able to run and play any time soon. Which was probably okay as he couldn't run very well with the leg braces on. But he knew what they were really asking him.

"Why? Are there more kids inside Mom waiting to be born?"

His parents looked at each other and burst into laughter. They laughed until they were crying but he wasn't sure what was so funny.

"Uh, yeah. Maybe. There might be more kids in there waiting to be born," his dad finally said.

It figured. He sighed. He loved his dad and his mom. He figured he'd learn to love Jeffery and any other kids that came out of his mom's tummy.

He knew he was lucky to have a family.

"Then I guess I like being a big brother just fine."

LET'S TALK

Romance

For exclusive extracts, competitions
and special offers, find us online:

MILLS & BOON
MEDICAL
Pulse-Racing Passion

Set your pulse racing with dedicated, delectable doctors in the high-pressure world of medicine, where emotions run high and passion, comfort and love are the best medicine.

Eight Medical stories published every month, find them all

millsandboon.co.uk